~ The ~
GREATEST ASSAMESE STORIES EVER TOLD

The GREATEST ASSAMESE STORIES EVER TOLD

selected & edited by
MITRA PHUKAN

ALEPH

ALEPH BOOK COMPANY
An independent publishing firm
promoted by *Rupa Publications India*

First published in India in 2021
by Aleph Book Company
7/16 Ansari Road, Daryaganj
New Delhi 110 002

This edition copyright © Aleph Book Company 2021

Copyright for individual stories vests with respective authors/proprietors
Copyright for English translation vests with respective translators and Introduction copyright © Mitra Phukan 2021

The acknowledgements on p. 291 constitute an extension of the copyright page.

All rights reserved.

This is a work of fiction. Names, characters, places, and incidents are either the product of the author's imagination or are used fictitiously and any resemblance to any actual persons, living or dead, events or locales is entirely coincidental.

No part of this publication may be reproduced, transmitted, or stored in a retrieval system, in any form or by any means, without permission in writing from Aleph Book Company.

ISBN: 978-93-90652-93-8

3 5 7 9 10 8 6 4

Printed in India

This book is sold subject to the condition that it shall not, by way of trade or otherwise, be lent, resold, hired out, or otherwise circulated without the publisher's prior consent in any form of binding or cover other than that in which it is published.

To Deep and Vandana Goswami, two of the most discerning readers I know, who can lose themselves in a story regardless of what's happening all around them.

CONTENTS

Introduction		ix
1.	Patmugi LAKHMINATH BEZBAROA	1
2.	Aghoni Bai BIRINCHI KUMAR BARUA	9
3.	Mistaken Identity SYED ABDUL MALIK	29
4.	Miyah Mansur BIRENDRA KUMAR BHATTACHARYYA	37
5.	Kathonibari Ghat MAHIM BORA	46
6.	Sweet Acacia SHEELABHADRA	59
7.	The Restless Electron SAURAV KUMAR CHALIHA	62
8.	Looking for Ismael Sheikh HOMEN BORGOHAIN	102
9.	Rats BHABENDRA NATH SAIKIA	115
10.	The Victorious Woman NIRUPAMA BARGOHAIN	123
11.	Values MAMONI RAISOM GOSWAMI	129
12.	Blood on the Floor APURBA SARMA	146
13.	The Captive HAREKRISHNA DEKA	158
14.	A Night with Arpita DEBABRATA DAS	174
15.	The Hunt PUROBI BORMUDOI	180
16.	Journey YESHE DORJEE THONGCHI	190
17.	The Green Serpent DHRUBAJYOTI BORAH	194
18.	Close of Day with Miss Havisham ARUPA PATANGIA KALITA	207
19.	The Journey KULADHAR SAIKIA	221
20.	An Incomplete Story RITA CHOWDHURY	229
21.	He Returns MANOJ GOSWAMI	236
22.	No Man's Land ANURADHA SARMA PUJARI	247
23.	Bak: The Water Spirit IMRAN HUSSAIN	256
24.	Providence MONIKUNTALA BHATTACHARJYA	274
25.	A Tale of Thirdness MOUSHUMI KANDALI	283
Acknowledgements		291
Notes on the Authors		294
Notes on the Translators		302

INTRODUCTION

What goes in, and what to leave out, when collecting the twenty-five short stories for this compilation? Obviously, it's a tough job, for this is not a large enough number when choosing a representative selection for a readership that may not be familiar with the particular flavours and nuances of the short story in Assam. That, of course, would be the problem that any person tasked with selecting a comparatively small number of stories would face, of choosing a few and discarding others, equally 'deserving', equally fit to be included in a collection of this kind. This must be the problem faced by all collators, who have to cull out narratives from the vast ocean of stories that is the heritage of all the many literatures, both oral and written, that enrich our land.

It goes without saying, therefore, that a collection of this kind is bound to be subjective in its choice of stories. A reader's response—and this collection emanates from a readerly response, not a scholarly one—is bound to be coloured by her own lived experiences, her memories, her education, her milieu, the stories she has herself read and appreciated, and, of course, her choice of reading material.

However, the selection of these stories, to the exclusion of others, was not just subjective. They are also, for the most part, stories that have, at one time or the other, struck a deep chord in the general readership. Many are stories that have stood the test of time, their relevance not strictly restricted to the age in which they were written. The human values, or, perhaps, the lack of them, that they highlight, the delineation of unforgettable characters, the ambience of the particular time and place that they are placed in, remain relevant.

The choice of writers, too, was difficult to make, because there are many others who are just as good. Leaving aside the question of subjectivity, when one talks of 'good' writing and writers, there was one criterion that also had to be considered. This was the fact of their having received prestigious literary awards, which is often—though admittedly, not always—an acknowledgement of excellence. But this was not the only criteria, naturally. What was perhaps even more important was the fact of their being read, and re-read, by people even today, by readers who acknowledge the 'truth' that lies at the kernel of a great story, whether a novel, a novella, or a short story. It is this 'truth' that the people I interacted with while choosing these stories said 'spoke' to them. This is the 'truth' they referred to, a truth brought out through the medium of plot, setting, and character. It is this 'truth' that moved them, has moved them, no matter when the story was written, or when they read it—in their childhood, youth, or in their later years.

Another criterion was the kind of influence that a particular story has had on subsequent writers. One such story, indubitably, is 'Oxanto Electron', translated as 'The Restless Electron' which was written in 1950 when the writer, Saurav Kumar Chaliha, was still very young. Because it was a complete break in theme and treatment from the stories being written at the time, it created a huge impact. It has become a classic, and there are stories, even novels, written today which take off on the theme of the story. Some even use the same characters of the original story, though, of course, the treatment is different. And even today, after the 'novelty' of that kind of treatment has become a thing of the past, the relevance of the story remains, as a story, grippingly told, with enduring truths at its core. It is also a very accurate depiction of the society and the economic realities of the time.

There was also the question of whether these stories would be representative of the author's work. Most, or perhaps all, certainly are. These are stories that are some of the author's best. They were all written during different periods of a writer's life. Some when the writer was a young person, just setting out on a writer's journey, but writing already with assurance and skill. Others written mid-career, still others towards the end, with the richness of a lifetime of experiences behind them; with complete and confident mastery of techniques at their command.

Which, then, would be the 'best-known' and 'greatest' stories written in Assamese? Which would bring 'instant recall' in connection with a particular author? Balancing the subjective with the general perception (if one can call it that) was not difficult, in the end, because both merged into one whole. Perhaps that is the greatness of these stories…their universality, their appeal to such a wide cross section of readers across decades, for well over a century.

An important point that needs to be emphasized here is the fact that these are 'Assamese stories in translation'. For a land that has numerous ethnic groups, each with their own culture, music, literature (oral or written), weaves, cuisines, belief systems, and so much else, this is a fact that cannot be stressed too much. These stories are from the storehouse of short fiction written in the language that we know as Assamese. There are rich literatures from other communities living here…Bodo, Bangla (mostly from the Barak Valley of Assam), Mishing, Nepali, Hindi, Dimasa, Singpho, Rabha, Sadri, and so much more. These are all stories from Assam, whether written or oral, but not Assamese stories, in the sense they were not written in this language—Assamese. To have included them in this collection would have been ideal, for they are 'Assamese' in flavour and spirit and emanate from the land as much as those included here; the only difference being the languages that the stories are couched in. But it would not have been practical, given the huge scope and size that that project would have had. Hopefully, there will be other collections in the future where these particular literatures, coloured by their locales, their languages, their cultures and individual histories, can be compiled, as well.

Another point that needs to be stressed is that even today, besides the rich stream of written literature of Assam, there still exists a vast body of oral literature, extant in stories, songs, and so on. Of course these are not watertight compartments. For instance, the well-known 'Tejimola' story of folklore has reappeared, again and again, in written literature, as a metaphor, as a reference, and also as a kind of take-off point to move the theme and metaphor forward, in the context of contemporary ideas, especially of feminism, regeneration, and ecology. This collection only brings to the reader short stories written by particular authors, that is, written literature of a particular genre.

Though all these stories are originally written in Assamese, many of them have the flavours of the particular kind of Assamese spoken and written in the author's specific region. This is seen especially in the use of dialogue, where regional variations in the language are more pronounced. Mamoni Raisom Goswami, for instance, used a specific kind of language heard and spoken in the rural areas of western Assam in the dialogues of characters based there, especially the working-class people. Sadly, these nuances of the language, which add so much to a story in the original language in which it is written, cannot really be conveyed through translations.

All the translators who have contributed their time and efforts to this collection are experienced in this field. Besides, they have that quality which a fine translator should have, that quality which cannot really be quantified, but is essential if the work is to read well in the target language. This is what one can perhaps call a 'sense' of the story. It means that the translator is empathetic to the theme, the characters, and the way the narrative unfolds. It also means that she has the originality to couch the language in a way that the reader can relate to. This is because the demands of contemporary English are very different from what the story in original Assamese could be. All the translators have been aware of that, and have always worked accordingly, balancing the needs of the original with that of the translated version. None of the translators of these stories have used the kind of stilted, difficult-to-access English that make translations read haltingly, at times. These are contemporary translations, in accessible language, mostly following the original conscientiously but sensitively, with the translators themselves having a thorough knowledge of both the source and target languages.

Translators of different genres have different kinds of challenges. It is not just about language; it is about the way that the target language is used in a particular genre, in this case, the short story. As Raymond Carver, the short story writer puts it, 'There is a compression of language, of emotion.' It is tempting for the translator to take the easy way out, and give in to prolixity, just a little. For to convey the exact pitch of a story requires paying close attention to not just what is put in, but also what is left out. The temptation to put in these bits with the aim of 'making things easier for the reader in the target language' is sometimes better not succumbed to, since this detracts greatly from the tone. And yet, some things that are taken for granted, for instance, the descriptions of culture in the source language, will need a little bit of unobtrusive 'explanation'. The best way, for me, is to contextualize it within the narrative itself, rather than have a glossary which creates a break in the attention of the reader.

One aspect that presents some difficulties to translators working at putting across stories from Assamese to English is the phenomenon of 'shifting tenses', if it can be called that. This is possibly true of other Indian languages also. The 'tense conventions' in Assamese are different from that of English, where the rules are much more rigid. In a single paragraph, the tenses of the verbs can shift, without, in any way, compromising the sense. It is a convention that is understood, even taken for granted, by readers. However, this shifting has obviously been done away with in the translations, in accordance with the 'logic' of the language. This perhaps takes away some of the nuances in the original Assamese, but there seems to be no way to avoid this. A translator's journey, in any case, is always an ongoing one, and we all learn from each other as we go along.

There is also the question of syntax, so different in both the languages.

Sometimes, unconsciously, one tends to use the syntactical conventions of the source language, without realizing how unnatural it sounds in the target language. The translators in this volume have all been aware of this, and have written accordingly.

The short story format has as many variations as there are writers. One of the chief characteristics is that it should have a 'single effect', or mood, unlike the novel, whose spaciousness allows different characters and incidents to reflect, or hint at more than a single effect. Length is the most obvious criterion that differentiates between a novel and a short story, but length is dictated by many aspects. The short story is much more than an incident, though it can describe, upfront, an incident. But the story must evoke, if not set out in so many words, different dimensions, beyond the incident itself. There is a limitation to the number of characters who can be brought in, because of the limitations of length. Besides, too many characters or incidents make the short story too diffuse to be categorized as such, and is material, therefore, for a longer work, a novella, perhaps.

The defining characteristics of a short story differ from place to place, and from era to era. Yet, there are also common characteristics which bind them together into a genre. As has been said by William Trevor in *The Art of Fiction*, it should be 'an explosion of truth'. The stories in this collection certainly are that.

One of the characteristics of the short story is that it lends itself more to stylistic experimentation than other forms of fiction. With some glorious exceptions, to carry this technical experimentation into a full-length novel will not always work. Saurav Kumar Chaliha's stories, to give an example from modern Assamese literature, showed his boldness in moving away from existing and contemporary styles. His 'Restless Electron' employed a new stylistic technique. This stylistic experimentation blended with the contemporaneity and realism of his theme and characterization.

However, brevity is not synonymous with lightweight in the case of short stories. If anything, its very conciseness requires more 'work' from the reader. While in a novel, the writer has the luxury of explaining things, the short story writer does not. Instead, the short story demands evocativeness, just as in poetry. Just as in a short film, the best short stories require the reader to figure out some things for herself. Stories such as 'Rats' by Bhabendra Nath Saikia are fine examples of this. The mother's reactions over time to the sack that was smeared with her dead son's blood, and how they change as hunger overtakes her, are not 'explained'. But the way they are described carry the story forward even as the reader imagines her motivations, and the final outcome. And of course, the human aspect, the compassion with which it is told, moves this story forward with delicacy and understanding.

In Assam, as in several other regions across the country, special editions of various publication houses appear around important festivals. In the case of Assam, it has been during Bihu and Durga Puja. These editions, which are quite voluminous and popular, showcase short stories of both established writers and talented new writers. It is not at all unusual to see these budding writers go on to become acclaimed writers in later years. Though longer stories, more novella than novel, also appear in these editions, it is the essay, the poem, and the short story that seem to be most popular. There are today journals such as *Prantik*, once edited by Bhabendra Nath Saikia, and now by Pradip Baruah, which have actually discovered and nurtured short story writers, and encouraged their growth to maturity. There are also awards such as the Munin Barkotoky Award which, for over a quarter century now, have annually awarded the best writings of authors below forty, many of them from the short story genre. Many have gone on to become acclaimed writers, still creating beautiful and relevant stories.

There are, of course, many different sub-categories within the broad format of the short story itself. There is the 'long' short story of over twenty thousand words. Yet, because of unity of mood, and 'effect', it is still defined as a short story. And then there are the 'short shorts', usually below a thousand words. These pieces are tightly written, with each word carefully chosen in order to convey the precise meaning as well as to evoke a larger world. And then there is 'flash fiction', and the 'micro story', which also fall under the definition of the short story, in spite of their extreme brevity.

The stories in this volume, however, fall into the category of the traditional short story, as far as length is concerned. Of course, some are much longer than the others, inevitable in a collection of this kind. Some, though not all, have the 'twist in the tale' that is sometimes expected by readers of a particular kind of short story. But this is just one of the styles. In all, there is a 'flow', inexorableness, and a chain of consequences dependent on the actions of the characters, and sometimes, of outside events such as war, poverty, or the death of a provider.

Given the popularity of these stories, many of them have been published and read elsewhere, in original Assamese, certainly, but also in other translations. However, these twenty-five stories in translation have never been seen together in a single collection. This is what makes it a very valuable addition to the storehouse of Indian literature in translation. For one of the ways in which we come to understand each other in this world is by accessing each other's stories. The specific cultural traits that shape behaviour, the milieu of a particular place, aspects of belief, cuisine, and ways of life, come alive through these short fictions.

Like many other literatures around the world, the short story in Assamese too has its roots in oral literature of the region. The oral literary tradition has always been a strong one. For one, literacy was, in the past, confined to the elite and the privileged. There are the 'folk tales', and the mythological stories which have always had eager listeners, and talented men and women who combined a sense of narrative flow with dramatic techniques, and sometimes even rudimentary dance steps and gestures, to keep their audiences engaged. There are the Pal Naams, group songs that are also narratives; the Oja Pali performances which narrate stories based loosely on mythological tales, but with a lot of extempore additions that vary from performance to performance. The mythological stories sometimes dealt with minor characters, who became the protagonists of these stories. With the spread of literacy in contemporary times, this tradition is becoming weaker. Technology, too, which has made content through the audio-visual medium easily available, is sadly contributing to the phenomenon of the skilled oral storyteller becoming rarer.

Assam, the land of blue hills and the red river as it is often known, has a written language that dates back, probably, to the seventh century CE. Recognizably 'Assamese' literature included, among the early known writings, the Charyapadas, which were Buddhist songs composed from the eighth to the tenth centuries. There are also poems written by Hema Saraswati (late thirteenth century) and Madhab Kandali (fourteenth century). Among the prose writings of Assam of the past were the 'buranjis' which were historical records of the Ahom kings. Though initially written in the language of the Ahoms, later entries were succinctly written in contemporary Assamese.

And there was Srimanta Sankardev, the saint poet of Assam, whose luminous compositions in praise of the Almighty were beautiful works in varied genres. There are the effulgent lyrics, the Borgeets or Great Songs, set to music, in praise of the Lord. There is the Kirtan Ghosa, which is a collection of poetic works meant for community singing. And there are the bhaonas, the plays, which were mainly written to propagate the Message of the Lord to the people, written in both Brajavali and Assamese languages. These writings, which were a part of the Bhakti movement, took religion to the people through literature, music, and performances.

As with most other literatures, the appearance of prose, in general, and fiction, in particular, in the form of brief stories and novels, was a progression.

Among the first influences that brought the short-story genre to Assam was *Orunodoi* in 1846—the journal of the Baptist Missionaries who set up the first printing press in the region at Sibsagar in Upper Assam. Though their aim was proselytization, they did bring in an idea of Western literary trends of the time. Writers wrote stories, mostly Christian parables, and also fables and moral tales from Indian and Greek stories in a rudimentary short-story format, sowing the seeds for more secular writings later. Anandaram Dhekial Phukan is a prominent name of this era.

It was during what is known today as the 'Jonaki Era' that the short story in Assamese began to flower. *Jonaki* was the very popular and influential literary journal started in 1889 in Calcutta. Not just the short story, in fact, many writers thrived during the decades of its existence, and brought in a richness of content in the genres of poetry, lyrics, drama, novel, and essays. It brought in romanticism, as well, in various genres. There was the revival of folk tales, which also, in their own way, paved the way for the short story. Indeed, Sahityarathi Lakhminath Bezbaroa, often known as the Father of the Assamese short story, began by putting together a collection called *Burhi Air Xadhu* (Grandmother's Tales). But these were more than tales. Through the prism of his sensibilities, they also had the elements of what is generally seen in a short story, by definition. There is a point of view, a flow from beginning, through middle, to end, complexity of characterization, a well-delineated setting, plot, theme, conflict, a climax, and a satisfying denouement, as also a brisk narrative pace. Later, of course, he wrote many masterly short stories, one of which, 'Patmugi', is included in this collection.

Among other early short story writers of the time, and also of the later *Banhi* and 'Usha' eras were Sarat Chandra Goswami, Dandinath Kalita, Mitradev Mahanta (mainly known as a luminous poet but also a short story writer), the well-known historian Suryya Kumar Bhuyan, and so on.

The writers of the Romantic Era had, in their stories, a combination of romantic love as well as a reformative mission, to correct the wrongs that they perceived in the social set up of the time.

The next important era with reference to the Assamese short story is referred to as the 'Awahon Age', once again named after a very popular literary magazine. Along with romanticism, the seeds of realism were also sown at this time. The writers and thinkers of the time were now exposed to the works of world literature as never before, as also the literatures of various Indian languages, too, especially Bangla. Several went abroad to study and returned with a broadened outlook on life, which, mingled with their original rootedness in their birthplace, saw a flowering of this genre, in all its many colours, in ways that could be said to be uniquely and truly 'Assamese'. Realism such as that found in the works of Maupassant and Chekhov found its way into the short story in the hands of these writers. The genre showed the realities of life around them, in characterization, and setting. The mores and traditions of their birthplace and motherland that often formed the backdrop to these stories, and the motivation, often, for characters behaving in particular ways, gave a depth and uniqueness to these stories, which, however, remained strongly universal in appeal. Among the popular writers of this time was 'Bina Barua', the pen name of historian, academic, and folklorist Birinchi Kumar Barua.

These pre-war stories of the Awahon Era gave way around the middle of the twentieth century to the great flowering of the short story in Assam. Just as World War II itself changed the world, the Assamese short story, changed in theme, mood, style, use of language, and many other aspects. With the world in turmoil, and economic ferment, the leading journal *Awahon* had to stop publication, putting an end to a glorious era. It is notable that during and after this time, Assam, too, changed irrevocably. The ferment of war, of the freedom movement, and of Independence brought new ideas, new ways of looking at things. People moved out of the villages, travelled the country and also, to an extent, the world, either as students or for work. Gradually, the area itself became more urbanized. All of this was naturally reflected in the writings of the time. Various journals began to come up which reflected the changing themes and styles of the short story, which were now seen as a wonderful vehicle for putting across ideas through the medium of fiction. The genre now went beyond Romanticism to Realism. One of the important writers at the cusp of this phenomenon was Syed Abdul Malik. His characters and settings were the poor, the marginalized, living, often, on the fringes of society. However, his gaze as a writer was that of a Romantic. Celebrated filmmaker, dramatist, and poet Jyoti Prasad Agarwala (1903–1951) wrote at this time. His thoughts and ideas continue permeate the literary landscape of Assamese even today, even though he is better known for his other works, rather than short stories.

During the 1950s, the popularity of the short story as a genre grew even more. A new vehicle for it was the popular journal *Ramdhenu* (Rainbow). This era is often called the Ramdhenu Era. Among the streams that influenced writers such as Saurav Kumar Chaliha were also Marxism and Socialism. However, a good writer is always known to rise above 'isms'. The imperatives of plot and character which are employed to illustrate, unobtrusively, the theme, inevitably create a world of their own. At the core of all great literature is the ism of humanism. And in this present collection, too, the stories, through the different eras in which they have been written, have a bedrock of compassion and humanity which permeates them. Though several writers of the time had strong leftist leanings, the lens through which events were crafted and characters created was humanist. In spite of the fact that these stories are set in Assam, and often in an Assam of the past, a rural Assam that is slowly vanishing, these stories themselves remain timeless and universal. Perhaps because of the format of the short story which requires a tight storyline, the background details in these stories are always suggested, and not overly detailed, which would perhaps have put off the reader not familiar with the setting or the time. And it is also, of course, the skill of the writers themselves that universalizes these stories. One of the best-known stories of this kind is Mahim Bora's 'Kathonibari Ghat', in which the sense of place is extremely strong. The wait for the ferry, the dependence of a woman on the men...throughout it all, the river, with its boats and ferries is a palpable and strong presence. There is also Birendra Kumar Bhattacharyya's 'Miyah Mansur', which, too, shows the strong links that people of Assam have with the river that bisects it, the Brahmaputra, along with its numerous tributaries.

It is, in fact, no accident that so many of the stories in Assam, in all the many tongues, have rivers as the backdrop. In fact, rivers in several stories are more than just the setting. They influence character, reflect moods, and are sometimes used as the objective correlative to human thoughts and emotions. The river...rivers...with their many facets are often metaphors in the poetry of the region. The lyrics of the land abound in references to rivers, as reflected in the setting as well as through allegory and symbol.

There is also, in many of these stories, nostalgia for the village that has been left behind. The rural landscape is romanticized and viewed through rose-tinted glasses, the past that cannot be brought back in these changed times. The urban landscape comes through as being mechanical and soul deadening in several stories of the time, though gradually, urbanization is viewed as inevitable, even desirable in some contemporary stories.

The short story, along with other forms of fiction, flourished through the decades, with writers such as Mamoni Raisom Goswami, Birendra Kumar Bhattacharyya, Homen Borgohain, enriching it greatly. Historical events that had a huge impact on the region, such as the creation of Bangladesh, and the war that took place in the neighbourhood of what was undivided Assam at the time, and its playing out through the decades, influenced many writers.

One of the major events in the seventies was the creation of several states from what came to be known later as Undivided Assam. Through a process that took some years, full statehood was granted to the states of Arunachal Pradesh, (which, earlier, had been administered as the North East Frontier Agency or NEFA) Mizoram, Nagaland, and Meghalaya. Naturally, since fiction holds up a mirror to the times, these events found an echo in the stories of the time. One of the fallouts was that some regions, after getting full statehood, changed their medium of instruction in educational institutions from Assamese. When children in the schools of Arunachal Pradesh were taught in Assamese, and when they went to colleges in Assam for further studies, they were more comfortable writing in this language, than in their own tongues, which sometimes did not have a script. Later, when the official language and the medium of instruction changed to English, while the dominant language of communication among ethnic groups became Hindi, the writers too stopped writing in Assamese. This is a sad development, because those fictions and poetry in Assamese, from places that were earlier a part of Assam, had greatly enriched the oeuvre of Assamese literature. A fine example of this is 'Journey' by Arunachalee writer Yeshe Dorjee Thongchi. Deceptively simple, it shows the changes that happen when 'development' takes place and education leads to a job where the old skills and strengths are lost, to the detriment of society as well as the individual. The moving narrative shows the rapid changes happening in the rural areas of the state. It is as much an allegory as it is the story of individuals.

Assam went through a period of great turmoil and unrest during the years of the Assam Agitation (1979–1985) which saw a degeneration in its later years into violence. Fear stalked the land and extortions, killings, and kidnappings were common. It is inevitable that the stories of the time should reflect these. Many powerful, hard-hitting stories emerged then, showing the effects of violence on the people and society, and highlighting the sufferings. Some of the stories in this collection, such as Harekrishna

Deka's 'The Captive', Manoj Goswami's 'He Returns', and Apurba Sarma's 'Blood on the Floor' are from this time. Though located in Assam, and reflecting the troubled times, these stories have a power that speaks to all.

Contemporary stories have a variety of themes. There is Moushumi Kandali's 'A Tale of Thirdness', which deals with gender identity. The yearning for nurturing a child is shown to be confined not only to women, as is often erroneously portrayed. This sensitively told story was groundbreaking because of its theme, when it first appeared. Anuradha Sarma Pujari's story 'No Man's Land' deals with the theme of borders and their human cost. This issue of borders, their porous nature, and the way humans negotiate them, is in any case a very complex and troubled one in Assam, and indeed in the whole of India's Northeast.

Indeed, many of the troubling questions, the burning problems of the time, are reflected in the short fiction of Assam. The relationship between man and nature, the rapacity and greed that destroys the environment, is reflected in Purobi Bormudoi's 'The Hunt'. Debabrata Das' 'A Night with Arpita' builds on what can be called the tradition of 'Train Journey Stories'. The romance of the train journey, the fact that total strangers are thrown together in close proximity, the realization that after the journey is over, they go their separate ways, possibly never to meet again, has fuelled the imagination of several writers of contemporary times. Perhaps this tradition can be seen as a kind of parallel to the 'Shipboard Stories' of Western literature. As the blue night light of the sleeping coach in a moving train envelopes the characters of 'A Night with Arpita', the story too shifts between reality and the unreal. The 'action' unfolds through the night, but we come across a sense of the trigger, the need which gave rise to it all only at the end.

The dreamy settings of Imran Hussain's 'Bak: The Water Spirit' are of a different kind. Alternating between reality and the spirit world, between belief in a world beyond observed actuality and the life of reality, this story weaves together different strands till we come to the horror at the end.

There is another important aspect that these stories depict: that of economic realities. Acute financial hardship, extreme hunger, and helplessness makes the mother in Bhabendra Nath Saikia's 'Rats' behave in a particular way, as it does Mamoni Raisom Goswami's Damayanti in 'Values' and Sushila in Nirupama Bargohain's 'The Victorious Woman'. When there is acute poverty, some of the most vulnerable are women and children. It is no accident that all three of these protagonists are widows, left without the financial support of their husbands after their deaths.

In Birendra Kumar Bhattacharyya's 'Miyah Mansur' the eponymous character, by his actions, shows that humanity is above considerations of class, caste, or religion. There is also Syed Abdul Malik's 'Mistaken Identity'. Written before India's Independence, it is reminiscent of Saadat Hasan Manto's narratives, though, of course, it has its own flavour and originality. The inhumanity of religious discord and the human cost of political actions are movingly portrayed in this true-to-life narrative, which is firmly rooted in the time it portrays. In the end, it is humanity that is killed. The author takes no sides, only depicts the tragic consequences of the actions of the time.

There are several women-centric stories in this collection, written by women, as well as men. There is Arupa Patangia Kalita's compassionate story 'Close of Day with Miss Havisham' about a woman for whom time stands still after the death of her husband, who used to look after her every need. An excellent delineator of character, Arupa Patangia Kalita creates a setting that brings to life the hapless woman whose world collapses once its centre, her husband, passes away.

Sheelabhadra's story 'Sweet Acacia' is as evocative as the delicate fragrance of the flower that permeates it. In a series of vignettes, the old man's past and present are presented with empathy. The juxtaposition of memory, which is a symbol of his past, its transference from the visual to the olfactory, with the harshness of the present, speaks of its significance in his life, even though the character in his memory herself probably did not think too much of it beyond a momentary period of annoyance. This brief story encapsulates the passage of time in a person's life, from youth to old age, in a compassionate way.

Nirupama Bargohain's story, 'The Victorious Woman', similar to Mamoni Raisom Goswami's story 'Values', places the theme of the 'Fallen Woman' in the centre. 'Fallen' in the eyes of society; the same society which does not lift a finger to help her when the support of her husband fades away. Both of them are beautiful, and in their desperation, this beauty becomes the only currency that they have to survive and overcome their circumstances. Mamoni Raisom Goswami's powerful story portrays how deeply ingrained caste values can become a motivating force for a destitute woman, a mother, for whom her Brahmin ancestry is, at this point, the only thing that she can take pride in. It explores the deep yearning of a man for a male offspring who will take his lineage forward, even though his wife, who is an invalid, is incapable of bearing a child. It also shows the depths to which poverty can make people sink. However, the two central characters differ greatly in their response and motivation. The trajectories of the stories, too, differ greatly, propelled by the finely etched characters.

There is also 'Aghoni Bai' written several decades ago by Birinchi Kumar Barua, which shows the stratagems and petty deceptions that the protagonist has to resort to, once her husband dies. Her beauty was a handicap in her youth, inviting all kinds of unwanted attention. With age, she became an almost sexless person, whose only aim in life was to somehow raise her physically handicapped grandchild.

In Mahim Bora's 'Kathonibari Ghat', the narrator comes to realize that the woman, whom he is meeting at the ferry-landing stage, is at a turning point in her life. As soon as she leaves the boat, when she reaches her marital home, a realization will come to her that a dreadful thing has befallen her, and she will, henceforth, be condemned to live a completely changed life.

The drastic change in a married woman's life which comes about when she loses her husband, and the cruelty emanating from societal pressures to which even parents succumb, is poignantly depicted in Rita Chowdhury's 'An Incomplete Story'. Completely neglected and ignored, treated with indifference and contempt, a woman's place in the household after widowhood is most pathetic. Yet she is helpless, and is at the mercy of her loved ones who have no regard for her emotions.

Harekrishna Deka's 'The Captive' is a poignant account of the relationship between a person who is kidnapped and the kidnapper. It speaks of the gradual process by which the relationship becomes more equal, and is a sensitive depiction of the Stockholm Syndrome. The end leaves us distraught, and touches a deep chord in our hearts. Written by a police officer during the darkest days of violence in Assam, its small details and character depictions, along with the minutely observed poverty as well as the beauty of the landscape that the captor and the captive pass through, make it one of the most powerful stories in Assamese literature. The alternate world of the kidnapper becomes a reality for the kidnapped, as his memory of his own world starts to fade, while the two of them move for months across the land. Perhaps the most moving aspect of the story is the fact that it is presented without judgements and without any moral pronouncements.

Another story set in those particular times is Manoj Goswami's 'He Returns'. This too has resonated greatly with the readership of Assam. Told in a very cinematic style, it is inevitable that it has been translated into the audio-visual medium several times. It shows the disillusionment of the idealist as he realizes that while he has been spending years away from civilization, the world has moved on. His friends, even the girl with whom he had shared a deep bond, do not now want to have anything to do with him. It is a true portrayal of the situation that confronts idealists and revolutionaries in today's world.

Set in the same time of terror and insurgency, of brutality and violence, is Dhrubajyoti Borah's 'The Green Serpent'. Though, on the surface, it is about two people, a rapist and his victim, it is also about many other things—ethnic violence, hatred that overrides human considerations, but also the regret and emasculation that stems from that hatred. The story moves above the particular to the level of the general, though the end is left ambiguous from the point of view of the personal.

Homen Borgohain's well-known story 'Looking for Ismael Sheikh' too deals with the effect that violence has on people. Though written decades ago, it remains contemporary in its relevance today as a tragic commentary on how we still resort to bloodshed in the name of religious beliefs. Through the twin stories of a prostitute and a cultivator belonging to different communities, narrated from the perspective of a government official, the inhumanity that exists all around is held up in a moving depiction. Their stories are mirror images of each other, but the suffering and the tragedy that unfolds are strikingly similar.

Apurba Sarma's 'Blood on the Floor' portrays the different worlds that coexist very uneasily at a particular point of time. The 'encounters' of the people with the Army, on the one hand, and the insurgents, on the other, and the organizations of which they are a part, play out against each other, with each believing that they are fighting for a noble cause. In the process, it is the innocent who are pulverized between the two. In this delicately narrated story, the realities of several different worlds, including that of academia, college life, and the world of cinema, face off against each other.

Bhabendra Nath Saikia's 'Rats' depicts how the demands of physical hunger can numb and help overcome grief of even the most devastating kind. The rats of the title are present at various levels in the story…literally, and in the mind, too. And, of course, there is the gnawing hunger that is described in Assamese as rats running around in the belly. A filmmaker as well as a writer, Saikia writes a story that is direct in the way it delivers a punch to the reader's sensibilities. And yet there is deep humanism in it, which even the extremely degrading and tragic circumstances of the protagonist's life are not able to erase.

Kuladhar Saikia's story 'The Journey' is very representative of his style and subject matter. Urban in setting, the wanderer in the journey moves across the landscape, desolate at times, in a series of shifting yet connected montages, with a canine for company. The dog's words and his own replies are, in fact, the protagonist's own interior dialogue. Atmospheric yet pulled together, the story describes character as well as, by implication, social compulsions and the pressures of a particular milieu.

Monikuntala Bhattacharjya's story 'Providence' is set in the time of the Indo–Pak War. It depicts the moving reaction of a father, a military man like his son, at the latter's death, and the way in which it happened. It is also an indictment of war and is deeply humanistic.

There is diversity in these stories that go beyond setting and character. Each one also exemplifies the spirit and the dominant mood of the times and of the people who lived at a particular time. Of course, several, such as Bezbaroa's 'Patmugi' are able to override prevalent modes of thinking, but by this very act of penning what was beyond the pales of social acceptability, the authors have been able to make a statement about the society of which they are a part. These stories are not simply reflections of their time and their era. They also depict how the times shape character, which, in turn, shape events; about the efforts of characters to break free from the restrictions of the times they live in, especially in some of the traditional societies that are described here, in this collection.

It is hoped that these stories will resonate with the reader, as they did with me, and with so many other readers in the language in which they were originally written. Painstaking efforts have gone into the attempt to put all this together, but the joy and satisfaction, at the end of the day, are immeasurable.

PATMUGI

LAKHMINATH BEZBAROA

We live in Doboka mouza. We are of the Kumar community. That is, traditionally, we have been potters. For countless generations, we have made our living by crafting and selling small earthen jars, pots, pitchers for adults, and rattles and small earthen utensils for children. But these days, our profession has fallen into a decline. Our land is now flooded with a variety of foreign goods. British toys have slyly chased away our rattles, earthen utensils, and vessels. The foreign utensils made of aluminium, iron, and china have banished our traditional pots and pitchers. Today, we have no other option but to abandon our ancestral profession and somehow manage to eke out a living by cultivating a bit of land. Here, too, foreigners are shoving us into a corner. We lack the strength in our bodies and the money in our purses to push back that shove. And, on top of that, it's as they say, 'Oil only falls on the oilman's head.' We are not able to satisfy those officials who arrange the distribution of land. For these reasons, we are now in these dire straits, on the verge of destitution.

Aloti Bai is also from our village. She is our neighbour and from the same caste. Patmugi is Aloti Bai's daughter. She calls me 'Dodai' out of respect. That is, she addresses me as she would her father's younger brother. I have seen her growing up in front of my eyes. She is now a comely young girl. Looking at her, can anyone guess that she is from an impoverished potter's family like ours? She looks quite as though she is the daughter of some high-ranking judicial officer.

A Brahmin boy came from the Bokota mouza and began to eye her. By God's wish, her heart, too, settled on him. He remained sweet to her. All of us tried very hard to reason with Patmugi, telling her not to go ahead with such a thing, but we could not change her mind. She did not listen to her mother's warnings, either. Finally, resigned to what had happened, we called a meeting of the Panchayat. The boy swore on his sacred thread before the Panchayat and gave a written statement that he would never abandon Patmugi while he lived. He said that since he was ready to forsake his caste for her sake, it should be quite obvious to the Panchayat that she was very dear to him. We, too, thought: since Fate had brought this impoverished, needy boy from a distant village to our doorstep, we should do something for him. Let him remain in our village, we thought, as one of our caste. In addition, an old woman without a male descendant would, in a way, gain a son.

But things are different these days. The sins of Untruth and Deceit have gained strength, and swallowed the world. One cannot rely on a person's word. If one tries to understand a person, going by the way he looks, or behaves, one will come to grief. One day, the young man, though dependent on a woman for his existence, after staying with the girl for a year, simply vanished. Nobody could say where he had gone, so suddenly. Unable to find him, the girl grew mad with grief. We, too, searched high and low for him, but could find no clue as to his whereabouts. Finally, exhausted, we thought that he must have met with an accident and died somewhere. Otherwise, why would this loveable young Brahmin boy abandon this beautiful girl? Nobody had heard the young couple ever quarrelling among themselves. His mother-in-law, too, had pampered him no end. And certainly, it was fitting that she did so. All the villagers were pleased by his calm demeanour, his charming manner of talking, his behaviour, and the way he carried himself. They all said, 'It is her good fortune that Patmugi has managed to get such an excellent husband.'

But now there were all kinds of speculations among the villagers, and the days were filled with talk of this nature. What can I say, what will you hear! The other day, a rumour reached our ears. We heard that he had gone back to his home in Bokota mouza. As soon as he reached there, he underwent purificatory rites, and reverted to his caste once more. After this, he married a Brahmin girl. Our Patmugi insisted that this rumour had been spread by an enemy, and refused to even listen to it. I said, in that case, let's settle the matter, by going and seeing it with our own eyes.

Off I went, walking through slushy lanes and muddy paths to Bokota. I was aghast at what I saw and heard there. The rumour turned out to be absolutely true. He had indeed committed this terrible act. I wished to meet him and speak a few words with him, but I could not even go near him. The people of that village had surrounded him for protection. Seeing me, they tried to catch hold of me, and beat me up. I managed, somehow, to flee from the place alive.

On hearing what I had to say, Patmugi beat her head and chest and wept bitterly. Her mother's condition was truly piteous. The old woman had not eaten anything for three days and was stretched out on her sleeping mat. At first I tried to tell them that it was best to bear what had happened, for what was done was done. But then I thought that if this kind of terrible betrayal was left unpunished, there would be no justice, no righteousness, and no dharma left in this world. With this thought in my mind, I, along with Aloti Bai and Patmugi, walked to Rongpur to lodge a complaint in the court.

It was the month of 'Sot', March–April. The sun beat down very strongly. After walking for a while, all of us began to feel very thirsty. We came upon an elephant apple tree growing by the wayside. Looking up, I saw quite a few ripe fruits on the tree. Patmugi said, 'Dodai! I am really thirsty. Please bring down a ripe outenga, we'll all eat it. My throat is parched with thirst.'

I climbed up the elephant apple tree, and plucked three ripe fruits. While I was coming down, I happened to notice Patmugi's upturned face. In the sun, her face was as rosy as a ripe kokum. Really, she was very beautiful. I had seen her, of course, very frequently, but I had never seen her looking as beautiful as she did today. After coming down one more step, our eyes met. I stood there, transfixed, and thought, 'Dehi Oi! What an unparalleled pair of eyes!' I could not tear my own eyes away from hers to look down where I was going. I don't know what Patmugi thought when she saw how I was behaving. Smiling softly, she said, 'Dodai! What are you staring at? Come down! Be careful, you will slip and fall!'

Hearing her words, I lost all control over myself. I had not been aware, previously, that she had such a honeyed voice. I don't know why, but I began to sweat profusely. Somehow managing to control myself, I slithered down to the ground. In the process, I scraped the skin of my chest on the tree's trunk. I noticed that Patmugi, who till just some time ago had been parched with thirst, was now quite energetic again. She was smiling.

What was this? Could anybody tell me what had happened to me? I was perplexed, unable to find a clue to the riddle. Patmugi's face, which had been quite shrivelled up with thirst till just a while ago, was now full of soft smiles. Her limbs, too, were now steady. Where had her tiredness gone? She was lively again, even though she had not yet put the ripe fruit to her mouth. What would she be like after she had eaten it? Would she suddenly possess unearthly powers to vanquish me completely? What was at the root of the sudden change in this girl who, till a few minutes ago, had been half-dead because of her Brahmin husband's deceitful and wicked ways? And why was I suddenly so unsteady? I had seen Patmugi since she was a naked baby. She, too, had always seen me around. One can say that I had carried her around in my lap and seen her growing up.

What was this that had happened to me today? And what had happened to her, for that matter? Was there some spirit in this elephant apple tree, who had pierced us with his arrows? I was an old man of two score and ten. Patmugi was a young girl of seventeen. She was my daughter's age. Sih, this was all quite disgraceful, quite sordid. I was ashamed to even think of this. Hari, Hari! What have you done to me? I have really fallen. I have a wife and children at home. Where has my discipline, self-control, gone today? Has the spirit of the outenga tree entered me, replacing the good spirits within me? Right, I understand. A spirit has entered my body. It's probably entered the girl's body, as well. The piece of outenga that her mother has cut for her remains forgotten in her hand. What is she thinking of, then, as she stares at me?

These thoughts went at the speed of lightning through my mind as though they were a mail train that goes breathlessly over the railway tracks. Patmugi called out, 'Dodai, eat the outenga. What are you worrying unnecessarily about? Come, let me see your chest.'

Saying this, she got up and placed a hand on my chest. She must have heard the thumping of my heart. 'Iss! The skin has been scraped away... luckily it's a surface wound, it hasn't gone in too deep.'

Hearing her words, I was quite abashed. What did she mean by saying that it hadn't penetrated too deeply? What did it mean? I began to take the piece of outenga she had given me to my mouth, but it bumped into my nose instead. Seeing this calamity, Patmugi began to laugh out delightedly. I felt exceedingly embarrassed. I said to Aloti Bai, 'I am not feeling well at all, Bai!'

She replied, 'Climbing that outenga tree at this noonday hour was not a good thing. The spirits, ghosts, ghouls, demons, all of them and more keep running around at this time.'

After concluding the elephant apple tree chapter, the three of us set out once more for Rongpur. On the way, I was nearly silent. Patmugi, however, kept chattering away. At this, her mother said, 'Patmugi! What's the matter with you? Why are you suddenly so delighted today? I feel nervous when I see the way both of you are behaving. I promise to slaughter a multi-coloured drake and invite the Vaishnavite priests, the bhokots, to a feast.'

While walking along, I thought, 'What is this? I never thought of Patmugi in such an impious way ever before! She, too, never had any such ideas. So why these difficulties today? And what can be the meaning of all those small smiles on her face? Has she somehow been able to read my mind? Is she that clever? How could she understand my condition? Now I am embarrassed to even raise my face and look at her. Is her delight due to my defeat? Truly, a woman's mind has been created with a strange substance. This little girl suddenly vanquished this dried up fifty-year-old. Odd, indeed!'

We reached Rongpur and went to a well-known lawyer there. Initially, we fell into the hands of the lawyer's assistant. This person harassed us greatly. With a glib tongue, he demanded cash for this expense and that. The money that we had carried with us dwindled quickly. Finally, when we did reach the lawyer and heard the amount we would have to pay as fees, we were disheartened. I told the lawyer, 'Deuta! We do not have that amount with us right now.'

The lawyer replied, 'Give me whatever you have with you. It will be fine if you bring the remainder of the money when the complaint comes up. You have a strong case. I will see to it that the deceiving boy is taught a lesson. The girl will surely get compensation.'

We gave the lawyer the remainder of the money. Suddenly, Patmugi told the lawyer, 'Deuta! I shall not pursue this case.'

When the lawyer asked her the reason, she replied, 'Enough is enough. I do not wish to get my husband punished.'

'Then why did you come here?'

'To get proof.'

'Of what?'

'The deceit, cruelty, and weakness of men.'

'Have you got the proof, then?'

'Yes.'

'Where?'

'I had got it before, and now, too, I have the proof. No more now, Deuta! For bothering you, be satisfied with the bit of money we have given you.' Saying this, she marched away.

The lawyer was stunned. He told us, 'This is no ordinary girl. She is very whimsical.'

Finding no words with which to respond to the lawyer, we paid him our respects, and followed Patmugi out. The lawyer's assistant called out to us, 'Hey, come here, I have something to tell you.'

Patmugi looked back, and replied, 'Whatever it is, let it be. I shall not listen any more.'

On the return journey, too, Patmugi behaved in the same way. She bustled about, laughing with joy. I was silent, so was her mother. When we reached the elephant apple tree beside the road again, Patmugi said to me, 'Won't you pluck another outenga? Even though I'm not thirsty now, perhaps you are?'

Without replying, I began to walk faster, with my head lowered. I ensured that Patmugi and her mother reached home, and then went back swiftly to my own house. Here, I had a thorough wash, and went into our prayer room. I lay down full length, head first, in obeisance before the stand on which the image of the Lord was placed, and pleaded with Him to forgive me for my momentary lapse that day. I do not know if I reached my previous state of balance. However, I did not go towards Patmugi's house for some time after that.

One day, Patmugi suddenly appeared. 'Dodai!' she said to me. 'Please forgive me. Men can never really know about a woman's nature. They cannot. It's true that men do not understand us. They say that even the gods do not understand women. A woman's biggest hope lies in getting a man. A woman can never hide her happiness at winning a man, no matter who he is. I have seen a lot in these last few days, and learnt a lot, as well. I do not want that wicked, dependant Brahmin boy any more. But I don't want to harm him, either. The only truth in this world is God. Worship is mankind's only work. People talk ceaselessly of dharma, of religion, and yet do so much that is irreligious. It's sad. Our revered saint, Srimanta Shankardev, has already told us what religion is, what dharma is.

> The true devotees all see Narayan...

through worship. Srimanta Shankardev has also told us how He should be worshipped.

> Friends or enemies...treat them the same
> In this lies the greatest devotion to Krishna

'Nobody can see the Almighty with mortal eyes. But He is very much present physically before the eyes of the entire world. The Almighty is satisfied with the devotee who works to remove the sorrows of the poor, and labours to improve the lot of the meek.'

> Envy, slander, pride, rid yourself of all....

'I have bound up my mind as though it was a stone pillar. Following Mahatma Gandhi's teachings, I have dedicated my life to the cause of Swadesh, and society, and especially for the betterment of the condition of the poor. From tomorrow, nobody will see me as I was in the past. Dodai! Bless this poor unfortunate niece of yours, so that her heart's desires may come true.'

Saying this, Patmugi knelt down to pay me obeisance and then went away. I kept looking after her like a fool.

∽

After writing this story, I showed it to a close friend of mine. This friend is quite fearless and is a reputed literary critic. I requested him to have a look at it, and said, 'Please give me your opinion on this in writing.' I was quite sure that he would speak well about it. If a noted literary critic were to praise this story, I would confidently send it off to a journal for publication. Out of a sense of fear, the publication would not say anything negative about it. And even if they did, our critic would take up arms on my behalf.

I am mentioning below the comments that my friend, honouring my request, wrote on the manuscript. Readers will immediately come to know that the fruit of my dreams was a mare's egg merely, a pipe dream.

My dear friend,

Even after reading through your story very carefully, I could make no sense of it. If this is to be called a story, then all the routine conversations that take place in our homes about daily activities should also be called stories. I ask you, where is the plot? There is no plot, no art, no beauty, no ethics, no morality, and no tradition. There is only the froth of the ephemeral. Aloti Bai's friend is an old man of fifty, and according to the village's relationship pattern, he is Patmugi's uncle, Dodai. There's an old woman in the elderly man's home, as well as his children. I get the feeling that the old man has a sense of values, and is quite religious, as well. The old man has seen Patmugi from her childhood. In all these years, the old man's mind had always been steady. It had to slip when the old man was dragging himself down the elephant apple tree? It's ridiculous, laughable. This has crossed the threshold of all that is both possible and impossible. The girl has recently been abandoned by her husband. She is exhausted after walking for miles in the hot sun. In addition, she is deeply hurt by the man's deceit and wickedness. In this situation, when she sees her respected guardian's mental turmoil, it seems she begins to laugh. Her tiredness vanishes. The burden of grief goes away after a while. The girl says that she will not lodge a complaint. And both the mother and the mature guardian listen to what she says, and obey her. What can be more ridiculous than this? And the reason that the girl gives for not filing a complaint is also unrealistic. And then, in the name of serving the country, she joins Gandhi's Congress. This may be your 'Midsummer Night's Dream', but it's not a story. Don't publish this. If you do, I'm telling you, you will be the butt of jokes; people will make fun of you. I am giving you my honest opinion, please don't mind.

Your friend, Shri

I have not obeyed my critic friend. My reason for publishing my story is this: if somebody without any 'critical faculty' finds something in this story, well and good. And there's no harm done even if nobody finds anything in it. At least the pages of *Banhi*, this journal that I edit, will be filled up. And those who keep complaining that there are no stories in *Banhi* will be given one. This will be a black leopard instead of a tiger, molasses instead of sugar, and dried leaves instead of pearls. At least it can be hoped that those who pant, 'Ha! A story! A story!' will accept this string sack on the end of a pole, in place of a palanquin. Will this hope materialize? I am saying here that even if, by chance, this string sack does break, the person sitting inside will surely not fall from too great a height.

Translated by Mitra Phukan

AGHONI BAI
BIRINCHI KUMAR BARUA

'Who's that, Bhubon? Who's opened the yard gate?'
Saying this, the lawyer's wife put down the teapot in her hands and rose from her seat in the kitchen that morning. She looked out at the vegetable patch and said, 'Of course, who else can it be? There are no greens left in the yard because of this old woman. She's come this early only to scrounge around in the vegetable patch. Bhubon, go and tell the old woman to come out from there.'

Telling the domestic help to do the needful, the lawyer's wife entered the kitchen once more.

After waking up in the morning, the children were beginning to fuss. The lawyer's wife hastily fried some ghila pithas of rice flour and molasses, and distributed them to the fretting children. But it was impossible to bring them to order. Moini grabbed a piece of Makhoni's pitha and stuffed it into her own mouth. Makhoni began to sulk. In a tantrum, she flung all the pithas away. Bhaiti complained that only five pithas had fallen to his share. These tantrums irritated the lawyer's wife greatly. What would she do with these stubborn children! If only their father had paid them some attention! His pampering had spoilt them thoroughly.

The lawyer's wife shouted, 'You wretched lot! Why don't you just eat? You want a taste of the bamboo stick on your backs, do you? That old woman will arrive any minute. Eat up everything fast. If she gets to see this, you've had it. Her greedy eyes will curse whatever you put into your mouths, and you'll all get running stomachs. You'll see the fun then.'

Bhaiti, who had been sobbing his heart out so far, said to his mother, 'Give me another pitha, Ai.'

Even before Bhaiti could finish what he was saying, Makhoni pulled the bowl she had kept aside closer to herself, and thrusting it towards her mother, wailed, 'Moini took one from my share, you'll have to give me another one.'

The mother shouted, 'This monster's belly is never filled unless she snatches food from another. She's growing up, and her gluttony is also growing....'

After her mother's scolding, Moini whined, 'Just because I looked at it, now she says I've eaten her share of the pithas?' Sulking, she immediately walked out of the kitchen. Sensing the seriousness of the matter, Makhoni and Bhaiti began to chew on their own pithas. In the meantime, Bhubon came in, after having washed the used bell-metal platters and bowls, the kahis and baatis, at the well.

'Oi Bhubon, so what was the old woman looking for in the yard? Has she left or not?'

'What can she be looking for….? She's bundled up the ripe areca nuts that had fallen on the ground. When I asked her, she said that no nuts had fallen at all.'

'Such a liar, that old woman! When will she get over her thieving habits! She herself can't eat them, yet she keeps gathering them….'

Even as the lawyer's wife was speaking, the old woman came up to the smaller kitchen away from the main one where the tea was being made. Pulling up a low wooden pira to sit on, she said, 'Okay, Ai, give me a drop of tea, I'll have that and leave. I've been meaning to come over for a couple of days now, but haven't been able to.'

The lawyer's wife had hurriedly taken down the kerahi on which she had been frying the pithas from off the fire. She wasn't paying much attention to what the old woman was saying. She noticed the old woman sitting quite near the hearth after she took off the utensil. Glaring at her, the lawyer's wife said accusingly, 'Can't you sit a bit further away? You've come here after roaming the whole wide world, and now you're sitting so close to the fireplace.'

Seeming not to be affected by the other woman's words, the old woman dragged her pira a little further away, and said, 'What wide world are you talking about, Ai, I've come hurrying to your place right after my bath. Come on, Ai, give me a drop of that hot water, I've not eaten anything since last night. I asked the Nazir's mother for a handful of athiya bananas; I just had a couple of them. Really, those bananas…they were full of seeds.'

The old woman chattered on, but the lawyer's wife did not have the time to pay her much attention. She held out a bowl of hot tea and some half-fried pithas to the old woman. The old woman wrapped up the pithas in a clean piece of paper that was lying nearby. This did not escape the notice of the lawyer's wife. 'For whom are you taking those?'

Sighing, the old woman replied, 'Heh, Ai, who am I going to take them for? That lame one, who else, she's there, isn't she? She told me to get some for her as I was leaving.'

The other woman's heart softened. She took down a few pithas from the corner shelf and gave them to the old woman, saying, 'All right, take these, and give them to the lame girl. You eat up your share here. If you take them home, your granddaughter will kick up a fuss.' After saying this, the lawyer's wife went out of the kitchen.

The old woman put one in her mouth. Then, looking around, she bundled up the rest along with the others. Bhubon, who was sitting nearby and eating some pithas, began to laugh.

Embarrassed, the old woman said, 'They're very tough, can't chew them.' She blew on the tea bowl of bell metal, and, contorting her face at Bhubon, said, 'This tea is also very insipid. It has absolutely no taste at all.'

Thus did Life play out that morning.

∞

It was a place that was still in the early stages of developing into a town. The population was very small. It could be said that there was nobody like the old woman Aghoni Burhi in that place. From the young to the old, everybody knew her. Aghoni Burhi was a living 'gazette' for spreading all the domestic gossip. Who was ill in which household, which home had guests, she knew it all. Aghoni Bai was in the know when a household held a prayer meet in which a group of women sang Ai Naams, songs in praise of the goddess, or when someone held a large religious gathering. The old woman somehow sniffed out all the details about these. What was the behaviour of the new bride at the government official, the Sirastadar's, house like? What was her manner of speaking? She knew all about the boastful son-in-law of Hazarika…Aghoni Burhi gossiped freely about it all in front of everybody.

This season, the tart garcinia plant in the yard of the official Keeper of Records was fruiting abundantly. People would pluck the fruit from the elephant apple tree with poles every day in Phukan's house. Cowherds had entered the Gossain's yard, and now after their ravages, the wood apple tree was completely destroyed. In the Barua household, they had put a net over the litchi tree, and saved the ripe fruits from the depredations of bats. She knew all this thoroughly, just as she knew what greens, what vegetables, were growing in which household, in which family's yard at that time. All she did was wander around from house to house throughout the day.

Sometimes, if necessary, the old woman also helped out somebody in need. Sometimes, she would pound the pestle to make flat rice in somebody's house. At other times, she would pound the coarse rice grains in another household. The old woman never used her general bodily weakness as an excuse to shirk any kind of work. The old woman was for many daughters and daughters-in-law of the town, their right hand, and quite indispensable. The Sirastadar's new daughter-in-law had felt a craving to eat taro greens. Barua's wife needed some fiddlehead ferns. Phukan's wife wanted to eat something bitter, but hadn't been able to, all this time, because she hadn't been able to find any xokota, the dried leaves of the jute plant. Gossain's daughter longed to eat posola, the cooked pith of the plantain stem, yet had not been able to get anyone to bring her the trunk of the specific athiya banana plant required to cook it. It was Aghoni Bai who was usually instrumental in fulfilling their desires.

One just had to mention it to Aghoni Bai, and next day the thing would appear. The old woman was an expert in fetching a thing from somebody's house, and presenting it to somebody else. She was notorious for being light fingered. But even though she heard this being said about her, she pretended not to have heard. Neither shaming nor insults, scoldings or abuse, affected the old woman. If these insults and scoldings became very loud and carried on for a length of time, she would mutter, 'I'm hard of hearing, I can't hear a thing,' and hurry away.

The old woman slyly gathered some litchis from Barua's yard, and put them in her bundle. Barua's son came out, and accused her of being a thief. Saying, 'What are you saying, son, I can't make out anything,' she rushed away to Phukan's place. She took out the litchis before Phukan's son. Coming out of the smoke-filled kitchen, Phukan's wife saw the litchis in her son's mouth, and asked who had given them to him. On hearing the boy's reply, she looked towards the old woman and said with annoyance, 'Sih! Who asked you to bring these? Are you trying to kill the boy by feeding him unripe litchis?'

'Ishh, they are hardly unripe now. People have almost finished eating them up.'

Phukan's wife's anger doubled at the old woman's words. 'Fine, let other people finish off eating them. Don't you come here and try to show your love for my son.' She snatched the litchi that the boy was sucking on, and flung it away. She then re-entered the kitchen. But there was no expression whatsoever of anger on the old woman's face. Throughout her life, she had been the target of this kind of contempt and insults. Where was the question of self-respect when she had to beg from others for even a scrap of food?

The boy was mortified at his mother's cruel behaviour. That litchi had been quite fleshy and juicy! Understanding the boy's dejection, the old woman consoled him, 'Listen, my dear, when they become really ripe, I'll bring you some more. These days, my eyesight is not what it used to be....'

The other day, Bhogai had been really angry. He was the old woman's neighbour. With his large brood of children, he was barely able to make ends meet. He had his own land, and his own cattle and ploughshare. He somehow managed to survive with these.

That day, Bhogai had had to leave for the potters' village on the banks of the river, on some community work. While returning, he had brought with him a fine pipe. In the morning, he had looked around for the new pipe to smoke his tobacco. It was not to be found. This could only be the work of one person. While going that way in the evening, the old woman must have pinched it.

Next morning, the old woman's house was thoroughly searched. Bhogai's mentally challenged son went in the morning to the old woman's house. The pipe was discovered inside an old pot in her house. Neither the old woman nor her granddaughter was at home at that time.

The old woman's hut could hardly be called a home. It was a small, tumbledown hovel. The roof had not been repaired with new thatch for a very long time now. It would be difficult to take shelter under that roof when the rains came. Of course, a few people had given her cause to hope, saying they would give her a bit of thatch for the gaps in her roof. But who knew what they would do when the time came? The walls, too, were in really bad shape. Here and there, patches had been made with bits of kerosene tins taken secretly from other people's houses, and pieces of wood. In some other spots, the holes had been papered over.

In spite of the condition of the hut, it had a door. Moreover, to complete the picture, it had an ancient lock, too, on it. She kept the key to the lock suspended from the waist of her mekhela where it danced during both her waking and sleeping hours.

The house had two rooms. One was a kitchen. She slept with her granddaughter on a broken bamboo platform in the other room. These rooms, though, were stuffed full of a variety of things. Small clay pots, earthen pitchers and cooking vessels, big and small tin containers, coconut shells, were scattered everywhere. The old woman could not tolerate cooking pots and pitchers being thrown away by other people. She would, therefore, gather up these earthen utensils which were now homeless, and give them space in her own house.

There was no similarity whatsoever between the old woman's past and present conditions. At this point, when she had set foot on the last step of the staircase of her life, she was afraid to look back on the treads of the past. She was almost four score years of age. She could barely stand firmly on the step where her feet were at the present time. In this situation, how could she look back? She had no time or leisure to ponder; she was engrossed in going forward. But how could she move ahead? Her lame granddaughter pulled her backwards all the time.

The lame girl was indeed her granddaughter. She was always known as 'Lengeri', the Lame Girl. If she did have another name, nobody knew it, except her grandmother. She was crippled from birth. She could neither stand up nor walk. She would go around town on all fours with her grandmother. Her mother had died quite some years ago and her grandmother had been around since her birth.

Aghoni's husband had passed away when her child, Loyoni, was not yet four. Since that day, Aghoni's life had taken a completely new turn. Nobody in the village ever saw Aghoni's laughing face again. The merrymaking of the girls who went to fetch water from the Kolong River decreased greatly. It was, as though, all this time, it had been Aghoni who had opened the container of laughter and had cast good cheer all around.

Since that time, Aghoni's life was full of hardships. Her husband had not had any close relatives. Leaving his own people behind, he had settled down on the outskirts of this town. He had earned small sums by doing odd jobs in various homes. With this, they had been content, and happy. He had been in the prime of youth. The thought of saving something had never even entered their heads. Why live at all if one could not spend one's money in fulfilling one's desires during one's youth? The body had strength; there was no reason to be afraid. If all else failed, he could at least work as a day labourer and earn enough for the needs of two people.

Aghoni's husband, Ratan, certainly got good opportunities. He was indispensible to Gossain for his ability to perform various tasks satisfactorily. Only Ratan came to Gossain's mind when it came to getting something done. Ratan had become close to Gossain's sons, too. He was in perfect harmony with Gossain's boys, who were his contemporaries.

Gossain's eldest son was a sub-deputy collector. He was very fond of hunting. Whenever he came home, he would set out on the old she-elephant on a hunt. His companion was always Ratan. Without Ratan, the elder son could never set out for a hunt. He had taught Ratan to fire a gun, too. He loved Ratan and always behaved with him as he would with a brother.

But Aghoni did not much care for these hunting trips. On the day that Ratan told his wife about killing a pregnant red doe, Aghoni made him promise not to go hunting ever again. Intoxicated by the power of his youth, Ratan had tried to make his wife see his point of view, using logic and reason.

'God has created these creatures for us, if we don't consume them, who will?'

Ratan would be without a moment of rest whenever Gossain's eldest son came home. It was as though his own brother had come home and he would become completely busy in searching out suitable spots for shikar. He would get up at the crack of dawn and go out to find out if wild ducks had gathered at the murmuring lake, or if the Bengali fishermen had got their boats ready. He would also gather information about whether haitha, the yellow-footed green pigeons, had come to roost in the fig trees of Barhampur; whether or not herds of deer had come to graze in the Laokhowa Reserve Forest.

The elder son was truly anguished when he heard of the death of his companion, Ratan. He kept writing home urging them to give Aghoni all possible help. Certainly, in the beginning, Aghoni got plenty of help from the Gossain's household. The sub-deputy collector's mother would generously give her whatever economic assistance Aghoni needed. But constant supplication can wither away even the great virtues of kindness and compassion. The world is, after all, a marketplace. People invest their capital where there is hope of some returns. Very few actually want to earn merit by giving alms to the destitute. In the sphere of practical domestic concerns, and in matters of giving and receiving, in particular, women have a sharper intelligence as compared to men. Because they move around in the wider world outside their homes, men have a broader vision. They only notice matters of larger import. But because they are restricted within the sphere of the home, women have not got this opportunity to develop a broader vision. For this reason, they notice even the minutest things.

Even though Gossain's son sent money for Aghoni every month, his mother stopped handing it over to her. What was the point of nurturing a potential concubine? And in any case, why was her elder son so concerned about Aghoni's welfare? Why was he always enquiring about this woman, who was in the prime of youth? No, such a thing could not be allowed to happen in Gossain's family. By any means whatsoever, by hook or by crook, Aghoni would have to be sent off from here. Who knew what this young man would do, in the heat of the moment? And come to that, why did Aghoni keep asking when her elder son would arrive?

After Ratan's death, life became harder than Aghoni had expected. It was a series of unending crises that came upon her, one after the other. Barely had she solved one problem, than another one would appear. Aghoni did not really have to worry too much about running the kitchen, for both she and her daughter ate little. She could make do with whatever she received by husking and winnowing paddy. Indeed, she was an expert at these jobs. There was no one who could get as much rice from a measure of paddy like her. The sound of her working the dheki, the threshing pedal, was so distinctive, that people could make out from a distance that it was Aghoni.

This frequent use of the dheki firmed and filled out Aghoni's calves. Her figure grew more and more attractive. This body threw her into many predicaments after Ratan's death. When she went out, young men's eyes followed her everywhere. Sometimes, if there was any chance to do so, a youth would come forward to exchange bantering words with her.

Aghoni tried her best to avoid them. But it was impossible. The young men would come forward on their own to talk to her. They would snatch Loyoni away from her by force. On the pretext of playing with Loyoni, they would come closer to Aghoni. She did not have the courage to scold those young men and send them off. It was not an easy thing to set fire to a hornet's nest. The consequences would be grave.

But on the evening that Hatbor's eldest son, Bhedo, came near her as she was immersing her pitcher in the Kolong's waters and asked, 'Aghoni, will you come home with me?' she felt that the skies had crashed down on her head. Without replying, and only partially filling her pitcher, she hurried back to her own hut.

And this was that very same Bhedo! Ratan had showered him with so much affection! After returning from a hunt, he would never rest until he had sent a portion of meat to Bhedo, sometimes even depriving himself of it. If there was some tasty morsel to be had, he would not eat till he had shared some of it with Bhedo. When Bhedo acted in the village theatre, it was Ratan who took on the responsibility of getting him a suitable costume. Ratan had borrowed Gossain's middle son's muga outfit for Bhedo on one occasion, and had got thoroughly scolded after it was badly stained with bamboo sap. Once, Hatbor had refused to permit Bhedo to go and see the bhaona and other festivities in Puronigudam. All the young men of the village were ready to leave; only Bhedo was missing. Unable to bear the sight of his gloomy face, Ratan had coaxed and cajoled Hatbor till he had yielded. Though he had been unwell, he had taken Bhedo to see the bhaona himself.

One by one, all those incidents came to Aghoni's mind. Today, when it was not yet three years since Ratan's death, this Bhedo, whom Ratan had loved as a brother, was now eyeing his widow! He wanted to set up home with Aghoni!

Aghoni found this intolerable. From dawn to dusk, she constantly felt this same lustful gaze on her. They seemed to be greedy, all of them, for the flesh on her body. They were all distressed that the full bloom of her youth would wither away and be wasted. Those young men were all busy trying to find a remedy for this state of affairs.

It became very difficult to stay alone at home after dark. Every night, somebody would come to her door and call her by name. She would clasp Loyoni to her breast and weep. She would try to wake the child from her sleep, as though it was Loyoni who would be able to protect her from the hands of these tormentors. She believed that no man could molest a woman before her own child.

Next day, while going to fetch water, Bhogai's daughter-in-law met her at the ghat and said, 'Hoi O Aghoni, why were you calling out to your daughter so loudly in the middle of the night? We could hear your shouts right up to our house.'

Aghoni answered softly, 'Ei, I thought some thief had come.' Immediately after the words had left her mouth, Aghoni felt she should not have said them. Perturbed, she fell silent.

Placing her pitcher on her hip, Bhogai's daughter-in-law gave a sarcastic laugh and said, 'Eesh, just imagine, thieves coming to your house! Your place is full of gold and valuables, isn't it?'

Aghoni thought, indeed, why would thieves come to her house? Next moment, sighing at a memory, she went down to the river to fetch water.

Aghoni decided that she could not stay alone like this anymore. She would have to go and stay in somebody's house. If she didn't have her daughter to think of, she would have drowned herself in the Kolong a long time ago. Of course, if she went into menial service in some household, there would be no place for her in society. All right, fine, if that was to happen, let it happen. But she just could not stay on like this, surrounded by people who had become her enemies. Who knew what would happen at any time! It was only Gossain's mother who could save her from this calamity.

Aghoni decided to broach the matter to her. But for some time now, she had not been treated well by Gossain's mother, either. Even if she asked for something, the older lady would send her off by saying, 'Not now, come later.' Even so, Aghoni looked for an opportunity to bring up the subject.

It was the month of Aghon. Dusk came early in these November days. It seemed as though it was dark just after the midday meal. Gossain's mother had finished her meal, and had spread the split bamboo mat in the yard, cutting betel nuts. Aghoni appeared before her, along with Loyoni. Gossain's mother gave Aghoni a betel nut and paan leaf to chew on, and asked, 'So what did you have for lunch today?'

'Ai, what food can I have, it was nothing much.... I made khaar with the matimah dail, the black pulses that you gave me the other day. I had rice with that khaar.' Pointing to her daughter, she said, 'This one doesn't put anything in her mouth unless it's a tenga, a tart curry.'

Gradually, after a few words, Gossain's mother said, 'Ok, let's talk, but why don't you also open my bun and loosen my hair while we do that? Some big lice are crawling on my head.'

Even before she could finish her words, Aghoni had loosened the older woman's hair from its confines, and ran her fingers through them. Almost immediately, she found a large louse. Aghoni took it out and cried out, 'Oh, Ai, this one has sucked so much blood, it has become very plump!' She called her daughter to her, and got her to kill the louse. Both the women talked to each other even as Aghoni continued to pluck lice.

Gossain's mother said, 'Get someone to have a look at your house this Phagun. You can take the few bamboos you may need from our yard.'

'Ai, how can I employ anyone to repair my house? Where shall I get the money to pay him?'

'But what will happen when the rains come?'

'I really can't say right now.' After a pause, Aghoni asked, 'Tell me, Ai, can I come and stay in the shed where the dheki is housed?' She looked fearfully at Gossain's mother's face.

'Where's the space in that shed? If there had been some space, wouldn't I have asked you to come and stay there?'

A ray of hope lodged itself in Aghoni's heart. Perhaps she could get a little space in the dheki shed if she told the other woman of her troubles.

With this simple faith, she said, 'Ai, it's become impossible to stay alone in the house now. Somebody comes and keeps knocking at the door, and throwing things. That's why I want to come and stay here in your compound.' Breathlessly, she said all this and then fell silent.

In a very wise tone, Gossain's mother said, 'Didn't I tell you long ago to find somebody and set up home with him? You only have one child, anyway. What has Medeu's daughter Jetuki done? Didn't she take her three children and set up home with another man?'

At Gossain's mother's words, Aghoni sighed and kept quiet. The search for lice, too, ended there. She had wanted to open up her heart and express her anguish. She could not. Indeed, not even a single tear fell from her eyes. She quickly tied up Gossain's mother's hair in a bun, and prepared to leave.

'Ai, I'll go now. I need to search out some wild greens and herbs for our evening meal.'

Understanding that Aghoni was saddened, Gossain's mother said, 'All right, go. If you can, try and come over tomorrow at some point. Don't feel bad about what I've said. I'm only speaking for your own good. You are a young girl now; you will not be able to control yourself for ever.'

Even before Gossain's mother finished speaking, Aghoni had bolted from there, like a cow who comes to graze in somebody else's yard and takes off when the householder comes out to chase it away. Hearing the creaking of the bamboo gate in the yard, Gossain's mother turned back to look, and exclaimed, 'Eesh, she's taken flight at the mere mention of it. What's the point of giving good advice to a low-caste person?' She took her bota of betel nut and went inside.

That day, Aghoni did not get around to plucking any wild greens. Indeed, she did not even cook anything for their evening meal. She lay down on her bed as soon as she entered her house. She did not lift her head even when she heard the doba and kanh, the kettle drum and cymbals being played in Gossain's house for the evening prayers. Several times, Loyoni whined for her dinner, but after getting a few slaps from her mother, she lay down on the split bamboo mat and fell fast asleep. Aghoni lay down beside her and wept throughout the night. Just because she was born into a poor family, did that mean that she had no morals, no emotions, and no right to love, at all? Memories of her girlhood, of her marriage to Ratan and his boundless love for her, kept coming to her mind, repeatedly. Aghoni had never thought even in her wildest dreams that Gossain's mother, knowing about her nature, would insult her in this way.

Of course Aghoni was aware of the gossip that was going around about her. But nobody had had the courage to say anything like this to her face. She did not realize when her weeping and her worries gave way to sleep, towards dawn.

Opening her eyes, she saw that the door leading out of the house was open. Loyoni was not there beside her. She hastily got up from her mat and rushed out. It was quite late in the morning by then.

Outside, she saw that Loyoni was sitting and playing with Bhedo. On seeing him, Aghoni lost her temper completely. Last night's worries and anguish came rushing like a storm to her mind. Without thinking, she caught her daughter by the hair, and began to rain blows on her back. Not understanding what her fault was, Loyoni was too afraid even to cry.

After punishing her daughter in this way, she turned furiously to Bhedo and said, 'Who asked you to come to my yard in the morning? If any of you ever come to my yard ever again, then the Almighty will curse you.' She began to pant in anger.

Bhedo, too, was stunned into silence on hearing Aghoni's furious words, that too in the morning. He looked around for a while, and then fell with a thud at her feet. Addressing her as his elder sister, he said, 'Baiti! Forgive me for what I said the other day. From today, I am once more your younger brother, Bhedo. From today, nobody here will be able to say or do anything against you.'

Aghoni's head began to spin. Unable to remain standing any longer, she sat down on the ledge outside her house, and began to weep. In the meantime, Bhedo picked up Loyoni, and took her to the road. Aghoni sat on the ledge and sobbed uncontrollably.

At that point, the lawyer's domestic help came by and asked her, 'Baiti, aren't you coming to milk the cow today? Its calf is mooing in hunger.' Only then did Aghoni come to her senses.

'I'm not too well today,' she replied. 'All right, I'll hurry up and have a quick bath, then go. You go on ahead.' With a long, heavy sigh, Aghoni went inside.

Bhedo was actually a good person. But people have their weak moments. For many, it becomes difficult to control themselves at that point of time. The sensual desires become so strong that it becomes impossible to discipline them at that time. Their conscience becomes weak, and they cannot judge the difference between good and bad. The rules of society, of religion, everything vanishes from their consciousness. They want to go on a rampage like a mad elephant, and satisfy the desires of their senses. They wish to destroy everything in their path like a violent storm. But just like Nature becomes calm and tranquil after a mighty tempest, in men, too, there is a state when everything returns to its natural state. When that happens, a man becomes a God. Immersed in repentance and regret, people come forward to atone for their past sins. They accept all the disrespect and insults that are thrown at them.

Bhedo, too, was now a changed person. Aghoni was saved from a very big danger in her life. She, who had no family to call her own, had now found a brother.

There is no uniqueness in a poor person's life. The days passed with difficulty for Aghoni and her beauty could no longer arouse lustful feelings in the youths of the village. Nobody could think of Aghoni as a young, fun-loving, cheery village girl any more. The Aghoni of today was a mature, sober, serious, poor widow who could not be called a beauty at all. There is a saying that strength and power do not fall apart. However, the learned pundits have perhaps not yet been able to decide whether beauty falls apart or not.

Even as the lustre of beauty faded from Aghoni, its radiance came and settled on Loyoni. The toddler Loyoni was growing up. She could now help her mother with some chores. As she grew older, she would leave her mother's side, and roam around the village by herself. All on her own, she discovered the details of what could be foraged in which yard and whose backyard contained what plants. Her mother would leave her to look after the house when she went to thresh paddy in somebody's house, or to fetch water. But instead of staying put in her own home, she would wander around the village, searching out whatever was available in other people's yards.

Even fit and robust young men did not go into the Sirastadar's wife's yard because it was a deserted, neglected place. It was in that yard itself that the last rites of the Sirastadar and his two sons had been performed. Being alone, the Sirastadar's wife could barely take care of it, though she was aware of even the fall of a leaf from a tree there. Nobody had the courage to pick up anything from that yard. Juicy fruits such as leteku, dimoru, poniyol, tepor would ripen and fall to the ground, and rot there. People thought that the place was haunted. Even when the Sirastadar's wife passed away, she would probably remain there as a demoness, living on a tepor tree.

One day at high noon, the place was still and silent. After having a frugal meal, the Sirastadar's wife had gone in to rest. On hearing some noise in the yard, she would wake up with a start, and shout, 'Who's there?'

At that moment, Loyoni quietly entered the Sirastadar's wife's yard, with a khorahi, a bamboo bowl in her hands. She felt extremely happy. There were so many ripe tepors and dimorus lying on the ground. Why did nobody come to gather them? With her limited capacity to think, she was unable to arrive at any answer to this riddle. Loyoni began to suck on a tepor. How much could she eat, how much could she gather! She would not be able to pick up everything today; she would have to return tomorrow to continue doing that. She would bring Maniki and Konsowali with her tomorrow.

Loyoni had assumed that her mother would be very happy to see the khorahi full of tepor and dimoru. She waited impatiently for her mother to return. Every now and again she would go out to the road and see if her mother was on her way back. Since her mother was not visible, Loyoni would turn back and begin counting, once more, the number of dimorus and tepors in the khorahi. After counting a few, she would invariably make a mistake, and put the lot back into the khorahi again.

When her mother returned in the evening, she asked, 'Hoi, Loyoni, who brought these?'

Proud of her achievement, Loyoni said, smiling happily, 'Okay, you tell me, who gave us these?'

'How can I say, am I a know-it-all?'

Since her mother was unable to give her the correct answer, Loyoni replied enthusiastically, 'Who'll come and give these to us? Your own daughter has gathered these and brought them here.'

Surprised, Aghoni asked, 'Where did you find them? In whose yard?'

'In whose yard has all this been lying around? I've brought them from the Sirastadar's wife's yard. I gathered them this afternoon. Ish, there are so many other....' Loyoni could not complete her sentence. Her mother grabbed her by the neck and began to shake her violently.

'Moroti!' she rebuked her daughter, 'Couldn't you go anywhere else? You entered that yard in the afternoon! You fool, don't you know that it is a haunted place?' Letting go of her daughter, Aghoni took the fruits along with the khorahi which contained them. Going out, she flung them, khorahi and all, outside her own compound. Loyoni was distressed, though not because of the blows her mother had rained on her, but because she had thrown out those ripe and juicy dimorus that she had foraged with such care. If only she had placed one in her mouth, her mother would surely have appreciated the taste of those fruits.

Another day....

There was a thickly wooded patch behind Gossain's mother's house. A wild bitter gourd creeper had climbed up and was now abundant with bunches of the vegetable. Because it was an unappealing and repugnant place believed to be the home of spirits, no young person of the village went there. That evening, Bhedo went searching for his brown cow, used for pulling his plough. Since it hadn't returned home, he went in search of it there. Suddenly, he saw a young girl with wild, tangled hair in that place. Bhedo shivered. Quietly, he began to retrace his steps. Abruptly, he heard Loyoni's voice, addressing him as her maternal uncle, 'Hoi, Momai, wait, I'll come with you.'

Startled, Bhedo looked back and asked, 'What are you looking for here? It's already evening!'

Loyoni went up to him and showed him the bitter gourd which she had collected. 'Momai, there are so many karelas on this plant! I couldn't pluck them all today. I'll gather a lot more tomorrow, and go to your house and give you some. But why have you come here?'

'The brown cow that we use for pulling the plough hasn't returned home. I need to plough my field tomorrow.'

'Ei, your brown cow did come this way. I had thought that I would chase it back to your house when I finished here.' Saying this, Loyoni rushed off to a nearby jackfruit tree. Bhedo had still not recovered from his fright. He screamed, 'Where have you gone, Oi Loyoni?'

The girl replied from under the tree, 'The brown cow went this way. Wait, I'll chase it back here.'

Bhedo said hurriedly, 'Ei, it's dark. Let it be now. I'll leave the bars of the gate open at night, she'll come home by herself.'

He had barely finished his sentence before Loyoni appeared, chasing the cow before her.

'Where was she?'

'Somebody had cut a branch off the jackfruit tree today. She was eating its leaves.'

'But how did you know that the jackfruit leaves were lying there?'

'I had come here in the afternoon. I took back a whole lot of leaves for our white goat.'

'What! You came here all alone in the afternoon?'

'Well, who'll come with me?' said Loyoni. She went after the cow which had in the meantime wandered off in a different direction, and brought her back again.

'Really, you're quite a girl.'

All this time, Aghoni hadn't been aware that it was now time to get Loyoni married. Of course, for a long time, she had nursed a hope that she would be able to get a good boy for her daughter. But she hadn't thought, even in her dreams that it would happen so soon. Loyoni would step into her fifteenth year after the monsoon month of Ahar ended, and that of Xaun began. Surely she was not yet of an age to get married? There was no sign of Bhola's daughter, who was three years older than Loyoni, getting married anytime soon. Bhola had three daughters who were ready to be married. Whereas she had only this one daughter. Where was the hurry to get her married in such haste right now?

But one day, while going to the Kolong to fetch water, Bhogai's daughter-in-law asked her, 'Hoi, Aghoni, is it true, your daughter is going to live with Podo?'

That was when Aghoni was jerked back to reality. Even though Podo was a boy from their village, he lived in some faraway place, Jorhat or Golaghat. He was some Hakim's employee. He had taken leave for around a month, and come home. He was not on very good terms with his father and stepmother. She had seen Loyoni chatting and laughing with Podo after he had come here. But as a mother, Aghoni did not believe that just because they talked, it meant that she was going to set up home with Podo.

Not getting a reply even after quite a while, Bhogai's daughter-in-law said with a derisive grimace, 'Why do you want to hide this from us? Podo has brought a lot of gold and money from Jorhat. Why should we go to beg for it? Instead of getting hitched in this furtive way, God would have been happy if it had happened after the proper rituals, pouring a pitcherful of water on the head.'

Unable to give any answer to this, Aghoni asked, 'Where did you hear this?'

Bhogai's daughter-in-law said furiously, 'Eesh, we haven't yet lost our eyes and ears, have we?' She picked up her pitcher of water, and, placing it on her hip, strode off, muttering something to herself all the while. She didn't ask Aghoni to accompany her.

The villagers expressed different opinions after Loyoni went to live with

Podo. Some people thought she had done quite a smart thing. Another lot of neighbours thought, 'No, that young girl is incapable of much planning, she couldn't have thought this thing out. This is all a plot laid by her mother. Podo has earned a bit of money, and Aghoni has noticed this. She's ensnared him with love potions and given her daughter to him.'

After this came to light, there was quite an uproar in Podo's house, as well. Podo's father had considered a particular person in the village who was quite well off. A bit of jewellery and a few other things would come to their house with his daughter if she was brought in as a bride.

On the evening that Loyoni entered Podo's home, his stepmother used very abusive language on her. She had already spoken to the wife of the merchant Rongai Mahajan in the village about bringing their daughter Maloti home for Podo, and was in the process of gathering a few things for the wedding itself. But here was Podo, suddenly bringing home that Aghoni's daughter. Aghoni, who was practically starving, and had just a dilapidated hut to call home! Furious, she hurled all kinds of invectives at Loyoni, 'Oi you cursed creature, daring to enter my house! You shameless whore! Get out of my house, right now. Otherwise I'll catch you by the hair and beat you up with the broom and throw you out. You'll come to know very well what your old mother-in-law is like very soon!'

Podo's father was a quiet and peace-loving person. He somehow managed to calm his wife and tried to make her understand. 'What can you do? Since she's come here on her own, you shouldn't abuse her. It's good, in a way. If we had gone in for a proper wedding, we would have had to spend a large amount of money on it.'

All the villagers had assumed that, leaving everything else aside, Aghoni would be delighted to have Podo as a son-in-law. But what happened was just the opposite. After her daughter left her house, Aghoni had nothing to do with her. She did not go even once to Podo's house to have a look at her daughter and son-in-law. She had no regrets about the fact that Loyoni had just gone away with Podo. But why couldn't she have gone with someone other than Podo?

Aghoni had quite a few reasons for disliking Podo. It seemed that when he was away from home, he was quite fond of liquor as well as bhang. He was known to be of loose character, as well. There were several scandals regarding him in the village itself. Staying in the town had changed his behaviour, and his manners and conduct were now quite different from theirs.

Aghoni's greatest disappointment and anguish was that Podo was a servant in another man's house, the Hakim, in Jorhat. The very same thing that made the villagers look up to Podo with respect, made Aghoni, on the other hand, look at him as a person of no worth. He was unacceptable to her. She had never imagined that Loyoni would elope in this manner, keeping her mother in the dark. The neighbours observed that Aghoni changed greatly right after Loyoni left. Aghoni went completely grey. She aged. The sorrow within her expressed itself through the changes in her body.

It was now almost a year since Loyoni had left home. And yet, not once did she come to her mother's house. Indeed, after her shameful behaviour, how could she come? She had not even bid farewell to her mother when she had left.

Now Aghoni came to hear about her daughter from others. It seemed that Podo hadn't come home for quite some time. He had stopped sending home money, too. From cleaning out the dung from the cowshed, to clearing the undergrowth in the patch of sugarcane, Loyoni had to carry out these chores herself. On top of that, she had to listen to her mother-in-law's abuse day and night. In addition, Loyoni was pregnant. But that did not excuse her from having to toil at these tasks. She could never escape her mother-in-law's curses and abuses.

Aghoni would come to know of these things and return home to weep in private. Her Loyoni, the same delicate Loyoni, whom she had sheltered from doing any kind of manual labour, was now being made to toil like this! Aghoni had not been able to bear the sight of her daughter working the dheki. That same Loyoni was now suffering, having to labour hard in another person's house, while her own mother was alive. What was this? Surely she could return to her mother's house? But how could she herself go to Podo's house to see her daughter? Yes, certainly she was her own child, the fruit of her womb. But even if there was no respect, motherhood had its own pride.

Aghoni was returning home one evening after winnowing husked paddy in Barua's house, with a basket of paddy on her head. She was surprised to see her door ajar. Who could have done that? Entering her home, she kept down the basket, and looked around. Hearing the creaking of the broken bamboo platform, she looked in that direction. Thunderstruck, she placed a hand on her head and sat down with a thud on the floor. This was her pretty, delicate daughter, her restless, lively butterfly, Loyoni! This was not a human body. It was a living skeleton.

Aghoni grew extremely angry at herself. Why had she not gone and fetched her daughter home, all these days? Was there ever a mother as cruel as her?

Loyoni came down from the platform, and, clasping her mother, began to weep. Both mother and daughter held each other and sobbed heart-rendingly.

That evening, the oil lamp was not lit in Aghoni's house. Both mother and daughter cried themselves to sleep in each other's arms. Starting up in her sleep, Aghoni pulled her daughter to her bosom. She forgave and forgot the disgraceful behaviour of her daughter in the past, all the stains and stigmas she had brought on them. Loyoni, too, snuggled into her mother's bosom like an infant.

Everybody knew that Loyoni would not survive for very long. If she could just remain alive till the child was born, it would be a blessing. But Aghoni's heart did not accept this. She began to try her best to give her daughter a new life. She went to the well-known kabiraj, Phukan, in the town, and, falling at his feet, began to wail. Phukan tried all kinds of medicines that he had at his command. But how could medicine men and other learned people hold back, with their potions, a person whose days were numbered on this earth? A month after giving birth to a crippled girl child, Loyoni, suffering from excessive bleeding, closed her eyes forever. Nobody was surprised.

There is no empathy in people for the misfortunes of the poor. Without the sympathy of others, the grief within one's heart remains bottled up, and creates a tumult there. But even with this grief, Aghoni remained alive, to look after her crippled granddaughter, and nurture her to adulthood.

The neighbours said to each other, 'Loyoni died, all right. But why did she have to leave behind this crippled child like a noose around Aghoni's neck?'

Today, Aghoni is not the beauty she once was. Nobody stops on the streets to cast a glance at her graceful ways. Today, Aghoni is a grandmother. She has a granddaughter. She is always busy in providing for her, in scrounging around for her food and clothing. She moves around other peoples' homes and yards, to see if she can get some good food for her grandchild. Once, Loyoni, too, had moved around in the same way in other peoples' yards, gathering fruits and vegetables for her mother's enjoyment. Aghoni was now echoing that.

Aghoni moves around, entering peoples' homes in the afternoons, getting news of their domestic concerns. Outside their hut, the lame grandchild sits by herself and plays a simple game with pebbles. Today, on seeing her grandmother returning home, she goes inside the house. From the anchal of her riha, Aghoni takes out the bundle of ghila pitha that the lawyer's wife had given her. The child hastily picks up one half-done ghila pitha and puts it into her mouth. Even before she has tasted it properly, she says, 'It's very tasty, Ai! The Ai from the lawyer's house has sent them for me, hasn't she? Tomorrow, I'll definitely go over to their house.'

A smile of satisfaction lights up her face. Seeing her smile, Aghoni thinks, 'It's good that you were born lame. You'll never be able to leave me and go off like Loyoni did.'

Translated by Mitra Phukan

MISTAKEN IDENTITY
SYED ABDUL MALIK

He had a small business, a business of selling products worth two paise. Before the war, his commodities had been priced at one paisa each, now it was two paise. He had to collect many items with a price tag of two paise.

He brushed the brass plates daily, in order to make them shine. The brass flower pots gleamed as though made of gold. He cleaned the electric bulb just above the level of his head. Only two cubits of space remained for him among the items he sold. Three lines of foreign cigarette tins, though all empty, brands like Players, State Express, Barkleys and so on. On some shelves, there were cardamoms and qiwam. Matchboxes were stacked beautifully, like bricks. A few small glass cases contained some rings made of American gold, buttons, shirt links, torchlight bulbs, and in front of his lap there was a plate containing paans, dried and cut betel nuts, zarda, qiwam, and two pots of a mix of khoir and lime. It was all quite elaborate, yet the items were priced at two paise only.

Niamat Ali's paan shop was on the main Mirjapur road. It had been there for a long time. It was open most of the time to facilitate the babus. He was always there in the shop with a smile, his two front teeth showing their gold fillings. He was born and brought up in Calcutta. His parents, wife, and children all lived in a small, dark room in a bylane, a gali nearby. He had not seen much of Calcutta except his dark enclosure. The two-feet-wide shop was his only domain, his Calcutta. Once in a blue moon he also enjoyed movies with his children in third-class seats, but he repented those luxuries soon after. He always promised himself not to waste money in this manner again.

There was a five-storeyed building just behind his shop. There, on the second floor, lived Jagatbabu. The building was very old and dilapidated in places. Jagatbabu was a storekeeper of a godown in the Sealdah Railway Station. He used to come and go by tram. But he sometimes walked, especially at the fag end of the month. His pay was forty-five rupees. He had arranged a broken chair and a table in a corner of his godown to sit on. His father, two brothers, a sister, his uncle's orphan child, and his own four children lived with him in his house.

Jagatbabu had been very gentle before. But now, after the death of his mother, he had become irritable. It was more apparent in the hot environs of his godown, which was made of tin sheets. Every day, before going to work, Jagatbabu bought a paan at Niamat's shop and packed two for office. He spoke to Niamat often. However, the time for his return was not fixed. Sometimes, it was eleven at night. He was more concerned with his work at the godown. Niamat spoke little. Jagatbabu liked his Bengali, spoken with a North Indian accent. He also liked his paan with that zarda and qiwam, and the way it stung his mouth.... Both of them liked it when there was a hartal, a strike. Yet, they could not enjoy it wholeheartedly. When Niamat's shop was closed during a hartal, he lost a day's earnings. That shop was his only source of income. Yet, he joined in the strike and walked with the processionists. He enjoyed it. He felt proud wearing the coat with a nickel badge with Pakistan written on it. His badge was the finest one.

Jagatbabu also liked the strikes. Though there was an apprehension that one day's pay might be cut, yet he joined in the strike. He shouted slogans vigorously. If he got an opportunity, he even took a flag from another processionist.

There was, however, one difference. Their groups were different. Niamat's shop was open when Jagatbabu went in a procession. He enjoyed looking at the people. There were good sales. And on the day when Niamat joined in a hartal, Jagatbabu too liked it. But as Niamat's shop was closed on that day, he had to go to another paan shop. When Jagatbabu met him after his office hours, he would say, 'It was a massive rally, Jagatbabu', and the latter would nod his head in appreciation.

Their lives were far from being political. Like many poor Indians, they lived with some dissatisfaction, no doubt, but with the casual ease common to many poor people in India. There was no turbulence, no brightness. They would withstand any calamity, even the death of their wives. It was 9 August 1946. The Hindus celebrated the anniversary of the Quit India Movement of 1942. Flags were hoisted, slogans were shouted. Lakhs and lakhs of Hindus were on the streets of Calcutta to celebrate it. As if everybody was now free and independent. Jagatbabu also went with the processionists, his head held high. He was happy. In 1942, he had not been sure about Gandhiji's movement, nor did he understand it much. But today, he felt proud to be a part of the celebrations.

When Jagatbabu returned in the evening, tired, he came to Niamat's shop. Before asking him anything, Niamat offered him a bottle of soda. Jagatbabu smiled at him while taking the bottle. Niamat said, 'Today, the rally was massive, was it not Jagatbabu?' Jagatbabu nodded.

'Was there any trouble?' Niamat asked.

'Why should there be any trouble? Were we quarreling with others? The British regime has to go. Why should problems arise if we say it?' Jagatbabu replied with a paan in his mouth.

'Oh yes, we will make our country free. Why should others mind it?' Niamat responded.

Jagatbabu laughed.

'There is a hartal of Muslims also on the 16th,' said Niamat.

'Oh yes, if both Hindus and Muslims fight together hand in hand, all their demands would be fulfilled.' Niamat was also a co-fighter with him in this war of India's Independence. 'If both of us fight together, the British will have to leave. Will they rule the hills and forests?'

'We will also get Pakistan, isn't it Jagatbabu?' Niamat asked. They did not know what Pakistan was. Jagatbabu had heard the Hindus saying that giving Pakistan to Muslims was not a good idea and that if it happened, the Hindus would suffer a lot. But seeing the eagerness on his face, Jagatbabu said, 'Oh yes, why not, when all the Muslims of India are demanding it?'

Jagatbabu felt very tired. He went homewards.

Niamat looked at the map of Pakistan that was hung on the wall of his shop. Two green areas on the map, that was Pakistan. He was happy. Then he looked towards the beautifully framed picture of Qaid-e-Azam, Jinnah. It was as if he was seeing it all. He had heard many things about Jinnah. He also uttered Zindabad after his name, along with others. Today he felt the largeness of that thin man's reach. He was the undisputed leader of the Muslims of India. He had fought for their existence, for many years. He was fighting for the poor people.

'Please give me a paan,' Niamat looked towards Jahir who was standing before him. He prepared the paan and quickly gave it. Then he asked, 'Jahirbhai, will Pakistan be formed one day?'

'Do you have any doubts?'

He went back home early that day. He declared to his family members that Pakistan would be formed and it was final. His father nodded.

'We are at the fag end of our lives. Let India be free now, during our grandchildren's time. We should be grateful to the Almighty.'

Niamat was excited. He came back to his shop and looked at Jinnah's picture again. He went to sleep late that night. Many thoughts came to him.

He saw lakhs and lakhs of Muslims in processions.

'Nara-e Takbir—Allahu Akbar.'
'Qaid-e-Azam Zindabad.'
'Muslim League—Zindabad.'
'Nara-e Takbir.'

Calcutta reverberated with the call that Adam had given when he was thrown out of heaven. Ibrahim had shouted those words when the Pharaoh had pushed him into the fire. The Prophet Noah had called out those holy words during the great deluge. Hazarat Mohammed called out the same thing in the Battle of Uhud. The cry was given by Imam Hussain in Karbala to the enemy Yazid. Every lane, bylane in Calcutta reverberated with the war cry. Islam was strengthened, 'Allahu Akbar Zindabad, Zindabad, Zindabad.'

Niamat's shop was closed that day. On 16 August, a direct action by the Muslims to fight the British imperialists was on. It was the month of Ramadan. The month of sacrifice, restraint, prayer, peace, and forgiveness. There was a white cotton cap on his head. It was a Friday. He wore a white kurta and a silk scarf around his neck. But he was empty-handed and without shoes on his feet. His old shoes were torn and he planned to buy a new pair on Eid.

Niamat went out, leaving his father at home.

'Nara-e Takbir.'
'Allahu Akbar.'

The procession passed through Mirzapur Street. All Muslims joined it except the old and infirm and children and women, who remained in their houses.

Jagatbabu had a holiday that day. So he went in the morning towards Howrah. He was going to find a bridegroom for his daughter.

Suddenly in the procession a rumour was heard, 'There are riots happening somewhere.'

The rumour spread like wildfire throughout Calcutta. 'Riot! Riot!!'

'Where?'

Nobody could say anything.

'Which way?' Nobody was sure.

'Between whom?' No one could find out.

'There—in the direction of Mirzapur Street,' somebody said.

'Nara-e Takbir.'
'Allahu Akbar.'
'Pakistan Zindabad.'

Niamat stopped.

He asked many people where the riots were happening. One person told him with certainty that it was in Mirzapur Street.

He thought about his home, shop, and children in Mirzapur Street. He started to run towards it. Reaching near his shop he saw that nothing was happening there. But in the other bylane, there was a great commotion. He ran towards his house. The noise was coming towards them.

At that point, he heard someone calling his name 'Niamatbhai!' It was Prasanna, Jagatbabu's brother. He went upstairs to Jagatbabu's apartment. Everybody was very fearful. Their faces were pale. They were all frightened and helpless.

'Where has Jagatbabu gone?' Niamat asked him.

'Towards Howrah.'

'They came thrice,' Jagatbabu's wife said.

'Who were they?'

'Goondas!'

'It is not safe to be here even for a moment. Let's get out of here! Quick!'

'They are coming again.'

'Quiet!'

All of them took their few belongings and came out of the house.

Niamat held Jagatbabu's three-year-old child with one hand and a suitcase in the other.

Quick, lest the goondas come running towards them.

Prasanna was helpless. He silently followed Niamat. Niamat was also not sure where he would take them. He was only thinking of how they could be protected from those ruffians, those goondas. Going through several bylanes, he reached a place and stopped in front of a house. He called out 'Fazalbhai, O Fazalbhai!'

The door was opened.

'Oh. Niamatbhai.'

'Let these people enter first, and then I'll talk.'

Niamat gestured to Jagatbabu's family to enter. All nine of them entered the narrow room in Fazal's house.

'Who are they?'

'She is my sister.'

Niamat then began to leave. He told Jagatbabu's wife, 'Don't worry. I will come again, Fazal is also my brother.'

'When will you come, Niamatbhai?'

'I will take you out when the situation is under control over there.'

'Prasanna go with him, otherwise how will Niamatbhai save his goods?' Jagatbabu's wife said.

'Prasanna, will you come? Together we can save some goods. There is no fear here. Fazalbhai is here.' Prasanna and Niamat went towards the road.

Jagatbabu reached his house about twenty minutes after Niamat had taken out his family. He had come rushing back on hearing the rumours about the riots. The whole of Calcutta was gripped by fear. Hindus murdering Muslims, burning their houses, Sikhs firing at Muslims, Muslims also counter-attacking. The innocent and the weak were murdered by the agitated mobs in the streets. Murders, rapes were happening in broad daylight. The fate of India, its independence, all went towards Lal Qila! The British were laughing at the people. 'Gandhi you go on your mission! We will give you ideas! Jinnah go on—we will supply you with weapons.'

Jagatbabu ran towards his home. His head reeled on seeing the empty house. All the doors were open and the things inside were scattered around chaotically. There was nobody inside. He trembled in fear at the sight. A great darkness fell upon him. He ran back hurriedly outside. Like a madman, he ran. And ran. He went towards the house of a friend of his wife's about a quarter of a mile away. He felt thirsty. He looked towards Niamat's shop. It was closed.

Nearby, in another bylane, the killings continued. There were loud, ugly screams. Noise, screams, cries; there was no Allahu Akbar, no Vande Mataram, no Jai Hind, only the sounds of machetes and lathis, and the shouts of terrified people. People were killing people, brothers decimating brothers. There were wild, beastly celebrations by some brutes in Calcutta.

Jagatbabu went on ahead. He thought that his family members were also in that chaos.

In the meantime, Niamat and Prasanna came back to rescue Niamat's family. They brought out the terrified family. He took with him a few items. The loud cheers of the killers were coming closer. There was no time to spare. Who could prevent the mob of arsonists? Niamat came near his shop. He remembered that there were several items of value inside. He turned back and told Prasanna, 'Brother, you continue towards that safe place of ours. I am taking some costly items from the shop.'

'Don't be late. The goondas are coming this way. Be quick.' Niamat's family went with Prasanna and soon disappeared at the turning of the bylane.

Jagatbabu returned. He did not find his family at his wife's friend's house. He felt that the sky was falling down on him and he went towards his own house.

'Where have you been?' Bisheswar Kabiraj asked him as they crossed the road.

'Everything is finished,' Jagatbabu was crying.

'Did it happen just over the road?' Kabiraj asked.

'Why?'

'Have you not sent your family members with Niamat?' He asked Jagatbabu with astonishment.

'With Niamat? When did you see this?' Jagatbabu was agitated.

'Why! Aren't you friends with Niamat?'

'Friends! What friendship is left today among Hindus and Muslims? Niamat is only a Muslim goonda.' Bitter thoughts came to Jagatbabu's mind.

Kabiraj had not finished talking but Jagatbabu ran like a man possessed towards Niamat's house.

'Niamat is a Muslim, Niamat is a goonda, Niamat, Niamat.' Oh, he had waited for this opportunity! Has he finished everyone? His little three-year-old son also?

Jagatbabu ran like a frenzied person. Niamat is a Muslim, he is the goonda who has killed Jagatbabu's family members.

Jagatbabu had a near collision with a man running from the opposite direction. But he did not stop. His mind was filled with one thought only, the deep conviction that Niamat had lured his family away and killed them all. Jagatbabu was possessed with rage. 'Oh my Purabi, could hapless Prasanna not save her?'

Jagatbabu reached Niamat's paan shop. Niamat was inside it collecting some valuables, rings, and so on. He saw the picture of Jinnah and taking it down, kept it inside his shirt. He was about to take out the bag with valuables when he felt a big blow on his head. He fell down on the floor.

Jagatbabu did not wait; he hit Niamat again on his head with a soda bottle. Great spurts of blood from his head spilled onto the items in the bag and on Jinnah's photo.

Incensed, Jagatbabu circled Niamat. After a minute or so, Niamat became conscious again. He opened his eyes, and saw Jagatbabu with the soda bottle. He looked at Jagatbabu and tried to say something. Jagatbabu came near him. 'They, they are with Fazal bhai at Chitpur Road.' He was bleeding profusely.

'Where?'

But Niamat, in spite of his best efforts, could not say anything more.

A military vehicle came and screeched to a halt near the shop. Jagatbabu was talking and lifting Niamat's head over his shoulder.

Suddenly, a sentry inside the vehicle shot a bullet from his revolver. It hit Jagatbabu's chest.

The vehicle went away. The white sentry gave a cry of victory. The veranda of Niamat's shop was awash with the blood of the two brothers.

Jinnah's picture still lay on Niamat's bloodied chest.

Translated by Syed Nazim Hussain

MIYAH MANSUR
BIRENDRA KUMAR BHATTACHARYYA

These men were not known to me. But I derived a kind of pleasure by looking at their comings and goings on the dock. Each mazdoor carried a bag of cement on his head and his head was wrapped with a white cloth sprinkled with sand. The kurta on the body and the short dhoti worn over the hips were also covered with sand. Their faces reminded one of the monkeys who had built the setu, the bridge, over the sea. The flow of the comings and goings of the mazdoors went on unabated.

The dock was known as Atara dock. The worker who was addressed as the sikani by others offered me a stool to sit on. He was the person who dealt with the invoice in the dockyard. This was the month of Ahaar, the monsoon season, and the sky was heavy with dark clouds. Soon, it began to drizzle. Due to the rain, the wooden planks of the bridge were sticky with mud. Down there, the mazdoors dipped their bodies in the water to bathe. Then my eyes fell on the wide expanse of the river Luit. A fishing boat was struggling against the strong currents of the river and slowly making its way along the edges of the small island known as Urvashi.

Gradually, some information came about the luggage. I saw my retainer pulling three huge parcels towards him and my heart danced with joy. These three parcels carried the fruits of three years of my hard labour. A writer, at times, may be drawn more towards his first published work than even his newly-wedded wife. In my excitement, I began to move around the heap of luggage lying on the dock. Having observed my restlessness, the sikani asked me, 'What is the matter, Babu?' In reply I smiled at him—the kind of smile one sees on a mother's face when she looks at her child for the first time.

Probably he could not discern what lay behind my smile. He rarely came across babus who smiled in this manner. So many parcels of books must have passed through these rough hands of his. But never had he regarded these parcels as being any different from the bags of cement, oil, cloth, or paper. Suddenly, an unexplained sorrow arose within me—the kind of sorrow that arises when one notices the intense differences that exist between men. The realization that he did not understand me as a person, my worth, brought a deep pain within me. Suddenly, the happiness of writing and publishing a book was no longer there.

There are many in this world who would regard my parcel of books to be just like any other parcel and this realization brought upon me a sudden quiver. There was no forgiveness for the sikani within me. Moreover, there is always an inherent desire in everyone to see their words in print and when obstacles come in the way or there are people who are not appreciative of this, then it becomes terribly hurtful. I wanted to move away from there and so ordered my retainer to arrange for a man to carry my entire luggage. I just wanted to make a quick departure.

But it was not to be. Seeing the sudden downpour, my retainer did not dare to go beyond the dock. He returned from the small wooden bridge near the dock and said, 'Kakaideo, do wait. Let the rain subside.' There was nothing I could do but agree and once again I came and sat near the sikani.

Suddenly, I noticed that the mazdoors were carrying tins of oil and wooden boxes without paying any heed to the rain. In this world around me now, there were only two useless individuals—me and my retainer. The rest were all occupied in doing some work or the other. One mazdoor was lying curled up over a heap of gunnysacks and snoring heavily. The poor man must have been very tired after a hard day's work. The white sand from the gunnysacks covered his body making him look like some kind of performer. The sight made me feel as if there was a stage right in front of me, where a scene was laid out—where men just work and when they don't, they sleep.

I took out a cardamom from my pocket and put it in my mouth. The rain began to pour even more heavily. Some mazdoors were shouting while pushing a large paper reel over the wooden bridge. With every push the reel began to move here and there like a drunken man being pushed around. In a way the scene was quite an entertaining one. The lean muscles visible on the bare legs of the mazdoors somehow seemed like they were able to maintain the weight of the bodies. I continued to stare at this drunken reel till it reached the sandy bank of the river. When the reel was finally loaded on to the truck, it seemed to lie there in a drunken stupor. While pushing the heavy reel up, the mazdoors, bearing the weight, let out a piercing cry that sent a shiver down my spine. Even before the shiver had subsided, I saw something—on one side, some trucks were moving on the main road, probably going to some printing press, and on the other side there were others returning to the dock. Not a word could be heard from the mazdoors. After all, the hard-working people rarely have any time to chat and relax.

I put another cardamom in my mouth, took out my handkerchief, and wiped my face. I looked around and saw that the sikani was no longer engaged with looking at the invoice but was staring intently at the rain falling on the river. He was sitting flat on the ground with his lungi folded to his knees. There was a pen in his mouth with the nib pointing outwards and he seemed to be perturbed by some dismal thoughts.

My thoughts suddenly turned from the busy dock to this man. What kind of a fire was burning within him? Why should a man like him, whose world comprised only of ships, invoices, port, and rice, ignore his work and the official notebook lying before him?

In fact, due to the rain, there were a couple of people reminding him to call out the numbers of the invoices, so that the luggage could be disposed of quickly, but it seemed as if he had turned a deaf ear to all their demands.

I looked at him and turned to where his eyes seemed to be fixed at. At a distance a boat seemed to be struggling against the heavy rain and torrential currents of the river. Instantly, my mind shifted from the dock to the heart of the boat. For a moment, I forgot about the dock, my enthusiasm for my book, and the silence of the sikani. My only concern was how to save the unfortunate men and women struggling in the face of death in the boat that was about to sink.

There was no sign of any other boat nearby. I was not aware if there was any boat at the dock at all. After all, who would dare to row a boat in this heavy rain? I became restless and began to tremble just as one would do in helplessness, at the sight of certain death right before one's eyes. I trembled in such a manner that my retainer placed a hand on me and asked, 'Kakaideo, why are you trembling in this way?' addressing me as his elder brother. Without uttering a word, I pointed towards the boat. Struggling against the currents of the river, in the midst of the heavy rain, the boat looked like a huge dolphin. Seeing the boat my retainer let out a shriek, 'Oh no! Babu, Nabou was supposed to have come from the other bank in this boat itself.' He was referring to my wife, whom he addressed with this honorific.

A shiver ran through me. I told him, 'Maliram, do you think Nabou would cross the river in a boat? I forbade her to do that.' In a quiet tone he replied, 'But Nabou had told me that she would come in that boat itself.'

This was disastrous! Why on earth did she have to come in a boat in this rainy season? I tried to reassure myself that she would probably use the ferry and not the boat in this rain. Who knows, she may not have come at all. There was no reason for her to do so. Why would she be so enthused about my book? Maybe she couldn't resist the temptation of bringing home her husband's first book. She could have at least spent a night at her mother's place. No, Anu's mother would not be so unreasonable as to allow her daughter to return in this heavy rain.

The more I tried to reassure myself, the stronger my doubts grew. Anu would always do as she willed. She would keep her word even in the face of this heavy monsoon rain. Having grown up near the river she would not be afraid of drowning in a boat.

My fear was so deep-rooted, that unknowingly I sighed loud enough to reach everybody's ears. Sharing my anguish, Maliram shouted twice, helplessly, 'Bhagwan, Bhagwan!'

In a moment all work came to a halt at the dock. A box remained on someone's head. The one who was about to lift another box stopped there itself. Someone let out a cry, 'Haribol!' The mazdoors gathered at the entrance of the dock. One could hear only sighs everywhere.

My own sorrow seemed to be all alone in the midst of this collective sorrow—there was no reason for these homeless people to be affected by my grief.

Disturbed by the noise, the sleeping mazdoor woke up and gazed in surprise at the perturbed crowd. It took him quite some time to analyze the situation.

The sikani, who was near me, was uttering something. I realized, with a little effort, that he was chanting the Aayat. There was no time for me to unravel the meaning of those words. Then suddenly I realized that there was a kind of profound peace on his face. His vigilant eyes were still on the boat. It seemed as if the traces of white on his beard reflected the wisdom of his age. An unperturbed face, in such moments of crisis, can always raise some hope in the heart. Even in these ultimate moments of death, it seemed as if there was still some hope left in rescuing those who were on the boat.

Gradually, the boat began to sink and the entire dock was filled with cries of desperation. For a moment I could not utter a word. Slowly, I leaned against Maliram and looked at the scene of drowning. A thought came to my mind that perhaps Anu was gradually entering the depths of the river and would soon be drawn towards the mermaids down there.

Unknowingly, my tears began to flow. There was hardly anything that I could do. Maliram hugged me so tightly that I felt too weak and helpless even to move.

There were loud shouts and mournful screams everywhere and in between could be heard the sound of the Aayat of the Koran. I felt as if my heart would stop beating altogether. The joy of being the writer of my first book was shattered to pieces. The only thought in my mind was, 'Let Anu be saved. Let her return to me.'

Suddenly, the sound of an engine reached my ears. Someone shouted, 'Motor boat! Motor boat! Save them, save them!' Maliram pulled me up a little and said, 'Look Babu, they are being rescued by the motor boat.'

Seeing the motor boat, a sense of hope awakened among the mazdoors at the dock. Each in their own way shouted words of encouragement. Pointing at the speeding boat, someone let out a cry, 'Faster, faster.' Someone pointed out, 'See, just see! A net has been cast to pull them out.' I saw a man, who was swimming, being almost pushed by the current to the boat itself. Serang, the captain, cast a net and caught hold of the man.

One could hear the echoes of fear, uneasiness, elation, and desperation which were let out by the mazdoors from time to time as they watched the men, who were frantically trying to reach the motor boat to save themselves.

The sikani was the only one who stood still. His chanting of the Aayat was over. With a grave and intent look, he continued to witness the conflict of man and the river Luit.

As I watched men being pulled up and saved by the motor boat, a kind of undefined gratefulness filled my heart. The boat appeared to me, at that moment, like a very benevolent God. There are times when non-living objects seem to assume life and act like a living being.

Gradually, as the boat drew nearer and the faces of the passengers became somewhat discernible, I searched intently among them for Anu. But there was no sign of her.

There was uneasiness in my mind and a kind of darkness filled my entire being. The boat touched the edge of the dock amidst the shouts and rejoicings of the mazdoors.

Suddenly, I heard the sound of a splash and the next moment I noticed that the sikani was no longer beside me. He had jumped into the river, and no matter how hard I tried, I couldn't locate him in the water.

The sound of the boat coming to a halt could be heard. I went closer and looked at the passengers. Anu was nowhere to be seen. I saw her maternal uncle who was all drenched and shivering. I called out loudly,

'Mama, did Anu come with you?' My shout seemed so strange that everyone on the dock and the boat became silent and waited in anticipation for my uncle's response. Initially, my uncle tried to explain with gestures that everything was over. Then he pointed his hands upwards and I understood that Anu had drowned.

When this thought dawned on me, I felt a sudden void and hardly knew whether I was dead or alive. My heart seemed to be beating furiously. I was inconsolable and like a small boy I wept, my cries matching the waning sound of the motor boat. Maliram again had me leaning against him, patting my back like a mother and consoling me. I felt that by losing Anu, I had lost the most precious thing of my life. My inner being seemed to have been drenched by the pouring rain. In fact, I wouldn't have minded even if the world had come to an end at that moment.

Suddenly, I heard a shout. I saw that the mazdoor who had been sleeping till the other moment, was shouting from a vacant part of the dock. He pointed his finger to a distant area and said, 'Sikani!'

I looked in that direction in surprise. I saw a pair of raised shoulders dancing its way towards us, from a distance of about half-a-furlong from the boat. Something foamy passed along near the side of his hands and on the other side a huge piece of log seemed to be floating away unmindfully.

But what was the sikani doing in the water?

I was surprised and it was not just me. There emerged a subdued cry of distress from all the people standing there. Why on earth did he jump into the water? Was he out of his mind?

Suddenly, his head emerged out of the water along with his hands and he let out a terrible cry.

The sound of the motor boat's engine shattered the silence of those who were a witness to the scene. When one looked intently it could be seen that the sikani's raised shoulders were just about to be caught in the current of a whirlpool!

'Faster.'

'And faster.'

'And faster. Faster. Faster.'

Each one of us looked unwaveringly at the motor boat moving towards the shoulders visible above the water. It was truly terrifying. Everyone let out a sigh as the boat neared the whirlpool. The sikani seemed to be fighting against Yama, the lord of Death. What a fearless battle it was!

Gradually, the scene became clearer. The sikani was pulled up by the net that was cast from the boat. There was again rejoicing among the people. Gradually, the motor boat returned and the sound of the boat increased the heaviness in my heart. There was no sign of Anu. Nothing in this world could bring back my Anu to me. I felt as if I had lost consciousness. Only my eyes shone like an earthen lamp lit before the sacred 'tuloxi' plant.

When the boat became more clearly visible, the mazdoor who had been sleeping earlier spoke out—'The sikani is not alone. There is a woman too.'

'A woman!'

I waited with a lot of hope as well as anxiety for the motor boat. My eyes were repeatedly looking at the approaching boat in search of the lost one.

As the boat drew near, I saw that the woman was leaning against somebody, almost like a sleepy person. When the boat finally stopped, someone said, 'She must have taken in a lot of water.' I noticed that the man who was holding the woman was Anu's maternal uncle.

The excitement of getting back my cherished one brought a quiver within me. I realized for the first time that one's heart could tremble even in happiness. As soon as the big wooden plank was placed near the boat, I rushed and almost pulled out Anu from her uncle's arms and held her tight. I called out, 'Anu, Anu!' But she was unconscious. I called her again, 'See Anu, my book has arrived. The one where you had done the proofreading. It's the book that was printed in Calcutta.' I almost believed that, even in that unconscious state, she would listen to my words.

In a moment I lifted her on my shoulders and like a mad man rushed over the wooden plank that touched the boat and then ran across the dock. Like a mazdoor walking over the bridge while carrying a gunnysack on his head, I got into the ambulance waiting near the bank of the river. Being overpowered by my emotions and feelings, I once again whispered in the ears of my unconscious wife, 'Anu, my book has arrived. We have to bring home the book together today.'

If it would have been humanly possible, I would have brought her back to life with all the warmth of my heart.

After three long days in the hospital, Anu finally regained consciousness. As I was leaning over her head, she looked at me with surprise and asked, 'How did I survive? I was washed away and the boat could not pick me up. Tell me who brought me out of the water. Do tell me.'

I seemed to have got my life back when I saw the smile on her pale face and the brightness return to her weak eyes. I kissed her dry and rosy lips softly and said, 'Anu, I haven't even enquired about the person who saved you. I completely forgot about that lifesaver who pulled you away from the mouth of the whirlpool.'

My mind dampened at the thought of being so ungrateful and I said to Anu, 'I am really very ungrateful. I will go at once and bring the sikani here to your bedside. When I got you back, I completely forgot about the person who saved your life. Really, how ungrateful I have been!'

Anu was really moved by my words and said, 'You really love me so much.' I smiled and without uttering a word, kissed her softly twice on her eyelids.

Anu asked me, 'Has your book arrived? Can I have a look?' I fetched the book from the outer room, placed it in her hands and told her, 'Now I will go in search of the sikani. Meanwhile, you can go through the book.'

Anu said softly, 'Please go and tell him about me.'

I rushed out at once to the dock.

Atara dock of three days back and the Atara dock of today. The flow of the mazdoors carrying the luggage continued unabated as before. But strangely, I did not recognize any one of them. There was sand all over their faces, bodies, and clothes. There was a mazdoor sleeping over a gunnysack, but bore no resemblance to the man who had been sleeping there three days ago. The weather was cloudy even today. The men who had come to take their luggage were standing near the sikani as before. But this was not the same one who was there three days ago. The man sitting here was completely different. The previous one had a beard and this one did not.

I asked slowly, 'There was this man—the one who used to sit here—where is he?'

The man was a little taken aback when I asked him about this person. He said, 'Tell me what you want from him. You can ask me.'

'No, no, I just wanted to meet him. He saved my wife from drowning.' I was really ashamed that I didn't even know the name of the man who saved Anu's life.

The new sikani replied, 'You must be talking about Miyah Mansur. He is no longer here. He left for Pakistan just yesterday.'

I asked him in a cursory manner, 'Did he ask about me?'

'No.'

'Sih! I did a very wrong thing. I didn't even find time to express my gratitude.' There was remorse in my voice.

The new sikani tried to console me and said, 'You can go now and please do not keep thinking about this. To save people from drowning is actually our Dharma. There is no need to be so grateful about it.'

'Can you just give me his address?'

'Babu, I don't know his address. Homeless people like us do not have any address. We keep moving from place to place.' With these words, he went back to his routine job of locating the customers' luggage by referring to the invoice numbers. The mazdoors, as always, were moving around and doing their work without paying any heed to the rain. Work and work. Work was all they knew.

But why only work? They were also aware of a liberal, selfless, and universal kind of love. It was this kind of love that enabled the man to save Anu and depart from the place without expecting any gratitude in return. My love, in contrast, seemed so selfish. I had completely forgotten about Mansur when Anu was brought to me. Not even once did I remember to express my gratitude. Sih, how ungrateful I was!

Till today I have not been able to convey my gratefulness to him.

I have been searching everywhere. I have been looking for Miyah Mansur in every dock. I will search for him in all the docks in this world. My fascination for this Aayat-chanting man, Miyah Mansur, whom I had come across accidentally on the dock, was no less than my fascination for the mermaids of the river Luit. Anu, I, and everyone will one day depart from this world, but Miyah Mansur will continue to live on the dock of river Luit forever. He will always save some unfortunate traveller even at the risk of his own life and, in turn, will leave behind many ungrateful people to bear the burden of unexpressed gratitude.

Miyah Mansur. In whichever corner of the world he may be, the writer Shri Amit Saikia and his wife Srimati Anu Saikia have placed him, with reverence, in that corner of their hearts where even the Divine Lord may not find a place. And it is not just Amit and his wife but many unfortunate ones who will place him in their hearts for all times to come.

Translated by Arunabha Bhuyan

KATHONIBARI GHAT

MAHIM BORA

Standing by the river one could see only the endless hillocks of coal dumped on the river bank, the scarred banks of the Brahmaputra devastated by rampant erosion, and the vast expanse of green jhau grass that is exposed as the river dries up and recedes, undulating constantly on the sand bars in mid-river. During the rains, the Brahmaputra reached up to the stone chips covering the government road running along the river bank. Now that the river had receded, one had to go down the sloping banks and walk quite a distance to reach the mooring point for the ferry, the ghat. Bamboo scrapings and mat-like structures of bamboo called tarzaas, made of interwoven strips of bamboo, were laid over the sand to provide a makeshift path for people to walk over. The lone tea shop, raised on bamboo stilts pitted deep into the sand and constructed over a bamboo platform, was standing out with its thatched roof amid the drab surroundings. Its door, made from patches of flattened kerosene drums, could be raised on its hinges to rest over a couple of bamboo props to form a roof over a tiny shed in front of the shop. In this shed, four squat bamboo posts supported horizontal strips of cleaved bamboo to form a good 'bench'. It was a useful bench, where one could sit, having endless cups of tea from the tea shop, enjoying a leisurely smoke or just talking one's time away with whoever was around.

I was, however, doing none of that—I kept watching the reflection of the setting sun that was looking like a huge bowl of sindoor, the vermilion powder that married Hindu women wear on the parting of their hair as a symbol of their marital status. The ferry was to come only at nine in the evening but I had reached the ghat while the sun was still shining. As I kept watching, tiny ripples of the river seemed to clutch at the sindoor with tiny little fingers to put the blobs of red on themselves and carry it all away. The ripples seemed to be in a hurry to bedeck themselves with the sindoor and attend some friendly gathering somewhere. It occurred to me that it looked as though somebody had angrily dumped a whole pot of sindoor right on top of the ripples to be carried away. With all the traces of sindoor thus carried away, the river, thereafter, reminded me of a woman with a bare forehead, from which all the traces of the vermilion powder had just been rubbed away....

My mind had become quite forlorn. Hardly any passengers could be seen around the ghat. There were a couple of Nepalis with their wives and a few labourers from the tea gardens. Till then, the ghat at Kathonibari had been humming with activity and was alive with the noise made by the tea gardens' vehicles carrying tea chests and coal. The tendrils of hazy smoke from the far off machine rooms of the tea gardens were already merging with the gathering darkness. The thickening dusk slowly descended over the black ghostlike mass of the motorboat with its deckhands, the small family who owned the tea shop and the few stranded passengers like me, as if our loneliness prompted the darkness to swallow us up.

My curiosity was suddenly roused by the tinkling of small bells accompanying a soft rumbling sound. Peeping through the gaps in the tea shop's wall of straw and jute reeds, I could see a bullock cart coming to a stop in front of the shop. The cart driver or garowan got down and slowly lowered the yoke from the necks of the bullocks. The bullocks immediately started sniffing the blades of grass that were sprouting from the soil here and there. The lively green of the curtain covering the front of the cart, hiding whoever was behind it, was visible even in the fading light and my mind also became alive and started quivering like the curtain. A sprightly lad of fifteen or sixteen jumped down from the cart. With the help of the garowan, he brought down a tin trunk and put it on the ground. The trunk was raised and lodged atop the garowan's head with a fair bit of pushing and pulling. The boy then led the way for the trunk to be carried and taken to the boat.

My mind started quivering again. I could clearly see even in the dim light a statuelike figure coming out of the cart—the last particles of light were still floating in the air before being swallowed up by the gathering night. Shaking off whatever was sticking to its clothes, the figure stood there looking at the river. The boy and the garowan came back and moved closer to the cart once more. Taking out a 'hold-all' and some other stuff from inside the cart, they slowly made their way again to the boat accompanied by the statuelike figure. My eyes kept following them.

A little later, the boy and the garowan came out of the boat. The boy handed over some money to the garowan and after asking him to reattach the bullocks to the cart said, 'Tell them that we have reached safely, alright?'

After instructing the garowan, the boy went back to the boat. The garowan gulped down a 'single' tea and a 'banana biscuit' from the tea shop in a frantic hurry. In response to a question from a labourer who spoke the same tongue as him, the garowan explained that he had to go back ten miles and it was already pitch dark.

A little later, he started on his ten-mile journey. For a long time, the thin glow of the cart's lamp that the garowan had lit at the ghat before moving kept blinking feebly until it disappeared around a bend in the distance.

The dim glow of a candle became visible at one end of the boat. The new arrivals appeared to have chosen that part of the boat. I too had chosen the same spot earlier and I had already kept my luggage there. In the whole boat that was the only comfortable spot. A hurricane lamp had just been lit on the spot from where the path to the boat began. A lamp of the same kind had been lit a little earlier in front of the tea shop as well. The candle on the boat and the two hurricane lamps formed the three pillars of light that defined the limits of the tent of darkness enveloping us. Somewhere not too far away, a loose lump of earth detached itself from the river bank and rushed headlong to fall into the river. Tuplung! Quite close by, in the shallow part of the river, one could clearly hear the sniggering of a few minnow-like selekona fish. I glanced towards the tall and ugly heaps of coal. I felt as if they were waiting to pounce on me like those man-eating demons of folklore.

I was quite eager to go back to my spot in the boat, to know a little more about the new passengers, perhaps. I went into the boat by walking over the sturdy logs that connected the boat to the land like a gangway.

In the pitch black darkness inside the boat, the medley of smells from tea chests, paints, dried fish, and burnt-out lumps of coal had burst forth with a maddening intensity as if they were all tipsy with lao-pani, the local brew. I felt as though somebody had yanked open at that moment, right under my nose, an old family chest that had been kept locked for ages. I liked the ambiguous smell that assailed my nostrils.

The ferry was due to arrive at any moment. The deckhands were busy finishing their meals before the ferry arrived. A little distance away from where I had kept my luggage, the Nepali family had spread out a blanket to sit on and had opened up their lungs to a full-throated song. A little distance away from them, on another blanket among the railings, a few Santhali men were seated in a circle and were hastily munching on something. Perhaps it was puffed rice. And bang on top of my stuff and belongings, a young boy had opened a hold-all and was lying on it, pushing my suitcase and my bed-roll to one side and flipping through a film magazine in the dim glow of the candlelight. By his head sat a girl—the statue I had seen alighting from the bullock cart—and she was looking at the magazine in a detached manner without really seeing it.

Not knowing what to do, I fiddled with my suitcase, giving it a little shake just for the heck of it. The girl raised her eyes towards me but it took her a little while to make me out through the glare of the candle's flame. She continued to look unseeingly in my direction. It gave me an opportunity to have a good look at her face, framed by the gentle glow from the candle. The boy was also looking at me with a hand over his magazine. As I bent down a little towards my suitcase, my face must have received a lick from the candlelight.

The boy sat up in a huff and the girl pulled up her 'sador' over her head onto the bun of hair at the back of her head to form a kind of hood, an 'oroni'. The gesture meant that the girl was married. The oroni was customarily used by married ladies to hide their faces.

The boy was saying, 'Is this your suitcase, this one? We moved it a bit, I hope you don't mind. All of us will squeeze in a bit to sit a little closer together. You may open up your bed-roll and set up your bed.' The boy's tone had such an air of familiarity that I was slightly taken aback. I have often come to grief in the past for forgetting faces, but no, I just could not remember seeing this one before.

'That's alright,' I said. 'You two (Oh! I had forgotten the oroni! I shouldn't sound so casual to a married lady!)... I mean, well, you please sit comfortably.... Don't bother about me. I'll manage.'

I did a little tricky manoeuvre with my fingers to push my dirty bed-roll out of sight behind my suitcase. But the problem now was: what to do with my prized possession—the discoloured suitcase with its crumbling paint, which was at this point acting as the shield, that now stood hiding the dirty bed-roll? Its lineage was excellent; its body was made of British steel. But who bothers about lineage anymore these days?

As I was removing them in order to make more room, the boy started complaining in a hurt, petulant voice, 'Are you trying to move away to a different place? We will mind that very much....'

The boy actually started rolling up his hold-all.

'Don't do that,' I said hastily. 'It is really more sensible that you both stay here and rest for a while. Who knows when the ferry will finally arrive? It's never punctual. And sometimes, it doesn't come at all....'

'That's all the more reason why we would like you to stay back with us. There are such few passengers today! On top of that, there are no local

Assamese passengers at all. My sister and I were in fact discussing that. If only we had someone….'

It was obvious the boy was as nervous as his sister. But I had done all that drama only to hide my dirty bed-roll and suitcase. Now that hiding them was no longer important, my bed-roll could make an unabashed appearance. So I opened it up towards the foot of their bed and sat down.

'I think it is time to go and get our tickets. Let me go and find out. Your tickets would be to which place?'

Actually, there was still lot of time left for purchasing tickets. But there was nothing else that came to my mind at that time.

'We have to go to Jorhat, eventually,' the boy answered after sitting down a little hurriedly.

'To Jorhat? But that's upstream! Today's ferry is going downstream!' I exclaimed, shocked. It was unbelievable that they did not keep track of such basic things. There was no excuse for them to make a mistake like that.

The boy looked quite smug as he put my worries to rest. Quite pleased with himself and tickled with the kind of pride that a fifth grader would feel when he had to explain something to someone in the sixth grade, the boy explained to me with a lot of unconcealed glee that they would go downstream and get down at Silghat and then catch a state transport bus for Jorhat. 'We have to reach Jorhat tomorrow by all means. It is really very urgent.'

I was attracted not so much by the meaning of the words as by the words themselves and the way they were delivered.

Though the newly-wed girl was staying a little apart because of her natural shyness, whenever I caught a glimpse of her face, I got an impression that she was also taking an equally active part in the discussions. I was, in fact, wondering about this quality of the girl, conveying an impression of being alive to the discussion without a single sound escaping her lips. She must have been married only recently, I thought. In the feeble light of the candle, I thought I could still make out traces of the paste of lentil and turmeric on her body, the maah halodhi of the bridal bath. The fragrance of the scented oil used during the wedding ceremony was still wafting out from the clothes that she wore. A full face, round arms reminding one of those long, rounded balloons, the bright fairness of her radiant skin, and the shade of the paat silk she was wearing, all combined to frame her like a painting. Such a combination of grace and beauty was rarely seen. Suddenly, I realized that the boy had asked me something, and not getting a reply was somewhat embarrassed and a little annoyed. Sensing his annoyance, I turned towards him and asked,

'Oh, what did you ask? About my destination? I am also going to Silghat. My home is very near Silghat.'

'That's even better. The ferry will reach Silghat sometime during the night. Meeting you was a big boon for us. Isn't it so, Baideo?' he asked his sister, addressing her as his elder sister.

Baideo was leafing through the magazine but her mind was with us. She kept staring at her brother in mute acceptance of what he had said.

A smile was stamped all over her face as if with some indelible paint. Even her brows appeared to be smiling. Her nose, chin, and eyes also were all swathed in smiles. How could such deep, dark eyebrows appear to be smiling so smoothly?

It was time for the ferry to arrive. I got up to find out. The boy was on the verge of taking out some money for the tickets. I stopped him saying that the bell for tickets had not yet been sounded and even if tickets were being sold, I could get them with my money. He could pay me back later.

'If there is still some time before the ferry arrives, maybe we can get some tea?' I asked tentatively as I was about to step out.

The boy looked at his sister. She poked the hold-all here and there with her fingers and then asked as if to herself, 'Where did we put the flask?'

That was the first time I had heard her voice. Deep yet somehow soft like butter—I don't know if that was an apt description for a human voice.

The boy went near the railing with the flask to give it a wash. Close by, a river dolphin surfaced for a while as if to find out how late was the night. Someplace nearby, a lump of loose earth fell noisily into the river. From the tea gardens in the distance the strains of the tired beats of the Madol drums came riding on the breeze.

I saw no sign yet of tickets being issued. 'Maybe the ferry got stuck in some sand bar,' the ticket master said with some annoyance. The last big earthquake had apparently left behind quite a few sand bars inside the ticket master's mind which had been disturbing his sleep ever since.

The family of the tea shop owner had already had their meal. The children were busy bringing down stuff from the bamboo platform to prepare their beds. In the makeshift shed in front of the shop they had put some mattresses on top of the bamboo 'bench' and the middle-aged, fat shopkeeper and three other men were engrossed in a game of bridge.

The moment I reached them, one of them blurted out, 'Oh! It's already ten, is it? It's time to leave.'

'Come on, play another round,' another one replied as he was shuffling the cards.

No one had seen me. I did not want to be a spoilsport and so I kept watching the game, unnoticed.

'One heart', 'One spade', 'One no trump', 'Two clubs', 'Three diamonds', 'Double', words like these kept popping up like the sounds of firecrackers. The game started and ended. The man pressing for a last round was the shopkeeper, and he had gone down heavily. By then, three of the men had got up, ready to leave. I could gather that they were from the tea garden—they came there every evening to play a few hands of bridge.

I was watching the shopkeeper with sympathy. His sad face had begun to look like a veritable 'spade' by then. Only then did he notice me.

'Do you need something?' He asked in a soft voice.

'I would have liked some tea. Can it be arranged?' I asked, casting a glance at the same time towards the children preparing their beds and getting ready to sleep.

'Of course. The ferry may not come tonight at all.'

A small boy had by now jumped down to stand by my side.

'One cup...?'

I extended the flask towards the boy—'Three'.

'Oh!—So, you have your family with you?' The tea shop owner went on. 'Please let me know if you face any difficulty. We can arrange food too should you need it. If you need hot water or tea during the night, please don't hesitate to come and take it.'

He was a very fat, dark, middle-aged man. There was softness in his face. His voice also had a hearty earnestness about it. I could make out from a few words he had dropped here and there that the boys had lost their mother and now, he with his children, had set up his small world here on the banks of the Brahmaputra.

I was taking a liking for the people in this world. They were so full of affection, concern, and sympathy. I felt very pleased with life. Saying a few words of thanks, I paid for the tea and came back to the boat after a gap of about an hour. From the ticket master I gathered that there was no hope of the ferry coming anytime soon. If it came at all, that would be towards late night, almost by morning. I proceeded towards our place through a narrow path between two rows of tea chests.

The party that had had the puffed rice earlier was now snoring lustily, their noses making the sound of puffed rice popping in a hot vessel. The song of the Nepali family had reached a crescendo sometime back. It had already petered out in a diminuendo and was now dying out altogether through a series of sleepy limb-stretchings and long-drawn-out yawns.

The film magazine had also gone snugly to sleep on top of the boy's chest, as if reassured of safety in somebody's company for the night. The sister must have spent the time sitting by the boy's pillow waiting for my return. On noticing me, she slowly woke the boy up, 'Barun, won't you like some tea?' Her voice did not have any trace of unnecessary urgency, nor did her actions betray signs of anything out-of-the-way. She had confidence in herself and also had faith in others. A lot of my diffidence and inhibition melted away.

'Barun!' I called out.

All three of us sat down for tea. I had brought with me three earthen tumblers from the tea shop. They took out some coconut laddoos and some assorted snacks from their suitcase. As I was about to retreat after taking my share, there were all-round protests. I remained sitting at the same place.

'Make up your bed comfortably, Barun. Hang up the mosquito net too. You will sleep more comfortably that way,' I told the boy.

'So, the ferry is not coming?' Both of them seemed to be asking at the same time.

'What will happen now, Barun?' the sister asked with lot of anxiety in her voice. I would not have believed if I had not seen it with my own eyes that even anxiety and worry could make one look so beautiful. But why was she so worried, I wondered.

'Do you have to attend to something really urgent in Jorhat, Barun?' I blurted out.

'We have to be in Jorhat tomorrow by all means.' This time it was the sister, who replied directly, with her head bowed, as she looked at the ground.

'We will think about tomorrow when tomorrow comes, what do you say, Barun?' Barun received a huge reassurance in my words and was visibly relieved.

'Yes. Baideo is worried over nothing. The telegram says "No worry". You have also passed your "minor" school exam, Baideo. Don't you know what "No worry" means?'

'But then what about the "Come sharp" part?' she asked, looking at her brother with a shy smile.

'Bhindeo is chicken-hearted. Even with a simple headache he makes a fuss as if he is about to die and asks for you. Actually, he can't live without seeing you all the time. That's why the "Come sharp".' The boy replied, referring to his elder sister's husband as Bhindeo.

The candlelight lighted up her face, now blushing with a radiant beauty.

'No worry. Come sharp'.... What mysteries were wrapped inside those words, I wondered.

'Is he ill or something?'

'Bhindeo had a bicycle accident. He is in the hospital. It has been two days since we received the telegram. I wasn't home; I came back only yesterday after my school holidays began. My father also couldn't leave as this is the plucking time in the tea gardens, the busy season.'

At my repeated requests, Barun finally made up their bed, spreading it out well. The mosquito net was also hung up with a lot of care to form a secure triangle. The sister lay down without uttering any more words. From snatches of conversation I could gather a little more information about Barun's world. He had, in the meanwhile, scribbled down my address too. A little later Barun was also fast asleep.

Kathonibari ghat was deep in slumber. The boat also seemed to be drowsily stretching out. From somewhere close by, the disturbing shuffle of feet of the ticket master or one of the deckhands came in, penetrating the silence of the night to reach our end of the boat. From the overhang of the river bank some more loose earth fell into the river with a deep rumbling sound.

It was the time of night when, on the opposite bank of the Brahmaputra, a predatory tiger, shrouded by the night in the Kaziranga forest, would be lying in wait by the side of the path frequented by prospective prey. I was sure about that. In the distant sand bars emerging out of the river and within its shrubs of wild grass of kahua and jhau, submerged by the dark expanse of the Brahmaputra, something mysterious would be dozing with frequent flickers of eyelashes. A few other equally mysterious creatures would be crowding in for a peek to find out the identity of the one that lay dozing on the sand. Sitting by the bank of the river close to the boat, a few young washerwomen with disheveled, unruly hair were possibly thrashing clothes and a sound like 'sap-sop-sapaat'...was carried down to us. It took me some time to realize that those were not washerwomen but waves breaking on the river bank!

From what I could gather from snatches of conversation, the boy, Barun, studied in Class IX in the school in the nearby town. His father—what was the name?—worked in the tea house of a nearby tea garden. He was 'Head, tea house' or something like that. The garden was ten miles from the ghat. Barun's baideo had got married one-and-a-half years ago. Now she was being called back after only a week's stay at her parents'. Minor injury but that 'Come sharp'?... Can't stand her absence. Must be very close to each other.... If only this night had happened to me one-and-a-half years ago! And I haven't had a bicycle accident.... Oh my God! What was coming over me!

The wind had snuffed out the candle. I enjoyed the darkness but thought it was possibly not quite proper to sit like that in the dark with a lady around.... I struck a matchstick. Finding a half-smoked cigarette, I lit that and then stretched out the lighted matchstick towards the candle.

I got a shock. The sister's voice. 'Maybe darkness can bring sleep faster?'

'You are not asleep yet?'

'I was dozing. Sleep seems to be eluding me.'

Quite natural. I did not light the candle. Leaning on the railings of the boat, I kept watching in the direction from which the ferry was to come. Candlelight wouldn't do. What was needed here was the light of the ferry.

I lost track of the time that passed. Suddenly, there was commotion. Sounds of 'Ferry', 'Ferry', 'Light', were accompanied by the ring of the bell for tickets and the thudding sounds of hurrying feet.

I hurriedly lit the candle. Baideo was sitting up. She woke Barun up by pushing him with both hands. Barun got up, still in a daze.

'The ferry has come, Barun.' It sounded as if after a long wait and a lot of anxiety I had given some prospective father the news, 'A son has been born'. I told him to roll up their bed and then went out for the tickets. A glance at the ticket master's face told me that there had been some mishap. A signal had been received from the ferry that a repair was needed. So tickets would be issued later. The ferry was limping closer. Barun also came to stand by my side. On hearing the latest, he went back to tell his sister.

Dawn was breaking.

I went down to the bank of the river. I had to think of some way out. These two had to be in Jorhat that day. After the morning ablutions, I had a strong cup of tea to chase sleep away. I asked for three cups of tea and got them to make some hot puris. The ferry came and one or two passengers came down. A little later I saw Barun coming down the sands with a boy by his side.

'Dada, dada,' he said, addressing me as his elder brother, 'Mamu has come. He has come by the ferry from Jorhat. Did I not say there was no need for worry?'

Mamu was totally worn out and looking weary from lack of sleep. He was a cousin of Barun's sister's husband. He was almost of the same age as Barun, perhaps just a little older.

'What news from Jorhat?' I asked looking at Mamu. It was Barun who shot back promptly, 'Good. He has been sent here to fetch us because of our delay.'

'Why fetch you?'

'If they want to go, I'll take them with me. Otherwise I can use the opportunity to take a tour of this place. So I came,' was Mamu's reply.

'So, what do you propose to do now?' I asked Mamu.

'"Nabou" wants to go back by all means,' replied Mamu, referring to Barun's sister with this honorific, signifying the wife of an elder brother. 'We will hire a boat to be on time to catch the first bus to Jorhat. The ferry got stuck in the sand. Something has gone wrong. It can move only after repairs. So waiting for the ferry will only delay things further.'

'Then Barun, go and arrange for your baideo's bath. Both of you go and get ready. I'll send over the tea and snacks.'

Barun handed over the flask to me and he and Mamu left my side. After giving them about an hour to get organized, I went back to the boat with the tea and snacks carried by a boy from the tea shop. I saw that Barun's baideo had already taken her bath and was chatting merrily with Mamu. The night's anxiety was no longer visible on her face.

'The moment I saw you, my heart started thumping violently with fear,' she was telling Mamu.

'I have already told you, you can go back to the garden if you are not too keen to go.'

'Oh no, no. You two may come back here after dropping me off at Jorhat. Good that you have arrived. Last night a gentleman had helped....'

I had reached the boat just then and she saw me. Hurriedly she pulled her oroni a little further down to cover more of her face and blushed a deep red.

The boy from the tea shop went back after putting the stuff on the boat.

'Where has Barun gone?' I asked Mamu.

'He hasn't come back from his bath,' Mamu's nabou answered. And then she got busy with pouring out the tea.

She pushed our share of tea and snacks towards me and Mamu.

'Not for me. I have just had it at the shop,' I said.

'No. You have to take it again.'

Ah! What sweet insistence! I went to stand a little further with the tumbler of tea in my hands.

'I have already arranged for the boat. It's better that we get ready fast. The tea will get cold. You need not wait for Barun. What do you say, Mamu?'

'Oh yes. The sooner the better. The bus for Jorhat reaches Silghat at nine.'

The boatmen from some western part of the country started rowing in tandem with the beat of a song Barun and Mamu were singing:

Brahmaputra Ganga Ma,
The wind is making our bodies sway
Off to Mathurapur we go
Bring the boat closer to the quay.

The boat went like an arrow downstream. I stared at Barun's baideo and Mamu's nabou (What about me? What was she to me?). She was all ears to the song that Barun and Mamu were singing. Keeping to the rhythm of the beats of the song, her smile too was waxing and waning. And that blob of sindoor on her forehead? What a glowing ember of vermilion! In the soft rays of the morning sun, her face was radiant, like burnished gold. No! It was more like a joint of raw turmeric. Gold was lifeless, her face was not.

A picture of a happy family came to my mind along with snatches of conversation...father-in-law, mother-in-law, brother-in-law...a husband who 'Can't live without seeing you' and that's why 'Come sharp'.... 'You too have passed your "minor" school exam, don't you know what "No worry" means....' 'No, you have to take it again.'

To my life, that of a vagabond, going from one tea garden to another, looking for a job, a day had come, a day among many, a night among many.... As Silghat approached, brought closer every minute by the speeding boat, my mind became more and more lonely, desolate, and empty.

Suddenly, I noticed the dot of sindoor on her forehead glow red like blood. She was leaning out of the boat a bit, and the glitter of sunlight bouncing off the waves passed over her face as flickering patches of light. It appeared as if the reflected flickers of light from the waves were trying to break the dot of sindoor into tiny little fragments and take it away to share among themselves.

The boat came up to the ghat. We had reached Silghat.

As soon as we finished our customary tea, the bus arrived.... It was a government bus—it ran by the clock. That was where we were to part ways. Barun and his baideo went up to sit on the second seat from the front. Barun was gushing out words of gratitude.

'If you ever come to Jorhat, do visit Baideo. I hope you remember the address.' His baideo also said much more than Barun through her earnest, honest gaze. 'And if you happen to go through Kathonibari ghat, you must come to our house in the tea garden.'

These were not mere formalities expressed in words, but an honest display of affection straight from the heart. The horn of the bus was blaring. Barun's baideo slowly brought her hands together up to her forehead in a namaskar. I offered my namaskar in return.

But where was Mamu?

Mamu was still seated in the tea stall. Requesting the driver to wait for a moment, I hurriedly approached the tea stall to send Mamu over.

Mamu was impatiently puffing away at a cigarette.

'The bus is leaving, Mamu.' Mamu threw away the cigarette and stood up.

'It was extremely nice meeting you....' Mamu kept looking at me with agitation sharpened by his hurry.

'We will surely meet again sometime. But the bus is leaving, Mamu. Go now.' I almost shoved him towards the bus. The horn was blaring again. Mamu was sweating with pent-up agitation.

'Yes, I'll go. I have to go anyway. But what do I do afterwards? Dada had a car accident. Everything was over the next day. I have only been putting up an act all the time.'

Mamu leaped onto the bus.

The wheels of the bus were spinning rapidly round and the bus soon went out of sight beyond the curve on the Kamakhya hill.

Translated by Jiban Goswami

SWEET ACACIA
SHEELABHADRA

It was faint and hazy, but unmistakably the scent of the sweet acacia. He knew fully well that there was no such tree in the vicinity—the fragrance had traversed over fifty years to make its way to him. Or perhaps it had been with him all along and had now found a release from its surroundings. The moment he tried to associate it with its context, it vanished into thin air like a bird shocked to flight. Choudhury sighed.

We dwell on memories and dream of the future—the past we have left behind and what lies ahead. The present remains meaningless. Truly, what is the present? Which segment in the flow of time can we dam and label as the present—five minutes? Five seconds? A hundredth of a second? A millionth? If the present does not exist at all, what is it? Nothing can happen in the present because every event requires a time span—it has either occurred or will occur. We exist either in the past or in the future. Our lives are merely memories and dreams.

Choudhury is ageing. There are things he is incapable of doing, or not interested in anymore. He can no longer play football, jump around, or fall in love. He has also lost his ability to dream about the future.

As he sits dozing in his easy chair, the scene appears bright and vivid, with details he had missed out earlier, probably because he had not cared to look for them. But the entire episode was tucked away somewhere in the recesses of his mind, and was now presenting itself, down to the minutest detail.

Yes, the birds were chirping on a nearby tree. Choudhury was a confident young man with the future in his grip. He was staring, intent and unblinking, with joy and admiration. The day had just dawned. He had just about opened the window by his bed when he was awe-struck by the sight.

The girl was bathing by the well. Secure in the knowledge that there was no one around, there she was, bathing in the open. The twin globes of her bare breasts jiggled in rhythm every time she bent to draw water.

Choudhury froze, his hand still on the bolt of the half-open window. He felt a pleasurable ache in his heart. The feeling was alien. At that very moment, strangely, he was overwhelmed by the scent of sweet acacia. It seemed to awaken a blurry new sensation within him. Eyes were for sight, ears for hearing. But what was the purpose of this new sense? The awareness of its power seeped slowly through his being and added another dimension to his three-dimensional world. He held his breath as he surrendered himself to this new feeling. The floral scent seemed somehow connected to his awakening. It seemed to have a colour, form, and physical existence of its own. It invaded his mind and made it bright and fragrant.

Choudhury was jolted out of his reverie by his eldest daughter-in-law—'Deuta?'

He was slightly irritated. 'What now?'

'Here, have your Horlicks.'

'How often do I need to eat or drink? Didn't I have something just a little while ago?'

His daughter-in-law did not contradict him. Everyone knew that his memory was failing.

Samar came up and stood by him. 'Who's this?' Choudhury asked his daughter-in-law.

'It's me—Samar', the young man replied.

'When did you come? Does your college have vacations now?'

Samar, the middle son, had arrived that morning on hearing that his father's health had taken a turn for the worse. They had spoken earlier in the day, but Choudhury seemed to have no recollection of the exchange.

The past, however, was crystal clear.

The year was 1931, and it was 7.13 in the evening on 14 January when his first son, Amar, was born. Choudhury was all tensed up until he suddenly heard ululation in the inner room. His younger brother started thumping on the wall, his mother smiled, and his misgivings melted away in an instant. He tried to restrain his brother, 'Hey, what are you trying to do? Break down the wall?' That was all he could say before uncontrollable laughter gave his mock anger away.

Amar's concerned voice brought him back to reality, 'What's the matter? Why are you behaving like this? Are you feeling unwell?'

'No, I'm fine.'

'Would you like some glucose and water?'

Choudhury was irked. 'How often do you need to ply me with food and drink? I just had something.'

Everyone seemed concerned. 'I forced him to have some Complan in the morning. After that, he's been snapping every time we mention food,' said the daughter-in-law.

Choudhury was no longer an old man dozing off in his easy chair. He was a young man of twenty-two or twenty-three. He opened his window as usual in the morning. Like an orchestra missing a beat, his orderly world was thrown into disarray. The girl saw him through a gap in the curtains. She made a feeble attempt to cover herself and rushed away. Choudhury's senses were in shambles. The scent of the sweet acacia was gone.

The glow that surrounded him seemed to fade and his world was suddenly grey. He had the reputation of being an upright young man. The mantle collapsed around his feet and left him totally exposed. There was nowhere he could hide. How could he possibly detach himself from everyone around him?

The girl was new to their household. But she would talk. No one would ask Choudhury for an explanation. They would draw their own conclusions. No one would believe him if he said that his pleasure was limited to witnessing ethereal beauty and that there were no inappropriate feelings. There was no way he could explain himself. Any attempt to do so would be like trying to touch the Mona Lisa with muddy hands.

Choudhury was weighed down by guilt throughout the day. His heart felt heavy, his mind numb.

On his way to the market in the evening, he saw the girl chatting with a couple of other girls from the household. As he self-consciously made his way past them, he noticed that she scowled in his direction. Then he heard her say, '...the eyes should be gouged out....'

No, there was no scope for forgiveness. Scandal was inevitable. He would remain tarnished for a lifetime, at least to one person. Sleep eluded him all night. In the morning, he opened the window as usual. The girl was bathing by the well, uninhibited and oblivious of her surroundings. His mind suddenly felt light and free. His world turned bright once again. Birds chirped in unison and a gust of wind brought in the scent of sweet acacia which enveloped his being.

Choudhury had forgotten all about the incident. He had no recollection of the girl either. However, the scent of the sweet acacia, detached from its backdrop, became a part of his being. And, fifty-odd years later, it filled the moments of his life with its fragrance.

Translated by Maitreyee Siddhanta Chakravarty

THE RESTLESS ELECTRON
SAURAV KUMAR CHALIHA

Strains of a song, a Rabindra Sangeet, broke Nikhil's sleep. It was a song he had never heard before. Straining his ears, he attempted, futilely, to make out its lyrics. He opened his eyes and saw the room already flooded in bright morning light. Through a hole in the window a narrow beam of sunlight was streaming into the room, its path vividly outlined by the particles of dust floating in the air. 'Rectilinear propagation of light,' the thought came to him like a reflex, without him thinking it deliberately.

The beaming smile of the girl on the wall calendar seemed to be greeting him. The polished blades of the table fan were blazing, as the sun's glare bounced off them and entered his eyes. He languidly stretched out his hand and pushed the window open. From a neighbouring house floated in the faint sounds of a school boy memorizing his lessons and the deep blue sky sent the exuberance of white clouds into the room. And drowning all other sounds, the strains of the morning's Rabindra Sangeet from a radio wafted in. His spirits this morning were deliriously buoyant for no apparent reason and listening to the song in the singer's dulcet voice made him feel as if his spirits and the lilting melody of the song were merging like two harmonic waves undulating in complete resonance. He put a cigarette in his mouth and was about to light it when he paused—the matchbox rolled off his hand to land on the bed with a mild rattle of matchsticks.

He suddenly recoiled when he remembered the night before. With enormous loathing he glanced at the glossy film magazine lying by his pillows. A sense of growing disgust gripped him as he glanced at the damp spots on his clothes and on parts of his bed. Abruptly, the lovely morning seemed to turn ghastly, spoilt beyond repair. Why was he shrinking away from offering a warm welcome to the soft rays of the morning sun? A sense of despair was rising in him....

The house was already abuzz with the hum of the daily grind. The wife of his elder brother, Bou as he called her, said to him while offering him his morning cup of tea, 'You must not forget to go and get that piece of cloth today. It can't be delayed any more and it has to be here today by all means. You have been avoiding it on one pretext or the other.'

'Hmm,' he muttered indifferently, sounding preoccupied. Last night's memory was tormenting him, making him uncomfortable. It was chasing him like the memory of an evil dream. He could not shake off the feeling of loathing.

'No more of your "hmms". Take the money and get ready to go now. Otherwise the two frocks will never be ready on time.'

…Yes, ghastly, hideous. But, somehow, he was not prepared to take the responsibility. But why was there this reluctance to admit guilt? Why this cowardice? Had his moral courage deserted him?

'Frocks?' suddenly he came out of his reverie and asked stupidly.

'Why? Don't you remember that Xonti and her kids are arriving day after tomorrow?' Bou said, widening her eyes in sheer disbelief. 'For Ila and Neela….'

Oh, yes. He remembered alright. His elder sister Xonti Baideo and her children would be arriving the day after. The faces of Ila and Neela floated up in his mind. They must be quite grown up by now, must be lovelier too.

'Oh, Bou, please help me, will you? Please tidy up my room a bit today.'

Bou couldn't control her laughter. Nikhil was obviously scared of his elder sister Xonti. She would not spare him if she were to find things in a mess in any part of the house.

'That's all right. Get ready now.'

'But Bou, why are you so worried? There's enough time.'

Bou made a face at him. Nikhil was a little surprised at her anxiety. But he could guess the reasons for her worry. Bou wanted to show her affection towards Ila and Neela, and hence the frocks.

'Manu's room also has to be cleaned up today. Xonti is so fussy about cleanliness. If she finds even a little dirt somewhere, we've had it,' Bou said and gave an innocent smile.

Why was he finding hidden motives even behind that simple smile? Why couldn't he take a simple smile at its face value? Why was he becoming such a skeptic? He could visualize Bou bracing herself any moment now to tighten her belt, so to speak, and get down to cleaning the house from one end to the other, after throwing the broom to Bimala to take care of the sweeping. Xonti Baideo would certainly make a snide remark that Bou was doing all this only to impress his father. Only to make sure that Deuta, as he called his father, would take note of how his daughter-in-law was sparing no effort, how she was dirtying her own clothes to make his daughter's stay comfortable, even neglecting her infant lying in her bedroom…. Xonti Baideo would also remark that Deuta was unlikely to realize that Bou was putting up only a show of fake sincerity, essentially for the benefit of others.... And to think of poor Deuta.... He would be so completely bowled over by Bou that he would feel genuinely grateful to her.

He wondered if Bou's smiling reference to Xonti's mania for cleanliness was also not an insinuation...that having to remain busy all the time in fulfilling other people's whims, was it any wonder that she had to remain overburdened with work at all times?

Why had he become so mean-minded these days that he couldn't avoid seeing evil designs even in the simplest of things...? Had Xonti or anybody else ever really put it into his head that Bou's care and nursing of Deuta was just a facade? That Bou was always after her own selfish ends and nothing else?

Ugh!

'How's Ranu's sore today, Bou? Have you applied Burnol again?'

'I have. The sore does not seem to heal at all.'

There were creases of concern on Bou's face. Her concern was quite genuine, Nikhil felt. Bou had, meanwhile, mechanically and in an absent-minded way extended another slice of bread towards Nikhil's plate. Nikhil looked at her again, and saw the concern on her face. He took a bite of the bread and wondered....What could have brought about this change in Bou?

'Our house always seems to be plagued by one disease or the other. And by the way, have you heard of Nabin's mother? She was taken seriously ill last night—they had to call for a doctor at two or two-thirty in the night.'

'Really?'

'Oh yes. She was given one or two lakhs of penicillin. Something like that, anyway.'

In a gesture meant to convey a hopeless confession of ignorance, Bou gave a shy laugh. Bou always found it incomprehensible and comic at the same time that this stuff called penicillin should come only in lakhs. The innocence in her self-deprecating laughter with the rustic simplicity of a village girl was quite appealing to Nikhil. Once more, Bou extended her hand mechanically towards Nikhil's shirt and pulled out and tidied the collar that had somehow gone into the neck of the shirt. Nikhil got up, skillfully protecting the packet of cigarettes in the pocket of his shirt from having any contact with Bou's fingers.

The sound of coughing came to his ears. A dry cough. That meant Deuta was awake. He must have had a bad night's sleep.

One could tell from the old man's eyes. He was beset with innumerable worries. Bou must have gone to him on hearing his cough. The sound of the wooden clogs, the kharam slippers that Deuta wore on his feet, merged with the rustle of Bou's ankle-length mekhela as she went towards Deuta's room at a brisk pace. Seeing her brisk business-like manner, all feelings of light-headedness vanished from Nikhil's mind in an instant and his skeptic self took over. 'Ah! Look at Bou. Just see how she has suddenly become busy ever since Deuta got up! As if she has no time even for a little rest,' he said to himself in a tone of skeptical sarcasm.... But he was quick to reproach himself, 'There you go again, Nikhil.... You are again becoming that petty-minded cynical beast....'

Water had been kept ready in a brass pot, a ghoti, for Deuta's wash but Bou came and changed the ghoti to a slightly bigger one so that Deuta could use more water if he wanted to.

'Maina,' the old man called out to Nikhil. For everybody in the house, that was the name that Nikhil was known by, his pet name.

Nikhil went and stood by his side.

'Take some money from daughter-in-law and go and get the pipe of my hookah changed. This one has become totally useless.'

'Alright, Deuta.'

The rubber pipe of the hookah had really become rotten. It was covered all over with blackish spots. The metal warbler, the gurguri, the bottom part of the hookah that contained the water and warbled whenever the smoke on its way to the smoker's mouth passed through it, was beginning to rust. The ear of the earthen chillum was broken. Whenever the old man puffed at his hookah, all these small irritants added up to make lines of annoyance appear on his face. He had hardly any respite even while sitting on his chair—every now and then he would fidget and glare venomously at the arms of his chair. The tiny pores in the wooden arms of the chair were probably infested with fleas and they were possibly biting the old man every time he put his hands on them. It was only the other day that Bou had killed the bugs by pouring boiling water on the chair but they must have colonized it again.

Nikhil's mind became agitated again. Where was Bou? Where did she vanish when she was needed? What was she doing, anyway? She must be busy with her fiendish children, as always, he thought.

A storm was raging in his head. There was that intense loathing for himself, triggered by the memory of last night's sordidness. Then there was this discontent with Bou, unreasonable maybe, but.... Suddenly, without any apparent reason, he felt a sudden disgust for the whole neighbourhood around him. The faces of all the opportunistic, selfish men living there suddenly flashed across his mind.

'Bou, the fleas seem to be breeding again. Deuta is getting bitten all over. I have to go and get a bottle of DDT today,' he said aloud as he went into the kitchen.

'DDT is good for nothing. Absolutely useless.'

That piece of wisdom came from Ranjan, speaking from inside the kitchen. He was looking vacantly at the black, soot-covered walls of the kitchen....

'Where did you spring up from so early in the morning?' Nikhil asked.

'Mantu has had a fever since yesterday. I came to borrow the thermometer.'

'What's wrong with him?'

'Cold and fever, what else? A thermometer needs to be earmarked just for his personal use.' Annoyance was writ large on Ranjan's face. It was quite clear that he could not bring himself to accept that even cold and fever merited being called ailments.

Bou looked a little worried. Ranjan had a feeling that she was not very comfortable in having to part with the thermometer. Who knows, it might get broken, or might even get lost. And if any of that happened, that would be the end of the thermometer. Courtesy would make it difficult to accept money or a replacement. Still....

Bou made an effort to sound genuinely concerned about Mantu's fever. Unseen by others, Nikhil made one of his disbelieving grimaces. Ranjan got a little flustered.

'Your kitchen has turned ghastly dark,' Ranjan tried to change tack. In Nikhil's opinion, Ranjan was an incorrigible pedant and Ranjan's next words seemed to confirm that. 'The walls have become so black; there is no scope for the reflection of light.'

'Yes. And the smoke doesn't have any way of escaping either; it has become quite a nuisance. My eyes smart and I can't help tears welling up in my eyes whenever I am in the kitchen,' Bou said.

'And this Maina, what is he doing? Can't he even get a carpenter to make the windows a little wider, a little better?'

Ranjan cast an admonishing and authoritative glance towards Nikhil. Ranjan then stooped down to squat inches above the floor on a low wooden seat, a pira, and thrust out his legs in front of him. Mantu's fever was not bothering him one tiny bit. His mind was already on other things. His eyes were fixed on the sun rays reflecting off the tea in the cup he was holding in his hands.

'Bou, look here, will you? Do you see this curve on the surface of the tea?'

'Where? Oh that one? Yes, yes, I can see that.'

'Do you know why it is visible? Hey, Maina, do you know why? It's called a caustic curve. When sunlight....'

'What's it called? Kasti what?' Bou laughed out.

'Enough! You need not flaunt your wisdom here. We can live without knowing that,' Nikhil's voice was oozing annoyance. Since morning, his temper was sore. He was in a vile mood.

'I cannot even tell one letter from another and now you expect me at my age to try reading from the tome of knowledge?' Bou said. 'Anyway, I have so much work to do; I do not have the time to listen to your gibberish.'

Bou went on to make her 'busyness' clear. Pulling towards her the moida, a curved chopper with its foothold placed flat on the floor, she started chopping vegetables on the chopper's blade. Her light laugh was intended to lighten the sting of her words, but it couldn't revive Ranjan's dampened enthusiasm.

'You people don't seem to be curious about anything. Take this Maina here, only thing he ever does is sleep or loaf around. I am telling you, Nikhil, you really have gone to the dogs'.

'So I have gone to the dogs, is it? And why, hah? Because I couldn't tell what is a caustic curve or whatever it is, is that why?'

'And why not? The earth would not have come to an end if you had shown some interest in what I was trying to say. People should have some curiosity about things they do not know.'

'Ah, now he is really upset for being denied the opportunity of flaunting his knowledge!' Bou seemed to be thinking as she lifted her face from the moida and threw Ranjan a mocking smile. Ranjan did not even notice it. But Nikhil suddenly became agitated. This Ranjan here was talking about curiosity. He, Nikhil, had been curious about a lot of things, and now he wished he had not. His curiosity had made him learn many dirty things; his friends had taught him some absolutely disgusting stuff. And now he was suffering because of his knowledge. He looked at Bou and wondered what must be going through her mind every time she saw his emaciated listless body. What she must be thinking on seeing his pimple-filled face!

'Ignorance,' he said slowly, 'is a blessing.'

'Only when it is foolish to be wise,' pat came Ranjan's reply.

Nikhil was devastated. He had never thought of it that way. For once, he looked at Ranjan with something bordering on admiration. Did Ranjan notice that by any chance? Hurriedly he averted his eyes.

'There you two go again!' Bou said, 'Now that you two have come together with all your daggers drawn, we've had it. How long will your lectures continue?'

Ranjan was trying his best to avoid the old man's gaze. But the old man's eyes were alert. Household worries had made him feeble, his eyesight was also getting weaker, but it was not easy to dodge him. Ranjan was often awe-struck by the old man, wondering at the kind of firm physique he must have even at that age. The old man, while moving slowly from one place to another, often seemed to totter and fall. But he never did. Whenever he saw the old man totter, Ranjan felt sad, and anguish darkened his face. Nikhil was taken a little by surprise and Bou got a bit flustered. Ranjan, on such occasions, made an effort to hide his feelings, bringing forth an amused smile on his face as if he was enjoying himself and he would then whisper, 'Unstable equilibrium.'

'Is that you, Ranjan?' the old man asked.

Scratching his head, Ranjan went to stand by the old man's side. He told him about Mantu's fever.

'When are you leaving? When is the university re-opening?'

'On the twenty-second. I am leaving on the nineteenth.'

'I hope you are doing well in your studies. You must get a First Class. Our Maina here seems to have ended up being nothing.'

Maina overheard that in the next room and let out a sigh. He said silently, he was sorry, but....

'You have to go to Shillong once, Ranjan. That is, before you go back to the university. Do you have anything important to attend to in the meantime?'

'To Shillong?'

'I want you to go and find out about Dhon. I received a letter yesterday from Bap. Dhon has again turned very violent, Bap said. Please go tomorrow, if you can.'

Ranjan stared at the lines of worry on the old man's face. He couldn't find any similarity between all the curves he knew and the lines on the old man's worry-laden face. He grew concerned.

Quietly, with enormous calmness, Nikhil's father explained everything to him. Dhon had remained paralyzed for nearly seven months. He would lose his mental balance every now and again. At times, he became almost insane. Then there would be endless worry, fear, and noisy scenes. His madness seemed to be getting worse with each passing day. The old man was incapable of going to Shillong; Maina also had a lot of things to attend to here. That was why he was asking Ranjan.

For a moment Ranjan toyed with the idea of suggesting Kon's name but a look at the old man's face made him lose his nerve. The old man was very angry with Kon, Ranjan knew. Calmness reigned on the old man's face, concern too. Stretching out his hand, he brought over the newspaper towards him, then groped around for the case where he kept his reading glasses. Ranjan noticed that though the case was lying quite close to his groping fingers, the fingers somehow did not go towards it. That meant he was not seeing things even close at hand, and not just because the things were small. That meant, Ranjan thought, the 'accommodation' of his eyes, or rather, the range of his eyesight was getting reduced. How could this Maina keep watching so indifferently this downhill slide of his aging father? Maina really was a hopeless, good-for-nothing boy. Something needed to be done for the old man, and done fast; there was no doubt about that.

The old man, too, was lost in his own thoughts. He also felt that something needed to be done. The possibility that old age would turn him into an invalid was unacceptable to him. But he had not complained to anyone nor had he appealed for help. He could never reconcile himself to the idea of taking advantage of a situation, of becoming an opportunist of sorts. And because of that attitude, he had suffered a lot throughout his life. He had spent enormous amounts of money for the benefit of others, had provided for them, but had received only a pittance in return. His health was going down with each passing day; his house was crumbling with the passage of time. His wife, Maina's mother, had died ages ago. His son, Bap, hardly ever enquired about his health or about his well-being and a hidden discontent against Bap was always raging inside him.... Even then he recoiled whenever he thought of baring his heart to Bap's wife, his daughter-in-law. And then there was Maina—the boy was yet to make up his mind whether or not to appear in the exams again after failing once and seemed content to be just loafing around doing nothing, without any concern for the family. But the thought that eclipsed everything else and kept agitating his mind, was the thought of his son Dhon losing his mind. In desperation, in order to raise some money for his son's treatment, the old man had sold off a plot of land. He was saddened to realize that no one seemed to enjoy talking to him anymore; everyone seemed to be avoiding him. With a frail and weak body, feeble and failing eyesight, the old man tried to get a feel of the pulse of the world only through the pages of newspapers....

'BANK STOPS PAYMENTS....' The bold bright headline seemed to be screaming from the second column of the third page. Everything seemed to go into a crazy whirl. His weak eyesight suddenly seemed to become even weaker, a shrill bell seemed to go off inside his head ringing loudly and just at that moment a flea sucked away some more blood through his palm in another painful bite. His ears could vaguely hear the ceaseless rattle of a sewing machine floating in from the two-storeyed building around the corner...the old man could not quite recognize the sound at first. The sun's rays were becoming paler, in the dimming light he could sense his daughter-in-law passing by his side carrying something in her hands; he could hear the shouts and noises of his grandchildren from somewhere close by—and he could sense that through the door near him Maina and Ranjan had shuffled out of the house.

Ranjan and Maina walked out of the house and came to a halt by the window. On the veranda of the house opposite, the advocate's daughter, Neeru, straightened and sat up in her cane chair. She seemed to become suddenly animated. She was preparing for her exams and while making a show of reading the book in her hand, she kept looking furtively at them. She was not a bad looking girl and dimples dented her cheeks whenever she smiled. Nikhil often got flustered by her gaze but Ranjan dismissed it as sheer coquetry. On seeing her this morning, Nikhil seemed to become suddenly angry. When a white cat suddenly leapt on to Neeru's lap without warning, Ranjan just managed to suppress a laugh. Neeru became confused, flustered, and diffident. Just then her married sister came out from inside the house and Neeru turned her attention back to her book.

'Your father's eyesight is gradually becoming worse.'

'Hmm.'

'What nonsense! What do you mean 'hmm'? What are you doing about it? Whenever I think of you, I just can't help becoming angry. What are you up to? What's got into you, anyway? Are your relations with your family only economic and biological?'

Nikhil did not say anything.

'Are you appearing in the exams this year?'

Just then there was a sudden burst of noise. The crowd of neighbourhood kids appeared from nowhere, bringing a lot of incoherent chatter with them. Ila's brother, a toddler, fell off her lap and a loud howl followed. Runu and Phunu were having a tug of war over a wooden horse. Phunu gave a resounding slap to Runu. There was another howl, louder than the previous one.

'Silence!' Ranjan bawled.

There was a moment's lull and all noise stopped. Then the chatter resumed with renewed vigour. Everyone now had a new source of entertainment. All the kids started shouting, 'Silen! Silen!'

'Boomerang!' Ranjan said with a hearty laugh. Nikhil too gave a forced laugh. The spirited liveliness of these young kids could make no impact on his dampened spirits. He wondered why he couldn't join them in their innocent laughter.

He started feeling totally worthless, someone who wasn't capable of doing anything in this world and was only degrading himself day after day. Two small boys ran down the road and together they set a kite afloat. The yellow piece of paper slowly soared up high into the air, its red tail fluttering in the wind.

In the Dutta household, the lady of the house stopped her work at the sewing machine and kept staring at the kite. Neeru threw a glance towards the scene but tried to keep the glance nonchalant as if she could not care less for that kind of stuff. A smile began to spread on Ranjan's face as some equations, some diagrams, and parallelograms of forces began to gambol around in his mind. He felt like explaining to Nikhil the theory behind kite-flying, how airplanes stay aloft in the air and many such things, but the look on Nikhil's face made him banish those ideas.

A look of disgust, of intolerable annoyance was clouding Nikhil's face. He found the atmosphere in their neighbourhood depressingly oppressive. He could see that the people around him were starting the day and had already become busy. He had seen and had thought a lot about their meanness, their opportunistic bent of mind, and their obsessive lust for money. He remembered how someone among their neighbours had been having a high fever continuously for ten days and how the learned advocate staying in the house opposite had not felt the desire to enquire even once how his sick neighbour was doing. Bribes had made Dutta and his wife become more and more bloated as days went by. Mahendra Barsaikia, carrying on the covert business of selling kerosene and corrugated iron sheets in the black market, was now busy getting a house of the latest design built. That old lady, Lalit's mother, was going from door to door spreading rumours and evil gossip. War-time contractor Khagen Das, a man becoming more and more mysterious with each passing day, was hitting the bottle really hard and was perpetually drunk. More and more new radios had invaded the neighbourhood; their combined cacophony making life miserable. The new glittering DeSotos and Fords were seen coming out of the neighbours' garages with slow turns of their shining wheels. But the conditions of bank clerk Ram Babu and the court's petition-writer Chandi Kalita had only gone from bad to worse and it was the same thing with many others of their class. Chandi Kalita's younger daughter had been wearing the same torn frock for the last three months, exposing her budding breasts, but it was yet to be replaced by a new one....

Indira Barua strolled down the road, dazzling in fashionable clothes and clever make-up. Rajani Sharma, the pettifogger, looked derisively at her through his window. Dutta's wife sniffed haughtily and made her sewing machine whir faster for no apparent reason. Third-year college student Abani, on the pretext of lighting his cigarette, kept standing at the paan shop looking at Indira. Indira was gradually earning a bad name in the neighbourhood.

Throwing one end of his sador over his shoulder, Professor Bhatta was getting up on his bicycle. Just then Jhunu came running with a football in one hand and a pump in the other.

'Would you please pump the ball up for me, dada?' Jhunu asked Ranjan. Jhunu was wearing white half pants and his cheeks were full and round like footballs. Girija Sharma, the manager of a nearby lodging house for single men, a robust gentleman wearing an expensive suit, got down from his bicycle. The gentleman had become rich after setting up a cloth shop.

'Jhunu, come with me. I'll pump it up for you,' Girija Sharma said. Jhunu ran along Girija's side. Nikhil meanwhile asked Girija if he could borrow his bicycle and when Girija agreed, kept the cycle. He was usually reluctant to ask for any favours from a man like Girija. He couldn't stand the tenants in his lodging house, they seemed so vulgar. Even then, he needed the cycle....

The cycle's tyres appeared almost deflated, not having enough air in them. Leaving Ranjan behind, Nikhil went to ask Girija for the pump. The door to the mess was bolted from inside. From inside came the protesting shouts of Jhunu. Nikhil knocked on the door.

After a pause Girija came to the door and opened it. He was drenched in sweat. After him, leaving the ball lying on the floor, out came Jhunu running, suppressing a sob and pulling up and buttoning up his pants as he ran.

'Hey, you!'

'Let this whole neighbourhood go to hell!'

Taken aback, Girija Sharma stumbled on the threshold and fell headlong on the ground. There he lay, the husband of a beautiful wife and the father of a son.

Nikhil tried to analyze the character of Girija Sharma, but held himself back. Was he any different or any better? 'Physician, heal thyself....'

He suddenly remembered an incident from a couple of months back. Their neighbour Ram Babu had a visitor, his sister-in-law. She had come only a few days ago and was still new to the place. She and Nikhil had known each other only for a couple of weeks.

One day, Nikhil, the well-bred gentleman, had climbed over the connecting wall to drop into Ram Babu's courtyard. But it was immediately clear to him that he had no guts.... He panicked and ran away....

Niranjan had talked about Freud. Talked about how pent-up repressed desires expressed themselves. Maybe what Niranjan had said was right. But how much Freud could he have? Freud, Freud, and more Freud! He would go crazy. Was it only repressed desires that caused one's actions? What about all the rampant obscenities all around him, the loudly advertised smut, titillating posters of film stars on both sides of the roads, the books and magazines on sex or on sexology strewn on tabletops everywhere, the sideways glances of the buxom full-breasted girls like Indira—did these have no contribution; were they in no way responsible for his depraved, warped mind?

Back home, Jati Babu came in from somewhere and sat down.

'I have very interesting news. Kamini Sharma has been arrested by the police this morning.'

This was too much information for Bou to ignore and curiosity got the better of her. She dumped whatever she was doing and came rushing to Jati Babu's side. 'Why? What happened? Tell us everything, won't you?'

'Opium smuggling. He has been caught for carrying on a secret trade in contraband opium.'

Hearing this latest news about the 'eminent patriot', Bou almost leapt with joy. She kept pestering Jati Babu for all the juicy details.

Deuta overheard everything from the other room. He knew Kamini

Sharma only too well. He kept quiet, but kept his ears cocked. Jati Babu continued, 'And it is people like these who are the pillars of our society. Corruption is spreading all over the place. This is quite natural. Capitalism is dead, and all these are part of the stench coming out of its rotting corpse.'

Nikhil made no comment. Bou was all ears, though she could not quite understand all that was being said.

'Captalism stands on its last legs,' Jati Babu repeated a line he had read somewhere. 'How long can such rampant corruption continue? There is a limit to people's patience.'

Nikhil was tickled. Had Jati Babu finally become a full-blown communist? He cast a look of mild reproach at Jati Babu's silk kurta. Bou was also looking at it. To Bou, the word 'communist' ('take that son of our second sister, for instance,' she often said) evoked the picture of a perennially shabby creature with a mop of unkempt hair on his head.

'You and your communist lectures somehow do not go together,' Nikhil told Jati Babu with a teasing smile.

Jati Babu was a bit offended. He could surely get the hint. 'The aim of communism is to enhance the standard of living, not to degrade it.'

Nikhil was forced to keep quiet.

Coming out of the house, he could feel the excitement in the air. The news had spread like wildfire and by the afternoon, there was a public meeting; a lot of new rumours were floating around and speculation was rife about the future turn of events. The informal but regularly held meetings of chat groups, the addas, in the roadside tea stalls were becoming quite lively and animated. The socialist cadres were becoming quite active and boys wearing Nehru jackets were pasting posters on the walls, demanding befitting punishment for Kamini Sharma.

'The activities of these Socialists are ludicrous,' Jati Babu commented and pointed derisively to one of the wall posters. 'They may as well be termed drain-inspectors if one goes by the spots they select to paste their posters. They like raking up petty issues. When it comes to the major ones, they resort to lies. Jayprakash keeps quiet when the talk turns to revolution. If an opium trader is caught, they make so much noise, as if some earth-shaking event has occurred. But after betraying the cause of labour strikes, they bring out their victory drums.'

It was Jati Babu venting his spleen, as Bou called it.

Nikhil wanted to tell him, 'You are all dalals, middlemen, with vested interests, who do the bidding of Cominform in everything; petty crimes like opium smuggling must be too trifling a matter for high-brows like you to bother about.'

Did that mean that he, Nikhil, had suddenly become a Socialist himself? He smiled to himself.

Politics can be really weird, he thought. It's the business of scoundrels—someone seemed to have said somewhere. Maybe it was just that.

What would Kon have said in a situation like this?

Maybe Kon would have said that Kamini Sharma should be shot dead on the streets in public. His speech would have then become more and more sharp, strident, and high-pitched; slowly the groups of dalals would have fled the scene (shouts of 'Halal the dalals'—kill the middlemen—would have rented the air). Things would have gradually turned intolerable for Jati Babu. The debate would have digressed to other territories—whether the time was now ripe for 'revolution', whether contesting elections was in line with Marxism, and at last, whether Stalin had betrayed the cause of a global revolution and if Trotsky was a German spy.

Who really was fighting for the good of the country? Nikhil became confused, he didn't know what to believe and felt ashamed that he was so dull.

Recently, he had been to his Mama's place, one of his mother's brothers. His Mama was the manager of a tea estate in Upper Assam. Nikhil had gone there seeking a little solitude within the quiet ambience of the tea garden, with its beautifully trimmed and well-maintained tea bushes. He liked the muffled sounds coming from the tea garden's machine rooms, the rhythmic beats of the jhumur dances of the tea-pickers, and the distant sound of trucks on the move carrying tea leaves. He imagined he could spend the time there comfortably reading books and watching the tiny birds perched on the telegraph wires outside. He wanted to read light literature, fiction basically. Jati Babu had sent over a copy of *Two Leaves and a Bud* along with a long letter and Nikhil had thrown them into his suitcase along with the Huxleys and the Hall Caines. He had read Virginia Woolf's *Jacob's Room*, Meredith, Hardy....

Before he could finish the books, there was labour unrest in the garden. Out of sheer curiosity, he had gone through the posters and leaflets of the Communists. Some of the posters talked about increase in wages, adequate living quarters, and some were full of invectives against a particular fitter of the garden. The posters of the Communists were printed ones. He also had read the posters calling for revolution pasted by the Panchayat Union—these were cyclostyled. He listened to the compromise proposals of the

Socialists, through speeches made from the top of trucks and by reading the reports of newspapers' 'Own Correspondents'. His uncle's residence was surrounded one day and he was manhandled. The Socialists and the Communists called each other names and there were meetings of the tea-garden labourers. There was also a meeting of the Tea Garden Board and a little later the police came in. There was firing and then came the Army. There were comments and remarks in the Press; there were arrests and boycotts, enquiry committees and tribunals....

He returned. Where on earth could one find some peace? Everywhere in the world, Jati Babu said, the 'exploited masses' (favourite words of Jati Babu) were up in arms—why should Assam be left behind? In fact, looking at the state of affairs and the environment, the agitation in Assam should have come much earlier....

Jati Babu said such agitations were the precursors of a revolution. Deuta said these agitations were nothing but the makings of 'lawless elements' (an observation in the editorial of his favourite newspaper). Kon had told Bou, 'We are passing through a revolutionary phase and these are its symptoms'. Ranjan was immersed in his differential equations; Bou was thinking of Runu's upset stomach.

Kon was running around avoiding the police, Jati Babu was going around with his scholarly lectures, Jawaharlal was talking of plans of all kinds, and thanks to the Socialists, the only thing visible on the walls of the streets were posters.

What were the people really seeking? Simple, they wanted to eat, to have the right to live as decent human beings. That was fine but why all this factionalism, why all these complications?

Jati Babu had remarked, 'Excuse me, but you are quite naive.'

Maybe he was. Maybe Ranjan was naive too. But Ranjan was not willing to accept that. One day he would criticize all the political parties and the next day he would praise them all after seeing one of their more logical statements. Jati Babu tried to explain to him the reasons for the turmoil and the differences of opinion among political parties. Ranjan said, 'Wait. Think for a moment about an atom. There is a positive charge at its core. Revolving all around that are negative charges. So you have in an atom the positive protons and the negative electrons. Apart from these two there are also the neutrons, chargeless particles. The world too has positives or good characters as also negatives or bad ones; it has its rights and its wrongs and it also has its independents, the neutrons, who can be called neutrals.

Every single thing has two sides to it; take the atom as an example. Why should political parties be different? Or men for that matter? Why should the society be any different? Good and evil, force and counter-force have many complex ramifications, inside the atom and elsewhere.'

'Agreed,' Jati Babu was not quite sure what Ranjan was aiming at.

'You are trying to convert me.' Jati Babu shook his head violently, but Ranjan continued, 'Fine. But if I do not have any interest in knowing what makes protons different from electrons, would you find that objectionable?'

'I am not sure that I have understood what exactly you are trying to say.'

'You will understand. I just accept that there are differences between a Proton and an Electron. I accept that as a fact of Nature and I don't ask why. I don't feel the need to write a thesis on that. I am not sure about you; you may need to go deeper into the reasons. But for me, what matters is, certain truths are emerging out of their inherent difference and we can use that difference for our benefit—these are borne out by facts and figures. Based on these differences we have, let's say, designed the valves used in a radio. Just keep in mind that protons and electrons can be obtained in trillions even in the tiniest piece of matter; the atoms in a drop of water, if converted to tennis balls, can cover the earth from end to end. Whenever we deal in large numbers, certain statistical models can predict their mass behaviour. That's why statistical models are applied in predicting the behavioural patterns of a huge population. The rules governing the behaviour of electrons also are entirely statistical. And if I can give you, based on those broad statistical laws alone, a new type of valve, which can give you much greater amplification, much enhanced fidelity, without breaking my head about the reasons for the inherent differences between individual protons and electrons and their inherent contradictions, (Nikhil laughed out: this was a show of pedagogy at its height; this was pedantry let loose), would you have any objections?'

'I wouldn't, but....'

'I am trying to tell you just that.'

'I haven't quite understood,' Jati Babu seemed a little uncomfortable. 'Of course, what you said is admirably dialectical. But that doesn't mean....'

'I have nothing further to add. So, think about it.'

There was no way of knowing what Jati Babu thought. Maybe he thought it better not to try and explain things any more to Ranjan. He could not decide if what Ranjan said was right or not. Was Ranjan an escapist or of a warped mind? ('I mean perverted.')

Who knows what people are really after? Suddenly, Nikhil came back to reality with a jolt. A bunch of college girls were passing by. He watched them mechanically. Maybe he felt lust for a while, and he was ashamed of that. As he came closer home, he felt that he was already in the grip of evil, perverted thoughts. Following his gaze, Jati Babu saw the posters of Hollywood's glamour girls on the walls. Exhibition of vulgar, lurid taste. In the guise of advertisement for adventure movies based in the South Sea Islands, obscenity was being openly flaunted. 'Cinema, Theatre, Literature, Radio—all these are the means by which the Capitalists aim to degrade man's good taste. These diversions are arranged by capitalist Hollywood so that people may stay away from revolutionary ideas, so that people become soft and do not allow revolutionary inclinations to germinate in their minds,' Jati Babu said.

To Nikhil it now seemed a strong point in favour of the communist propaganda. He did not have the courage conviction to counter it. Memories from his past came to him—memories of Neeru, memories of that Khasi woman from Shillong. He remembered how his teacher Mahibulla had one day severely beaten up his daughter for the 'crime' of exchanging glances with boys through the window of their residence and how the offending window was kept shut from the next day onwards. Branding the entire social system a culprit seemed ridiculous to Nikhil. Whom would he make responsible for his own bizarre thinking and his insane dirty thoughts? Or would he accept Jati Babu's versions? Would he take a leap from Freud's 'healthy mind' to the Communists' 'healthy society'? Jati Babu said, 'A man's mind is shaped by his environment.'

...Environment? In his case, the environment was his neighbourhood, and that's what has been shaping his mind, he thought wryly.

And maybe it was true.... Even then he gritted his teeth in impotent rage against a force he knew so well; he became angry with himself for not being able to have the naivete of a Jati Babu with his simplistic analyzes. He looked around for the comfort of a shelter and he found that by apportioning equal blame to all of them as 'partners in crime' for his degraded state. He felt a sudden urge to draw all the curtains in his room and cry...his thoughts were distorted thoughts, like that of a madman's; he had burnt all the letters from Makhani, had burnt a huge number of cigarettes, and had kept staring at the rising spirals of smoke. Only then did he have a sense of self-satisfaction...as if he had finally arrived at a firm decision with a firm mind...by deciding to ignore them all—

'She also lieth in wait as for a prey, and increaseth the transgressors among men...her house is the way to hell, going down to the chambers of death....'

'Interesting!' Jati Babu suddenly cried out. 'Who has removed the paper that was pasted here some time ago?'

Someone had torn away the paper pasted on the wall that detailed the Kamini Sharma incident. On the wall, exposed by the part that was torn away, the picture of a Hollywood star was now in full view without any obstruction.

'The police tore it away,' the owner of the paan shop told Nikhil, while handing him his pack of cigarettes.

Jati Babu gave a meaningful glance towards Nikhil as if the episode had suddenly exposed all that was rotten with the social system.

'Even the police like glamour girls.'

Jati Babu's smile appeared leering to Nikhil, he could not quite appreciate the humour. Maybe the owner of the paan shop could. He gave a hearty laugh, showing his teeth, red with betel nut stains.

The leer gradually faded from Jati Babu's face. Under the glare of the fluorescent light in the stationery shop, Jati Babu at that moment did not seem to be a bad sort to Nikhil, and when Jati Babu started buying trinkets for his wife from the stationery shop, Nikhil thought his face was definitely softening. He then appeared to be a social creature fully devoted to his wife.

Jati Babu too had a world of his own and Nikhil suddenly realized with a start that even pickpockets, scholars, lechers, communists, capitalists had family lives of their own. Ranjan had said, all men need a support around which their minds can take shape; an occupation that makes them feel that they have discharged their responsibilities—that could be the reason that men have families. Marx too had his family, but would Jati Babu agree to look at that from a purely biological point of view, he wondered. Ranjan had said that he had a theory but he did not want to prove it because it was only his personal belief, though a strange one. Even the droplets of water in a cloud needed minute particles of dust, some nuclei, maybe electrons or some form of support, to facilitate cloud formation, Ranjan had remarked philosophically while trying to explain Millikan's process for determining the electric charge of particles. A base or a foundation is a must for stability and for facilitating the formation of something. Inside Wilson's cloud chamber, too, dew drops form over electrons under the same principle: there is always a support, a family, a wife, politics, mathematics, or a violin...something to lean on while going forward in one's own trajectory.

That implied very impulsive decisions, irresponsible decisions, Nikhil thought.

'Putraarthay kriyatay bharyya'—a wife is for making children, Niranjan had remarked with a sarcastic smile on his face. Jati Babu had objected and had launched into a severe criticism of our ancient reactionary philosophers and the scriptures. His remark that there was no liberation for women in a capitalist society and that women would be emancipated only in a socialist state, earned a lot of admiration from Bou that day. Bou's words and actions made that clear.

Waves of anxiety swept the evening away for Nikhil.

Back home, there was an uncomfortable silence. Had Deuta already gone to bed, Nikhil wondered. The light in his father's room was switched off. Indistinct strains of an orchestra were wafting in from the radio of the nearby lodging house. He stumbled and almost fell over the threshold of the main door. A tired Bimala was dozing on the threshold after the day's work with her head on the wall. He was alarmed—had the noise of his stumble roused Deuta from his sleep? The light streaming out from the front of the advocate's house across the road was falling on their door and he could vaguely make out the dozing figure of Bimala. In Neeru's house, light was visible through the window panes of Neeru's study room. She must be busy studying for her exam.... Deuta, hopefully, hadn't woken up. No sounds were coming out of his room, so he surely wasn't awake. He tiptoed past his father's room and cast a glance at its curtains. Deuta was possibly asleep. With very high blood pressure, too many worries, anxieties, and feeble eyesight, there was nothing else for the old man to do except get into bed once it was dark. Sometimes, a few aged gentlemen from the neighbouring houses dropped by, sat in the dark on the front veranda and talked in soft voices, discussed things, and expressed their thoughts. None of the excitement on the brightly lit road going past the front of the house reached the old man who lay on his bed like an invalid towards the end of a long, hard life....

He walked into the kitchen. Phunu, his nephew, still drowsy after being roused from his sleep, was being fed by his mother. Fish bones were continually getting stuck in Phunu's throat and he was looking helplessly up at his mother with sleepy eyes. Bou, however, could not pay him much attention; she appeared distracted.

Leaning on a doorpost of the kitchen, Nikhil listened as Bou narrated the bad news. Everything seemed to have gone haywire. No news could be worse than the news of a bank failure, he thought.... Deuta's worried face came floating to his mind. Even at a moment like this he couldn't imagine any sign of anxiety on that face. His father believed that hard times are bound to come in our lives but we must learn to bear them with patience; we must confront bad news and sorrows with equanimity; we must face God's tests with calmness if we have to succeed in the end—that was his philosophy, his attitude towards life. Why couldn't he as a son learn to follow his father? In fact, his father did not feel the need to talk about the bank failure; he had accepted it quite calmly. His father's unconcerned, sedate face came to his mind, brighter than ever before, and he wanted to bow his head in respect. He also wanted to say spontaneously, 'Deuta, I too am fully prepared to face the hard days ahead, I am your son, and I will not shrink from my duties today thinking of the difficulties likely to come tomorrow.' Sufficient unto the day is the evil thereof....

But what held him back? 'But yet the pity of it, Iago—O, Iago, the pity of it, Iago!' Trying to bow his head, he had halted, he remembered he was a worthless, idle, immoral son; apart from getting immersed in useless sentimentality, he also had responsibility towards a house without a mother, a family whose daughter was dead, and which was deserted by a son. He had an insane brother and he was, for all practical purposes, the eldest son of the family (because Bap, his elder brother, had almost no link whatsoever with them).

But what could he do, what was he good at?

Had Deuta kept everything aside and gone to sleep, seeking some peace of mind that way? He peeked into his father's room through the gap in the curtains. He could hear the sound of soft conversation inside the room. The mosquito net was still not pulled down over his father's bed and all around the room, large old trunks and almirahs could be seen standing like dark hazy statues. Rays of feeble light came in through the window near the head of the bed and fell on the large old table with books and papers lying on it. A smell that was redolent of the past, which had a whiff of antiquity, hung within the room. The room was filled with the aroma of tobacco. Deuta was sitting on his bed and smoking; rumbling sounds were coming from the warbler of the hookah. Sitting on a chair by the bed, Karuna Babu was trying to blow life into the dying embers in the chillum and with each blow, the embers glowed bright red for a while and lit up the two faces for a moment or two with a reddish hue before getting swallowed up again by the darkness. At any other time, Nikhil would have thought of them as two characters coming out of the pages of a Dickens novel.

Karuna Babu had a lot of respect for his father, and though he considered it a presumptuous audacity to try and comfort the old man at his time of distress, he was always keen to give his father company. Over the years, Karuna Babu had come to know Deuta well and had found in Deuta an ideal man—someone who had not allowed countless storms to wither him or to put stains on his character. Someone who had had enough opportunities but did not do anything dishonest or unfair; he had helped whoever he could but had never asked for anything in return and had never regretted that. For instance, right in front of the old man's eyes, that gambler, Naren, had gone off to Mumbai, without repaying any of the debts he owed the old man, causing him great loss. But the old man....

'I could never expect that he would disobey me like this.'

Nikhil's heart gave a sudden lurch. Was the old man talking about him?

'What else can I tell you? It's a fault of the times. Or, rather, a sign of the times.' Karuna Babu's words added to Nikhil's confusion and seemed to tangle up the web even more.

'He should at least have spared some thought for the family. He knew our condition well enough,' Deuta was sounding dissatisfied without being accusatory.

'Why are you feeling bad about it? He has a conviction. His conscience is prodding him to do this. He has not gone underground just for the fun of it.' Karuna Babu was trying to make Deuta look at it from a different angle.

Deuta did not say anything. Neither of them spoke for a while and the only sound that could be heard came from the hookah. Deuta did not want to stand in the way of anybody's faith. But he felt that before plunging into anything, it was better to complete one's education. But no, the present generation did not want to see it that way; they didn't see any merit in that. As if education was not worth anything. 'Servile education,' they said. The old man did not want to get into a debate on our education system. Maybe Kon was getting more appreciation from the old man than Maina during the last few days. Kon, at least, was doing something or trying to do something. But what was Kon doing in reality? Goondaism, dacoity, murder? At least, that's what one kept hearing. How could the old man support such things? He had been praying to God to bring his errant son back to the right path, to make him see sense but had God listened to his prayers? The old man's heart was filled with dark anguish at the thought that his own son had degraded himself to the level of an inhuman brute....

'They have created only lawlessness in the country. That's what people are seeing in their actions, anyway. Where is their allegiance to the country?'

'It's true that we are seeing it that way. But how many of us have tried to understand the reality? My mind says that boys like Kon—and why speak of Kon alone, but all, all of them from different political parties—have been forced to do this out of ideological compulsions.' Karuna Babu tried to sound genuinely convinced of what he was saying.

'Violence,' the old man said slowly, 'is always sinful. The cause doesn't matter.'

'That is a matter of opinion,' Karuna Babu at last gathered up his courage and said. The old man was somewhat taken aback by his unfamiliar assertiveness. 'They say, or rather, a large group of people say that the government today is completely fascist. There is no scope today of openly forming groups, be it among farmers, among labourers, or among the middle class. No one has a right to organize a meeting and no right to express one's thoughts in a newspaper. Apart from an armed struggle, or seizing power through a revolution, they can, therefore, find no other option before them. Violence may be necessary for that. They say, "The ends justify the means".'

The old man's response was laced with sarcasm. 'That would mean that all these murders, lootings, arsons are, in the end, justified.'

'A revolution involves atrocities,' Karuna Babu gathered the courage to respond.

There was an uneasy silence for some time.

'I did not really stop him,' the old man said slowly. 'If he wanted to go and fight for a cause, I did not have the right to stop him. But he took a very drastic step.'

Nikhil immediately started feeling a lot lighter, as though a very old secret was suddenly revealed by the old man. It was almost a confession. The clouds dispersed from Nikhil's mind and the old man's words sounded like a shower of blessings, like a goodwill message of approval for all that Kon was doing. It struck Nikhil, as if to remind him afresh that Kon was his own brother, with whom he had a blood relationship. Deuta's approval for Kon's actions (even if it was given unwillingly) would surely be sensed by Kon, in whichever inaccessible, inhospitable place he was, fearing for his life or spending his days in near starvation. The strains of the indistinct orchestra suddenly became louder; someone must have increased the volume of the radio. As if a sudden burst of joy had come floating in to rhyme with the tone of Deuta's words....

Karuna Babu came out of the room. His glasses were slipping down, and he pushed them up to the bridge of his nose, threw a backward glance towards the old man's room and then asked Nikhil, 'Where is your Bou? Alright, don't bother; there is no need to call her. Listen—tomorrow morning before eight, go and fetch Nalini Doctor. I have already briefed him on my way here.'

'Nalini Doctor?'

'Your father's blood pressure needs to be checked.'

Nikhil silently appreciated Karuna Babu's words of concern. Karuna Babu, however, was not aware of that. He was still feeling abashed for saying all those high-sounding words to the old man. He had given quite a lecture to justify what he said, maybe against his better sense, to drive away the bitterness from the old man's mind.

Karuna Babu's asthma was getting worse, he told Nikhil. Nikhil accompanied him to the front door and then came back. Deuta had not gone to bed yet. Every now and then, glimpses of his face could be seen, lit up by the feeble glimmer of the embers that glowed every time he puffed on the hookah. He must be engrossed in thoughts.... Maybe he was thinking, where was Kon at this time? What would the life of somebody always on the run be like? Was he fine, was he in good health? What did he get to eat? Then the old man would suddenly remember Dhon. He would recall Dhon's desire for higher education, how he wanted to send Dhon abroad. By association, he would then remember Maina's friend Amal, whose ship had left Bombay on the tenth of last month. Maina himself had brought him the news. He, Dhon, the bright student of the other day, was now insane. Suddenly, the old man would imagine a bomb going off somewhere, there would be the roar of a pistol, scenes of farmers snatching the rifles from the police—who had poisoned the minds of those poor farmers, those peace-loving Assamese people, to do such things? Then there would be a commotion, a loud noise; smoke and the smell of explosives would fill the roads and Kon would be caught.... The old man would possibly imagine that Kon was getting severely beaten, kicked on the chest by boots.... An unknown terror would grip the old man, he would start feeling momentarily forlorn. He had not seen his daughter Xonti for a long time. She would be arriving any moment now. She would bring in a whiff of fresh air with her and he would feel good for a change. One could imagine that even in the dim light, his eyes would be suddenly straying to the wall, trying to make out Gandhiji's picture hanging there, one hand raised in a gesture of peace. He would vaguely make out the calm look of the face in the dim light and his mind would suddenly turn bitter—he had lost faith in humanity. Man had crucified Jesus, had shot dead Abraham Lincoln and, going further down to the level of brutes, had finally killed Gandhiji too.

What would people in the world live for now?

The shadow of war was hanging over their heads, with the terrifying prospects of atom and hydrogen bombs. The human race had become diseased, opportunistic, violence-prone....

...The embers in his chillum would be slowly dying out.

Nikhil thought he could hear the door to Manu's room being opened. He saw that the whole room was filling up with all sorts of knick knacks, various small articles. He suddenly remembered that his elder sister Xonti, Xonti Baideo, as he called her, was on her way home and that's why a room was getting cleaned today by his sister-in-law, his Bou and the odd items were removed from there and being dumped in this room in front of his eyes. The entire house was looking much cleaner and tidier; Bou must have taken a lot of pains. He cursed himself; how could a young man like him loaf around doing nothing while Bou did everything? Bou had said nothing openly, but surely she was piqued at his apathy. He suddenly felt a liking for Bou and realized that, all said and done, she was still the wife of his elder brother. He wondered how she was managing the family even after taking care of her own unmanageable kids. Had he ever faced difficulty over anything as long as she was around? Xonti Baideo kept making innuendos that all Bou ever did was just a 'show' to impress Deuta. But wasn't it because of Bou that Deuta never had trouble over anything? If the messy family affairs were making Bou feel overwhelmed, could she be blamed for that? Where did that leave him, he thought. He recalled Bou's face as she was feeding her child, Phunu: her face seemed so preoccupied. The news of the bank failure and the sudden blow to the family finances had shattered her as much, even if one believed that she was not really as simple as she made out to be. Her life had become inseparably entangled with the fortunes of this family. The family's happiness was her happiness, its sorrows her sorrows.

Her eldest child Makhon was sleeping at the reading table with his head on the books. The electric bulb's holder had some problem and the bulb did not work ('Will have to show it to Ranjan', he thought). The only light in the room came from an oil lamp and the kerosene burning in it was red and dirty. Light from the lamp was falling on Makhon's sleeping face and was getting heated by it. A list of algebra formulae was stuck on the room's wall and a lizard was crawling over it; a shirt carelessly draped over the arms of the chair had slipped to the ground. Radios were blaring from neighbouring houses. He suddenly flew into a rage against all his neighbours. They kept their radios on at all hours of the night and the day, disturbing the boys and girls of the neighbourhood in their studies, distracting them from their preparation for the exams. Easy money! That man, Bhuban, living in the same neighbourhood, had died the other day after suffering from typhoid: but none of them would switch off their radios for a moment. Maybe this is the 'curse of civilization' that Jati Babu talked about. He lowered the lamp's wick to reduce its brightness, trying hard not to disturb Makhon. He then ambled into the kitchen.

Bou was not there. He found her dozing in her own room. The wooden planks of the bed had become infested with bed bugs in the last few days, so she had pulled the mattress down to the floor to lie on it. Keeping Runu, her youngest child, clasped to her bosom, she was lying down by the side of her children and had dozed off. Moonbeams were streaming in through the window. Bou's face, serene in sleep, suddenly brought to his mind the image of eternal motherhood—moonlight was falling on the feeding bottle lying next to her hand, making it shine like a piece of glass. He could make out the closed and frayed old prayer book, the *Kirtan Ghosha*, lying by the side of her head—its dog-eared pages were stained red with blots of sindoor. Bou sometimes used to leaf through it when she was alone....

He stood still for some time.

Bou was not in deep sleep. Somewhere in the distance people were singing a community prayer or a *naam*, the sound of its halting rhythm was coming in through the window. In her semi-wakefulness, Bou could faintly hear the accolades sung for Lord Krishna, '*Gopala Govinda Jadunandan, tomara charane lailo saran.*' The familiar, haunting tune carried a sense of boundless peace and made Bou forget the complications of life, her eyelids were getting heavier, and she was forcing herself to stay awake to keep listening to the soothing words of the song.

She suddenly woke up with a start. Maybe a mosquito had bit her on the forehead. She could hear Maina calling, 'Bou, O Bou, wake up. Is dinner ready?'

The sounds of khol and tal, the local drums and cymbals, gradually died out in the distance. The choral prayer songs, the naam-kirtan, were winding up. When he went back to his room, he switched on the light and started writing a letter. He had not written to Makhani for a long time. She surely couldn't have forgotten him so fast. He had now come to the conclusion that his diseased warped mind was at the root of his unreasonable dissatisfaction with her.

The old days came back to his mind like a flashback—college and the cultural functions; the girls and the 'posturing' of the boys. A sense of anarchy pervaded everything and his days were spent within an intellectual circle. Then there was Makhani and her singing. A bit of Communism, a dash of poetry, a sprinkling of hypocrisy, and a few years filled with self-deception.

He remembered Kon and Dhon again. Amal was now sailing to foreign shores. An image of Misra's restaurant came floating in from the past. He remembered their intellectual circle and their chat groups, the addas. The partitioned enclosures inside the restaurant came vividly to his mind. They had placed the restaurant virtually under siege those days. The load of unpaid bills kept accumulating and was making them break into sweat; the sarcastic comments of Misra's partner, who also happened to be Misra's elder brother (who had this habit of making constant attempts to pull up his trousers above the waist though the trousers refused to stop slipping down) were making the intellectual circle thoroughly embarrassed. Even the waiters of the restaurant found their predicament amusing and broke into teasing sniggers.

Nikhil and his circle of friends had always enjoyed listening to songs on the radio and the editorial board of their cultural magazine had caused many a tempest in the tea cup within its walls. They tried to keep away from the self-centred crowd outside and maintain their distance from all economic and political complexities. None of them could ever be seen in any of the meetings within or outside the college, they never took part in any procession and the moment the radio started a news bulletin, their faces would cloud over with annoyance. Life was an unending series of highbrow thinking, poems and dramas, girls and love letters.

There was no shortage of unpleasant incidents. They used to enter the restaurant after skillfully avoiding the placard that read: 'No sales on credit'. There were often signs of unconcealed annoyance on Misra's elder brother's face and the waiters would also hint at their unwelcome habit of spending hours over a single cup of tea. Misra would sometimes switch off the radio, or one of the two lights overhead just to insult them, and their own voices would then sound mocking as they pronounced dramatically, 'Light, more light....'

Yet they were proud to have created a splendid atmosphere away from the squalor and the noise of the world around them. There were times when a noisy procession of labourers and middle-class men would pass along in front of the restaurant or when the restaurant would be violently shaken by the roar of passing vehicles. An annoyed Misra would then keep switching the radio on and off. There they sat, ridiculing the radical ideologies and the communist propaganda or heaping abuse on the roaring vehicles of the capitalist tycoons and remained cocooned in their narrow but lively environment. An environment that was secure, calm, and devoid of tensions. There would be times when all the lights of the restaurant would go off, a fuse might have blown somewhere and a few cups and plates would then tumble with a clatter in some corner, there would be a bedlam of confused noise and a few high-pitched shouts would ring out in the darkness and the strains of the Bhimpalasi raga coming out of the radio would suddenly die out. But the circle of friends would remain unfazed; a matchstick would flare up in the darkness; a succession of long white cigarettes would appear one after the other, only the tips of the cigarettes would glow in the darkness to throw bizarre misshapen shadows of the cups and plates and men on the walls of the darkened restaurant and their circle of would-be bohemian intellectuals would sedately wait for the return of lights (and Ranjan would have failed to repair the flaw that night to restore the electricity and would have felt the uselessness of his knowledge, feeling for the first time a little disrespect for his education with its huge chasm between theory and practice).

But all this was ultimately in vain. As time went by, the members of their circle drifted apart and no one kept track of what happened to whom. Amal was on his way abroad, Jatin was in jail, living on the daily ration of a C-division inmate. Others became school teachers, clerks, or lecturers in colleges, all moving in their own orbits. One of them, Himangshu, vanished without trace. Then one day, as Nikhil was standing outside a movie theatre, listening to the songs on the loudspeaker outside, he suddenly came across Biresh. Both were so overwhelmed that they couldn't find their voices at first. Then Biresh opened up in fits and starts. He took out a packet of expensive State Express cigarettes from his pocket, requested Nikhil to give him company in watching a movie in Special Class. In the bright lights outside the movie theatre, his face glowed, and his expensive suit glittered. When Nikhil, watching this rather grand appearance of a mere clerk working in the government's supply department, frankly expressed his skeptical disbelief, Biresh came clean without the slightest discomfiture and said that yes, he took bribes and that he did it willingly, did it 'on principle'.

'Loot while you can, brother. Look around you and you will see everyone busy all the time scheming and finding ways to loot,' he had told Nikhil.

Biresh had sold out to the materialist's hedonistic outlook. They talked of many things that day. They took stock of their friends, talked of the life Jatin was leading in jail, how Makhani was faring, talked about Amal and his trip abroad, ridiculed their own past and their obsession with intellectual refinement and commented on the horrible state of affairs of the world, where he, Biresh, had embraced corruption as a way of life. Nikhil wondered what had happened to their buddy Narayan Hazarika.

'Narayan Hazarika? Why, didn't he commit suicide long ago?' Biresh replied.

Nikhil was stunned and couldn't speak for some time. 'There is a tide in the affairs of men,' he said feebly.

'What? Oh, Shakespeare? I have forgotten all that a long time ago.'

Naturally. How could Shakespeare survive under the combined assault of files, accounts, and Marwari businessmen? The loudspeaker outside the movie theatre fell silent, signalling that inside the hall the prelude was over and that the movie was about to begin. Biresh bade a hurried goodbye.

Nikhil, thereafter, wandered about the streets as if in a dream. The world seemed to be drifting away, and he too seemed to be drifting with the current. There is a tide.... All around him people were creating a jumble of noise. What were all these people thinking? He wondered. From Ranjan's point of view all they were doing was creating sound waves. Narayan Hazarika.... So the world had at last managed to kill him. That was the end of an immense potential. He suddenly realized the truth of Ranjan's words, that the world was nothing but the interplay of waves. Sounds and songs are nothing but air undulating in waves, sunshine and heat are also mere waves.... Electromagnetic waves. Even the electrons are waves, waves of probability. Radio is wireless transmission of waves. Every single event in the world, every single thing in it is a sequential chain of waves—coming in and going away as a propagating series of vibrations and they would continue coming in and going away one after the other. Narayan too came and he also went away. Maybe Deuta too....

The train too had come in and gone away. Standing on the railway crossing with Jati Babu and Ranjan, he had observed the signal in the distance. The rich man's government had again increased the train fares, Jati Babu had commented. Ranjan did not respond, nor did Nikhil. Jati Babu must have realized that he had said something totally inane. There they were, like three young kids waiting to see a train as though it was something they had never seen before. All three were amazed at the thought. All three saw the distant signal turn red, Nikhil couldn't think of anything to say, Jati Babu hesitated to symbolize it with the coming of a 'Revolutionary Red', Ranjan was not inclined to comment that the colour red too was a wave and had a wave-length of 6563×10^{-8} centimeters. All three remained standing, smoking the cigarettes bought from the nearby shanty of a Nepalese shopkeeper. It seemed as if in the stillness of the silent night in that lonely spot, the eternality of arrival and departure had somehow become replete with emotional overtones. The humongous monster of a machine, resembling a one-eyed titanic Polyphemus with shrill whistles, full of crowded unromantic compartments ('Ease of travel is not meant for commoners,' Jati Babu said) and with loud back and forth movement of its pistons ('Thermodynamic cycle,' Ranjan said) sped past them and they stood rooted to the spot, as if thunderstruck, till it passed.

As if a huge wave had undulated past....

'Difference is only in the mode of manifestation of the waves and in their lengths and it is the difference in wavelengths that makes things look red or yellow and is the root cause behind x-rays differing from gamma rays...' Ranjan said in a rambling tone.

Ranjan is a wise fool, Nikhil thought.

'It's beautifully dialectical,' Jati Babu said. 'Transformation of quantity into quality and vice-versa is part of a principal law of dialectics.'

Jati Babu is a parrot, Nikhil concluded.

The night was already deep; the community prayer songs were over long ago. The world was asleep. The sound of his father's coughs could be heard every now and then.

It was very late in the night when the mysterious Khagen Das car could be heard coming back. Out opium smuggling? Maybe not. Maybe his face was showing signs of excesses during the night. Excesses of wine and women....

His father's cough was weak but clear. The sound of Khagen Das car engine was fading out. Night has a certain power to inflict pain.

'But the night will also end at last.' His head seemed to be reeling, as he recalled the train that took Makhani away to her in-laws. Its wheels seemed to be still churning inside his head.

It was wheels again that transported him from pain to pleasure. Phunu's new tricycle came and banged against the door. Its three wheels carried a heady feeling of speed, added to that was the free-flowing laughter of a child. (His brother-in-law, Xonti's husband, had presented Phunu with a new tricycle).

Words were gushing out non-stop from Xonti Baideo, his elder sister, like a veritable fountain. Ila and Neela had gone to hide behind their mother's mekhela on hearing Nikhil's voice, their unruly hair constantly flopping down on their foreheads. Phunu and Runu were carried away by the fun of it all and were shouting the roof down. Bou was trying to control them by whacking them with Makhan's wooden ruler in her hand and they went to hide behind the door. His brother-in-law had brought them savoury biscuits and he was smiling. Bou too was smiling. Even his father had a ghost of a smile playing on his lips.

His elder sister, Xonti, had become plumper. Ila and Neela were adorable. His brother-in-law, whom he addressed either as Bhinihi or Bhindeo, was a huge man, huge in face, wearing a huge bush-shirt and sporting a massive moustache. He and Makhan became thick pals in no time, his Bhinihi being a sports aficionado. Those two didn't talk of anything but sports all the time—

In just two days, the house was transformed as if by magic. Xonti Baideo wept a lot on seeing the state of the house and that made Bou wince, as she thought, 'Oh look at her crocodile tears!' New curtains had replaced the old ones at the doors, cobwebs had vanished, and his brother-in-law had bought a whole bunch of fruits from the market for his father. Xonti Baideo made arrangements so that the old man would get a steady supply of fish fingerlings every day. Fish fingerlings are said to be excellent for weak eyesight. It was like a slap on Bou's face.

Ranjan came in with the bad news: Dhon's condition was worsening. He was beating up whoever came near him and his blows had already resulted in a cracked skull for the doctor who had come to see him. Deuta quietly took to his bed, Nikhil's Bhinihi stopped his sports talk, and Xonti Baideo started weeping all over again.

'We are destined for bad luck,' she said in between sobs.

'Pessimism will solve nothing,' Jati Babu tried to console.

The evening progressed silently with excruciating slowness. Bhinihi started a description of his travels to break the embarrassing silence. He talked about the exquisite beauty of the Ajanta and Ellora caves. The atmosphere thawed a little after some time. Nikhil did not open his mouth; Ranjan made no comments.

Ranjan gave the impression that he didn't want to be on talking terms with him, Nikhil thought.

'I have heard everything,' Ranjan told him. 'What were you up to with that Khasi girl, Bluebell?' Nikhil bowed his head like a culprit.

Nobody could get Dhon out of their minds. Suddenly, Bhinihi realized that no one was paying him any attention. Xonti was still sobbing, Bou was looking askance at the new curtains, a little dissatisfaction visible on her face, Ranjan's and Nikhil's faces had the look of eternal foes, and Jati Babu was cocking his ears trying to pick up some sound from Deuta's room. Maybe he was feeling sad for the old man.

Bhinihi suddenly stopped his monologue.

'And then? What happened after that?' someone asked him.

'No—let's stop here for today.'

Nobody objected. Time ticked away in embarrassing silence.

'Ranjan Kokaideo, would you please help me with a problem in geometry?' Makhan said almost in a whisper, maybe he too was aware of the tension in the room. Ranjan heaved a sigh of relief at getting a chance to do something that he liked.

'God knows what is in store for Deuta,' Xonti broke the silence, while wiping the tears away from her eyes.

'Yes, one feels bad even thinking about it,' Bhinihi said with a sigh. 'No one to take proper care of him—and at his age.'

Bou was hurt by these words. Bhinihi had said it with simplicity but realized immediately that he had been unfair and was angry with himself.

Bou and Xonti exchanged a quick glance. Ranjan and Nikhil noticed it but did not like it.

'Kon too had to end up doing this,' Xonti said with some heat. 'They are brewing trouble even over our own land, Deuta was telling me today. Our tenant farmers tilling that land have stopped paying us with rice.'

'That place has already been declared as a "Disturbed Area" since day before yesterday,' said Bhinihi, having nothing else to add.

Bhinihi said, 'That place is reeling under full-fledged terrorism,' Jati

Babu chipped in, 'they have burned down the zamindar's residence, looted the barns of the rich—'

'That's what you work for, anyway,' said Nikhil.

'No, not us. Communists do not go for that kind of stuff. Communism and terrorism are not the same.'

For a while, there was silence.

'That is the end of whatever little rice we had got from that land,' Bou said.

'By making Deuta face this at his old age, Kon has....' Bhinihi suddenly stopped before proceeding further.

'People like Deuta are selfish,' Nikhil blurted out all of a sudden. 'What if the paddy is lost? It is going to be lost, anyway. It is better to forsake with grace what is anyway going to be lost.'

Everybody was stunned by Nikhil's outburst. Xonti became quite angry.

'How can you say that? Have you ever wondered how this household is managing itself?'

'For greater interest—'

'For greater interest, yes,' Jati Babu said slowly, 'but what Kon is doing is termed terrorism by us.'

Ranjan was livid and came down heavily on both Nikhil and Jati Babu.

'Don't you know, Nikhil, the condition of the social system with which your father had to struggle to become a man? And you, Jati Babu, you had said it yourself that theirs was a time of oppressive repression by the British. The social system of those days could give no certainty, no assurance to one's life or to one's survival. And men like Nikhil's father had struggled greatly to find ways and means to earn a livelihood in the midst of that hopeless situation. If today those ways and means, like that hard-earned piece of land, and the little rice it earned, are wrenched away from their hands, can those men be anything but sad? Are they to be held responsible for their attachment to their hard-earned private property?'

Jati Babu and Nikhil stared dumbly at each other.

'And you, Jati Babu, are you also not responsible for not being able to convince the old generation to look at things from your point of view?'

Jati Babu was silent.

'Do you seriously think that Jati Babu is going to do the convincing and dissuade the terrorists, do you?' God knows what prompted Bhinihi to make that sarcastic remark. Everybody was taken aback. That sudden leap from the world of football-cricket to the world of politics was a gigantic one.

'But Jati Babu wants only communism, I thought—' Bou said, confused.

'You bet I do,' Jati Babu became somewhat angry, 'Don't Kon and his mates call it terrorism? If not, what do they call it?'

'Partisan warfare,' Ranjan replied.

Jati Babu came to a complete halt. He frantically foraged in his mind, with its store of theories, to come up with some rebuttal.

'Is Jati Babu a communist?' Xonti questioned, surprised.

'But in my opinion,' Ranjan said, 'considering the state of the country everywhere, if someone is a true communist, he would either be in jail or would have gone underground.'

It was like a slap on Jati Babu's face. Bhinihi fidgeted with embarrassment. Bou did not quite understand what had happened and Xonti Baideo made an effort to make her smile look sympathetic. Nikhil thought Ranjan's words had exposed Jati Babu's hypocrisy. But Ranjan regretted saying what he had.

The room was filled with an oppressive silence. As if to put an end to it, something went wrong with the electricity and the room was plunged into darkness. Inside his already darkened room, Deuta couldn't have known of the power outage. The baby in Xonti's arms started howling and Bhinihi dislodged the metal platter kept on the table for offering betel nut and it tumbled to the floor with a loud metallic clang.

'These electric lights can be a real nuisance—' Xonti Baideo said in irritation.

'Yes, can be very irritating at times,' Bou commented.

Bimala came in and lit up a lamp before going out again.

'Why does this happen?' Bhinihi asked Ranjan.

'Because the flow of electrons is cut off,' Ranjan tried to make it sound complicated.

'That's Greek to me,' Bhinihi said.

'Let your electrons go to hell,' Nikhil said.

'If you can make the light come on again, then I would say you really know your stuff. What do you study, anyway?' Xonti Baideo said.

'Just theoretical Physics. What else?' Nikhil said tauntingly.

'My theory is far superior to your practice.'

Ranjan's tone made both Xonti Baideo and Bhinihi suspect something. What practice? What could be Nikhil's practice? They stared at each other questioningly.

'Asking electrons to go to hell sounds good coming from you. Since you are already in hell.'

'What's going on here? What is it?' Bhinihi asked. Xonti Baideo was all ears. Bou was intelligent enough to maintain a deadpan face.

'Nothing, nothing really,' Ranjan tried to divert the topic, 'Just a manner of speaking. Who hasn't gone to hell these days, anyway?'

Yes, who hasn't gone to hell, Xonti Baideo wondered. Anima had dropped in today. Her old college friend, Anima Mazumdar. These days she was a radio artist and a lecturer of Botany. She had turned so cynical. She was still single. Her simplicity of the old days had almost disappeared, as also the enthusiasm and liveliness. Xonti had been overjoyed at meeting a classmate after ages and thought she would have a welcome break from her world of feeding bottles and oil-cloths to take a trip down memory lane. But—

Jati Babu wanted to leave. Karuna Babu's asthma had worsened; he wanted to go and call on him.

'Why don't you stay for some more time?' Bou asked Jati Babu.

Jati Babu wasn't keen. Ila and Neela had gone to sleep on the bed in a corner of the room. He looked at them and seemed to go into a reverie. Bhinihi became engrossed in his newspaper. He read about someone commenting on jet-propelled planes used in the Korean War. He wanted to ask Ranjan what jet propulsion was all about but decided against it. Deuta had asked him about it that morning and he had no answer. Deuta had gone through the newspaper at noon and had asked Bhinihi to keep him company. Bhinihi had gathered that according to Deuta the Congress had gone to the dumps after Gandhiji's death and that he did not like what the UN was doing in Korea and Kashmir. It was becoming clear with each passing day that the General Assembly was under the total control of the US. Why didn't the Americans leave Korea? People there could decide their own fate themselves. Bhinihi had commented that people in the Far East had been harbouring an intense hatred against the whites for a long time. He had narrated to Deuta an incident in a Japanese harbour that he had heard from a much-travelled customs superintendent…they talked of this and that for quite some time but the old man had a feeling at some point that Bhinihi wasn't really enjoying it. The old man's face darkened in a sulk like a small boy's; he might have realized that he had become a relic of the past, with hardly any historical use for anybody. Pretending to feel sleepy, he had made Bhinihi go away. Bhinihi felt relieved but he too guessed the real reason behind the old man's action and started to feel guilty.

'No, I had better leave. I must call on Karuna Babu once. I have to call on Nabin's mother too,' said Jati Babu who seemed to be in a hurry to leave.

'What is Nabin doing these days?' Xonti Baideo enquired.

'That rascal has become an informer,' Bhinihi suddenly burst out. 'He was treating Neela to coffee today and kept asking her if Kon had come to visit his elder sister. Lucky that Kon hadn't. I couldn't get the drift of his questions at first and realized it much later. There is his mother fighting for her life and here he is, busy spying.'

'What option does he have, poor chap? Their finances are at rock bottom. And on top of that his mother's condition….' Nikhil sounded as if he was pleading for Nabin. 'Their economic condition is so bad.'

Jati Babu theorized, 'This is the way Capitalism degrades people. Just think about it. Nabin, of all people. Someone living on the same street, besides being one of your friends for so long—'

Suddenly, Jati Babu stopped in mid-sentence. He felt ashamed of himself.

Xonti Baideo vented her ire on Nabin; why did he have to bring the little girl into all this? Bou too said a few words in anger. Nikhil was saddened by this attitude towards the little girl. He remembered how Jati Babu had spoken one day about individual freedom and how India was lacking it. Think of the moment when a baby is born and a new child comes to our planet. Just imagine for a moment the environment of bitterness through which the child would have to grow. A few demons have laid siege to the planet—their penetrating Machiavellian gaze is keeping everybody under surveillance. This child will watch his own shadow with suspicion as he grows up on this lovely earth and all around him would be the dark spectres of suspicion and fear, distrust and hatred….

Would the shadows of suspicion and hatred engulf the beautiful innocent faces of Ila and Neela too?

Jati Babu took his leave. He left with an uneasy mind. Who could have made someone like Ranjan understand the nuances of 'partisan warfare'? Did Ranjan read and appreciate Lenin? His gaze had strayed to Deuta's darkened room. The old man, a victim of bourgeoise propaganda, was asleep. The old man's mind was full of resentment against the new generation but what had he got for himself from the old system? Who, in the pursuit of their ideologies, had failed to win over this simple, honest old man and people of his older generation as their valued allies? Who were the people watching indifferently as this old man and people like him were getting sucked into the vortex of cunning propaganda? What was the advantage the Leftists were gaining through this kind of propaganda? The Fascist administration was not going to help them anyway. The likes of Kon said that in the absence of any scope for spreading ideologies through propaganda, what became more effective was a demonstrative action of some kind, a show of confrontation. But Kon belonged to an opposing faction. In the whirlpool of political representations, Jati Babu's ideas became more complicated; he became more confused.

Conflicts liberate thought—'Action releases thought from its blind alleys and vicious circles....,' they say. Still terrorism is heinous. Talking of action—does action have to mean terrorism?

Bhinihi, who was walking by his side, said, 'Our people have always been getting bashed up. Kon and his mates say that it is time to remind the people of that so that they also learn to give it back. It's a policy of replying to bloodshed with bloodshed. It has become necessary to shake off the lethargy and inertia of the people.'

'Looting of banks or looting the paddy in barns, do these shake off the inertia of the people?'

Nikhil, meanwhile, was trying to get to the root of all this complicated stuff. He remembered Goethe. He suddenly burst out aloud, taking everyone by surprise, 'In the beginning was the Act.'

The one most surprised was Ranjan. He was yet to get over the shock of Nikhil's affair with the Khasi girl, Bluebell. His head was reeling from thoughts about Deuta, Bou, Xonti Baideo, and Nabin. It was as though sanity had disappeared from everybody's minds, as if everyone was getting involved, even if reluctantly, in all kinds of muddles. Strange unexpected words were coming out from unexpected mouths. He too was forced to listen to Jati Babu about the reasons behind the bank failure. Thoughts of Dhon, Kon, Anima, and Makhani were messing up his mind. Everywhere there was instability, breakdown, and uncertainty. The sun was dying; Nikhil's father was dying. The fluid was evaporating from the milk in the saucepan; alpha particles were spontaneously being emitted from radium all the time; restless electrons were being scattered through the grid inside the valves of the radio. There was no certainty anywhere, waves acted as particles and the very next moment particles behaved like waves, as if a state of anarchy was inherent everywhere...people were revolting, becoming restless, lawless; like the electrically charged particles breaking laws while confronting a potential wall, like Dirac breaking laws of mathematics with the delta function....

'Ranjan, aren't you going home? It's quite late.'

'I am leaving shortly. What will I do at home, anyway?'

'How are you doing in your studies? Exams are....'

'All right, more or less. I feel like leaving this place soon. The mind can't be at peace here.'

Xonti Baideo responded with a smile of sympathy.

'I have decided to go away soon. I think I will leave day after,' Ranjan said.

'Day after? What is the hurry? Won't you stay back for the music function that Anima and her friends are organizing? Ila and Neela will also dance there, you know, the organizers were so persistent about it, wouldn't take no for an answer. And then Anima also plays the sitar really well, they say.'

'Oh, I forgot. I am yet to start work on their dresses.' Bou suddenly remembered that Anima and her friends had requested her to cut and stitch two multi-coloured sadors for Ila and Neela for their dance performance. 'Xonti, the sadors have to be stitched this very night. Hope you won't go to bed before they are ready.'

'I will get them enrolled in Uday Shankar's dance troupe once they grow up,' Bhinihi said with some pride. Xonti Baideo too swelled a little and Bou smiled. 'Everyone says they dance quite well for their age.'

Nikhil would have liked to watch the much-applauded dance of Ila and Neela but he shrank at the thought of the brightly lit atmosphere at the function. Two beautiful girls with their soft innocent faces would dance, Anima would play the sitar in the orchestra, people would enjoy the show and they would break out in smiles. In the bright light the smiling faces of men and women, Bou and Xonti Baideo, Ila and Neela would appear enchanting and romantic. Jati Babu would give comments from his cynical perspective in sync with the music, Girija Sarma would drool lustfully in anticipation of opportunities, and Ranjan might try to comment in a humourless flat tone that the music was really just a collection of Fourier waves. Girls with their breasts thrust out would move by his side, he would become excited; maybe 'unclean' thoughts would start moving around in his mind again. Khagen Das was the man financing the function and he wondered what kind of atmosphere would be generated by the man's arrogant attitude and by his condescending smile.

Would the function coincide with Janmaastami, the birth date of Lord Krishna? Bou was trying to count the days. She wouldn't be able to spare enough time in the function, she thought. What with so many chores remaining undone at home, she would have to come back early. Once back home, maybe the refrains of some prayer songs would come indistinctly to her mind. Being alone in the empty house with her children, her mind would keep straying every now and then to the light and laughter of the function.

(That's what had actually happened. Bou was feeling quite dejected, Nikhil too. As if someone was humming the strains from a prayer song describing the night Lord Krishna was born: *'Tonight a hailstorm is raging'*).

'It's becoming so warm, the lamp gives out so much heat,' Bou said.

Ranjan said, 'It's a sheer waste. The lamp is burning too strongly.'

Bou lowered the wick.

Ranjan waited for a while before saying, 'The waste is in the lamp itself. Of the energy generated by burning the oil, we use only two percent for our reading and for seeing things. The rest goes to waste, without any use to us. You have seen for yourself how much heat is generated.'

'What is science doing about it?' Bhinihi asked.

'They are trying to invent a light that does not generate any heat. I am just thinking, how can I stop this huge wastage of energy or reconvert it to light and supply it to places where it is needed? Theoretically, that's possible. Because all types of energy, be it light, heat, electricity, magnetism or sound, can be transformed from one form to another. Just imagine how the world would glitter with bright light if I could do that.'

'Utopian,' Nikhil said, but he realized immediately that he shouldn't have said that.

Bou grinned but Xonti Baideo hadn't paid any attention to what Ranjan had said. Bhinihi did show a little interest but that did not stop Ranjan from feeling deflated. Jati Babu came to his mind; he would have remarked that today's scientists can invent nothing that can be of any use to men. Capitalism had made scientists slaves of financial interests. In the manufacturing industry, from razor blades to the atom bomb it was the capitalists who had the last word. Let's say you had devised the capability to flood the world with millions of lumens but who in this world would allow you to apply the process?

Ranjan felt an irritation caused by something he couldn't quite put a finger on, and he left with irritation simmering within him. Besides, with Bou's cooking almost over, everyone would get up now for dinner and it was better to leave before he too was asked to stay back. Xonti Baideo was dozing in the chair, Bhinihi broke into a long-drawn yawn, and Nikhil went out of the room. Coming in from the kitchen, Bou saw Xonti already asleep, the feeding bottle lying by her side, still full of milk. The entire house was silent as though nobody lived in it. No one was speaking and no one was making any sound. A breeze was blowing and the curtains were fluttering. Bou's face suddenly softened. She picked up Xonti's baby in her arms and started feeding it milk from the bottle.

Many days later Nikhil woke up with a start to find Xonti Baideo caressing his cheek. He wondered why the usual blaring of the radios was absent and his sense of surprise became stronger. He got up and went out of his room to find that Bhinihi and Ranjan were seated at the dining table grinning away, Xonti Baideo was grinning, and Bou was grinning too. Ranjan pointed towards the rickshaw on the road where Girija Sarma could be seen going somewhere, with the radio loaded on the rickshaw. There was something like a doorbell on the socket for the fan and it was making an intermittent buzzing sound.

'He is carrying the radio to the repair shop,' Ranjan said with a broad grin. 'I would give my shirt to see the faces of the men in the repair shop when they look the radio over. They will scratch their heads, because there is nothing to repair—because nothing is wrong with the radio. The root of its trouble is here. Have you seen the buzzer I have fitted here? Its buzz is interfering with their radio and all they can hear in it is a series of buzzes. They are foxed.'

'You and your tricks, Ranjan!'

'Serves them right. I have silenced them quite scientifically. No child in the neighbourhood could study because of their callous indifference.'

Nikhil didn't bother to find out what a buzzer was or how it worked. All he did was to break into a grin like the rest of them.

'There may be a little time before breakfast is ready, isn't it? Let me complete my shave till then,' Ranjan said and sat down to use Bhinihi's shaving set as if it was his own.

'My shaving set got nationalized, is it?'

Jati Babu heard that as he was entering but he wasn't smacked by the sarcasm. He laughed out loud.

'What sound is that?' he asked.

'Rehearsal for the musical evening. The orchestra for Ila-Neela's dance performance.' Xonti Baideo was smiling from ear to ear. 'Anima has already taken them out in the morning.'

The orchestra was rehearsing in a neighbouring house. This was rehearsal for the second function. In the first, Ila and Neela had come out with flying colours.

Doctor Nalini came in just then. That meant there wouldn't be any time for tea. Everyone streamed into Deuta's room. In the doctor's instrument for measuring blood pressure, the column of mercury kept climbing rapidly.

All the faces showed signs of concern. The doctor's voice was reassuring. He told Deuta, 'Now you take complete rest. There are enough people in the house to take care of you, so take it easy.'

'Yes, I need some rest,' Deuta said and his gaze fell on Bou. He became thoughtful.

The doctor took his leave. Everybody followed him out of the room. Deuta, however, asked Maina to stay back. 'Bowari also needs some rest,' he said, referring to his daughter-in-law. 'With all these kids around, how much can she take? Make it a point to visit the doctor again and tell him about her. Maybe he will prescribe a tonic for her.' Outside the door to his room, Bou suddenly broke into a sob away from others' eyes. In the adjacent room, Xonti Baideo murmured, 'Deuta is so very simple, so very naive. He takes things so much at their face value.'

The light atmosphere of moments ago didn't remain the same. A shadow was already passing over it. Everyone again sat down for tea. Bou went into the kitchen. Ranjan suddenly jumped to his feet. Runu could be seen trying to climb the staircase. But he was struggling with the high first step, failing every time he tried to put one foot on it. Ranjan reached his side, watched for a moment, thinking that Runu was about to give up trying. Nikhil seemed to wake up from his sleep all over again and he too jumped to his feet and leaped up. He went and helped Runu raise his foot over the step.

Going up the stairs became easy after that. Runu started climbing rapidly—one step, then the next—and at last he put his foot on the very top of the staircase.

The orchestra rose to a crescendo in the neighbouring house. Bou came out with Xonti from the kitchen. Bou's eyes were still moist, Nikhil noted. He looked up at Runu whom he had pushed along the path of success, heard the joyous laughter that came out from the child's throat, and listened to the orchestra reaching its climax. A smile started forming in his heart and pushed itself up to his lips and he clutched Ranjan by the hand and pushed him onto a chair by the tea table. He felt like saying something to Bou and Xonti Baideo,

'Give us this day our daily bread,' he said.

Translated by Jiban Goswami

LOOKING FOR ISMAEL SHEIKH

HOMEN BORGOHAIN

I was completely oblivious of time, place or people. Standing in the middle of the busiest road in town, I shouted with all my might, 'Ismael!' startling everyone around me. I had started running even before my shout died down.

Perhaps there is no forgiveness for even the slightest lapse in life. Destiny is but the immutability of an unknown, preordained scheme of things. If I had not shouted, I would have met the man—he, whom I had been looking for relentlessly for the last five years—at that very spot. But hearing my cry, Ismael vanished, as if by magic. I had made a colossal blunder.

But I had to seek out Ismael. Now that I had spotted him, he wouldn't be able to elude me. Even from a distance I had noticed him dart a frightened glance at me before disappearing into a narrow lane off the main road. I dashed to the entrance of the lane.

Two young men were standing there, smoking beside a paan shop. Noticing my agitation, they whispered suspiciously amongst themselves. A secret fear gripped me at their mysterious behaviour, the sort of fear that a lonely wayfarer would feel in front of strangers speaking a different tongue in an unknown land. I looked at them briefly and quickly stepped into the lane. Immediately, a wave of bizarre, wild laughter broke out behind me.

Advancing a few steps, I stopped. It was only about three o'clock but evening shadows seemed to have gathered already inside the lane. I surveyed my surroundings. There were two huge buildings on both sides. At the point where the buildings ended, a wooden fence barred my way. There was no other way beyond the fence, save for a small opening big enough for one person to squeeze through. Probably the passage opened out to some house on the other side, even though it obviously wasn't meant for public use.

I wondered whether Ismael could have gone that side. I had to follow him, but to tell the truth, I was somewhat nervous of squeezing myself through the small opening in that sunless lane. Nonplussed, I stood rooted to the spot. Suddenly, I heard the loud guffaw of a woman on the other side of the fence. Laughter is also a kind of language. I realized that the woman's laughter was strangely similar to that of the young men's I had heard recently. For a few moments, my mind was engrossed in the intricacies of linguistics and speech communication. The mantle of mystery, it seemed, was being lifted gradually. I made my way in.

'Arre, kutte ka baccha.'

Before I could identify whom I had collided with on my abrupt entry through that opening, I was thus pleasantly greeted—the offspring of a dog. The reek of alcohol assailed my senses.

Startled, I took a step back and looked at the man. I felt my blood turn cold. His eyes were red and inflamed, and blotches covered his entire face. The sunken nose in the middle of his hideous face gave him an even more ghastly appearance. Clad in a blue lungi and a black coat, the man stared at me for some time, the unfeeling look of a professional killer on his face. Then with a shrill, broken laugh he advanced towards me.

'Arre saala, don't you recognize me? I'm your....'

Mouthing a foul word, he announced his glorious identity and came forward, apparently with the intention of grabbing my hand. My whole body trembled with fear and terror. I felt that it was not a flesh and blood human being who was standing in front of me, but a putrid lump of flesh over which crawled fearsome, poisonous insects, whose very touch would make my limbs fall off. As he approached me, I closed my eyes and raised my hand as if to hit him. At the same time I yelled out, 'Don't touch... don't you touch me!'

Opening my eyes I saw that the man had stopped, his swagger and bellicosity gone. The horrible abjectness and anguish of a lowly beggar appeared on his face. His disease-inflamed, bloodshot eyes filled with tears.

'So you—you know too?' he asked in his broken, ugly voice.

'What are you talking about?' I questioned, feigning ignorance.

'Kutte ka baccha, haven't you seen my disease? You'll get it too. Go away from me, run, bhago yahan se. Here everyone is sick, rotting away and stinking. I've been doing business with them for the last ten years. They gave me the disease, and now they close their doors on me. Bloody whores, all of them...thu thu!'

I suddenly remembered that I had to find Ismael. He must be quite far away by now. Taking out a packet of cigarettes, I lit one up and offered another to the man.

'Did you see a man go by a little while ago? A bearded man wearing pyjamas?' I asked him.

'Arre saala, why are you looking for someone else when I am here? No one knows what goes on in this neighbourhood better than I do, understand? But you must give me full five rupees.'

It was futile to bandy words with this creature. So, ignoring his offer I moved forward quickly. Immediately, I could hear squeals of ragged laughter behind me. It seemed that laughter was the lingua franca of the strange inhabitants of this blind alley.

Suddenly, a bunch of women burst into laughter in unison. I started. The lane ended near three rows of houses, together forming a horseshoe. Four or five women were standing in the open space in the middle, puffing bidis. Cheap cosmetics were thickly layered on their callous, expressionless faces. The smell of cheap perfume and cheaper sex emanated from their bodies and underclothes, and they loomed as lost, spectral sentinels on the frontiers of a ghostly twilight of consciousness.

I asked, 'Did you see a man come this way just a while ago?'

Hearing my question, they leaned against one another and laughed. It was as if my question was completely meaningless, as if I had spoken the language of prehistoric men. I wondered if Ismael could possibly be lurking inside one of the houses here. Once again I asked politely, 'Did you see a man come this way?'

A skeletal figure spoke up in a cracked, mannish voice, 'What kind of man, Babu? Has he made off with anyone? If he has, let him. There's no shortage of females.'

Her companion's guffaws drowned the rest of her words.

I was at my wits' end. I had quite clearly seen Ismael come this way and there was no other way out either. This was the only place where he could be hiding. But these women would not reply to any of my questions. What should I do? Probably there was just one way. I would have to go inside these houses and search them. Finally, I resolved to do just that. I advanced towards the first house.

The door was closed. Clearly the probability of someone hiding there was greater. I was about to push the door open when the women gave an anxious shout, 'Ei, there are people inside!'

I halted in my tracks. Peeping through a crack in the broken door, I caught a glimpse of what was going on inside. I realized that it would be inhuman to disturb the man inside at this moment.

I approached a second door. Finding it slightly ajar, I shoved it open. A beautiful girl was dabbing on make-up in front of a mirror.

Hearing my footsteps, she turned around to look, and then turned back again. Mechanically applying lipstick on her lips, she asked in a muffled voice, 'Will you, Sir?'

I did not reply. Her gaze and the indifferent expression on her face held me spellbound. Two obscene words came into my mind like bullets.

She finished applying her make-up and rising, came forward to stand in front of me. She was really beautiful and the proud yet melancholic expression on her face made her even more attractive. I looked at her lips, ravaged by the predatory kisses of countless men. She must have forgotten the number of lips she had kissed, but how could she forget the provocation for those kisses?

'If you won't, Sir, then go. If you stand at the door like that, others will be scared off.' She said these words very simply and calmly.

'What are you? Nun or prostitute?'

'I have not seen a crazier person than you. It seems that you're not quite right in the head. Why are you asking me these questions?'

'If I see an Alberto Moravia novel lying half-read on the bed of a girl who peddles her body in such dingy surroundings, and it becomes clear that she is the reader of this novel, wouldn't I feel the urge to talk seriously with her?'

Her gaze went to her bed where Moravia's *Women of Rome* lay. A shy and slightly guilty smile, of someone who has been found out, appeared on her face.

'You are the second one.'

'What do you mean?'

'You are the second person who has come here and talked the language of human beings. There was another one, a college student.'

I noticed that she was now using the more respectful address term 'aapuni' instead of 'tumi.' Perhaps my proximity had brought her closer in touch with humanity, making her forget the mercenary in her. I felt like paying homage to her as a human being. I said deferentially, 'If you permit, I'll give you some books in a few days' time. Now I have to leave. Nomoskar.'

For a while, the girl stood as if stupefied. When she saw that I was really about to leave she came to her senses and said hastily, 'Wait, wait, where are you going? I meant it in a different sense. Please stay a while.'

'Why?'

'Why did you come to this basti?'

I thought that it would be better to tell her about Ismael in some detail. Perhaps she was the only woman in this place who could help.

'I came to this locality in pursuit of a man who has been evading me for a particular reason. I have been on his trail for a long time, almost five years. Today, I suddenly spotted him on the street and called out excitedly.

But hearing my cry, he ran away into this lane. I ran after him, but after reaching here, I myself am lost. Tell me, is there another way out of this house?'

'No.'

'Then he must be hiding in one of these houses. But who would allow him to do that?'

'For a bit of money, who wouldn't? But why is he running away from you? And why are you hunting him?'

'That's a long story. And if I narrate such a lengthy story, I won't be able to find Ismael because he would bolt in the meantime.'

'How do you know that he hasn't already fled while you're here?'

'That's true. I got so carried away talking that I forgot my main purpose. Would you please make some enquiries anyway? I still feel that he is lying low around here somewhere. He must be thinking that I wouldn't follow him to a place like this. In fact, it's more likely that he would stay here until nightfall, instead of going out onto the streets and risk being caught.'

'What is this man to you?'

'Nothing.'

'An enemy?'

'No.'

At my answer the girl sighed deeply. Then she said, almost to herself. 'Who knows what lies at the end of this quest?'

Her tone startled me. 'What do you mean? Whom are you talking about?'

'About you, about me. Don't you feel prickled with curiosity even after seeing a prostitute who reads Moravia?'

'Of course. But I don't want to offend you by prying into your private affairs.'

'I understand your feelings. Therefore, I voluntarily want to tell you about myself. I don't know why you have been hounding your quarry for five years, and what you'll do when you find him. But a man is also searching for me, and he too has been looking for me for nearly five years. I've seen him, but he hasn't seen me. If he sees me, and that too in these surroundings, he'll probably kill me instantly. I'm not afraid of dying. But I dread the shock that the man will get when he sees me. You're chasing a man, and I'm escaping from a man. Do you notice the similarity between your quarry and me?'

I was astonished. Really, I hadn't been prepared for such a dramatic encounter. All this time I had been standing, but now I wanted to sit down.

Whether the woman standing in front of me was a poor prostitute or an affluent lady, whether the room in which I found myself was a library or the chamber of a working woman—such questions seemed totally irrelevant. At that moment, the intimacy between two suffering human beings, harried by a stroke of fate, appeared more important. I was standing in front of a woman and was talking to her about life's conflicts, sorrows, hopes, and dreams, and these were the same for her and for me, as they were for the rest of humanity.

The realization raised a flood of emotions in my heart. Sitting down on the bed, I asked sympathetically, 'Who is this man who has been searching for you?'

'My father.'

Again, I was startled. Hiding my surprise, I requested, 'Please regard me as a friend and tell me your story. Your words have really kindled my curiosity.'

'I'll tell you. I also have my own reasons for telling you the story. For a long time I was looking for a person with whom I could discuss this problem. But how could I expect to find such a friend among the scavengers who come sniffing for the flesh of women? God has delivered you to me today. Please sit for a while. I'll be back soon.'

Parting a curtain, the girl went inside. I lit a cigarette. When she came back I couldn't recognize her. She had washed away the layers of make-up, taken down her bizarre hairdo, spread out her hair, and put on a white sari and a white blouse. It was a metamorphosis. I looked at her silently with respect and admiration.

'Don't hope to hear a long narrative,' she warned and started her story. 'Life's events don't occur rationally, or as one plans. But while describing such events, people enrich them with emotion, imagination, and logic. I'll not do any such thing. About five years ago, I got separated from my father at Sealdah station in Kolkata. We had taken shelter there as refugees from Purbo Banga, Bangladesh. That shelter was completely temporary because no one sat there to hand out food. When I saw my father—a Brahmin and a scholar in Sanskrit—scrounge leftovers from some whore because of the fire in his famished belly, I plunged into a dark abyss, not in disgust, but in inconsolable grief. In one leap, from the temple of a Brahmin, I reached the hovel of whores. I thought all transactions with him were over. But it wasn't. One day, while strolling down the streets of Guwahati, I saw my father, Ananda Charan Mukhopadhyay, who had never touched anything except vessels of worship, pulling a rickshaw with two women passengers on it. I can't give the precise count of the number of tremors that shook the earth at that moment. I immediately covered my face with my oroni, and my father passed me by. Seeing his roving, helplessly yearning gaze, I understood that he was constantly searching for me. After that incident, I was really frightened. I shuddered when I imagined what my father would do when he found out that his daughter, who had committed the Bhagavad Gita to memory, was making a living selling her body. I was even more frightened because most customers come here on rickshaws. If by some twist of fate my father happens to come here, and I am caught at an unguarded moment....'

For some time she remained silent. Not finding anything worthwhile to say, I kept quiet too. Suddenly, a hint of a smile appeared on her face. Throwing a sharp look at me, she asked, 'Feeling sorry for me?' I did not reply.

She continued, 'I've talked with only one other human being about these things. That college student. Do you know what he said? He was not, or rather, he did not see any reason to be particularly saddened by my father becoming a rickshawala or by my turning to prostitution. People from the lower strata of society are being forced to change their occupation every day. Today's peasant or labourer becomes tomorrow's rickshawala due to the swings of fortune. If we don't lose any sleep over the fate of a thousand rickshawalas, why worry about just one? If a Brahmin learns that one from his own caste has become a rickshawala, he will probably rant and rave because he will take it as a sign of erosion of his caste. Do you know what else my friend said? If one Brahmin becomes a rickshawala, it is a matter of rejoicing for society, although it might be a tragic event from a personal point of view. For five thousand years, Brahmins and other high-caste people have been living off the labours of others, without doing anything themselves. In the beginning, the justification for such idleness was the pursuit of knowledge. But later it became a big sham. After 5,000 years, cracks have started appearing in the once rigid class divisions. Now, if even one Brahmin pulls a rickshaw for his livelihood, it's a good thing. Only through such harsh shocks can there be a revolution in the social consciousness.'

'The emotion with which you recount this almost leads me to believe that you're glad that your father has become a rickshawala.'

'I try to make myself hear these words every day. I must fortify myself like that, otherwise I'll go mad.'

I realized that the room had become dark. Perhaps dusk had fallen. Looking at the girl I could see that she was oblivious to the passage of time. On the pretext of smoking a cigarette, I lit a match and saw tears flowing from her eyes. I put out the match. It was useless illuminating unappeasable grief. Darkness was preferable.

She spoke up, 'I'm very keen to know why you've been seeking that man. Is he as unfortunate as I am?'

I suddenly decided that I should narrate Ismael's story to this girl. A girl who could discern the social implications of her own father becoming a rickshawala would discover yet another historical truth in Ismael's story and would get the strength to harden herself further.

'The name of the man I am seeking is Ismael.'

'Ismael?' The girl was startled. I had expected that. All Hindu refugees who had run away from Purbo Banga during communal riots react in the same way, with shock, when they hear the name of a Muslim. Nevertheless, I asked her, 'Why are you shocked?'

'Muslim goondas have devastated our lives. Because of these hoodlums, I am a whore despite being the daughter of a learned Brahmin. When I hear the name of one such goon, why shouldn't I be shocked? What did he do to you?'

'Listen to my story. The man I am looking for is called Ismael, and like you, he too lived in Purbo Banga. I don't know his past history very well. I only know that he was a landless peasant under some zamindar. One day, he heard that hundreds of peasants like him were migrating to Assam, where several lakh bighas of land were lying fallow. In their homeland there was not an inch of land from which they could eke out a living. Slaving for the landlords, they had approached the threshold of certain starvation. Without hesitation, Ismael joined the band of fortune-hunting exiles.'

Looking at the girl, I continued, 'You yourself had to leave your homeland. How did you feel when you had to sever all ties with the soil to which your entire being was intimately connected? Let me tell you on behalf of Ismael—surely, just as Ismael felt, just as his wife and children felt.'

The girl protested angrily, 'What are you saying? They left their homeland voluntarily. No one killed them and hounded them at the point of a sword like they did to us. How can it be the same?'

'When Ismael left his home, his wife had rolled on the ground in their compound and cried. When she took her farewell from a bottlegourd creeper that had climbed up to her roof, her heart had broken into tiny pieces. Yet you are saying that they left their homeland of their own free will? Didn't an invisible sword chase them away too?'

'Who drove them away?'

'The conspiracy of history—a history whose course has been guided through the ages by a handful of landowners and capitalists—the landed people and those with money. Why is it that Ismael and his kind had no claim on the land that they had made fertile with their heart's blood? Why did they have to leave their own country? Because more of them were born than the number of slaves necessary to keep the machinery of oppression going; they were chased away like cats and dogs. The tears that sprang to your eyes and Ismael's wife's eyes at the moment of being exiled from your motherland have no religion. Those tears are neither Hindu nor Muslim.'

'Why do you forget that Muslims chased us away in the name of religion? They inflicted unspeakable atrocities on all Hindus, rich and poor alike. It's those Ismaels of yours who presided over the Hindumedh Jagya, to slaughter the Hindus.'

'You should also not forget that the blood that soaked the streets of Dhaka in 1947 had a religion—that religion was Hinduism. The blood that drenched the streets of Delhi at exactly the same moment also had a religion—the Muslim religion. But as a woman, don't you understand the difference between blood and tears? The source of tears is humanity, and tears flow spontaneously at the prompting of the heart. Therefore, it's pure and true. But blood erupts due to violence and hatred, it's impure and false. The dharma of the Impure and the False is Adharma.'

The girl fell silent. It was now her turn to question herself.

'Moreover, you were not chased away by Muslims or even by communal frenzy. You were hounded out by the same conspiracy of history. You said a little while ago that you had been persecuted in the name of religion. Do you know what religion is? In every period of history, a bunch of landlords and capitalists have been depriving the poor multitudes of all comfort and pleasure by dangling before them the promises of eternal comfort in an illusory heaven. In the Bible, it is clearly written that only the poor can go to heaven. This is the neat arrangement put forward by the rich. If you people, the lowly slaves, serve us by shunning all pleasures and comforts in this life, you'll be able to regale yourself with meat, wine, and courtesans in heaven for eternity. Only the poor and the beggars will be given passports to heaven and since we rich people are destined for hell, let us enjoy ourselves in this life. But no scripture has been able to explain why the cleverest section of society, the rich, have chosen the transient pleasures of this life in exchange for an eternity in hell. Do you know what religion is? At one time in Europe, the Pope was pimping paradise to fill his empty coffers. He was selling gate passes to heaven! According to Islam, one earns God's blessings by making a believer out of a single kafir, an infidel. Why worry yourself sick about the salvation of others? And why do you have to tempt others with the prospects of God's blessings? The reason lies not in religion but in the incipient Arab national consciousness, and in the interests of the expansionists of Arab capitalism. Because of this injunction in Islam, millions of 'Infidels' from Spain to Indonesia were made to believe in Allah at the point of a sword, and lakhs of poor soldiers laid down their lives for the holy cause. I don't know whether those unknown soldiers ascended to heaven or not as a result of their sacrifices, but history bears testimony to the fact that a handful of emperors and nobles enjoyed paradise on this earth itself. The rich treasures accumulated in Hindu temples through the ages could deliver millions of people from poverty in this life itself, but the custodians of heaven—the Brahmins—are seated, embracing the gates of those temples, preventing any such deliverance. In the name of religion the Muslims of Purbo Banga plunged their hands into the blood of Hindus. Do you know what drove them to it? The history makers made them drunk on wine, the wine of religion. Without being drunk, can someone rape a woman about to give birth to a child?'

Having delivered this long sermon practically in one breath, I raised my head and looked at the girl. It seemed as if she had no more questions to ask of me, and no logic left to argue with.

'Listen to Ismael's story,' I resumed my account. 'They came and settled in the heart of the deep, impenetrable jungles of Assam. From birth to death, their lives were one perennial struggle with Nature. They were the brave children of this earth. No blow could break them. Every year, the wild waves of the Brahmaputra came during the season of floods, and swept away their precious homes, built with blood, sweat, tears, and infinite love. Every year they built their homes again with renewed vigour. About twelve years went by like this. But, in 1954, Nature hatched a new conspiracy against them. Massive erosion by the waters of the Brahmaputra resulted in the loss of thousands of bighas of land. Before they knew it, in two swift years, the insatiable river had claimed Ismael's village and paddy fields. Then, like ghosts being joined by devils, a cholera epidemic swept down on the homeless creatures, huddling on the trees. A big chunk of the population died. Among them were Ismael's wife and a twelve-year-old son. Ismael was left with a couple of children, both of tender age. You told me a little earlier that events don't happen according to plan. It is people who add their own imagination, emotion, and logic to these events. Like you, I won't do any of that. But I feel like shedding a few tears for Ismael.

'Anyway, after losing everything to the fierce hunger of the Brahmaputra, about a hundred families from Ismael's village petitioned the government for land. There was no response. There was no fallow land where they could quickly build their homes. In desperation, they decided to break the law for the sake of survival. They started encroaching on government land for grazing. That is where I came in.'

'How?' she interrupted.

'As a government official, I was entrusted with the task of evicting illegal encroachers like Ismael. One day, I headed a campaign against Ismael and the other villagers. With me were armed policemen, peons, and ten or twelve elephants. According to the dictates of the law I had to demolish their homes with the help of the elephants.

'On elephant-back, I assessed the situation from one side of the village. A plain covered with the kahua, khagori, and ulubon reeds stretched for miles, and on a cleared patch in the middle, there were a few thatched huts. Against the vast and lonely background of the wilderness, made profound by the unceasing roar of the wind, the huts looked so tiny and their inhabitants looked so frail and helpless that I wanted to reassure them by clasping them to me, instead of ordering the pitiful dwellings to be razed to the ground.

'But I heard myself give the order for the demolition to begin. Ten elephants bore down on the huts. The women and children started wailing. Their cries were scattered in the wind.

'Suddenly, a man rushed toward me like a lunatic. Raising his hands to the skies he started crying loudly, "In the name of Allah huzoor, spare my home. Both my children are suffering from smallpox. If they do not have a bit of shelter in the chill of this month of Magh, they will die this night. Their mother and elder brother have left them, huzoor, and they haven't had anything proper to eat for a long time!" Saying this he fell on the ground. I immediately ordered that his home should not be demolished. But the Mondal informed me that the work was already done.

'Hearing this, Ismael stood up. Suddenly, his unbearably grief-stricken face and eyes grew hard. "Khuda, it was for this that I roamed all over the world, left my home for a foreign land, pushed my woman to death by cholera. Today, you didn't even leave a roof over my children's heads for them to die in peace." Thus addressing an invisible God, he moved away slowly. There was nothing more I could do. I wrote down a few details about this man, including his name. Then I came back to my quarters after finishing the demolition work.

'Getting up the next morning, I opened my front door and was greeted by a sight the memory of which will haunt me for the rest of my life. On my veranda lay the corpses of two children, their faces horribly disfigured by smallpox. Everything was clear; there was no question of not understanding what had happened.

'Afterwards I made enquiries and learned that on the night of the demolition, Ismael had disappeared from the village with his two children. Gradually, everyone came to know about the children, but till now no one has any information about Ismael. Perhaps no one felt the need to find out about him. But I must seek him out. For the sake of humanity and on behalf of the barbaric and brutal laws of human beings, I must beg forgiveness from Ismael. Otherwise, even in my death I will not find peace.'

Ending Ismael's story, I lapsed into silence.

I had hoped that the girl would say something, but she too remained silent. The room had become completely dark.

'Won't you light a lamp or something?' I asked. But she did not reply. I realized that she did not want to attract any customers by illuminating the room.

I must find Ismael, I quietly vowed to myself. But at the same time I was tormented by the thought of this girl sitting still and speechless in the dark. I was chasing a man and she was running away from a man. I had come looking for Ismael, but on the way, I had found this girl who traded her own flesh. I wanted information, but I came to know about Ananda Charan Mukhopadhyay. But strangely enough, they were all the same, their stories were the same. Although they might not comprehend it, they were all sacrificial victims of the same conspiracy of history.

How can I keep searching only for Ismael now, leaving this girl all alone in the dark? Now I must also find Ananda Charan Mukhopadhyay. After finding him who else would I have to look for? I wondered who had the might and the perseverance to search for the millions of Anandas and Ismaels of this world. Actually, by knowing one you knew them all. Now it was necessary to look for the enemies of Ismael and Ananda, the foes of humanity.

It was very late. Getting up to leave, I asked the girl, 'Won't you light the lamp?'

This time too she neither uttered a word nor made any move to light the lamp. I felt that after listening to my story she wanted to re-examine whether Ismael was a Muslim or a human being. Her mind had flown away looking for Ismael Sheikh.

Translated by Pradipta Borgohain

RATS

BHABENDRA NATH SAIKIA

All the women who lived in those sheds rushed out. They tried to find out what exactly was happening. They behaved very much like a blind man resting with his cane propped nearby does, when he suddenly hears some confused and troubling commotion. His first reaction is to seek out and grasp his cane, and only then try to find out the reason for the turmoil. Normally, these women did not bother to find out where their children were or what they were doing, their attitude being that they would turn up when hungry. So they did not worry.

But today, as soon as they became aware of the tumult and confusion, all the women ran out of their huts, frightened and anxious. They began to rush around, each one screaming out her children's names. One of them might have clearly seen her son standing nearby, but she did not rest satisfied with that. She went there, dragged the boy out from the crowd of onlookers, and clasped him tightly with both hands. Only when her son was safe in her arms did she try to find out the details of what had happened. Within two minutes the women had found their children, and the shrill voices that were screaming out their names stopped.

Only the voice of Moti's mother gradually got louder. And louder. Her high-pitched voice could be heard clearly over the tumultuous din created by the crowd. In the beginning, she had called out to her son, Moti, like the other mothers, and had run hither and thither looking for him. But as time passed, and there was no sign of him, she grew more and more panicky. She started running around anxiously, calling out his name in distress.

His companions said that Moti had been with them right there.

'He was here?'

'Then where is he now?'

'Are you sure he was here?'

'Exactly where, where was he exactly?'

She went around asking every boy and every girl in an agitated voice. She ran to each of the children, asking them all in great anguish, hoping to hear that Moti might have strayed away without their knowing. But the children told her categorically that Moti had been right here with them—in the place that was now full of heavy sacks, two-and-a-half maunds each.

This was an open space near the narrow road leading to the huge warehouses. There was another dirt road, slightly wider, bordered on both sides by the establishments of various businesses. From that, this small narrow lane had somehow emerged between two houses located there. There was a long wall of corrugated sheets, marking the compound of a soap company bordering one side of this road, and on the other side was this open space. A bit further on, this road split up and spread out among the many large warehouses. These were the storehouses that fed thousands of people in the city. The relationship of these to the city was as vital as the relationship of a handsome youth to the horrible looking entrails of his stomach. They were ugly, but inevitable and unavoidable.

Numerous huge trucks roared into that narrow lane, carrying hundreds of tonnes of foodstuff. These they unloaded into these warehouses, after which they carried hundreds of tonnes of produce to some other place. Most rickshaw drivers found it difficult to turn their small vehicles on this road. The truck drivers alone knew what skills they called up as they managed to manoeuvre their huge trucks in that small space. Sometimes, if one vehicle created chaos by not being driven properly, there would be a traffic jam in the lane, and the filthy, stinking environment would be overwhelmed with the riotous shouting of drivers and their assistants.

The appearance and size of the drivers matched the size of their trucks. Indeed, it seemed as though the truck-building companies had taken the measurements of the drivers first, and then fitted the vehicles to suit their bodies! Their eyes were always red, perhaps due to driving throughout the night, or maybe because of something they had imbibed. As far as possible, these drivers preferred to sit comfortably and quietly in their seats and rest; it was the handymen, their assistants, who created a loud confusion. These handymen would sit on top of their loaded trucks, yelling at each other, trying to find out who was to blame for the road block. Sometimes the traffic jam would continue for hours together. That narrow space would become overcrowded with trucks, and vehicles lined up, one after the other, on the main road. No one would agree to shift his own vehicle even a little bit to help break the jam. 'Why should I? Let them do what they like!' and the driver would leave his truck and go to spend his time in the tea shop nearby. Sometimes, the trucks would enter the lane at midnight, heavily loaded, but the warehouses opened their doors only in the morning. On such days, the area would become still more filthy and smelly and sometimes both drivers and handymen would sleep, like babies in their cradles, inside their trucks.

A peculiar thick, slimy green and black liquid covered about half of this open space. Originally, this was probably plain rainwater. But over time it had got mixed with green moss, motor oil, and such other substances, and had turned into this peculiar colour and consistency. When the small children got dirty playing in the nearby open space, they cleaned themselves in this water.

On the other side of this open space there was a line of shacks built with bits of bamboo, straw, sacks, packing boxes, and so on. Sometime in the past, a few daily wagers employed to load and unload the trucks had occupied these poor shanties. But now the owners of the warehouses employed labourers on a regular basis, and no one from these huts got those jobs. So, they had left. Now, there were women living here with their children. There were no men living here permanently, and the few men seen around, at times, were not the fathers of these children. Most of the women, except a few like Moti's mother, were old. Some of them went out in the morning to beg; two of them worked in the hotels nearby, cleaning rice and grinding spices; and one of them kept herself busy selling snacks of puffed rice mixed with salt, oil, onions, and chillies.

But it was the children who helped the women most in earning their daily bread. They spent almost the entire day on the roadside, armed with woven bamboo baskets of various sizes and shapes. When there was no serious work to be done, they spent their time playing, screaming, and crying. But when the empty trucks returned after unloading their consignments in the warehouses, and when they were held up due to a traffic jam, and were forced to stop right here, then these children immediately jumped onto the trucks. Quickly they swept the floor of the vehicles where the sacks had been loaded, put the sweepings into their bamboo baskets, and ran home to their mothers. When these sweepings were carefully cleaned out, the women would be able to collect quite an amount of rice, lentils, and other commodities. The drivers and handymen were quite happy to let the children do the sweeping because their vehicles were cleaned in a trice. And the boys and girls were happy when there were traffic jams. If the traffic jams were long-drawn, they were still happier, because they got time to sweep all the trucks, and every child got a chance.

The children had organized an iron rod each, and had sharpened one end of it. If the loaded trucks happened to get held up in a traffic jam, they jumped onto the trucks and pierced the sacks with their rods. They pushed their fingers through the holes made by the rods, and took out rice, lentils, sugar, and other such goods. If the handymen saw them and gave chase, they laughed with great merriment at them, and ran a little distance away. But after a little while, they came scampering back again and fearlessly re-started their work.

And if the drivers and handymen happened to go to the tea shops, the children had a field day. They, therefore, prayed that there would be many more such jams. Whenever they saw two vehicles approaching from opposite directions, they would clap and shout, 'Come on, come on, get into a traffic jam!'

But today, there was no such big traffic snarl. What had happened was this: a truck was coming towards the godown heavily loaded with huge, plump sacks of rice. And a truck belonging to some cooperative store was coming out from the godown loaded just as heavily with sacks of rice, lentils, sugar, flour, salt, and other raw food items. Both drivers were aware of the truck approaching from the opposite side but each hoped that the other would go to the side and stop, allowing him to proceed. Therefore, neither of them stopped, and ultimately both vehicles stood face to face. The two drivers started to quarrel and shout at each other. This went on for some time, and the children started yelling their slogan of, 'Come on, come on, get into a jam!'

Normally, when only two trucks were involved, the drivers took the advantage of the open space, and managed to use their skill to manoeuvre their vehicles and go on their way. And indeed, after arguing for some time, the drivers did start to do just that. But they were both still rather angry, and they saw no reason why they should give way to the other driver. After backing just a little, with a huge roar and emitting a great deal of smoke, both vehicles again advanced. The children, seeing the situation, started screaming out their slogan again.

And the trucks did get into a jam. The trucker from the cooperative society did not give as much leeway as he could have; and the trucker carrying the sacks of rice tried to go as much to the side as it could. The vehicle, loaded very high with heavy sacks, slid off the road and into the soft mud by the side. It leaned dangerously to the left—and, in an instant, the tragedy had occurred. The truck veered to the left, and one by one, many of the sacks toppled over and fell down heavily. The children ran in confusion and chaos over the mud and slush. Only, as Moti screamed in terror, and tried to run, a sack fell on top of him, and squashed him. Then another sack fell on top of that…then another and another….

A large crowd of people came from the main road to see what had happened. They started to look for Moti only after his mother had gone almost mad with anxiety and grief. One by one, the sacks were removed. At first, one of Moti's feet appeared. The foot looked quite normal and natural. But after the last sack had been removed, they all looked the other way. The only thing that could be seen was blood, a lot of blood. No one had the heart to even try to remember the childish body of the boy.

The police came. And for that day, all loading and unloading was stopped in the warehouses. It was getting darker anyway, and the trucks lined up on the main road to wait for daybreak. The women surrounded Moti's mother and held her while the police collected the remains of the boy's body and took them away in a bundle to the police hospital.

Gradually, night fell. The two trucks that were involved were taken to the police station. The sacks of rice lay where they had fallen. A few loaded sacks had fallen from the other truck also, on the opposite side of the road, against the corrugated sheet wall. These were laden with salt and lentils.

Most of the children had become quiet and still, and were sitting despondently in their common courtyard situated at the centre of their huddle of huts. The older ones sometimes talked quietly with each other. None of them could sleep much that night, and although they went to bed so late, most of them woke up very early next morning. Probably they had been awake since before dawn. The older ones came out at daybreak armed with their rods and bamboo baskets, and went near the fallen sacks. They collected rice, salt, lentils, and sugar. But they were careful not to go near the sack covered with Moti's blood.

Later that morning, some labourers came, with a few well-dressed men, and started removing the sacks under the supervision of the latter. It was not known which of these well-dressed persons took the decision, but it was noticed that two of the labourers carried the blood-stained sack, and delivered it to Moti's mother's hut. She, who had spent the night sitting on her string cot, jumped up in distress, and cried out, 'No, no! I don't want it!' She clasped the sack, and started wailing in grief and in helplessness. The labourers had turned the blood-stained side of the sack towards the wall, and as they dropped it, the weak wall trembled under its weight.

For quite a few days, Moti's mother continued to shout, 'Take it out, take it away. I do not want it!' The neighbouring women grieved for her, understanding her sorrow.

This woman had no parents. She had lived in her paternal uncle's house and helped in cultivating lentils and gram. A man had said he would marry her and had brought her here, but he was not a good man. After Moti was born, he heard of some drug-dealing business, and went away in search of it. Moti's mother waited for a long time, hoping he would come back. The drivers and handymen who came to buy the puffed rice snacks at the next hut, had said to her, 'What are you saying? He will never come back again. And what sort of woman are you, sitting here thinking of him, when there are so many other men here!' The others would laugh when they heard this, and Moti's mother would get angry.

True, she was a bit scared of living alone. But she was afraid, not of other people, but of herself. Indeed, sometimes the natural needs and instincts of her body and age troubled her greatly, and threatened to overwhelm her. But she had always been able to overcome these feelings by clasping Moti to her breast. If somehow she could manage to pass a few more years like this, she thought, she would approach the age of 'beggarhood'. At least she could change herself into a beggar by wearing dirty, torn clothes like the older beggar women. And even if she could not beg, it would not matter, as long as she had Moti with her. A son was a far more important possession than a husband! She just wanted the words, 'Ma, Ma', ringing in her ears always, that was all.

But this sudden loss, this loneliness, and the empty hut almost drove her mad. She would sit alone, staring at the heavy, full sack and quietly weep her heart out. After some time, she simply sat there, stiff and silent, not even weeping. Some neighbour would sometimes bring her a little rice and lentil gathered from the sweepings, or from what they had got from begging. She would cook them, but leave them untouched. Sometimes, she did not even bother to cook. The handyman of the truck from which the sacks had fallen on Moti, often came to visit her. He would bring her a packet of sweets, jalebis and other sweets, too, from the nearby tea shop. But she would never talk to him.

The days passed. Moti's mother was always hungry. But the neighbours did not always bring rice and lentils. And, gradually, she came to realize that the torture of hunger was very acute and sharp. She had noticed as she lay on her string cot, that some rats had started making holes in the sack leaning against the wall, and every morning, the floor near it would be strewn with a few grains of rice. Sometimes, her eyes would dampen as she swept the grains of rice. One day, after lying for a long time on her cot, hungry and desperate, she slowly got up. She brought her bamboo tray and held it against the sack. Poking her finger through the hole made by the rats, she slowly eased out a little rice. The hole was small, and it took a long time to collect enough for one meal.

The hole in the sack got bigger with the constant poking of her fingers. Or perhaps the rats themselves had made it larger, getting the help of human hands? However that may be, after a few days it could be seen that there was quite a lot of rice strewn on the floor. Moti's mother did not like the idea of rats spoiling the rice, so she folded a piece of torn cloth, and placed it over the sack, and placed her bamboo tray against the sack so that it pressed against the hole. Later, she took to getting up whenever she heard a scraping sound. Maybe the rats had made another hole in the sack?

Sometimes the handyman would come and say to her, 'How can anyone eat only rice? Let me get you some lentils or something.' But she would refuse.

In time, the sack became lighter and thinner. It was becoming difficult to bring out much rice with her fingers, even though the hole had become much wider. After some time, Moti's mother could put in her entire hand through the hole. Then, after some more time had passed, she found that she could find no rice even after pushing her arm in, right up to her elbow. Whatever rice was still there had become embedded between the stitches of the sack.

One morning, Moti's mother undid the stitches at the top of the sack, and putting it upside down on the floor, gave it a few good shakes. She was able to collect sufficient rice for the night meal. She swept up the grains, and putting the rice on her bamboo tray, cleaned it properly. She then put the sack out in the sun. The side of the sack which had been leaning for such a long time against the wall now fell flat on the ground. In the evening, she took the sack, shook it out, and placed it on her cot.

After eating her meal that night, she lay down on the cot. It had become quite chilly, and Moti's mother always felt cold at night. In past winters, Moti used to curl up to her in bed, and surrounded by his warmth, she had not felt the chill. Today, too, she did not feel the cold seeping in from below because of the piece of sacking, which was why, probably, she felt warm and comfortable.

And when she felt comfortable and warm like this, she would feel as though something was biting her and pinching her, like the rats. After a while, she felt that if the handyman came to her at this instant and asked her, 'Let me get you some lentils, or something,' perhaps she would say, 'Yes. Get it.'

If not for herself, at least for the sake of the other Moti who would come in the future.

Translated by Gayatri Bhattacharyya

THE VICTORIOUS WOMAN
NIRUPAMA BARGOHAIN

When I came home for the summer vacation, my sister, Charu, informed me with a bright face that Sushila was victorious at last—she had won her case.

I was elated. I would have felt sick at heart if Sushila had lost the case into which she had pumped money almost non-stop for the last two years. But didn't I hear during the Puja vacation that she had exhausted her resources and was thinking of withdrawing the case? In that case, wasn't Sushila as poor as we had thought her to be? I felt puzzled when I thought about this. At last I blurted out a question to Charu:

'Where did she get the money to fight her case, Charu?'

A mysterious smile appeared on my sister's face. After hesitating a bit, she unfolded her narrative, prompted by my eager and impatient queries. After listening, I was stunned and silent for some time. Only a little while ago, Charu had said that Sushila was victorious. Victorious? How empty some words suddenly sounded.

I visualized Sushila with her arrestingly beautiful form. With that memory, her life story also came to me with a rush. Only, now a sense of irony seemed to hover around it.

Our father was a moujadar of the village—a land-revenue collector. We were better off than most other villagers. We garnered grain from several bighas of land. My eldest brother studied in a college situated in a nearby town. I passed my matriculation examination from the village high school doing pretty well too, I imagine. Otherwise, would my folks send a girl child to town to study, no matter how affluent we were?

Just before I went to college, Sushila had come into our lives. This poor widow had been engaged to sow seeds in our land. Before Sushila, there were other women who had done this job for us. We had never paid them much attention. But with Sushila, things were different. She was so attractive and had such a glowing complexion that everyone's eyes lingered on her. She was quite young too and we couldn't help thinking about the harsh fortune that had brought the eternal night of widowhood into her life. Piqued by curiosity, I once summoned her to me. She came and stood before me with a very diffident and obliging air. 'So you're Sushila?' She just nodded. 'Who else is there at home?' I asked, simply for the sake of making conversation.

'I've a couple of little ones. I stay with my old mother-in-law and the two of them. Except for them, there's no one else.'

'Who looks after you then?'

Perhaps detecting a trace of sympathy in my voice, Sushila felt encouraged to recount the story of her life to me. Squatting by my side, she told me everything in a manner free of any constraint or reticence. Her husband had died two years ago—he sank while he was in the prime of life. Some terrible disease had got its claws into him, and being poor, and without brothers who might have helped in getting him treated, it was all over very soon. After her husband's death, Sushila thought of going to her mother with her two children. But in whose care was she to leave her old mother-in-law, wracked and desolated by her bereavement? Also, her mother-in-law was not like other mothers-in-law. Since the day Sushila entered her new home as a bride, her mother-in-law had showered affection on her as if she was her own daughter. Apart from the fact that this would be a gross sin, wouldn't her husband in heaven be grieved if his wife abandoned his mother now?

Listening to her talk in this manner, I instantly formed a good opinion about this woman. Initially, I had felt only mild curiosity, but now I felt positively drawn towards her.

'You worshipped your husband, did you?'

Feeling that 'worship' might be a more appropriate term than 'love' for a woman of Sushila's social standing, I used that particular word. However, I didn't expect that her response would be so intense. She gave me no verbal response but tears welled up in her eyes at my query. I was rather taken aback. Getting over my nonplussed state after a while, I asked gently,

'Don't you have a piece of land of your own?'

With a deep sigh Sushila said, 'We do have a bit of land. But since there's no one to till it, we have let it out to someone else. From that we get only a handful of rice, which doesn't last us the whole year.'

I ran out of questions after this, and so closed the session with some cheap consolation, 'May God look after your children. One day they'll take away your sorrows.'

'That's all the blessing I need, Baideo. Yes, I indeed hope that God guards and nurses my children. I've borne the pain of parting from my husband only by thinking of them. I don't need any wealth or comfort—all I want is that my little ones should be safe and sound.'

Later, when I heard that this poor woman was facing a great calamity, I felt a sense of overwhelming sympathy for her. Yes, she was facing a calamity because she was embroiled in a legal battle. During one of my trips home, after enquiring about various odd matters of the household, I asked my mother about Sushila. In fact, whenever I came home, one of the first things I asked was always about Sushila. I would not even wait to meet her, and wanted to know about her the moment I arrived. She had certainly fascinated me. In response to my question, my mother heaved a little sigh and said, 'Can you hope to hear any good news about a poor creature like Sushila? Such a good soul, never did anyone any harm, simply living from day-to-day with her two little ones. But the Almighty had to thrust her into this awful ordeal of a case.'

'Case? What case could Sushila possibly get involved in?' I asked anxiously.

'Yes, who could ever imagine that a creature like Sushila would have enemies, people who would do her harm? Well, she stopped coming to our house for a while. I thought that either she, her two sons, or her old mother-in-law was down with something. Before I could find time to go and call on her, she herself landed up one day, moaning and groaning about something awful. "Well Sushila, whatever's the matter with you?" I asked. And she said that a man named Harekrishna, from our own village, had thrashed her so badly that she had been confined to bed all this time. Apart from feeling sorry for her, I was also perplexed, why should the man beat her up? Sushila did not elaborate but said that the man had been abusing her for some time now, and one day she gave a sharp retort, not able to put up with it anymore. Because of that, Harekrishna had assaulted her in this way....'

'But what about the case?' I asked with real concern and anxiety. This piece of news had made my heart heavy. 'The case? She herself started it. She went to town and filed a case against Harekrishna. After that they announced a date and she rushed to court. Real harassment for her, I can tell you. Not just that—she's pouring money down the drain too. Also, when a woman has to exhibit herself in court, where is her honour? She wails and tells me all this. But what can I do except dole out a few rupees from time to time? And what good is that pittance, when fighting a case is like keeping an elephant? So, by starting the case, the woman has brought ill luck on herself.'

'Why did Sushila leap into this without careful thinking? How can a lonely widow like her lock horns with a man?'

'That's precisely what I told her. She replied, with loud wails, that she had done this at the instigation of the village folks. Now she is burning with regret. She had never imagined that a case could drag on like this for so long and bleed one white like this. What expenses! Just the doctor's certificate cost her a hundred rupees!'

'A hundred rupees? What are you saying?' I was amazed. 'Isn't that our government doctor?'

'The very same. It's our Bipin doctor who took a hundred rupees to give Sushila the certificate.'

I was stupefied. Since he was a government employee, Bipin should have examined Sushila and given the certificate free of cost. What a heartless monster! But surely he wasn't the only one. Many others must have sucked the blood of poor villagers in a similar situation. I seethed with helpless rage.

'But Ma, where did Sushila get all this money?'

'Where do you think? Hers has been the usual fate of poor villagers who get sucked into legal cases. Selling her cows, hawking what little she wears on her hands and ears, pawning the land—nothing is left.'

I was subdued by this barrage of information. I lost all further curiosity to delve into the pathetic details of Sushila's case.

But I wanted to meet Sushila. I told my mother, 'Ma, do call Sushila once.'

Sushila was accordingly sent for and she materialized almost immediately.

'Sushila, here, have a seat.' I made her sit on a stool on our veranda and fetched one for myself too. At other times when I came home for the vacation, Sushila greeted me with a winsome smile on her beautiful face. But this time she started crying the moment she saw me.

After the first wave of emotion had spent itself, Sushila ran through her sad story, and I had to listen to the agonizing details again. Hearing it from her lips, I felt the agony of this story even more keenly. I also got acquainted with the exact nature of the abuse that Harekrishna had unleashed on her. I had formed an idea about what must have transpired from the very fact that Sushila didn't elaborate on this before my mother. For some time, Harekrishna's lewd eye was on Sushila, despite the fact that he was married with children. Being well-to-do, he thought that he would tame Sushila with the power of his wealth. For one year, he tried to do just that. He hailed Sushila with temptations: he would keep Sushila like his own woman, nurture the children like his own, and even see to the comfort of her old mother-in-law. Perhaps not all of those were false or empty promises. In this region, there was a tradition of even married men adopting and looking after someone else's wife and children. But it was not a question of whether Harekrishna would break his promise to Sushila or not. As she told me, her entire frame shuddered with fear and loathing at his proposal. She had simply sent him the reply that he should not pollute her ears with such sinful and scandalous talk in the future.

After saying all this she broke down, lamenting for her lost husband. She felt the pangs of eternal separation even more piercingly now. If he had not left her destitute like this, she wouldn't have had to listen to Harekrishna's foul proposal.

But Harekrishna was not one to give up so easily. He badgered Sushila with his proposal for an entire year. He set all possible snares for her. One day, her patience ran out. When Harekrishna accosted her on the road and began his rant again, she turned on him and lashed him with her tongue. After listening for a while, Harekrishna grabbed her by her hair, pushed her to the ground, and started kicking her mercilessly.

After narrating this, Sushila burst into tears. I remained silent, devoid of any words to console her.

After crying for some time, she told me the tale of the case. Then she wiped off fresh tears that had erupted from her eyes. She had already wasted so much money on this case—how much more money would she have to rake up? The outcome was also completely uncertain. Harekrishna was trumpeting his boast that he would win the case. He was in cahoots with the police, who frequented his house. After all, he had the power of money.

After quite some time, I spoke, 'Why did you have to fight a case with such a powerful man? Since you're such a destitute person you should perhaps have borne your persecution in silence, blaming your fate.'

'Baideo, I admit that I made a big mistake. I went into this unthinkingly, at the instigation of the villagers. Now I can't get out of it even if I want to. I have not been able to keep track of the way my brother-in-law has been running my expenses either.'

'Brother-in-law? What brother-in-law are you talking about?'

'Why, a distant brother-in-law of mine is fighting this case on my behalf. He accompanies me to town, fixes witnesses, and gives money to whomsoever necessary—apart from selling my clothes and pawning my land and ornaments.'

So this fellow, this 'distant brother-in-law,' was robbing the poor woman blind in the name of helping her. I just sat there, choking with helpless rage and sorrow.

Next time I came home, a few more months had passed by. This was the time when my sister, Charu, greeted me with the news of Sushila's victory. As I listened to the full story, I was assailed by emotions other than the sort associated with unqualified jubilation.

The story was brief enough. There came a time when Sushila's resources dried up completely. Then her 'brother-in-law' acquainted her with contractor Bishnu Saud. Sushila's money problems were miraculously solved.

As the mistress of Bishnu Saud, she lacked no funds to fight her case: the case that she had filed against Harekrishna because the latter had given her a dirty, sinful proposal of making her his woman.

After telling me about Sushila's story, Charu went away. But I sat stock still, wondering about an account of defeat that came camouflaged as a story of triumph. How did Sushila plummet from the heights of morality on which she seemed perched? But no, I didn't feel any curiosity to listen to that story.

Translated by Pradipta Borgohain

VALUES

MAMONI RAISOM GOSWAMI

Pitambor, the merchant, sat dejectedly in front of his house. He had still not taken off his mud-plastered shoes. Indeed, he had a weakness for his pair of old leather shoes. At one time, Pitambor had been a fit and well-built man. Now he was about sixty years old and although that was not an age that could be said to be 'old' for a man, all kinds of worries and discontentment weighed him down, and these had taken their toll on him. His face sagged and he had a haggard look about him. His head was always downcast; he could never look directly at the person he was talking to. The way his head invariably hung down, it seemed as though he was scrutinizing the ground, searching intently for something.

A big teak tree had recently been cut down, and Pitambor sat on the stump looking at the children with their improvised fishing rods, trying their luck in the gutters that lined both sides of the road. The incessant rains of the last few days had made the entire village muddy and slushy. The sides of the dirt road had become covered with all kinds of vegetation, both edible and useless, and the frogs were having a great time jumping from one ditch to the other.

Pitambor was looking intently at one particular boy who was trying to untangle his fishing line from an arum plant, when a deep voice suddenly caught his attention. He looked up to see the priest, Krishnakanta, standing near him. 'Pitambor,' said the priest, 'you have been sitting there engrossed in looking at those children for a long time. You were sitting exactly like this when I passed by some time ago, and you are still sitting in the same place in exactly the same way, staring intently, and with a peculiar longing, at those children. Is it because you do not have any children of your own? "Whose beloved child is being chased to the waters? Call out and bring him back so that I can kiss him!"—Is that what you are thinking? By the way, is your wife any better? Is she able to leave her bed and do some work now?'

'No. How can she move about when her hands and feet have become swollen? I have already taken her to the hospital in Guwahati at least twenty times, but she is no better.'

'There seems to be no chance of your ever having any children of your own then? So your family will become extinct,' said the mischievous and malicious priest.

Pitambor sighed in dejection. What else could he do?

Krishnakanta stood there silently for a while. He was dressed in a knee-length, old dhoti, a tattered and worn-out warm kurta, and an equally old 'endi sador'. His cheeks were hollowed as he had only two front teeth left—all the others had fallen—so that when he spoke, his face took on an odd and twisted shape. His eyes had a malicious glint, and a sly look, and his balding pate only intensified his cunning look. He came near Pitambor and whispered, 'Have you given any thought to what you will do if something happens to your wife? Have you thought about marrying again?'

Pitambor was about to answer when he happened to look up, and his eyes fell on Damayanti. She was the widow of the priest, Shambhu, who had died not too long ago. Everyone knew that she was a woman of loose character, and after her husband died, she had become the centre of attraction for all the young men of the village.

Krishnakanta called out to her, 'Where are you coming from, Damayanti?' he asked.

'Where do you think I am coming from?' she replied. 'Don't you see the 'endi' silk worms in my hands?'

'So you have started hobnobbing with that Marwari businessman, have you?'

Damayanti did not reply and instead, started to squeeze out the water from the bottom end of her sopping-wet mekhela. As she bent down to do so, her blouse rode up to her breast, exposing her slim, soft, and fair waist. Neither man could resist looking at this attractive spectacle, but the priest quickly averted his gaze. After she had squeezed out the water, she calmly walked away, without even bothering to look towards the two men.

'They say that she has no inhibitions and even eats fish and meat,' said Pitambor. 'Yes, I heard that too,' replied Krishnakanta. 'She has put all the Brahmins to shame. She does and eats whatever she likes, and does not care for any traditions or rules. In the beginning, after Shambhu died, when she cooked fish for her two daughters, she used to go down to the river and bathe and then cook separately for herself. But now, I am told, she does not bother and even sits with the girls and eats the fish.'

'Yes,' replied Pitambor. 'I have seen her taking fish from the fishmonger woman in exchange for paddy.'

'Dear me!' ejaculated Krishnakanta. 'What is the world coming to! A widow buying fish in exchange for a bit of paddy!'

'Softly, Purohit, softly,' said Pitambor. 'You do not need to publicize the fact that a Brahmin widow is eating fish. Such things are common these days, even in orthodox places like Dakhinpaar and Uttarpaar. And I do not really think it is such a sin. These old rules should be abolished.'

Staring at the departing figure of Damayanti for some time, Pitambor asked, 'Bapu, what is the condition of your clients these days? Has it changed at all?'

'What a surprising question, Pitambor! You know everything and yet pretend not to know! Don't you know that it is because of the quarrel between my brother and myself over our clients that I am in this poverty-stricken condition?'

'It is mainly because your brother went around telling everyone that you do not know how to read Sanskrit,' replied Pitambor.

Krishnakanta jumped up in anger. 'Tell me,' he shouted, 'how many priests are there these days who can recite the mantras as clearly and correctly as Narahari Bhagabati? He and I studied at the tol, the school for priests, together. He was the one who got the caning, not me. No, no. The main reason for our poverty-stricken condition is the attitude of the clients—of those people who ask us to go and conduct their pujas for them. We priests who know how to conduct the rituals and pujas should not have been in such an impoverished condition. In the olden days, there was no problem getting at least one sacred thread, a pair of dhotis, and some money from each of our clients every month. But nowadays everything is different. People want to perform the rites and pujas, but are unwilling to pay the priests. Only the other day, one of our oldest clients, Mahikanta Sarma's two sons were taken to Kamakhya temple for their upanayan, the sacred thread ceremony. One of my clients in Maisanpur, Surja Sarma, held the shraddha ceremonies of his mother and father together on the same day. People are gradually starting to ignore the Nandimukh shraddha, the shraddha ceremony of nine ancestors which is such an essential part of the wedding ceremony. And, of course, the smaller rituals and pujas, like the naming ceremony, house blessing puja, Basanti puja, purifying a house by holding a 'hom', organizing a purifying and sanctifying holy fire if a vulture happened to roost on the house…these have become things of the past. Time was when a man had to undergo a purifying ritual if he lost his sacred thread. But how many Brahmin boys today even chant the Gayatri mantra!'

Pitambor had been listening to the priest's lecture without saying a word.

His mind was still on Damayanti, and her lovely, silky-smooth back exposed when she bent down to squeeze the water from her soaking-wet mekhela. He thought that he had never seen such a beautiful woman's waist or back before. And it was not as though he had not seen or touched a woman's body before. He had married his second wife just two months after his first wife had died, mainly because his first wife had died childless. But this second wife was a sick woman. Soon, she became almost completely bedridden due to acute rheumatism. Pitambor had taken her to doctors in Guwahati many times, but to no avail. Ultimately, the woman had become thin, more like a skeleton than a living woman. She lay in her bed all day, quietly watching her husband's behaviour. The man seemed to have almost lost his mind, longing for a son to carry on his family name. People said that he was waiting impatiently for his sick wife to die. After a few years, he had given up going to the hospitals in Guwahati, and had given up all hope for a son and heir. The priest was now in front of him lamenting his lot in life, but Pitambor hardly heard him. His wife had signaled to one of the servants from her bed, to go and give a 'mora', a cane stool, for the priest to sit on, but Pitambor was not even aware of when the servant had come and gone!

'You are so absent-minded, thinking all the time only of the fact that you don't have a son and heir, that many people here in our satra have started saying that you are becoming unbalanced, that you are on the verge of insanity,' said Krishnakanta, referring to the religious and cultural institution. 'There are hundreds of people in the world who do not have children. It is nothing so terrible. And why don't you think of what our gurus have said—that families, sons and so on are, after all, transitory things, and hence valueless—simply manifestations of "maya".'

Pitambor simply lowered his head in dejection. The priest noticed that his hair was greying, that his eyes were circled with small cobweb-like wrinkles. The man had become completely unmindful of how he dressed and his shoes were caked with layers of mud.

Krishnakanta was overwhelmed by a sense of pity and compassion for Pitambor. Just a few years ago, the older citizens had called him the 'gora soldier'. He was so well-built, fair, and fit. There was no dearth of money or means, but the poor man had no peace of mind. His granary was full, but there was no one to enjoy it.

Suddenly, Krishnakanta said something almost unheard of! But before saying it he looked all round to verify that there was no one nearby. But the door of Pitambor's bedroom was wide open, and he could see the skeletal body of Pitambor's wife lying on the bed. Her sharp eyes, he noticed, were shining with a peculiar brightness—as though she was trying to find out what the priest was saying to her husband. Krishnakanta was shocked to see that a single glance, even from a distance, could be so keen, and could express such heartfelt sadness. Even so, he whispered to Pitambor, 'If you think that you can help me with some money, I too will help you to get what you so desire.'

'How?' asked Pitambor. 'How will you arrange things?'

'Don't worry about the arrangements. There will be no problems,' said the priest.

'What do you mean?' Pitambor asked curiously.

'What I mean is that I will arrange matters so that when you meet her, there will be no question of her not conceiving. I have found out that she has aborted and buried the results of her illicit and guilty pregnancies four times!' Krishnakanta said with confidence.

Pitambor almost shouted, 'Bapu, are you talking about Damayanti?'

'Yes, yes. I am talking about Damayanti,' replied the priest. 'Our Brahmin girls have started going across the Dhaneswari river to marry Sudra boys. Don't you know that the Gosain of Mukteswar Satra's son has gone and married a Muslim girl? It seems that our Gandhi Maharaj has shown this path—that caste and community do not matter. That is why I am thinking about this matter of Damayanti for you.'

Pitambor jumped up in excitement. 'What matter are you talking about?'

'If you so desire, you can make Damayanti your own woman.' Krishnakanta glanced towards the open bedroom door again. The eyes of the woman lying on the bed were wide open and it seemed as though they were burning with a fierce fire. She was staring at Krishnakanta.

Pitambor ran and tried to clutch the priest's hands, but the latter hastily stepped away. He had just bathed and was on his way to the Adhikaar's house. He had been asked to bathe the image of Murulidhar in the Adhikaar's temple, because the regular priest there had gone to Guwahati. It was a very important duty and he had to be clean and untouched by any other person, particularly one who was not a Brahmin. But the priest's words had opened an unthinkable world for Pitambor and he did not know how to thank the man.

'So Pitambor,' said Krishnakanta, 'It seems that you have been thinking about this for some time.'

A happy smile played over Pitambor's lips. Once again, Krishnakanta glanced towards the bedroom. The woman's eyes were now shut, but it seemed as though she was undergoing some terrible suffering and pain. Touching the priest's feet, Pitambor spoke humbly and pleaded, 'Bapu, do this for me. Everyone knows that she goes out at night to bury the things she aborts. I know it too. But she is a Brahmin woman and I am a Sudra. If she comes to me, I will place her on a pedestal and worship her.'

A sly and crooked smile spread across Krishnakanta's toothless mouth. 'It will not be easy. I will have to negotiate, I will have to get the two girls to agree to it, and for that I will have to bribe them with sweets from your shop.'

Pitambor got up hurriedly and went inside. The eyes of the woman lying on the bed flew open. She had probably just shut her eyes and was not asleep. She saw her husband go to the small, wooden box that was placed on top of a stool, and open it; she also saw him going out to Krishnakanta again after a while.

'You will let me know everything soon, won't you?' he said to the priest.

Taking the twenty rupees from the Mahajan, the wily priest went away with a mischievous smile....

Seven days passed without any word from Krishnakanta, while Pitambor waited eagerly every day for him. He had seen Damayanti a number of times; making her way to and from the Adhikaar's house to deliver the sacred threads she spun from the finest cotton. It was only now that he looked at her properly and discovered that he had never seen a woman as beautiful as her.

Her mother, they said, was from the village of Routa situated on the banks of the Dhanasri river. After seeing Damayanti now, Pitambor came to the conclusion that the Brahmin girls from near the Dhanasri river must be among the most beautiful women in the whole country. Her father, the priest Purnananda, had once lost a couple of his ploughing bullocks, and at that time he had had many clients in comparatively distant places like Maisanpur, Gargora and so on. Searching for his precious bullocks, Purnanada had gone to the village of Routa on the Dhanasri river side. No one seemed to know why he had to go so far to find his cows. But it was then that he had seen and married the beautiful daughter of Bhagawati of Routa village. No priest of the area had ever before married a girl from so far away....

It was the month of June, and the rivers and wetlands were overflowing with water. Both sides of the dirt road were full of shrubs and climbing plants that invariably came with the season. The road running in front of Pitambor's house was now covered with mud and slush. But in spite of the muddy and slippery road, Pitambor saw Damayanti walking along, plucking the edible greens such as the tasty 'kolmou' or water spinach which grew in abundance on the roadsides in the wet weather. She had lifted her mekhela up to her knees, and was accompanied by her six-year-old daughter, who was completely naked. Damayanti's legs and hands were soft and shiny, and healthy, like a new mango plant. Her hair which cascaded down her back was a reddish bronze colour, very much like the colour of rusted cannons, he thought. Oh, yes, the exact tinge of an old, rusted, iron canon! Pitambor remembered the huge iron cannon that was found when they were digging a well. It was said that the Burmese soldiers had left it behind when they had to retreat. He remembered that a group of students had come after some time and hauled it away.

After looking at her for a while, Pitambor plucked up the courage to speak to her. 'You will get sick if you walk about in this foul weather, on this dirty, muddy road,' he said. She turned and looked at him, her face and eyes expressing a surprised curiosity. But as earlier, she did not utter a word in reply. 'If you had only asked me I would have sent my servant to get you all....' But before he could complete his sentence, she turned to look back at him again. Pitambor felt as if her eyes that were blazing with a fiery look would burn him to ashes.

Without wasting any more time there, he walked rapidly away and sat down on his usual seat on the stump of the teak tree. He glanced towards his house and saw that his wife had taken to her bed again. She had tried to get up that morning after a long time. Her wasted limbs creaked with a ghastly sound when she tried to lift herself up, and she felt dizzy, so that she had to go back to her bed again. Now she lay there staring at her husband coming and going. Pitambor gazed at her with a cruel, and at the same time, somewhat embarrassed look. It was time for him to go and give her one of her medicines, and he was quite aware of it. But he did not get up—he simply sat where he was, looking down, contemplating his shoes. There were only four people in their satra who wore shoes—the clerk of the satra office, the two sons of the Adhikaar, and he himself. He bent down and tried to clean his mud-caked shoes with his handkerchief, and then again looked up at the road to see if Krishnakanta had come. But there was still no sign of him. As he sat waiting impatiently, a bullock cart came creaking into his compound. It was his tenant farmers bringing his share of the paddy they cultivated. On any other day, Pitambor would have rushed in enthusiastically and counted the baskets of paddy. But today, seeing that his master was absent-minded and indifferent, the servant came and counted the baskets and stored them inside the granary himself. After some time, having rested and partaking of some refreshments, the tenant farmers came as usual and took their leave from Pitambor. Also, as usual, they had some complaints about Pitambor's tight-fisted attitude. But nothing moved him today; he sat where he was, silent and indifferent.

Looking inside, he saw that his wife was lying with her eyes open. He noticed that someone had replaced a tumbler of water near her, and he remembered that the time for her medicine was past. But he got up anyway and was about to go and give it to her when he heard Krishnakanta's voice. Forgetting about his wife's medicine, he quickly put on his shoes once again and hurried to the gateway where the priest was waiting for him.

His wife's eyes, he noticed, seemed to be unusually weak—the fire that normally gleamed in her eyes whenever she looked towards him, seemed to be slowly dying out. 'Mahajan,' the priest called out.

'Yes, Bapu. Tell me, have you any news?' asked Pitambor.

'You will have to go to meet her on the coming full moon night in the dhekal, the room containing the dheki,' he said, referring to the wooden pedal for cleaning and pounding rice. 'It's located behind her house.' The priest looked furtively all around, and continued. 'I have found out that she is not pregnant at the moment. Her daughter told me this after I had bribed her with sweets. It seems that it is not yet a month since she terminated her last pregnancy. The girl is too young to understand these things. It seems that she had helped her mother by holding an oil lamp while the woman finished her job. She also told me that this time her mother had used a spade belonging to a Brahmin boy from Chataraguri. This boy used to come cycling from his home to study in the college near here. He is a boy from a well-to-do family, but of loose character. He came, and instead of going to college, he hid his books inside a basket of rice in Damayanti's hut and spent his time with her. He used to spend the money for his college fees buying things for Damayanti. The foetus she buried this time was this Brahmin boy's....'

'Listen Mahajan,' the priest continued, 'I have spoken to her about you. At first she was quite angry, "That Sudra man," she said. "How dare he even think about such a thing! Does he not know that I am the daughter of a good Brahmin priest?" I replied that everyone knew that she was a Brahmin woman. But now that she had taken the sinful path, there could be no difference between castes. I also told her that no Brahmin would stoop to marry her now. They would simply exploit her body and then cast her aside like the useless husks of the sugar cane stalks. I told her that you would marry her with all due rituals, as soon as your ailing wife died, that your wife is even now as good as dead. After you marry her, she would live a good and prosperous life, I told her. Do you know, Mahajan, when she heard all this, she went into her hut and cried her heart out, I do not understand why…. She came out after some time, wiping her tears and said, "I do not keep well these days, and it would be a relief if I could lean on someone's shoulders." I replied that it was not surprising that she did not feel well, after having aborted no less than five or six times within a short time; that if her case happened to come up in a Panchayat meeting, no one would even consider going near her, because anyone found to be giving her even a tumbler of water would be fined a sum of twenty rupees!'

'"What other option did I have?" she wept. "My daughters were starving. The Adhikaar's wife used to ask me to do small jobs for her in the kitchen. But now she says that I am not fit to work in her kitchen, that whatever I touch will become impure and contaminated. Before I used to be asked to spin and make the sacred threads, the 'laguns'. But now the Brahmin families of this area will not allow me to make the 'laguns'. They say that I am corrupted. The tenant farmers know that I am all alone with no one to look after me or my interests. So they too have started behaving like monsters. What do they care that I am a lonely Brahmin widow with two small daughters? How can I fight them? I own some acres of farm land in Satpakhila, but I have not been given my share of five maunds of paddy ever since my husband died. I have not been able to pay the revenue tax for that land for three years, and the land could be auctioned off any day now. What was I to do? I had to think of feeding my two daughters…."'

But in the meantime, Pitambor was getting more and more impatient. He almost yelled, 'Yes, yes, I understand all that. But what about me, my case?'

'Yes, I am coming to that,' replied the sly priest.

'She said, "He is a Sudra belonging to the fourth caste. Having relations with him…." But finally, she told me that she would meet you on the full moon night in the dhekal behind her house.'

Pitambor could hardly contain his joy. And taking advantage of that Krishnakanta said, 'But you will have to give me about one hundred rupees.

Damayanti says that she needs a mosquito net, and the two girls will have to be given sweets from Bhola's shop....'

Pitambor hurried inside and went towards the small wooden chest he kept in a corner of the room. His wife opened her sick eyes and followed his every move. Suddenly he shouted at her, 'What are you staring at? One day I will come and pluck your eyes out!'

Krishnakanta sat outside listening and understood what was happening inside the bedroom. He was a sly fox. When Pitambor came out and handed him one hundred rupees, he whispered, 'If necessary, give your wife a small pill of opium that night. She lies on that bed listening to everything, and understands everything. It is better to be careful.' And laughing meaningfully, the sly Brahmin priest took his leave. The woman on her bed simply shut her eyes.

Krishnakanta walked back a few steps and said, 'Damayanti is very keen on money. She acts like a tigress where money is concerned.... Never mind, you will be able to hold her hands intimately.'

The Mahajan felt rather guilty, and looked back at his wife. But no, she had heard nothing. She was asleep. But her dry forehead glistened with perspiration.

It was the full moon night of the monsoon month of Ashaar. Pitambor wore an endi kurta and a fine Santipuri dhoti. Across his shoulders he had thrown a sador of fine cotton. After a long time today he brought out the mirror with the wooden frame and scrutinized his face. He had shaved that morning, and now out in the sunlight, he could see fine wrinkles covering his face, and he was somewhat disturbed. It seemed to him that the wrinkles were a net and he was the fish trapped in the net of his wrinkles....

In due time, he walked towards Damayanti's house. It was located near the bridge on the Singra river, beyond the forest of teak trees. Very few people of the satra lived here, and it occurred to Pitambor that Damayanti was able to live as she did only because she lived in an almost deserted area.

He looked up to see some mushroom-coloured clouds floating in the sky, looking for all the world, like cannons. And that round moon! As though it was a deer shorn of its skin. As though someone had come and wrapped her dotted skin around the cannons. A skinned deer—her meat shaking uncontrollably without the skin to bind it in place! Lovely fresh vigorous meat!! This skinned deer suddenly transformed into Damayanti. A completely nude Damayanti! There were her lovely breasts—like a pregnant goat's stomach. Her body was the colour of tender bamboo stalks, and her lips? They were soft and lovely like freshly-cut mangoes oozing sweet nectar.... Pitambor could not stand there any longer looking up at the sky, weaving fantasies about the woman. It was deathly quiet and completely deserted. It was the night of the annual 'bhaona' performance, and the entire village had gone to see it. Indeed, she had purposely chosen this night!

He heard some jackals howling from the thorny shrubs nearby, and he walked rapidly to Damayanti's hut. He took off his shoes and sat on the plinth. A heady fragrance of the Champa flower floated out from somewhere. Damayanti lay with her younger daughter on a small cot set between the basket meant to store rice and a dome of ripe jackfruit. The girl was drowsily writing the letters of the alphabet on a slate with a dirty, old lamp with a broken chimney as the only source of light. Leaning against the wall, Damayanti was watching the man. After a while, she beckoned to him to come inside, and sit on a mora, that was placed nearby. A small earthen lamp filled to the brim with mustard oil, burned nearby. For some reason Pitambor was afraid to look at her body in the pale light of the lamp—he had a peculiar feeling that everything might be over if he did.... It was all a land of illusion, he felt. Was this Brahmin widow in front of him a real woman?

'Have you brought any money with you?' Pitambor was startled into reality. He had not expected her first question to be so very materialistic.

'Whatever I have is yours,' he replied and handed her a cotton bag. She took the small bag and put it inside a cane basket that was hanging on one of the posts of her dheki ghar. In the meantime, the girl who was writing the alphabet went and lay down with her sister and instantly fell asleep. There was a very low cot in one of the rooms that was used to store the baskets of rice. Damayanti's husband, who had been a priest, had been given those baskets during the shraddha of the Adhikaar's brother.

Pitambor followed Damayanti and sat down on that cot. After a while, she came to him....

Two months passed by. One day, after the Mahajan had left her, Krishnakanta happened to see Damayanti bathing in the river, and made fun of her, 'Why Damayanti, I never saw you coming to the river to bathe after you spent the nights with the Brahmin boys of Dudhnoi Bongora!'

Damayanti did not reply. But the sly priest was not put off. 'I suppose it is because this one is a sudra...?'

Again she did not reply, but she suddenly jumped up and going to a corner, she began to vomit violently.

For some moments, the priest stood where he was, dumbfounded. Then he said, 'This must be Pitambor Mahajan's child then?'

Again she was silent. But Krishnakanta continued, 'That is very good news. Poor Pitambor will be very happy; he was almost going mad at not having any children! Then I will go and give him the good news.' After a pause he said, 'Listen, you must not worry or feel bad. Our Gandhi Maharaj did not believe in all this business of caste. He said that all men are equal and the same. Just you wait and see, Pitambor will marry you with all the proper rituals as soon as his wife is dead. I am sure that you are aware that the villagers were getting fed up of your way of life, and were thinking of having a Panchayat meeting about it. I don't think you know that some time back one of the things you aborted and buried beneath the clump of bamboos, was dragged out by a jackal and deposited in one of the priest's courtyards. And have you any idea how much that poor man had to spend to get himself purified—and for no fault of his own!'

Damayanti started vomiting again.

'Be careful, Damayanti,' warned Krishnakanta. 'Do not do anything this time. Even after knowing all about you and your repeated abortions, Pitambor is willing to accept you. If you do anything this time to damage the child within you, I tell you, you will go straight to hell. No one and nothing can save you.'

And Krishnakanta went to give the Mahajan the best news he had ever heard. 'Pitambor, if she does not go and abort this child, you can be sure that she will not be unwilling to marry you.'

As usual, Pitambor was sitting on the stump of his favourite tree. He had not even bothered to take off his mud-caked shoes. Hearing the priest's words he started trembling in sheer excitement. He would be a father! Can it be true? Would he really be a father at long last? But of course it must be true. The Brahmin priest himself had told him so.

He stood up, deeply agitated, and started walking about aimlessly.

Krishnakanta said, 'What is the matter with you! Why are you walking up and down like a monkey! But of course you have more than enough reason to be happy and excited! It is not a small matter to become a father after thirty years of waiting! A very great fortune indeed!'

Suddenly, Pitambor came and knelt down in front of the other man. 'Bapu,' he pleaded, 'please see that she does nothing to frustrate the dearest desire of my life. You well know what kind of men my father and grandfather were. Only a sufferer can understand the despair of a childless man! Besides, she is a Brahmin woman from a priest's family and now she holds my life in her hands! What will I do, Bapu, what will I do?'

Krishnakanta lifted one hand as if in blessing and said, 'I will keep track of her and what she does, like a vulture keeping track of a corpse. Do not worry. I will also warn the old woman who helps in these dreadful things. But I will need some money to bribe her too.'

This time Pitambor did not have to go to his small box to get the money. That morning he had sold all the fruits from his seven jackfruit trees, and the proceeds were still in his pocket. He took out the entire bundle of notes and handed it to the priest. Extremely pleased at the way his plans were going, Krishnakanta put his hands on Pitambor's head and blessed him.

Now when Pitambor went to the bedroom, his eyes fell straight on his sick wife's eyes. And in spite of himself, their sad and desolate expression moved him to compassion. But the next moment he regained his composure and forced himself to anger. 'Hey, you sick and barren woman! How dare you stare at me like that?' And he yelled out to his servants, 'Come, come! Lift this bed. Take it to the small room next to the dheki room. Come, hurry up!'

No sooner said than done! Along with four of his servants, Pitambor carried the bed with his wife still lying on it, and put it inside a small, dark room without any sort of ventilation, near the room where the paddy and the dheki were placed.

Since his affair with Damayanti, Pitambor seemed to have almost forgotten that his wife needed at least some looking after, and had to be given medicines regularly. She was just skin and bones now, and seeing that their master did not bother about her, the servants too had started to neglect her. They were even careless about bringing her food on time, and often did not bother to bring her a glass of water with her meals let alone give her the required medicines on time. The poor woman's throat would often become parched and dry with thirst, but she would not utter a word of protest. People said that she looked more like a corpse than a living woman. Even now, when her husband brought her to this small, dark room and left her there, she kept quiet. But surprisingly, even in the dank darkness, her eyes shone brightly, and it seemed as though she saw, and understood, everything that was going on, more clearly than if she was out in the open.

The very thought of fathering a child made Pitambor delirious with joy. He lived in a world of joyful imaginings—the child in Damayanti's womb seemed to him to be already a boy, then a young man. In Pitambor's imagination, the boy walked along the banks of the Dhanasri river, holding his father's hands! The ever joyous and sparkling golden thread that binds fathers to sons seemed to stretch happily far into the distant horizon, where all was sheer happiness, where the ties and traditions of family were an unbroken saga of joy....

Pitambor got a couple of his trusted servants to bring down an old wooden box from its perch near the roof of his room. When he was sure that he was alone, he opened the box and took out a bundle tied in an old gamosa. In the bundle were a few pieces of half-burnt bones, the ashthi of his long dead father, and entwined in the dried up bones was a chain of the precious poal or coral beads that were so much a part of the traditions of Assam. Pitambor remembered how, as his father lay on his deathbed, almost choking with the effort to speak, had said, 'Keep this chain of my poal beads carefully. Your son will wear it, and then his son, and then his son's son, and so on. It will be the living symbol, the everlasting flag of our clan....' The old man died before he could complete the sentence. Pitambor took out this chain now, then wrapped the pieces of ashthi in the gamosa again, and put the bundle back in the old box. Finally, he called in his servants and had the box put back in its old place on the shelf.

Days turned into weeks, and weeks into months, and Pitambor became more and more impatient to hear some news. He had heard that a foetus that was five months old could not be aborted and he calculated that it was now three months since she had conceived. As he waited each day without any news, it seemed to become more and more unbearable. Each passing day loomed in front of him like a mountain he had to cross in order to gain access to his happiness and survive.

Almost every moment he seemed to hear the Brahmin woman's footsteps approaching him, and he imagined that she was whispering to him, 'Mahajan, hurry up and prepare for the wedding rituals. I can no longer hide my condition. Do you not see how big my stomach is? Hurry up. Get the wedding preparations ready.' Again, 'All those things about Brahmins and Sudras, about Hindus and Muslims, are just a lot of nonsense. We are all human beings, and you will find that the same red blood flows inside all of us.... Get the rituals for the wedding ready.'

She seemed to walk with ghungroos tied to her feet and she came to him with tinkling feet. He imagined her lovely fair and slim legs....

'Mahajan,' she seemed to whisper, 'nowadays I do not bother to go and bathe in the river after I sleep with you. Go, get ready for our wedding....'

Three months passed by uneventfully, and the Mahajan still dreamt of walking along the Dhanasri river banks with his hands on the shoulders of a handsome youth—his son!

It was the late monsoon month of Bhadra and often violent storms lashed the villages. A storm had been steadily gaining momentum since that afternoon. Going inside to shut the door of his wife's room, he noticed that her eyes today burned more brightly, more malevolently than usual. They looked to him like a shining snake that passed by him in the dead of night. As the storm raged, the lamps were blown out, and all other sounds were drowned out by its sheer ferocity. Pitambor shouted for his servants, but no one could hear him. The only sounds to be heard were the rumblings and thundering of the storm and of trees being felled, either being struck by lightning, or being blown down by fierce winds.

There, another tree had crashed down! Which tree was it, Pitambor wondered. Somewhere in the distance, he saw a streak of lightning that had definitely struck another tree! He could hear the frightening sounds of the tree being split down the middle and crashing to the ground. He went outside to see which tree had fallen and what disaster this terrifying storm had caused.

In a corner of the grounds, the fruits of seven of his coconut trees had been heaped up waiting to be sold. Now he saw his servants running about trying to salvage them and store them inside the dheki ghar. Some of the fruits which were still on the trees thudded on to the ground, being blown down by the wind. No one could hear anyone else, but gradually the storm began to calm down, the rumblings and thunder died down, and a heavy rain lashed the village. Lighting the lantern again, Pitambor could now see the heavy raindrops, but he could still hear the tinkling sounds of Damayanti's anklets as her feet came towards him....

Suddenly amidst the rain, Pitambor heard someone calling him by name. Picking up the lantern, he hurried outside, and saw the priest coming towards him, completely drenched and shivering. Pitambor was frightened. Only some extreme news could have prompted the man to come out in this terrible weather. Krishnakanta held an umbrella over his head, but it had so many holes that it afforded no protection whatsoever. His dhoti had been drawn up to his knees, and only a thin 'sador' that was dripping wet, covered his bare body.

Holding up the lantern Pitambor shouted out, 'Bapu! What brings you out in this foul weather, so late in the night?'

Somehow, Krishnakanta managed to come and sit down on the plinth of the house. Leaning the torn umbrella against a post, he took off his sador and tried to wring it dry, and wiped his wet face with it. Then pointing a shaking finger at Pitambor he said in a choking voice, 'Pitambor, when your first wife died, there were three inauspicious stars in the ascendant, three puhkars. Three or four?'

'I do not remember,' replied the Mahajan. 'Why?'

'When three puhkars are found at the time of death of a person in the house, even the dubari grass dries up, and dies. When your first wife died, there were three puhkars. And as a result, the ill effects are still there. Everything is dead and gone!'

'What has happened, Bapu? What is wrong?'

'She has destroyed it, Mahajan, she has aborted! She refused to carry the seed of a Sudra man! She belongs to the highest Brahmin clan, a woman from the Sandilya gotra! She has spoiled your seed, Pitambor, she has finished off her pregnancy!'

(The youth holding Pitambor's hands let go and fell into the depths of the Dhanasri river. Who was it who had fallen? Was it Pitambor, or the young man? Dear God, who was it that tumbled and fell headlong into the deep waters of the river!)

Soon after this, Damayanti heard a sound near her house in the dead of the night. Someone was digging something beneath the clump of bamboos behind her dekhal. She shouted, 'Who is it? Who is there?' and woke her elder daughter. The six-year-old girl and her mother stood near the window, listening. The sounds of digging came from the same place where the two of them had gone in the dead of night two days ago and buried that thing the woman had ruined. Mother and daughter had gone out that night and dug a hole with the spade the Brahmin boy from Chataraguri had given them. The young girl had quivered in fright when she heard the jackals howling nearby. And today, the unmistakable sound of digging came from that very same place. Thud, thud! Thump, thump! Standing near the window, the two of them saw a lantern burning in the spot, and in the light of the lantern they saw the figure of a man, a strong, well-built man digging away at the very spot where Damayanti had dug just two days ago. Indeed, he was digging up the same hole!

Damayanti's entire body and soul trembled at the sight. The man was

Pitambor Mahajan. He had hung his lantern on a bamboo, and was digging fervently at the spot. The man had assumed a terrifying aspect and he was hacking at the earth like a mad man. She trembled in fear and terror. Should she shout? Yes, of course she must. Such a terrible thing was happening in her own house—of course she must shout!

'Mahajan! Mahajan!' she shouted. But there was absolutely no response. He simply kept on digging.

'Mahajan, why are you digging up my ground?'

Pitambor looked up towards the window, but did not utter a word.

Damayanti went almost wild with agitation. 'Yes, I buried it. But what will you find there now? It was just an unformed lump of flesh.'

Pitambor lifted his head and looked at her. 'It was my child! I will at least feel the flesh of my flesh! I will feel my child, my son and heir, with my own two hands!'

Translated by Gayatri Bhattarcharyya

BLOOD ON THE FLOOR
APURBA SARMA

...the voice of thy brother's blood crieth unto me from the ground

In trying to explain a favourite poem by a noted poet, he held forth at length on the glory of human life—from English to Assamese literature, from God to nature, and from nature to human beings. He was a young professor, passionate about, and well-read in, poetry. Before him were eager young faces, looking up in rapt attention. Outside was harsh reality, a stench in the air, heart-rending news, and hopeless anticipation.

The sight of these innocents pained him. In trying to shelter them from reality, his lectures took them on flights of fantasy—into a world far from the confines of the classroom where they could breathe in their own rhythm, be happy and carefree, and experience uninhibited awe. At times, he got carried away and forgot what he had set out to do. That too was necessary.

A peon brought in a slip saying he needed to receive a phone call in the Principal's office, and he reluctantly left the class. The bespectacled man of indeterminate age was sitting at his desk, chin resting on his fists, listening to a sorry-looking visitor, and taking no notice of the new entrant. The fluorescent lights above him reflected off his shiny, bald pate, grey moustache and sideburns, making him look like a cartoon turtle. The visitor stole a quick glance at the doorway and went back to finding the lost thread of his narrative.

He lifted the telephone receiver from the table, listened, asked a few short questions, and placed it carefully back in its cradle. Then he walked up to the Principal's desk and waited uncomfortably until the visitor finished speaking.

The Principal unclenched his fists, picked up his all-powerful pen like he was taking up a weapon, stretched back in his chair, peered at his visitor through his thick lenses and said, 'Your son has failed to clear the hurdle of the finals despite two years of effort. Why trouble him further? The admissions are closed; there's nothing we can do. Go get him to till the fields and get married. You may leave now.' He dismissed his visitor, turned to him and said, 'What, heh? You seem to be receiving lots of calls these days?' The tone implied more complaint than concern.

'It was a call from home, Sir. I believe my mother is unwell.' He paused, wondering if his hasty explanation sounded convincing.

'Really? But what good will your going do? Ask her to consult a doctor. How old is she?' He returned to his turtle-like stance, this time armed with his pen.

'She's not too old, Sir. I'm her eldest. She is consulting doctors but seems to be quite sick. Tomorrow being Saturday....'

'Fine, then. You can leave tomorrow afternoon and return on Sunday. You can't afford to miss classes at this point of time.' He spoke like a well-wisher.

'No, Sir. I think I'll take the day off tomorrow so that I can return the day after. I have one more class left today, but Pallavi can take care of that,' he found himself saying with more confidence than he felt.

'Well, then. Go if you must. Ask your Head to make arrangements for tomorrow's classes. And don't forget to submit your leave application.'

'Yes, Sir. Goodbye, Sir.' His landlord now had a telephone; if he gave Jugin that number, he wouldn't need to receive calls in the Principal's office and make up all those stories.

He rushed through his preparations, got a friend to drop him at the station, and barely managed to catch the only bus that crossed his village. In three hours, he would be home, well before dark. He tossed away his cigarette and mentally ticked off his to-do list. The leave application was submitted and a neighbour was informed, since the landlord was out and the maid couldn't be contacted. The gas cylinder is due tomorrow—it would probably go back. Had he shut the kitchen window? Well, too late now....

His co-passengers were a stern-looking elderly man in a dull white dhoti-kurta with a day-old stubble and betel-stained lips, and a Marwari family—three little girls about two years apart and an infant, probably a boy, in the mother's arms. The man wore a small vermilion mark on his forehead, chewed paan, and had a dab of lime on the tip of his index finger. They had two suitcases and a huge bag. The girls squabbled. One suddenly jumped up and demanded, 'Papa, I want some too,' and her father responded with, 'Shut up and sit down!'

As the bus settled into a steady speed, he stared out unseeing. His mind, which he had forced shut all this while, opened up and he heard Jugin's voice, 'Can you come over? They have come again today.'

'They' had ransacked the house but, thankfully, not hurt anyone. His two sisters weren't at home. Jugin was calling from the booth at the crossroads and was afraid to speak in detail. He too refrained from asking anything— the Principal was all ears. He tried to visualize his home, and his parents' drawn looks post the harassment. And where were his sisters?

'They' had first come about a month and a half ago. He was home for the summer vacations and was playing a game of carrom with his companions in Kandarpa's shop at the crossroads when they heard a truck. 'The Army is here,' someone said.

It was his turn to play. The words pierced his heart but he feigned nonchalance. 'I wonder where they are going.'

'These guys are always driving around. Keep playing,' said one of his companions.

'Someday, they'll get blown up, truck and all—boom!' murmured another.

The game was on the verge of a climax when he heard someone call him through the din of animated spectators—'Romen!' It was Jugin, his friend and neighbour.

'The Army has entered your home. Come along.'

Someone restrained him. 'Wait. It's not safe for you'.

'They are totally unreliable, these maniacs!' added another. He hesitated for a moment, then freed himself and rushed homeward with Jugin at his heels.

A few Army men milled around the truck parked across the street. Some elderly people—not a single young man—gathered as a group of women and children watched from Jugin's courtyard. He saw his terrified mother and two tearful sisters among them. An officer stood at the door and a host of army men conducted a search as his father watched.

Nobody had been harmed yet, so it was probably safe. Stepping onto the veranda, he read the officer's name badge—Major Y. S. Yadav. On being asked to identify himself, he replied that he was a neighbour. The officer sensed his split-second of indecision and asked if he was sure he wasn't Niren's brother. Trembling inside, he realized he had made a mistake. In a pleasant, unaffected voice, he replied, 'I'm not.'

Search done, the officer asked for Niren's photographs. They knew that he came home often, he warned, and asked that he be brought to the Army camp next time. He ordered Romen to visit him at his camp that evening and got into the truck.

Pushing aside all proffered opinions and advice, he arranged for a cycle to visit the Army camp. Jugin insisted on accompanying him.

Major Yadav was a thorough gentleman. He offered him a chair, and a cigarette which he politely refused. Blowing cigarette smoke through his mouth and nostrils, the Major turned to him and asked in chaste Hindi, 'How are you related to Niren Barman?'

'I'm his elder brother.'

'The college professor?' He knew.

'Yes'.

'Why did you lie about it this morning?'

'I was afraid.'

'Was it fear or a conviction that there was nothing to fear?' smiled the officer.

However reassuring that sounded, he could not respond. His throat was dry.

'He comes home every now and then.' There was no telling whether Major Yadav was complaining or merely offering a piece of information.

'I haven't met him. We don't want him to come. We have no relationship with him any more. That's the absolute truth.'

'Your family likes him to visit. You should speak to him. He'll listen to you.'

'My father has tried to reason with him, but he won't listen. We can't force things; so we've just let go.' It was obvious that the officer did not believe a word.

'Try and explain to him that this is a dangerous path that leads nowhere. And it affects all of you too, right? Fear, hardship, tension....' This time, the Major spoke in English, enunciating each word clearly.

As he saw him off, he suddenly asked, 'Do you have any of his photographs?'

'No, I don't,' he replied truthfully.

Outside, Jugin asked, 'What did he say?'

'He wants us to get Bapa to surrender.' They returned home in silence.

During the rest of the vacation, he stayed home, read a few books and, with great effort, completed two sets of notes for his students. He tried to write a little, but wound up almost before getting started. On his brief and rare sojourns to the crossroads, he remained content with watching the others play. One evening, just a few days before the vacations ended, Jugin came up to him and whispered, 'Bapa is here.'

'Says who?' he asked in shock.

'My brother says someone saw him at the crossroads.'

'What about the Army surveillance?'

'He manages to walk right through them since they have no idea what he looks like. Who would think that puny little guy....' There was pride in Jugin's voice.

The entire evening, he sat in the dark outside, lost in countless scattered thoughts. It was imperative that he meet his brother. But what if someone had tipped off the Army? An endless stream of pictures flitted through his mind—some from the past and others, outlined, from the future. The darkness enveloped everything. The past, present, and future were all lost in its depths. How had the years they had traversed together, probably less than twenty, shaped them into men? Where were the people, the village, the society...? What had caused their downfall?

'Where's Dada?' His sister's voice inside the house jolted him back to consciousness. Dinner was ready. Emerging from the darkness, he questioned himself—who are you waiting for? Bapa? Or Major Yadav's demon troops? Both had taken up tools of destruction in the name of protection. He needed to get inside before his sister found him. He rose and tried to shake off the darkness, only to realize that reality was far removed from his philosophical dreams.

Later, he lay awake in bed, his mind in turmoil. It was as though he was awaiting something—unrest, uncertainty, fear, persecution.... Every aspect of life was measured against the yardstick of death. What had life descended to?

He heard a sound and sat up. His mother had woken. Bapa was home. He remained still, his chest tight. Then, silently creeping out, he saw his mother hold a torchlight as Bapa stood eating dinner out of a plate he held. Who was his mother's informant? Jugin? Or his brother? They sensed his presence and looked up at him, startled.

'Come and see me when you're done eating. We need to talk.' He returned to his room, imagining he heard Major Yadav's truck. Was that what he wished for?

His mother followed him in. 'Don't be too harsh on him. Explain nicely and he will understand.' She received no reassurance in response.

What if the Major were to appear right now? Would it be right to leave everything to chance or fate? What did his philosophy say? As an educated, thinking, aware, mature social being, what was his stand?

Bapa walked silently into the room.

'Sit'. But his brother remained standing; perhaps he didn't have much time.

He dived straight in, 'Give up all this. Don't you see what is happening to the household?' He concealed his helplessness and managed to sound resolute. 'Think about our parents and sisters. I'll go crazy if I have to handle everything on my own.' That was the best he could do. He waited for a response—anything profound, wordy, and debatable, be it about logic, ideals, or philosophy. But there was nothing forthcoming.

'You don't understand, but the path you have chosen is endless and leads nowhere.' He realized that he was merely repeating what the Major had said. Still no response. I should stop here, he thought to himself. Let Bapa sleep over it; he needn't reply right away. 'Think about it. Don't worry, I'll talk to the Army.' He was loath to admit that he had already done that. He looked at the quiet, immobile form before him. Both stood inert, as in a still-life painting. Even the air around them seemed to swell and become motionless.

His reverie was broken by a loud commotion. The bus, now almost empty, screeched to a halt. The handyman thumped its sides and the driver yelled at someone outside. The seat next to him was vacant; the Marwari family was gone too. In their place were two young men, probably college students, who kept staring at him. In the seat ahead of him was a woman trying to nurse her crying baby.

Through his window, he saw the familiar sights of village houses, greenery, the broken bridge, and the dry river. Almost home, he was overcome by a wave of nostalgia and anxiety. Pulling out his pack of cigarettes, he saw that there was only one left. He had finished the rest without realizing it.

As he walked through the village paths in the twilight, avoiding all possible eye contact, he received some curious looks and hesitant greetings to which he responded curtly. Jugin was waiting at the crossroads. Together with him and another friend, he walked wordlessly towards his home.

He stopped short at the gate. The black steel trunk from his college days, an old wooden chest and an old suitcase lay open across the courtyard. A random pile of quilts, another of books, and his sister's harmonium lay on the veranda.

'What's all this?' he asked Jugin in surprise.

'They were looking for papers and photographs and left everything like this.'

'How come no one has considered putting them back since morning?' His words came out louder and sharper than necessary.

'They want the MLA to see this. The man is at some meeting; he should be here anytime now,' was Jugin's unconvincing response.

His father appeared on the veranda.

'What will the MLA do? I wonder who comes up with these weird ideas.' He realized that he was screaming and quickly controlled himself. 'Here, put everything back in. Call Dhon to help. And tell your brother to stop sending word to the MLA.' Inside the house, he was greeted by an even bigger mess. The beds, tables, cupboards and even the kitchen had been ransacked. His mother slowly tried to salvage her kitchen; his father watched in helpless silence.

The evening felt unbearable. There was nothing he could do but fret. He walked over to Jugin's gate and they both smoked in silence.

'Do you think you should have a word with the Major?' suggested Jugin tentatively.

'What good will that do? I have already told him that we have no connection with him. What more can I say? This annoyance will continue. There's no way out.'

'No, but this time, they have....' Jugin hesitated.

'What have they done?' He glared at his friend.

Jugin avoided his gaze and stammered, 'Well, something.... With bad intentions.'

'What is it?' he asked sharply.

Cornered, Jugin nervously said, 'They were asking about your sisters.'

He froze. His heart turned to stone. Both breathing and speech became impossible.

Jugin tried to reassure him, 'They were simply asking...'

'What were they asking?' The question seemed to form itself out of nowhere.

'They were asking Prasanna,' Jugin stuttered.

'What were they asking?' he demanded in a stern, suppressed voice.

'They were just asking where the girls were—"He had two sisters; where have they gone?"'

'Where were they?' His voice still carried suppressed anger.

'They had escaped through the back door and were in our house.'

Defying all advice, he cycled to the Army camp in the evening. Jugin perched himself on the rod in front. The armed guards let him in after getting the requisite permission. Jugin waited outside.

'What have you done now? I have already told you we have nothing to do with Niren Barman,' he started even before he sat, trying not to sound harsh.

The Major offered him a cigarette, which he accepted. They both lit up. The officer relaxed in his chair and answered, 'Your brother was home the night before last. Yesterday, we erred in our timing. We should have gone earlier.' He paused and continued, 'We are a misunderstood lot. We don't harass people for no reason.'

He grabbed his chance, 'Today, your men asked about my sisters. Why is that?' He did not attempt to hide his displeasure.

'I had warned you that you too may be in danger. This is the sort of thing I meant,' said the Major. 'If we don't find your brother, we might pick up your father on the charge of sheltering or collaborating with him. And you know how the questioning might go. If we do find your brother and there is shooting involved, an innocent family member could become a victim. The problem is that I can't be present in every raid party. And our soldiers can get inhuman. Not that I can blame them. You are aware of the circumstances under which we work. Often we are mere machines performing our tasks. Tell me, what can we do? That is why I had asked you to reason with him and bring him to us.'

'So arrest him and try him under the law. We have no objections to that.'

'We have our problems,' sighed the officer.

The prime problem was that they didn't have a photograph. Another was the young man's popularity. Besides, he was the most inconspicuous terrorist—lean, calm, and innocent-looking—and managed to walk freely through their ranks. 'The circumstances will decide what happens and when. No one can predict any action or outcome,' he added gravely, stubbing out his cigarette in the ashtray.

Jugin was curious. 'What did he say?' he asked, but received no response. There was no one with whom he could share what Major Yadav had said. Once home, he handed over the cycle to his friend and slowly said, 'Ask your brother to send word that he shouldn't come home. There will be trouble if he does.' Then, without looking back, he blended into the darkness.

Before retiring for the night, he entered his father's room. The old man was lying in bed and sat up when he saw his son. His mother, preparing her bed, also went still. There was an uneasy silence in the room as his parents waited for him to speak.

'Don't let him come home. There will be grave danger if he does.' No response. He turned to his mother. 'Do you get what I'm saying?' he asked impatiently.

'Of course I get you. We don't allow him to come. But what do we do when he lands up in the middle of the night?' she responded in a pained voice.

He checked his rising temper and said, 'Don't let him in at any cost. It doesn't matter if he feels offended or goes back. You don't understand, Ma.

One more visit and everyone will be in trouble. Pita, please explain to her.'

His father coughed and, speaking with forced strength, said, 'We have given up trying to reason with him. Let destiny take its course. Tell the Army to do whatever needs to be done. We don't have a problem with that.' His voice trailed off. All three people stood still in the dimly-lit room, tortured, shamed, helpless, and ready to face whatever fate the future had in store.

He returned to bed and lay restless in the dark, the scene from a little while ago etched deep in his mind: three characters, still as statues in spite of their heart-rending condition, playing their predestined roles of a family lost in the present as they faced a hopeless future. But what play was this? Was it one where these responsible people were mere puppets and Major Yadav the indisputable hero? Were these emotions scripted, or were they real? He replayed the scene, fast-forwarded it, analyzed it, and finally switched it off before burying his head in his soft pillow. But the hazy kaleidoscope continued with the shadow of the Major hovering over it, larger than life. 'Who is this Major Yadav?' someone asked him from afar, making him uncomfortable.

The uneasy situation at home prompted him to leave in the morning instead of the afternoon. He gave Jugin the landlord's phone number and asked him not to call him at the college again.

At the crossroads, he turned towards the Army camp instead of the bus station. Haunted by the Major all night, he felt the need to talk with him once more.

The officer, still in his nightclothes, sat smoking at a table on the camp veranda. He offered him a chair and a cigarette and waited patiently for him to speak. What had he come to say anyway?

'I'm leaving, Mr Yadav,' he said, trying to sound casual.

'All right,' said the Major. 'Here, have some tea.'

'No, I need to go,' he said, but showed no sign of leaving as he sat nervously puffing on his cigarette. Suddenly, he said, 'I have barred him from coming home.'

The officer lowered his eyes and toyed with the cigarette pack on the table.

'I'm really worried about my family,' the words finally tumbled out.

Yadav nodded in understanding, looked directly at him and asked, 'Aren't you also worried about your brother?'

He bit back the involuntary answer that almost escaped his lips. What was he doing? Here was an all-powerful man who, he hoped, would protect his family. But why would he do that? He felt that his head would explode. He had never had to face such a situation before. The Major had already made his wordless assessment. Nevertheless, he pleaded, 'Tell me, what can I do? I tried my best. Yesterday, my father told me he was helpless. He...' and he stopped short.

'That's really sad. But I suppose that is the reality now,' said the experienced man.

'Mr Yadav, do what you will, anything you need to. But I don't want my family to be harmed in any way.' That was the best he could do.

'I can sympathize with you, but I can't give you any assurance. Everything depends on circumstances. Let's wait and see.'

He realized that it was time for him to leave.

The staffroom was empty. He felt strangely relaxed after his last class and craved a cigarette. In the ten days or so since his return, he had gone about his work but had cut himself off socially. Which world was real—the simple world of his near and dear ones back home where two sets of people created hell on earth while promising heaven, or the world he had created, based on academic ideals, vivacity of young students, fake friendships, meaningless conversations, aimless existence, and unsolvable problems? Weren't the two essentially the same? Neither felt real. Both were created by social, moral, intellectual, and nostalgic value patterns. He existed somewhere in between, detached from both, in an imagined vacuum where he tormented himself with endless questions of ethics, logic, truth and untruth, reality and illusion. Every once in a while, trapped in a dilemma, he screamed silently like a fictional character—'Am I my brother's keeper?' Then a trail of familiar questions jolted him back to reality and made him cringe.

Each time he calmly ventured into a philosophical realm, a disturbing question kept surfacing from nowhere—'Who is Major Yadav?' He groped uncertainly for an answer. The Major was a power backed by the law. He was the nation, the authority. Then another question cropped up—'Who empowered him to wreak havoc?' He shuddered, turned away from his thoughts and stepped outside.

This morning, he rose a little later than usual. The bright rays of sunshine shimmied straight to his heart and made it dance. On the back veranda, the pair of birds that came to his courtyard for their daily dose of crumbs flew onto the clothesline and demanded their due. 'Sorry, I woke up late today,' he said lightly. They looked around and, a little warily, started pecking at the crumbs he tossed on the floor—people could be nice! He was surprised but proud of their trust in him. In spite of nicking himself while shaving, he left for the college with a light heart. The whole world seemed brighter. Even Goswami, the incorrigible borrower, offered him one of the cigarettes he extracted from his shirt pocket as they were leaving the canteen.

Emerging from the library in the afternoon, he saw a few students waiting for him and figured that they needed something. 'What's the matter?' he asked.

'Sir, are you taking the major class today?' asked one of them.

'Why did you think I wouldn't?' he laughed. 'Come on.'

He took his time with the class. Later, he overheard someone say, 'Two hours! Go provoke him some more.' He smiled to himself. It was four in the afternoon. Everyone had left. The watchman was waiting to lock up. He stepped out.

Peeking through the Principal's open door, he received a loud welcome, 'Come, come in. Where were you all this while?'

'I was in class, Sir.'

'Good. I am glad that the course is progressing well this time.' The Principal seemed to be in a good mood. Should he push his luck and ask for some leave?

'Yes, Sir. I have almost completed mine.'

'I like that. You must earn your bread. See if you can do something for yourself too. I mean further studies and such. Trivial timepass gives nothing in return. However hackneyed it may sound, all that glitters is not gold—you get me?'

He nodded in agreement. 'True, Sir. That has been obvious all along.' He let a few seconds pass before he meekly asked, 'Sir, may I go home on Friday?'

'Why?' The man was suddenly serious.

Faking concern, he said, 'I'm worried. I haven't heard from my father in a while. You know very well that....' Was it his mother who was supposedly sick last time?

'Do you have any leave left?'

'Of course, Sir. I've hardly used any. I try and go home only on the weekends....'

The man seemed satisfied. 'Fine, then. Don't forget the application.'

He returned to his room and rested for a while. Jugin hadn't called, so all must be well. He would see them all on Friday. He changed and went out to see his friends.

He found them at the restaurant, puffing on their cigarettes. 'It's my treat today,' he announced. 'The old man has sanctioned two days' leave and that calls for a celebration. Hey...' he turned to the waiter, '...get paranthas for everyone.' He gloated about how he had manipulated the Principal and, with a flourish, tossed a pack of cigarettes onto the table.

After dinner, he leaned back in bed, turned on the TV, saw that a channel was airing an old black-and-white movie he had seen years ago, *Bicycle Thieves,* and settled down to watch it again. The last scene of the warm, tender hand of a child gripping the care-worn condemned hand of the father seemed like a ray of hope amidst cruelty, poverty, torture, humiliation, and the hopelessness of human life. It was especially poignant and tugged at his heartstrings. He fell asleep at an odd angle, with the TV remote, his pack of cigarettes, and a matchbox by his side.

Once awake, he looked at his watch and sprang out of bed. It was ten minutes to his morning class. In the next five minutes, he picked up the newspaper from under the door, tossed it on the table, rushed to the bathroom and got ready to leave. Then he heard the landlord's call, 'Barman, there's a call for you.'

Damn! Why on earth had he given the Principal this number? Just so he could call if there was a five-minute delay? The two-day leave would now be gone. He picked up the receiver and spoke impatiently, 'Hello?' It was Jugin.

The soft, broken words pierced his heart like bullets. The world went dark. He clutched hard at the telephone table, his mind in a whirl. He tried to sit, but there was nothing to sit on. He knelt, groped at the wall for support, and sank in a heap onto the floor. His heart seemed to stop beating as the words hit him. Jugin fell silent...the connection was cut. His world shattered and became empty. Time stood still.

Translated by Maitreyee Siddhanta Chakravarty

THE CAPTIVE
HAREKRISHNA DEKA

He had been bicycling since afternoon. It was now almost dusk. He felt extremely tired. If only he could rest for a little while....

It appeared that the youth who was bicycling beside him understood what he was feeling. Suddenly raising his hand, he gestured him to a stop. The youth also got down from his bicycle.

As he got down, he noticed the picturesque surroundings. The place was near the highlands. A stream came tumbling down from the hill and flowed past a huge rock. The sound of the brook as it murmured and gurgled on its way floated across to him.

Pushing his bicycle towards the rock, the youth gestured towards him, indicating that he should follow. As he neared the rock, he observed it closely. The water was bright and clear. As though a young girl from the hills had come rushing headlong down the slope, chuckling happily to herself. The simile rose, unbidden, to his mind. These days, his mind would search for metaphors and similes whenever it was confronted with something that was unfettered and unimpeded.

The youth stood on the rock, and surveyed the surroundings. He then took the bag down from his shoulders, and, looking towards him, said, 'There is no danger here. You can rest for a while.'

The word 'danger' created a strange affect in his mind. How many shades of meaning lurked behind the sense of a word! His eyes strayed to the shoulder bag that the youth had put down beside him. Even though the youth had kept its contents hidden from him, he could guess what was inside. This object inside the bag ought to have evoked fear in him. It should have been the very symbol of all that was to be feared. However, strangely enough, he ceased to worry when he heard the youth's words. Without his realizing it, the youth's feeling had spread to his mind. There was no danger here, and so there was no need to be alert. Neither soldiers nor security men would come here. But, for him, what danger could there be from soldiers and security men? Was he not endangered by the contents of that bag, instead? Yet, surprisingly, as soon as the youth said that there was no danger here, his mind had been emptied of all fear. And the other strange fact was that when they had been bicycling to this place, and indeed, even now, the contents of that bag imparted a sense of security, a sense of reliance, not just to the youth alone, but also to him.

As if to prove that there was no danger, the youth said, 'I am feeling quite warm. I'll have a dip in the water. Will you come?'

He was also feeling the heat. It was not yet summer. Still, the weather was hot, and he felt the oppressive humidity. But he did not wish to bathe at that odd hour. It would be inconvenient if he were to catch a cold or a cough. For him, as well as for the youth, it would be inconvenient. And also for the organization to which the youth belonged. They had to change their halting places frequently.

Shaking his head, he conveyed his refusal.

The youth took out a homespun towel, a gamusa from the bag, and plunged into the stream. The bag remained on the rock. The stream had only a moderate amount of water. Unconcernedly, the youth began to bathe.

Once more, his eyes strayed to the bag. How carelessly the youth had left it lying there! Sometimes, he was amazed. It was as though the youth and he had secretly developed some kind of understanding between themselves. The weapon inside the bag was the sign of a relationship between the youth and himself. But for quite some time now, it was as though a change for the better had overtaken that relationship. This changed relationship was illustrated by the carelessly-thrown bag. It was a portent not of danger, but of something else. He was a prisoner of faith; the youth trusted him not to attempt an escape. If he so wished, he could pick up the weapon inside the bag and escape. But he knew that he would not do so. This incident of the carelessly-thrown bag seemed to change the very nature of his captivity.

There was a grassy patch beside the rock. Near it was a tree which shaded the grass. He went to this patch of grass and lay there on his back. He thought that he would rest till the youth finished his bath. He looked at the branches of the tree above him. A beautiful bird of many colours was sitting silently on one of the branches. He remained gazing at the bird. An often-heard phrase came to his mind. 'Free as a bird.' He was not very familiar with the world of nature. He could not identify the bird. Perhaps it was a kingfisher? It had a long beak and a blue body. Perhaps there were fish in the stream. That was why the bird could not leave the place. It was bound by an invisible bond. As free as a bird!

The youth came splashing out from the water. The kingfisher suddenly took wing. Perhaps it had been frightened by the sound of the youth's footsteps.

The youth put on his clothes again. Having wrung out the wet gamusa, he put it back into the bag. He slung the bag on his shoulder, and, looking at him, said, 'Come, let us leave. We must reach the village before it gets dark.'

Both of them climbed onto their bicycles again. He rode in front, the youth followed. The hostage and his keeper. Both were now pedalling with the same idea in mind. A safe shelter from the soldiers and the security forces. It was as though he himself had arranged his own captivity. When news of the soldiers' approach reached them, he felt the same anxiety as the youth and the others of the youth's organization. And when they came to know that the soldiers had moved away, or when they reached a safe shelter, along with them, he, too, felt the same relief.

The narrow path became somewhat broader. This meant that their destination was not too far away now. He noticed the tracks made by bullock-carts on the path. The youth's bicycle was now moving alongside his own. He looked at the youth. His face was calm and unconcerned. It was as though he was confident that there was now no possibility of either the security forces or the soldiers coming here. The unemotional state reflected in the youth's face spread to his own mind. Once more, his eyes strayed to the carelessly-slung bag on the youth's shoulder. It was as though the lethal weapon inside that bag was only fulfilling a formal purpose. The weapon was no longer a harbinger of death. It was not just the sign of the relationship between the youth and himself: it was also its symbol, a symbol that expressed authority. But was it only that?

He was a prisoner at one end of the metallic gun-barrel. But, at its other end, the youth, too, was a prisoner. He suddenly remembered the kingfisher, and the phrase came to his mind again. As free as a bird! But the bird itself was bound to the water in the stream by a strange relationship. He himself was a hostage; the youth was free. But the youth could not abandon him and go away. Side by side with his own captivity, the youth, too, was a prisoner. Until he himself was free, this youth would remain a captive. The power of this lifeless gun mutely controlled their relationship.

Abruptly, the youth halted. From beside a nearby tree, two other youths came towards them. He was a little taken aback. He had not even realized that two people were standing nearby. The youth with him gestured that there was no need for alarm, which meant that the two others were also from the youth's organization. They had a bicycle with them. The youth who had accompanied him asked them something in the ethnic tongue. He appeared to be satisfied with their reply. Once more, he climbed onto his bicycle. The youth asked him to get up on his own bicycle again; the other two also climbed on theirs. All three bicycles now began to pick up speed.

It was almost dark when they reached the village that was their destination. He saw a bamboo platform beside the path leading into the village. Some youths were sitting on this bamboo platform. They had no lethal weapons in their hands. However, they had with them a couple of stout wooden sticks. A kerosene lamp was placed in a corner of the platform. Possibly these boys were there to guard the village. The youth who had accompanied him dismounted from his bicycle and talked to them in their own language. They conveyed their agreements with nods of their heads. Sitting on their bicycles again, the youth and he pedalled towards the village. The two other youths, too, moved along beside them.

It was a tribal village, in a remote area. Looking at the huts there, one could surmise that the economic condition of the villagers was far from sound. The huts had roofs of thatch and bare walls of dry reed with slits between them. It was almost dark. The villagers were busy herding their cattle together. The few people that they encountered showed no curiosity when they saw the strangers. Possibly the youth's organization often brought people to their village in this way.

Signs of extreme poverty were visible in the huts, as well as along the paths of the village. But it looked as though the same poverty had not yet managed to affect the healthy appearance of the few people whom he saw. And the signs of acute poverty that were apparent in the other huts were not quite as visible in the hut before which they eventually halted. Actually, it was not one, but two huts. A one-room hut was beside the main one. Even though its sloping roof was of thatch, its walls were attractively mud-plastered. The compound was clean, and a large storehouse was visible in a corner. There was also an indication of a large plot of cultivated land behind the house. This plot was full of jackfruit and banana plants as well as areca-nut trees and betel creepers. A stout bamboo fence encircled the house, while a bamboo gate barred the entrance.

Looking at him, the youth who had accompanied him, said, 'We shall stay here tonight. This is the home of the village headman. Quite safe, in fact.'

The other two youths pushed aside the gate and, entering the compound, called out for the headman. However, the village elder had gone out and had not yet returned. His son came out of the house instead and conducted them formally into the one-roomed house in the corner.

Inside was an armless, rough-hewn chair. He was asked to sit on it. On one side of the room was a low, wooden cot. Though the sheet that covered the bed was coarse, it was clean. The mild aroma of the plaster of dung and fresh earth was still in the room, which meant that the house had been cleaned not very long ago. The household had received news of their approach on this day itself. Of course, the decision to come here had been taken in haste. They usually shifted during the night. But only that morning they had come to know that a group of soldiers would reach their original hiding place that very afternoon. That was why they had fled on their bicycles in broad daylight. The news of their approach here had been conveyed this morning through a messenger.

The headman's son brought a small bucket of water along with a brass jug and a clean gamusa, and requested him to wash his hands and feet. He was taken to a corner next to the house, which was enclosed by bamboo screens. A large stone slab was laid out in this enclosed space, so that bits of earth would not spatter around. Because it was dark already, a kerosene lamp had been hung from the bamboo screen. Looking at the still undried bamboo of the screen, he realized that these arrangements had been made for his benefit. For them, he was a visitor. Did they know, he wondered, that he was a prisoner? How could they possibly imagine that this man, who seemed to move about so freely, was actually a captive?

After washing his hands and face, he felt quite refreshed. Wiping himself thoroughly with the gamusa, he entered the room once more. This, too, was illuminated by a lamp. The youth was waiting for him there. As soon as he entered, the youth got up from his chair. Even though nothing was said, he understood that there was respect in the gesture.

Instead of sitting on the chair, he went and sat on the bed. He said to the youth, 'Sit down.'

The youth said, 'You must be very tired today. Rest. We may have to stay here for a couple of days this time. Afterwards, we shall go to a safe camp in the hills. We shall have to cross dense jungles. It will be a difficult journey. So rest here for a couple of days and regain your strength.'

The youth took out two tablets from his pocket, and, offering them to him, said, 'Have these.'

He recognized them to be vitamin pills. He did not need vitamin pills for his health now, but, along with the tablets, something else seemed to come to him. Was it the warmth in the youth's gesture? Or some kind of fellow-feeling? Another symbol of their relationship? He wanted to say something, but the youth went out to the veranda without waiting for his reply. He seemed to think that it was necessary only to have that silent communication between them.

As the youth left, he noticed that the bag was slung on his shoulder. It was his constant companion. The weapon gave notice of its identity from inside the bag. It was now an inert tube, the sign of the tense relationship between them.

From the veranda, the youth shouted, 'I shall remain outside.'

But he knew that the youth would not remain outside. The words said to him, in a subtle language, 'I have a duty. I shall perform that duty. But I also trust you. Don't escape from here and break that trust. My duty is inextricably linked to your cooperation.'

The youth's words, 'I shall remain outside', reminded him once more of the relationship between them. Strange, the power of these words! Even amidst the numerous opportunities for escape, these words had shackled him. But had these words conveyed the same meaning during the first few days of his captivity? Of course during those first few days, they had had a powerful strength of a different kind. These words had then evoked mixed feelings of fear, agitation, helplessness, and insecurity.

He heard the sound of footsteps outside. A middle-aged man came inside the room. He understood that this was the head of the household. A small girl followed him in. In her hands was a platter of food. He caught the whiff of cooked chicken. The headman himself had brought a jug of water. With a great deal of care, the headman placed on the floor a mat that lay in a corner of the room. He put the jug beside it, while the little girl arranged the platter on it. Formally, and with humble gestures, the headman then asked him to come for his meal. The headman had brought a gamusa in his hands. This he placed on the mat.

The headman said, 'There is little in our house to offer you. Please don't mind this simple food. The news that you would be coming reached us very late. It is my good fortune that a great leader such as you is staying in my house.'

From the headman's respectful words, it was apparent that the youth had explained his captive's identity in this manner. The headman told him to leave the platter outside the room after he had finished his meal. Turning up the lamp a little, the headman then left the room.

He was extremely hungry. Even though the rice was parboiled, it tasted quite good when he mixed it with the chicken curry. Washing his hands and face on the platter itself, he took it and, opening the door, went out of the room. Sure enough, there were no guards outside. There was no way in which the door could be locked from the outside, either. Keeping the platter in a corner of the veranda, he re-entered the room and closed the door after him.

Sitting on the bed, he took out the notebook from the satchel that he carried with him. For the last three months or so, he had been keeping this journal of his captivity. The youth had brought him this notebook when he had expressed his desire to keep a journal. Out of his total captivity of seven months, he had kept a record of his daily experiences for the last three months. He had also written down, as far as he had been able to, a record of the time before. Those entries, of course, were from memory.

As soon as he closed the door from inside, a sense of captivity engulfed him. When he closed the door, it was as though he had willingly made himself captive. He also felt as though this self-imposed captivity was normal for him. So long as the door had been open, he had not felt like this. The murmur of voices from the other house had created the impression of some link with it. That link was now severed. The room was lonely and silent. There was no opening now on any side. He felt at peace after imprisoning himself.

By not remaining there, the youth who had said, 'I shall remain outside', had placed the prime responsibility for his own captivity on him. As long as the door was open, he had had a sense of unease. What if his mind hindered his feet from discharging that responsibility? What if his mind tempted his feet: 'The open sky is out there, there is freedom outside, go, get away!' And what if his feet really went out through the door? What if they, his feet, refused to accept the bond of that unseen trust? But no, he had shut the door. He had accepted his captivity. He had accepted the discipline of the words, 'I shall remain outside.' And the strange thing was that he felt at peace.

Rifling through the pages of the notebook, he glanced through the previous entries before writing down the experiences of that day. It had become a habit with him to read about the events of the past almost every day. In this manner, he wished to preserve intact the memories of that time.

He had written down the experiences of the first day in the very first page of the diary. On that first day of his captivity, they had put him inside a house and locked the door from outside. 'We shall be outside, don't try to escape.' How harsh, how fearful the words had been that day! They had dragged him out from his own familiar world, and pushed him into another one. The memory of the moment made him shudder. That moment, when another vehicle had stopped before his own. Four gun-wielding youths had dragged him out from his own car, and had forcibly pushed him into the back seat of another vehicle, which had then moved ahead with great speed. That had been a terrifying moment. In a world without reason, he had experienced the danger to his very existence. Later, however, he had realized that the logic of the youths' world was not the same as the logic of reason in his own ordered existence. He had heard them say several words which he himself used, or had read. However, since he could not understand their language, those remained just gestures for him. But even those gestures had the power to create a sense of fear in him. They also used some bookish English and Assamese words. Nation, state, revolution, imperialistic power, national consciousness, government, public, freedom, rights—in their world, the meanings of these words were completely different. The meaning of the word 'security' was also different in their world. This was because they had their own interpretation of the law. The entity that he had always thought of as a 'nation' was not, for them, a nation at all. They had created their own nation. In their eyes, his nation was an imperialist power. He had assumed that he was a citizen of a free country, but they said that he was the lackey of this imperialist power. Those laws which he had always thought of as a haven of security were perceived by them to be the means of state terrorism. Their act of kidnapping was, for him, an act of terrorism; but they viewed it as their duty to their nation. The government which he thought provided them with social and political security was for them an illegitimate government. It was, for them, but a sand bar across the mouth of a river, to be swept away by the flood-waters of revolution. He had read of many revolutions. But with the barrels of their guns pointed at his body, these youths seemed to aim the revolution at him.

They had, of course, reassured him that he himself was quite insignificant. Their dissension was against the 'illegitimate imperialistic national power.' He had been taken hostage because he was the symbol of the repressive security arrangements of that government machinery. The national power accorded importance to symbols such as he, for that power was a repressive force. Repressive acts were carried out in the name of security. If the mask of security was lifted, that power would be revealed in its true self.

They had some demands to make of that machinery which called itself the government. (Some day, they would overthrow that power, but it would take time for the revolution to mature. Therefore, it was necessary for them to get the illegitimate government to accede to some of their demands in this way.) That other nation would grant them their demands, for it was to that imperialistic power's self-interest to have him freed. Because if he died, the mask of security which that power used as an excuse would be ripped apart, and that power would suffer a loss of respect.

However, they had not presented their reasoning in quite that manner. But from what he could understand of their language when they talked with each other, their logic was of this kind. He got the impression that the ideas in the world that he lived in were controlled by a kind of linguistic centre. This was as though surrounded by an electromagnetic field, which held a positive charge for him as well as for people like him who thought in the same way. The linguistic centre of these youths was also surrounded by what, for them, was a positive charge. Both of them were surrounded by positive charges from their perspectives: when both the positives approached, they repelled each other. Even with his bureaucratic attitude (he was an important government officer) he could vaguely discern that both these worlds were deeply influenced by economic realities, and this had become intermingled with politics.

And he had been afraid. He could see no escape, no way out, from the distance, the gulf between their world and his, or from the emptiness that enveloped him.

For a long time, the meaning of their words and their reasoning was hidden from him, like the words of a riddle. They did not inflict any physical torture on him at all. Though their manner of speaking was rough, they were not exactly disrespectful towards him. Once in a while, they also allowed him to exchange letters with those at home. But their ways of thinking clashed repeatedly with his own. He had not been able to trust them. He would feel as though, at any moment, the muzzles of their guns would discharge their bullets into his breast.

But even greater than this physical fear had been the tremendous mental tension that he had felt. The physical hardships that he went through were, of course, quite considerable. Every day, they had to change shelters. He had no settled place to stay in. Nightly, they would wander through the fields, wade through the chest-high waters of rivers, and march through dense jungles and marshes. Yet, he would have shrugged off these physical hardships if he had only been able to trust them. Pushing him into various rooms at night, they would stand guard outside. Occasionally, they would push him inside with the words, 'We shall remain outside. Don't try to escape.' Each word seemed weighted with ridicule, callousness, and cruelty. Each word seemed to express not just his own helplessness, but also that of the national power. As it wounded him, each word became synonymous with terror.

He had been unable to comprehend how a functionary could become the symbol of the government machinery. Yet, they had assumed that by capturing him, they had unerringly dealt a devastating blow to the power of the government. They had thought that the bugle of revolution had been sounded loud and clear.

He had formed the impression that the youths were being guided by a grave error. And, like him, even the youths themselves did not understand what the outcome of that error would be.

He had not understood, either, whether the ideas in his mind were logical or erroneous. But his mistrust of the youths had grown. This mistrust also had a simple reason behind it. His guards had been changed almost every week. By the time he came to know one group of youths who guarded him, they were changed. There was no conversation between him and the youths. Only sometimes, when one or two youths who appeared to be some kind of leaders had come, only then had he had the opportunity to talk. Looking at the unemotional faces of his guards, he had been unable to fathom their thoughts. He had been unable to trust them. Just as they assumed him to be the symbol of the government, he, too, had thought of each one of them as a diminutive symbol of terrorism.

But four months ago, everything had changed. The change had seemed to come from the very day that this youth had come and taken charge. Even within their own positive magnetic fields, both had seemed to discover small negative charges also. This had allowed their minds to meet.

He did not know whether or not the youth was part of the higher echelons of power. But it was apparent that the youth was not just an ordinary guard. For, on many occasions, he took independent decisions without waiting for orders from above. The youth's pronunciation of English words had given him the impression that he was highly educated. Though of a different ethnicity, he spoke Assamese fluently. They talked mostly of everyday matters. Sometimes, however, each of them expressed their opinions and talked of their ideals. The youth professed deep faith in their revolution, but would listen attentively to what he himself had to say. There was never any callousness or disregard in his words.

On the very first day that the youth had taken charge, he had made an arrangement that had seemed to change the very nature of his captivity. Till then, the door had always been locked from outside after he had been put into a room. When the guards were nearby, they had always trained their guns at him. This youth had had no gun in his hands on the first day when he had come to him. He had not brought along other guards, either. He had enquired into his well-being, and had also given him news of his family. As he was leaving, he had said, 'Latch the door from inside. I shall be outside. Don't be afraid.' He had gently shut the door behind him.

'Don't be afraid.' These words had had a strange affect on him. The emptiness, the sense of discord that he had felt all these days, had seemed to vanish in a moment. Because the words 'Don't be afraid' followed them, the meaning of the sentence 'I shall be outside', too, had seemed to change. The difference between the two sentences 'Don't try to escape' and 'Don't be afraid' seemed to represent two completely different ways of viewing the same situation.

However, the other circumstances remained unchanged. He had to be shifted frequently from one place to another. They had moved from village to village at night, stung by mosquitoes and bugs. There was no question of staying anywhere for any length of time. For the organization that the youth belonged to believed in always being in a state of extreme alertness. The change was in his own mental condition. He was a hostage, the youth was his keeper. Yet, somehow, without their being aware of it, this relationship had now changed. In spite of the difference in their ages, there developed between them a bond of companionship.

The youth had never behaved like a guard. Certainly, he always carried a gun in his bag. No doubt, the gun was the sign of their relationship, but that sign had undergone a basic change. From a sign of terror, it had become a sign of trust.

And so while wandering on their journeys from village to village, through hills and valleys, sometimes he was the youth's teacher, while the youth was his disciple. Every now and again, the youth would mention some famous writer. At these times, the fact that he was very well-read had been a great help. He had been happy to be able to talk about those writers and their work. The youth then listened to him like an attentive student. But when the subjects were those relating to nature, rural life, agriculture, farming, and so on, the youth became the teacher, and he the student. He had no clear idea about the relationship between man and nature. In a strange way, this life of captivity helped him to augment the store of knowledge that he had had in his state of freedom.

After reaching a village, on one occasion, he had fallen seriously ill. The high fever made him pass out several times. Even in his semi-conscious state, he had been aware that the youth had secretly gone and fetched a doctor from a distant city. On becoming conscious, he had seen the youth sitting beside his bed. On his face there had been an expression of great anxiety. When the fever had finally subsided, he had come to know from the head of that household, that the youth had not stirred from his side until he came around. The youth had given him his medicines, heated water for him, sponged down his body, put cold compresses on his forehead, and had even cleaned up his excrement, all in an astonishingly compassionate way. However, the youth had not expressed any emotion after he had recovered. He had merely said, 'Your family was not informed of your illness. They would have been worried. Hope you don't mind.' He had mumbled his gratitude.

After his fever had subsided, they had to remain for quite some time in the same village till he had recovered his strength. During this period, the two of them had discussed a variety of topics. At that time, he had expressed a desire to keep a journal. He had thought that the youth would not agree to his keeping an account of his captivity. But the youth had readily agreed, and had brought him a notebook the very next day. After writing down his entries, he would always show them to the youth, who would read them. Sometimes, the youth would nod his head, as though he had been able to catch a glimpse of his soul through these entries in his journal. After his illness, he had felt a greater sense of uncertainty. His conscious mind had not been aware of this. But the youth, reading aloud from his journal, had pointed out to him how the uncertainty of his subconscious mind was revealed in these entries.

After he had gained some strength, it was necessary once more for the youth to change their halting places frequently. Sometimes, while pondering on the uncertainty of his ever being freed, he would become restless. This would be reflected in his journal.

One day, while reading these entries, the youth had said, 'You are impatient to be free, aren't you? But look, your government is not concerned about you at all. We have sent them some terms and conditions. We can release you as soon as those conditions are met.'

He had asked, 'And if they don't agree to your terms?'

On hearing his question, the youth was at a loss for words. After a while, he had said with a smile, 'In that case, you will have to become one of us. Would you mind?'

In the end, he had stopped thinking of freedom. He had accepted his captivity as the normal condition of his life now.

Around this time, the youth had relaxed the vigilance that surrounded his captivity. After saying, 'I shall be outside', the youth would go somewhere else instead of standing guard outside. From the very beginning, the youth had always carried his gun around unobtrusively, so that it had remained invisible to him. Sometimes, he would leave the bag containing the gun lying near him. It seemed as though without any outward sign, the youth was giving him numerous opportunities to escape. But on the other hand, even in the midst of these unlimited opportunities, the youth had seemed to bind him to himself with an invisible bond.

Around this time, also, the news that groups of soldiers, as well as the police, were searching these areas thoroughly for him had begun to trickle in. But he had not viewed these bits of information as something to be happy about. When news of the soldiers' approach would reach them, he, too, would become anxious. His mind, too, would clamour to go with the youth to a place of 'safety'. A part of his conscious mind understood that this kind of behaviour would be considered illogical by everybody in his own world. Even then, whenever he heard of the approach of the soldiers seeking to free him, he would think of safety as a distance between those soldiers and himself. Safety, for him, was the gun in the youth's hands.

Even today, when they received the news of the approach of soldiers, they had immediately fled to the shelter of this village. After settling him down in this room, the youth had gone off somewhere else, perhaps to the main house, to sleep. And in the meantime, he had latched the door and accepted his captivity willingly.

As on other days, now, too, he wrote down the events of the day. Swallowing the two tablets that the youth had given him with a draught of water, he lay down on the rough bed. The safety of the bed seemed to embrace him.

He woke up at dawn to the sound of birdsong. Unlatching the door, he went out to the veranda. The head of the household seemed to have been waiting for him to emerge from his room. With much ceremony, he brought a cane stool and, placing it in the veranda, requested him to sit on it. The little girl who had brought him his food the previous night, now brought him a bowl of black tea along with molasses. The others of the family appeared to be keeping a respectful distance from the 'leader.' Even though there was no milk in the tea, he quite enjoyed sipping it from the bowl along with the molasses.

The two youths who had brought them here the previous evening, now appeared on the bicycle. They looked around for the youth who was his guard. On hearing their voices, the youth came out from the other house. They informed him at once that this place was no longer safe. They had met some soldiers just a few kilometres away. The soldiers had stopped and searched them, and had asked them if they knew whether some strangers had come this way. They, however, had sent the soldiers in the direction of a distant village.

Listening to them, the youth said, 'We shall have to move camp today. These villages are not safe any more.'

For some time now, he had been on the verge of asking the youth a question. Because of a sense of hesitation in his mind, it had remained unasked. But today, he abruptly questioned, 'What will you do if the soldiers surround the house and try to rescue me?'

The youth seemed unprepared for this sudden question. He did not answer immediately, but remained staring at him. After a while, the youth asked softly in return, 'Tell me, what will you do?'

This question in reply to his own startled him. He did not know how to reply.

The youth continued, 'If those circumstances arise, I shall have no choice but to execute you.'

On hearing this, he remained staring dazedly at the youth's face. This same youth had nursed him devotedly to health through a serious illness, yet he was now talking quite unconcernedly of executing him!

The youth seemed to understand his feelings. He said, 'You are not our enemy. But don't have any illusions. A government seeks legitimacy by protecting its citizens. But we have to prove that your government cannot ensure the safety of its citizens. Your death will not be caused by me, or by our organization. Your government will be the cause of your death. If our revolution is to succeed, it will be my duty to kill you if those circumstances arise.'

Strange logic! He knew that no law of any country would ever accept this logic as just. But in the youth's world, it was this logic that had entrenched itself. He felt that the youth had no other alternative than to take this stand. The thought of his own execution had caused an upheaval in his mind. But this upheaval now subsided. He felt quite calm. He seemed to leave his own sphere of logic and step into the youth's world. Even the words 'revolution', 'legality', 'justice', and so on acquired different meanings in this other world.

It was decided that they would begin their journey to the camp that very evening.

In the meantime, the youth sent off some village lads to check the safety of the route along which they were to travel. One of these boys brought back devastating news while they were having their afternoon meal. The soldiers had, in the meantime, searched out the camp, and had destroyed it that morning. There was, therefore, no question of going there now. Even though this hamlet was no longer as safe as it had been before, they would have to spend the night here. Tomorrow, they would move again in search of a place of safety.

The youth busied himself in strengthening the security arrangements for the night. Just before dusk, several new faces appeared. He got a hint of their weapons inside their bags. The youth who was his guard gave them many instructions and they went off in various directions to guard the paths entering the village. The youth also sent the headman and his family to another house for the night.

The youth said to him, 'We shall make special arrangements for this night. For your own safety, I shall have to spend the night in your room. Several of our freedom fighters will stand guard around the house. If we can see this night through, we can go to another place in the morning.'

From the youth's words, he understood that the 'freedom fighters' had come to this village to secure his captivity.

They had their evening meal even before it grew dark. After a while, darkness engulfed the surroundings. The youth was with him in the dim lamplight of the room. The silent, lonely surroundings seemed to throb. The youth did not speak. Extremely alert, he remained standing beside the door. Today, he carried the lethal weapon in his hand openly. He himself remained sitting motionless on the bed.

Looking at him, the youth said, 'Go to sleep. I shall remain awake.'

But he remained sitting where he was. Even if he wished to sleep, would sleep come to him this night?

Perhaps he dozed. He woke up with a start when one of the youths, who stood guard outside, banged the door and entered the room. This boy said something to the youth who guarded him. He then went out again, after shutting the door behind him.

The youth said, 'The enemy has surrounded us on all sides.' He looked at the youth. Their eyes met. The youth's gaze was steady and unblinking. He now gestured to him to leave the bed and come forward.

He heard some explosions outside. He realized that the sounds were not those of crackers. They were the sounds of gunfire. He got down from the bed and stood before the youth.

The youth trained the gun at his breast.

He realized that the final moment of his captivity had arrived. Could the final moment be this long?

Just then, he heard the sounds of several guns being fired at the same time. He thought, 'So this is what death is like.'

But why was he still conscious?

Everything seemed to happen at once. He saw great gobs of blood gushing out from the youth's mouth. His body was riddled with bullets. The gun slid from his hand, and his lifeless body crashed to the ground like a felled tree.

The final moment of his captivity had not turned into the moment of his death. For the youth had not fired his gun. He had lowered it instead. And at that very moment, countless bullets had crashed into the youth's body.

Several soldiers rushed into the room. One of them extended his hand towards him. He said, 'I'm Captain Batra. Thank God! You are safe.'

Captain Batra had an RT set in his hands. The instrument crackled and Captain Batra spoke into it: 'Operation successful. Target safe. One terrorist killed.'

Terrorist! The word crashed against the magnetic centre in his skull, where it exploded loudly. Two words seemed to drag themselves agonizingly out from his mouth, 'Aaah, no!'

He sat beside the lifeless body of the youth. Placing his hand on his cold forehead, he remained staring at the youth's open, lifeless eyes.

Captain Batra did not stop him. Standing beside the dead body, Captain Batra paid his formal respects by touching his cap with his hand.

Translated by Mitra Phukan

A NIGHT WITH ARPITA

DEBABRATA DAS

The side berth was created by lowering the backrests of the two single seats along the aisle of the compartment. Crouching in one corner of that berth, chin in hands, eyes looking out of the window, could the expression on her face be called disinterest, or was it heartache? On the other hand, she had not the slightest curiosity about what was going on inside the compartment. Wrapping the loose end of her sari tightly around the upper half of her body, she had even withdrawn her feet into the cavity created by the wrapped lower end of her sari. Her presence in the compartment seemed more like an absence; she seemed completely oblivious and unaware of her surroundings; her look betrayed a sense of resignation or, perhaps, of surrender.

Having installed myself in the compartment, the sense of capitulation that was evident in her demeanour, attracted me to her the very first time that I looked at her closely. I told myself that if I wrote a story someday on the girl, I would name her 'Arpita', the one who offers herself. Arpita what? Ganguly or Acharya, Roy or Majumdar? Because on hearing Hindi strewn with Bengali words spoken by the girl's father (who had animatedly complained to the waiter about the quality of the fish served with the meal), I was certain that the girl was not an Assamese disguised in a sari; she was actually a Bengali. Regardless of whether she was Assamese or Bengali, she was basically a girl, a more or less pretty girl, and she was presently in another world, completely oblivious to her surroundings. Her entire being was concentrated on a point in the darkness of the world outside the compartment, a point that could easily be defined as infinity. Her absent-minded beauty tugged at my curiosity. Puffing at my Charminar cigarette, I kept staring at her, from my middle berth, in the 3-tier compartment.

Just then Kiran returned from the washroom and broke my reverie, 'What is this? Why are you already in bed? You don't mean to go to bed so early, do you?'

This story is actually the story of Arpita and me. I am the hero, Arpita the heroine. Apart from the two of us, there is no need for anyone else in this story. The problem, however, is that in order to be able to describe the chain of events, the inclusion of some redundant characters becomes necessary; their presence in the story is not essential, but without them, it is difficult to narrate what happened. Among those unnecessary characters, one is my friend, Kiran Debnath; we work in the same office and it is on official work that both of us were travelling by train to another city. We had to travel at very short notice, so we had no reserved train seats; therefore, the second unnecessary character, Krishna, becomes necessary. Krishna lives in our neighbourhood; a young man barely out of his teens, he had recently joined the NF Railway as a Train Ticket Inspector, or TTI in short. The moment I saw him at the train station, I was relieved—we wouldn't have to travel in the crowded, unreserved compartment, after all. Since Krishna was there, with his help, we would get at least two sitting seats for ourselves. But luckily, there was not a huge rush that day and after doing the rounds, Krishna arranged two sleeping berths in a 3-tier compartment for us. The sleeper charges for a night were five rupees fifty-paisa each, so eleven rupees in all. I gave him three five-rupee notes. He forgot to return the change. A little while after the train started, another uniformed ticket checker came and wrote out our reservation slips.

The fourth unnecessary character in this story is Arpita's father, who, after finishing the long and animated argument with the waiter about the stale fish served for dinner, turned his attention to his daughter, who was still staring out of the window. He told her to lie down and go to sleep and gave her other sundry bits of advice; all were met with monosyllabic answers. He then climbed up to the upper berth above his daughter and in a little while, with his snoring, gave proof that he was fast asleep. This is also the last time I will mention these unnecessary characters, except for Kiran.

I told Kiran that we had a lot to do the next day. We would have to go through all the documents and records at our branch office in the town we were travelling to. It was not clear whether we would have any free time at all. So, instead of sitting up chatting till late into the night, since we had secured two sleeping berths, it might be wiser to go to sleep. Like a good boy, Kiran immediately obeyed my directive and went to sleep in the lower berth below me.

To tell the truth, I was not at all sleepy. If I had wanted to or if we were somewhere else, I would have easily chatted with Kiran for an hour or two. But at that moment, in that situation, the desire to single-mindedly enjoy the distracted attractiveness of a beautiful girl made me give up the wish to chat with Kiran.

Arpita sat immersed in herself on the rattling train, on that otherwise still night, ignoring the silent presence of the other passengers sleeping in the compartment. No exam results had been declared recently. Then why was Arpita so single-mindedly distracted and sad? Was her pain intensely personal? Could it be that some sly lover had deviously cheated her and had gone away, after having made a thousand promises of many-hued rainbows and of eternal love? Or was there some complication with a recent wedding proposal, the partner that her parents had chosen for her had seen her and approved of her but was demanding a huge dowry from them, as a result of which it was completely impossible for her to leave her parents' home? What could it be? What was her real story? Where were the keys to her closet of sorrow? What was the reason for her lack of faith in the present, evident in the way in which she was sitting, betraying the proud hurt resulting from all the injustices that may have been done to her? What was the real shape and form of the actual reason for her sorrow? Although many alternative scenarios were racing around in my mind, I was not sure when, but at some point, my eyelids dropped and I fell asleep. Even then, Arpita was sitting motionless in her earlier position and staring out of the window.

The lights of the compartment had been switched off a long time ago. Only the blue night lamps were aglow here and there. There was blue light in the compartment. Blue is the colour of sorrow, an artist friend had once told me. Covering her face and head with blue light, the girl kept sitting there, carelessly, inattentively. That was the last memory I have of that night before I fell asleep. Arpita engulfed in blue. Arpita engulfed in sadness. That night I woke up twice. The first time, I got up on hearing a strange sound. The sound of sobbing. The sound was coming from Arpita's bed. Opening my eyes, I saw Arpita lying on her berth with her face to the wall weeping noisily. (The death of a loved one? Failure in an exam? The desertion of a lover or some complication at her wedding?) Not able to decide how proper it would be to try to console an unknown woman in the middle of the night when everyone else was asleep, I fell asleep again. In the corner of my mind, however, there was a sort of unhappiness about my helplessness, at my inability to do anything to stop her from crying.

The second time I woke up just like that. Raising my left hand to look at the time, my eyes moved in the direction of Arpita's bed. O God! The bed was empty! Where did the girl go at this hour? To the washroom? Yes, she might have gone to the washroom. When the panic in my mind receded, I looked around the compartment. Arpita's father was fast asleep. So was Kiran. I waited for a couple of minutes. When Arpita did not return,

I got down from my berth and started walking towards the washroom.

My heart missed a beat at what I saw. The door of the compartment near the toilet was open. Arpita was hanging there, precariously, dangerously, holding on to a rod of the door. If her grip on the rod slackened even momentarily, she could easily be thrown out of the train that was moving, definitely, at forty or fifty kilometres per hour.

The first thought that struck my mind like lightning on seeing Arpita's body, hanging there between life and death, was suicide. The girl was about to commit suicide. At that moment, the length of a whole corridor separated me from her. There was no way for me to rush and stop her. Moreover, my senses were still benumbed, having woken up just moments ago and seeing such a ghastly sight. I completely forgot the responsibility I had of rushing to her and pulling her back into the compartment.

But rather than being condemned to being a silent and helpless witness to a sad death, something unusual happened in front of my eyes. Arpita, who was hanging outside the compartment, holding on to the rod of the door, flung herself inside the compartment, still holding on to the rod with both hands. Hiding her head between her arms, she started to weep. Perhaps she was sobbing on realizing that she did not possess the courage, or perhaps the cowardice, to commit suicide. The tragedy did not happen. I started breathing again.

I, who had stood frozen like a statue all this while, moved forward now. I put my hands on her shoulders. She raised her tearful face and looked at me. I tried as hard as I could to bring signs of concern, sympathy, and kindness into my eyes. Turning towards me, Arpita embraced me with both her arms and started crying uncontrollably. My shoulder was now the support for her body. My heart became the custodian of her grief. I tried very hard to fulfil my role adequately as her rescuer and her refuge. I slowly ran my hand over her hair...sometimes also over her shoulder. Having handed over the care of her body and her pain to a kind stranger, she was still sobbing, engrossed in regret at her total failure. By then, I had been raised to the level of a great soul. It was as if I had sucked in all the pain of all suffering humanity into my broad bosom. As if all deprived and desperate humans had found, through my reassurance and support, their path to liberation, an alternative to suicide, the base to start all over again. I embraced Arpita passionately. There had been no exchange of words—either of complaint or of reassurance—between us. We were both quiet in our togetherness. As if silence was a shelter adequate for both of us.

Embracing each other, we stood there silently, in the corridor in front of the washroom. For the wretched girl, it was enough to know that there was at least one supporter left in this cruel world. And for the fake that I was, it was enough that I had been able to reassure one wretched soul at least. It was surprising that not a single person from our compartment woke up although such a lot had happened. Tomorrow, when I would tell Kiran this strange story, he would be astounded and surprised. He would be sorry for not having woken up and for not having paid more attention to the girl. And then, slowly, he would forget the incident.

I looked at her again from my berth. She had fallen asleep with a strange look of calm on her face, like the still landscape after a huge storm. I could not fall asleep again. I was feeling hot. I took off my kurta, put it under my pillow, and lay down again. The mixed smell of Arpita's lipstick, powder, and sweat on my kurta began to bother me. I looked at Arpita again—her sleeping body had the innocent beauty of a child. There was no sign of sorrow in it now. There was a deep sense of peace in her countenance.

We reached our destination very early in the morning. We disembarked with our bedding and luggage. Arpita was still fast asleep, totally at ease. Her father was sitting by her feet and smoking his 'mixture' nonchalantly. Kiran and I followed the coolie to the gate. I don't know why but suddenly I turned and looked towards our compartment. Arpita's face was at the window. In the meanwhile, she had woken up from her sleep and was sitting up. She was looking exactly in my direction through the window. Our eyes met. There was a strange expression on her face. I was caught out. What was it in her eyes? Was it gratitude or was it disdain at my running away from her quietly—contempt? I could not decipher the meaning of her expression. Both I and the hero depart from the story at this point, just like that.

There remains some difficulty about the reliability of the incident described. Even if everyone else believes it, after reading the story, at least Kiran will laugh unbelievingly, 'You have really made up a big story, I was with you all the while, so much happened and I did not get even the faintest inkling. You have really made up a very nice story.' And I will respond immediately, 'No, no, I did not make up this story, it really happened....' Not allowing me to continue, he will say, 'Don't tell such lies, at least not in front of me, do you understand? If it had really happened, you would have told me the whole thing at least the day after, wouldn't you have? The whole story is a figment of your imagination.' Then I will put on a sly smile and reply in this way, 'My dear friend, some unusual incidents in one's life are such that they have to remain within oneself, they cannot be shared, even with one's closest friends...that is why....'

During my student days, I had done a lot towards trying to remove pain and poverty from this world, from our country—I had gone to our tea gardens, to the factories and mills. Wading through the flood waters in Lakhimpur and Kamrup, I had tried to go to the farmers and labourers to figure out their source of pain and sorrow. Now it all seems like child's play. Now I am a civil servant. I have sold my mind, honour, and conscience and am spending my days in great comfort. Still, at times, I think that maybe I could achieve some satisfaction if I did at least something for suffering humanity. That is why I created this incident above, to see myself in the role of the rescuer and comforter of the poor and sorrowful Arpita. Regardless of whether Kiran and the others believe me or not, if such an incident had happened that night, I would have gained peace in being able to comfort Arpita. Of course, I am not completely sure that I would have had the courage to behave like that with Arpita in the middle of the night, in the absent presence of a compartment full of sleeping people. I would have probably not silently concealed Arpita's mistake or her shame at wanting to commit suicide and would have probably raised a ruckus, and on hearing that commotion, perhaps Arpita would have got desperate and she might have actually jumped out of the train.

Translated by Meenaxi Barkotoki

THE HUNT
PUROBI BORMUDOI

A dying afternoon in late Aghon. There is a light mist in the December air. The trees have begun to shed their leaves. With their hands clasped tightly together, and their heads resting on their knees, the trees seem to be huddled up to ward off the chill. It is colder at Biswanath Chariali than it is in Guwahati. Here, the cold is a definite presence. It creeps silently through the many layers of warm clothing, and enters the body.

Sitting in the Maruti Gypsy driven by Rahim, an experienced chauffeur, three people are talking about the cold weather. They are Engineer Choudhury, Dr Saikia, and their friend, Hazarika. Hazarika is the contemporary of Choudhury and Saikia, and their companion at card games. They had come from Guwahati to Biswanath Chariali yesterday. Amol, a relative of the doctor's, is accompanying them for the first time. He has recently joined service, and is distantly related to the doctor, being a nephew to him. At this time, they are journeying towards Ahmed's house.

The vehicle is moving forward slowly. Both Hazarika and Choudhury know the location of Ahmed's house. In accordance with what has been planned beforehand, two youths have already been sent ahead to Ahmed's house. Ahmed is probably ready to receive them.

The two middle-aged men have come from Guwahati in order to hunt at the Pabhoi Reserved Forest. These days, they get bored rather easily. After amassing vast fortunes, and earning the respect of society, they sometimes feel a great sense of despair when they begin to think that they have completed their life's work. At times such as these, they feel weary of life. It is to escape this feeling that they sometimes come to hunt game. As kings and emperors of the past came out on royal hunts, so, too, do these men come out on hunting trips, in order to escape despair, weariness, a feeling of emptiness, and the clamour within their hearts. They themselves cannot gauge whether they are relieved of these feelings of despair and of the clamour in their hearts after they return home from the hunt.

Biswanath Chariali is gradually turning into a small city. After crossing this small city, the vehicle enters a small rural path. Age has descended on the leaves of the trees lining both sides of the lane. The trees are beginning to shed their leaves. The dreary winter sky is visible through the bare branches of the leafless trees. The soft winter sun is slanting down the western sky. The van is moving forward on the twisty, unmetalled village road towards Ahmed's house. Every now and again, flocks of wild geese fly up, blocking the sky from view.

Amol, the doctor's distantly-related nephew, had landed a job as soon as he had finished his studies. He is but a youth, as unformed as a tender cucumber. He has been intently observing the skies and the hazy, greyish villages. It is impossible to gauge his thoughts. The faces of the people sitting in front clearly reflect their feelings. Joy—the joy of the hunt. A kind of gravity has descended on their visages, like the kings and emperors of old and like them, these men, too, are nonchalant and unconcerned. They are indifferent to a man ineffectually trying to ward off the chill with his woollen clothes by the side of the road.

The vehicle is going towards Ahmed's house. Ahmed is an expert shikari, a hunter. There is no other shikari to rival Ahmed in this region. The passionate hunters in the vehicle hire Ahmed whenever they come for a shikar here. Ahmed's domestic condition is not very satisfactory. He can barely support his wife and three children. He once had a bit of cultivable land, but it is not in his possession now. Ahmed's only income comes from hiring himself out as a shikari. Ahmed says that his wife and children do not approve of this mode of earning a living at all. But he is not fit for any other kind of work. He has, therefore, taken up this livelihood only because he has no other option. As soon as his son grows up and begins to earn, Ahmed will give up hunting and set up a small shop.

The vehicle moves forward slowly, and stops at the entrance to Ahmed's house. The men alight and sit on a bench on the veranda. Ahmed's wife comes out with a bota, a salver of areca nuts and betel leaves in her hands. Her face is crushed under some kind of mental strain. Ahmed, the shikari, comes out while the men are still chewing on the areca nuts.

Hardship and privation have put a stamp of sorrow on Ahmed's six-foot frame. He is slightly stooped. The veins stand out in his arms, the skin on his face is wrinkled, and more than half the hair on his head is white. Ahmed is wearing the baggy and rather soiled khaki outfit that is his costume while he is out hunting. On his feet is a pair of boots. In one hand he carries his gun, while a bandolier is strapped across his chest. There is not a single bullet in the bandolier.

The engineer, Choudhury, takes out the bullets from his pouch, and slots them, one by one, into Ahmed's bandolier. For a while, Ahmed leans on the gun, as motionless as a statue carved from stone. The two youths who had been sent ahead to help with the arrangements have already carried hot cases containing parathas and chicken curry, as well as bottles of drinking water, into the vehicle.

All of them climb into the Gypsy. Ahmed's wife remains looking after the departing men with a pitiful look in her eyes. She has covered her head with the end of her sari. Her face is not clearly visible. But her eyes, glistening like those of a deer hiding in the forest, can be seen from quite some distance away.

Slowly, the wheels begin to turn. As the vehicle moves, it leaves behind its tracks on the dusty, unmetalled dirt road. Clouds of dust are churned up. The dust covers the leaves of the trees and the vegetation by the wayside in a thick layer. The vehicle crosses the small city of Biswanath Chariali once more. It is a bustling place, as busy and full of activity as a house where a wedding is taking place. The vehicle reaches the crossroads at Pabhoi, at the place where five roads meet. Rahim, the driver, comes to the back seat. Hazarika will drive the vehicle from this point onwards.

The Gypsy moves ahead on the winding lane that goes past the Dholi tea estate. There is an aroma of fresh tea leaves. The shade trees over the tea bushes are bare of leaves. The lane itself is damp. It had drizzled here a few days ago, and the lane still retains some of that moisture. The lane is topped with cinders. From afar, it looks like the black border on the sari of a young female tea garden labourer. The aroma of the sweat of the toiling labourers mingles with the fragrance of the tea leaves. A few clumps of bamboo are scattered here and there by the side of the cindered track. The ground under these stands of bamboo is damper, for the shade has prevented the sun from falling on it. This late afternoon is preparing to curl up under a quilt. A rooster can be heard crowing from the labour lines. The setting sun waits just over the topmost branch of the bare trees. It will climb down in a short while, and reach the spot where the sky resembles an upturned bowl. Soon, birds will fly home and settle on these bare branches to raucously discuss the events of their day. The sky is ablaze with the glow of the setting sun, like a variegated canvas. It seems that a dexterous hand has just now painted the scene, with its setting sun, bare trees, tea bushes, and the smoke-grey evening curled up in that December chill.

Gradually, the dust raised by the hooves of the flocks of homeward-bound cattle subsides. A few labourers warming themselves on small bonfires in front of their homes are visible. A couple of dogs are curled up near the warmth of the fires. The sun vanishes into the upended bowl of the sky. For a while, the light from the sun remains hanging on the leaves and branches. A little later, the light descends to the earth, and merges with it. Even as one watches, darkness possesses the path that snakes through the tea bushes.

The vehicle is new. It moves forward noiselessly. Ahmed begins to relate his hunting tales, as he has done on previous occasions, also. The others have heard them all several times before. They listen to him quietly this time too. This is Amol's first hunt. All this time, he has been looking out abstractedly at the world outside the vehicle's windows. Now, with the same abstractedness, he enters the world of Ahmed's hunting tale. Choudhury opens a bottle of liquor expertly, unhampered by the shaking of the vehicle. He pours out the drinks and the soda, and hands out the glasses to everybody sitting on the front seats. He then passes the half-empty bottle to those sitting at the back.

Glasses, bottles, and packets of savouries begin to move up and down the length of the Gypsy at regular intervals. Hazarika, sitting on the driver's seat, steadily empties one glass after another of alcohol, even as he drives on slowly. Amol is the youngest of the lot. In addition, he is, after all, also a nephew of some kind of the doctor's. He hesitates at first. But he is told that none of the usual rules or relationships are valid when out on a hunt. On a *shikar*, all family relationships, age constraints, education, money, or power become meaningless. All are equal. All are the same—hunters, shikaris.

The others sitting in the front and back of the vehicle are all people who are in full control over both mind and body. Only Amol is of tender years. Gradually, he, too, begins to exert control over his mind and body. Gradually, he begins to lose his diffidence and inhibitions about drinking or smoking in front of his seniors. As soon as the inflammatory liquid burns into his belly, his mouth, too, begins to spout equally inflammatory speeches. Like the drab time of the day that wishes to curl up under the quilt, the dank thoughts in his mind vanish. He seems to come awake under the spell of some supernatural power. First, he begins to whistle a popular Hindi film tune. Later, he is heard singing the same song.

Outside, donning the garment of darkness, Nature waits motionless. At times, the music of the whistling wind outside can be heard over Amol's Hindi song. The trees are getting denser. The tea garden has been left far behind. The lights of the vehicle beam forth for a long distance through the shadows of the trees on the road ahead. The light of the headlamps and the shadows of the trees dance together deliriously in an endless line.

The van moves forward at a slow and steady pace. The chiaroscuro of light and shade, too, moves forward. The play of light and shade looks like the madwoman who sits at the crossroads with her unkempt, matted, and unmanageable locks. At other times, it resembles a serious, affectionate, and loving patriarch. Occasionally, the aroma of damp earth and the odour of the forest permeate the atmosphere, adding enchantment to the damp winter evening. In the beam of the vehicle's lights, a few trees in the distance also resemble wise and holy sages immersed in deep and inviolable meditation.

It is quite dark when the Gypsy halts in front of the check gate at the entrance of the Reserved Forest. The light clumps together in the dense mist. A truck carrying timber waits in front of the gate. The truck driver is speaking in low tones with the gatekeeper. The gateman allows the truck to leave, and comes towards the Gypsy. Once more, words are murmured in low tones. Both the passengers in the car and the gateman know very well that the check gates at the entrances of reserved forests are there only to facilitate the entry and exit of timber smugglers and those who hunt wild game illegally.

After an understanding is reached at the gates, the vehicle enters the unprotected Reserved Forest. The jungle becomes even denser from this point onwards. Sometimes, the vegetation encroaches upon the dirt track. The trees meet in a green canopy over the track. The ground beneath the trees is piled with the dead leaves of winter. There is a rustling sound as small animals, frightened by the sound of the vehicle and the beam of its headlights, flee over the dead leaves. Ahmed listens to the variety of rustling sounds, and, differentiating between the various kinds, says, 'This is a rabbit, this is a fawn, this is a leopard, this is a jackal, this a civet cat. Now this is the patter of the feet of a wild cat.'

Ahmed is a very experienced shikari. It is said that there is a tigress in this very jungle with which Ahmed is on familiar terms. Ahmed avers that he can recognize the sound of her footsteps even in the dark. She, too, recognizes Ahmed's footsteps. She never harms him. Once the tigress, along with two of her cubs, was napping behind a bush by the side of the track. The cubs were playing with the tigress's twitching tail just as kittens frolic with their mother. One of Ahmed's companions had said, 'Shoot her between her eyes....' Ahmed had replied, 'She is a friend of mine, till today she has not caused me any difficulty. I warn you, don't shoot her, or else....' It was only after the tigress had left with her cubs, twitching her tail and glancing back at Ahmed, that the other men had breathed easily again. It seems that there is also an elephant here in the jungle that Ahmed knows very well. He steps aside whenever he sees Ahmed, leaving him free to move on.

The bottle has not yet been emptied. Ahmed is chattering nineteen to the dozen. Amol has stopped whistling Hindi film tunes and is listening intently to Ahmed's words. A thick cover of darkness has eclipsed the jungle. It is only possible to guess what is going on, or what creatures lurk, in the areas left untouched by the beams of the vehicle. The two youths, Robin and Madhav, who are sitting near Amol, are quiet, though it is not really possible to know whether they are asleep, or merely silent. The stony banks of a small rivulet are visible in the light. The moon, which is today in its dark fortnight, is getting ready to appear in the skies. It looks as though the moon is trying very hard to break through the bank of fog. The vehicle stops near an enormous tree. The real journey will begin from this point.

The base of the tree is quite clean. Ahmed removes a few dead leaves and twigs from the ground, and sprinkles water from the nearby rivulet on it. He places a plantain leaf on the sanctified ground, and lights a packet of joss sticks. He removes the remnants of previously lit joss sticks, and leans the small axe, the machete, the hatchet, the guns, and other weapons that he has brought with him, against the trunk of the tree. The boy named Madhav also places a bottle of liquor on the plantain leaf. Nobody ventures on a hunt without worshipping at this place in this manner. This is worship of the hunt, and of the goddess who is the presiding deity of this jungle. Questions of religion and caste do not arise in this worship at all.

After concluding the homage, all the men pile back into the van and open bottles of liquor. Even though Ahmed, too, is drinking, he keeps warning the others, especially the youths. Not much, merely, 'Just remember, you have come out on a hunt, don't cross the limits.' At Ahmed's warnings, the bottles and the glasses are put away.

Game is not usually sighted at dusk. Wild animals leave their lairs only at night. The foreign liquor has kindled the men's spirits. They are hungry, as well. Ahmed's wife is famed for her expertise in cooking. The mouth-watering aroma of hot parathas and chicken curry cooked with cashew nuts escapes the hot case and fills the interior of the car, announcing her culinary abilities.

After they have eaten, the men rest awhile. The group now becomes active and alert about the real purpose of this trip. A searchlight is connected to the van's battery. Ahmed reverentially closes his eyes and places his gun to his forehead. Only then does he hoist it onto his shoulders.

In the front seat of the Gypsy are Choudhury, Saikia, Hazarika, and Rahim, the driver. Even though the space is cramped, they always sit in this manner. The hood of the car has been rolled back, leaving the top open. The two youths, Robin and Madhav, are entrusted with the responsibility of focusing the search light, alternately, with each other. Both stand up in the vehicle. Their hands are on the roof of the unhooded vehicle. One has the searchlight in one hand. Like an expert soldier, Ahmed stands between them. Amol has absolutely no experience of hunting; hence he is not entrusted with any task. Today, his role is that of a spectator.

The vehicle moves forward. To Amol, it seems that it is moving at the slow pace of a heavily veiled young bride who is welcomed across the threshold of her new home by her mother-in-law. At this slow pace, the smoothly running engine of the Gypsy appears, to him, to have become absolutely silent. Robin and Madhav beam the searchlight on both sides of the track alternately. The powerful beams of the light penetrate the dense jungle. The light glistens on the dry leaves and the bare branches of the denuded trees. Drops of midnight dew hang from the branches. The light falls on the dewdrops, too, and is reflected back, creating a beautiful sight. Amol is looking with great absorption at this dark forest with its necklaces of dewdrops.

The moon of the dark fortnight climbs overhead, and lights up the land like a searchlight. They cross another part of the same rivulet that they had come upon previously. There is hardly any water here in winter. The vehicle crosses the ankle-high water quite easily. The radiance of the moon and the beam of the searchlight create ripples of light on the pebbles. A large flock of thousands of waterfowl can be seen in the beam of the lights as they sit on the trees by the bank of the river. The glistening black backs of the waterfowl reflect glorious prisms of light. For a single instant, the sound of the beating of waterfowls' wings is heard. The sound vanishes in an instant, and the flock sinks back into sleep once more.

The vehicle makes a low sound as it rumbles over the rocks strewn on the river bed. As soon as it crosses over, there is silence once more. The rivulet, calm in this dry season, is left behind. The waterfowl remain sleeping. The vehicle moves on towards even deeper forest after crossing the river.

Rahim, the dexterous driver, is now at the wheel. Ahmed, the skilled shikari, is sweeping the lighted area of the forest with alert eyes, on the lookout for game. Suddenly, Ahmed taps the hood with his hand. Hearing the signal, Rahim stops the car. As soon as the vehicle rolls to a halt, the lights are switched off. The forest is now lit up by the light of the moon overhead. Amol does not know who else has observed it—probably, everybody has. But he thinks that only he has seen it. A pair of eyes glistens brightly in a part of the forest that the moonlight has not been able to penetrate. Unable to contain his excitement, he whispers, 'Eyes, eyes!' Ahmed scolds him roughly, 'Keep quiet!' Amol relapses into silence.

Once more, Ahmed taps on the rolled-back hood of the Gypsy. One should not utter any sound once game has been sighted. At this signal, Rahim moves the car slowly forward. Madhav aims the searchlight towards the pair of eyes. In the glare of the light, the eyes glow even more brightly. They stare unblinkingly. What are they looking at? What do they see? Do they see Death? Or do they see ambassadors who bring Death to those eyes?

Ahmed jumps silently out of the sluggishly moving vehicle. He moves slowly forward. Taking cover behind a tree, he raises his gun and takes aim at the centre of the pair of gleaming eyes. A heart-rending scream is heard synchronously with the sound of the gun. The sound of something moving heavily into the distance, and then falling down, is heard. The beam of light follows the sound. Ahmed reaches the quarry. A huge deer is lying in a pool of blood. Its heart has spilled out of its body. Wildly, a life tries desperately to leave the body. Ahmed places the barrel of his gun on the body of the supine deer. Once more, there is a bang. A life leaves the body. Ahmed immediately cuts the veins on the deer's hind legs. There is nothing left for Ahmed to do after this. He returns to stand near the stationary vehicle. He lights up a cigarette, and begins to pace up and down.

Ahmed and Robin jump out as soon as the gun is put back into the Gypsy. The deer had not been able to escape very deep into the forest. Amol, too, gets down. All three of them stagger to the vehicle, dragging the deer behind them. The carcass is lifted to the back of the Gypsy.

The vehicle begins to move once more, this time, on its return journey. The faces of the hunt-loving passengers in the car are wreathed in victorious smiles. There is no reason now for them not to talk. The men sitting in the front and back of the vehicle begin to talk ceaselessly.

Ahmed's wife does not like him to hunt. Once, long ago, Ahmed had mistakenly fired at a pregnant doe. A fawn had been found inside the doe when it had been cut up. After this, Ahmed had not gone hunting for a very long time. As a result, his small son had succumbed to a slight fever, and died. Once, a headstrong youth had shot a suckling doe. A small fawn had died along with its mother. The fawn was roasted and eaten in the jungle itself. Ahmed's verdict: 'A tender fawn is not tasty.'

Rahim is not usually very loquacious. Now he, too, begins to narrate a story. A doe was washed down in the floods. She entered a village. The villagers gave chase to the doe, which entered another village. The people of the second village chased the first lot of people. A fight between the two groups of villagers ensued. In an effort to save herself, the doe entered a clump of bamboo. A small village boy killed her by hitting her with sticks.

Amidst the telling of these hunting tales, the vehicle reaches camp once more. The youths begin to skin the deer, and cut it up. The moon of the dark fortnight sinks into the western sky amidst revelry and laughter. The birds awake from their slumber. Dewdrops begin to fall from the leaves and branches of the trees. The forest is covered with a mantle of white fog. The sky and the river, too, awaken. A ripe wood-apple, the colour of freshly husked paddy, is seen hanging at the edge of the eastern sky.

In the morning, all of them wash themselves in the clear waters of the small rivulet. One of them collects dry twigs and boils water for tea on the bonfire. After eating biscuits and savouries, washed down with tea, the group returns to the vehicle once more. A packet of venison is kept aside for the gatekeeper.

Once more, the Gypsy moves forward. The group of people appears to be somewhat tired. After dropping Ahmed off, they will rest for a while at the Dak Bungalow. They will start for Guwahati only towards the late afternoon.

The men are sitting motionless in the Gypsy. Nobody says anything. The huge deer is now only some lumps of flesh. It is probably because of the sleepless night that he has spent, and his tiredness, that Amol begins to ramble unintelligibly. He wants to compare the deer's eyes with those of Ahmed's wife. Hers had glistened on her half-veiled face. The same pair of eyes. Lustrous, glistening eyes full of love and affection, pitiful eyes. Eyes that cowered with fear and insecurity. Yes, the same eyes, with the same glance, thought, language, and the same yearning.

Amol has not slept at all through the night. Besides, it is for the first time that he has come on a hunt. He feels the pangs of grief in his breast. The hunter's aim has settled unerringly between the animal's eyes. No prey can escape the hunter after he has taken aim. Neither wild animals, nor Ahmed, the hunter, nor, indeed, any other person, can do so. Amol himself has not been able to do so. He is a prey to grief, poverty, and sorrow, to disappointment and anger, to insecurity and betrayal. And, most of all, we are all prey to lovelessness and to cruelty. We cannot escape the hunter after he has taken aim. We are all going to morph into lumps of flesh at some time or the other. Day by day, moment by moment, a desert is encroaching upon our hearts. A desert full of chaos and confusion. Everything is being captured by the arid sands. We are all prey to that arid desert within each one of us.

Amol looks back. Behind him, the dirt track disappears into the forest like a winding river. He presses his arms to his chest, as hard as he can. He will have to save his soul from the desert. Each one of us will have to save our souls. Yes, each one of us.

Translated by Mitra Phukan

JOURNEY

YESHE DORJEE THONGCHI

After spending Sunday at home, you feel extremely lazy to go back to work on Monday. After spending two months of leave at home, I also felt a similar laziness to go and rejoin work. Moreover, I had to leave behind my newly-wedded wife and go all alone to a far off place where I was posted. It was, therefore, natural for me to be all the more unwilling to leave.

Even then I prepared to leave. There was nothing much that I had to carry. It was a hilly area and there was still no motorable road; it was unlikely that there would be one in the future also. So, while coming on leave, I had not brought anything except a trunk. When I came home, there was no need to carry any bedroll; my intention of coming home this time was for my marriage. So, according to tribal customs, my parents had arranged new bedclothes for me.

In due course, my marriage had taken place. After marriage, one month passed in the twinkling of an eye. And my two months' leave was over. At first, I thought of taking leave without pay for some more days and staying at home; but I decided against such a thing. I had started a new family life. With the responsibility towards my parents and my home weighing more heavily on me, the responsibility towards my own self had also grown. I had also incurred a large debt due to my wedding. So I had to go back and rejoin work.

While coming home, I had a Nepali woman porter carry my trunk for me. Now I was having trouble finding a porter. Had it been some other time, someone from the village itself could have carried the trunk. But as it was the season for cultivation, everybody was tied up in their own fields. Nobody had the time to sit back even for a moment. On the other hand, modern education had made me useless, rendered me averse to physical labour. Otherwise, for a young person like me, carrying this trunk weighing twenty or thirty kilograms on my back and walking for a day should not have been a big task. Then again, for a highly-placed government officer like me, it was considered to be below my dignity to carry a load on my back. For two or three days, my mother and father ran from pillar to post, searching for a person in every household of the village, but nobody came forward to carry the load for me. Eventually my father said, 'Don't worry about anything. I will leave you at Dirang myself.'

I objected to the idea. Because how would it seem to have my father carry the trunk for me? What would others think of me? What would they say? But my objections had no effect on my father. At last it was agreed that my father would carry my load.

On the day of our departure, a lot of people assembled at our place. They were there to bid me farewell. On the other hand, any delay would mean missing the bus at Dirang. Finishing his meal early in the morning, my father had already started off with the trunk on his back. When I went out after bidding good bye to everyone, it was twenty minutes past ten by my wristwatch. I thought that by this time my father must have gone far ahead. So I started walking fast.

But I did not have to go too far. After walking for three or four miles from the village, I caught up with him. He was waiting for me. As I reached near, he said, 'You are very late. Will you carry on now or take some rest?' As I had walked fast, I felt tired. Also, from the village I had had to walk uphill to this point. On my shoulders I carried my tiffin and liquor flask. After drinking all the liquor brought by the people who came to bid me farewell, I felt a heaviness in my body and my limbs became numb. So before I said anything, I sat down on a rock. Seeing my condition, my father laughed at me.

'Has this distance already tired you? Sit down and rest a while. If you do not hurry, the bus will leave.'

Father kept quiet for some time. Then he looked at the sun and pondered over something, his sight gradually lowered and fell on my bag. Wiping his dried up lips with the palm of his right hand he said, 'I am feeling very thirsty.'

I handed over the liquor flask to him. Father took a mug full of liquor from the flask and handed it back to me. Then making loud gulping sounds, he finished his drink in one go and returned the mug to me. Adjusting the belt of the load round his head, he lifted it up on his back and started walking. I also started following him. Our journey began. With my trunk on his back, father walked ahead and behind him it was me with just a tiffin bag. He trudged along the narrow paths of the hill, up and down; no one uttered any word, as if we spoke different languages, strangers unknown to each other who were moving towards some unknown destination.

I could not guess what father was thinking along the way. But I did not feel comfortable walking along with him in this manner. At times, it occurred to me that I was not doing the right thing by putting my burden on my father's back and walking along with ease myself. I tried very hard to tell him to hand over the load to me, but some kind of shyness prevented me from saying so. Maybe that shame came from my education, my high official status, my sense of self-respect, and such things. I felt that if I carried a load on my back, he would laugh at me; the world and its people would mock and sneer at me. I would demean myself in front of my father and the whole world. Father had given me a good education. I had transformed his hopes and dreams into reality. Now my parents were proud of me. Because of me, my parents had earned more respect in the village and society. Naturally, they did not want to see me carry any load on my head. Instead, it was better for him to carry my load. Father had carried loads his whole life. Therefore, he was stronger than me in this respect and more experienced. Since childhood, I had lived in a school, college, and university hostel. We were never taught to do any physical work. Therefore, in spite of having a young body with immense youthful power in my arms, I was worthless, averse to physical labour, and lacking in physical work experience. I could have very well taken the load off my father and carried it myself. But there was no way to do that. So I silently followed my father and he carried my trunk on his back and walked on ahead of me—just as quietly as I did. On the way he stopped to rest twice, we had our tiffins; but there was hardly any exchange of words between us.

Finally, we arrived at Dirang. The bus coming from Tawang had not yet arrived at Dirang so I took my father to a tea stall. We sat at a table facing each other. He seemed to be tired. Seeing my father's condition my heart filled with love. Even then I could not say anything. I ordered two cups of tea. Hardly had the tea cup touched my lips, when I heard my father's voice, 'Do you have an old pair of shoes?'

I lifted my head and looked at him. Father repeated what he said earlier. 'Why?'

'The road is very rocky, you know, one can hardly walk, it hurts.'

I looked at my father's bare feet, covered with a permanent coating of dirt, feet that never wore shoes. It had cracked up in such a way that they did not look like human feet, but those of an elephant. I had never noticed them until now. I had not even noticed if the road was rocky or not. Since I had my hunting boots on my feet, I did not have to think about that. Only after seeing my father's condition did I realize.

I took out my purse and counted the money. I still had forty rupees with me. A pair of canvas shoes would cost me about twelve rupees. With the rest of the money, I could easily manage to reach Bomdila.

But father objected to that and said, 'If you have an old pair, just give that to me. There is no need to spend money buying a new pair.' Even after a lot of persuasion, my father refused to buy a new pair of shoes. At long last, I gave my old hunting boots to my father. I took out my pair of leather shoes from the trunk and put them on. After getting the shoes, my father's face lit up radiantly.

In due course, the bus coming from the direction of Tawang halted at Dirang. The passengers jostled among themselves for seats. Even so, the conductor managed a seat for me. Putting my head out of the window, I looked at my father. He was standing by the side of the vehicle.

'Take care and write a letter as soon as you arrive....'

Father wanted to say something more, but the bus started to move. In a matter of moments, he was left behind. Through the window, I looked in the direction of my village. At that moment, I saw the path by which we had come down a few moments ago lying lifeless like a rope in the bosom of the mountain.

Father would go up on that road after a while. This time, we had started our journeys in opposite directions. I was starting a journey seated in the cushioned comfort of the vehicle while my father was beginning a journey walking along a rocky path with his tired legs.

Translated by Surajit Borooah

THE GREEN SERPENT
DHRUBAJYOTI BORAH

When her mother found her, her eyes were closed and her face bore a very strange expression. She was lying face upwards in her grandmother's elaborately carved bed. The sador had fallen off from her chest, and the clothes of her lower body were gathered around her middle—the hem of the mekhela barely covering her nakedness. Her beautifully sculpted legs were lying bare over the crumpled bed clothes—with one leg stretched out straight and the other slightly folded at the knee. There was a stain in the upper part of her thigh—the stain of a blood-mixed fluid that had dried over the skin. A hand was laid across her chest—as if trying to cover the bare virginal mounds. The other hand lay near her body—a hand smooth and white as the core of a banana tree; a hand stretched out in lazy abandon.

The mother first looked at her with a sense of incredulity. Gradually, her mouth gaped into the beginning of a scream. Then her hand went to her lips and the contorted fingers stifled the scream welling up from the deep recesses of her being. With a sharp inhale, the scream went back inside her body and started a turbulent swirl inside. She felt as if her legs were turning into soft mud under her body—as if her knees would give way—and she would collapse on the floor.... She started to shudder violently. She saw two fine tendrils grow out of her daughter's closed eyes—the tendrils soon became two saplings with thin hanging leaves and yellow flowers. The saplings then began to tremble and dropped yellow flowers all around. She wanted to call out to her daughter, but hesitated and stopped. She felt as if her daughter lay exhausted—that her body had gone soft; the muscles had lost their tautness, the bones had become rubbery, and the sleeping body had assumed a strange posture on the bed. And her lips, the slightly parted lips with the corners turned up slightly—were holding on to a ghost of an enigmatic smile. The closed eyes looked sated and a tired satisfaction shone on her face.

A primeval sound of pain and terror, a gurgling sound like the cry of a wounded animal escaped from the mother's throat. The shivering saplings disappeared, coiled back into the eyes of her daughter leaving turbulence in the air and images of scattered yellow flowers all around. The mother then rushed to her daughter and fell over her with a cry and shook her violently. She pulled up the clothes and covered the bare breasts. She looked keenly at her daughter's nakedness and saw a thin line of blood at the angle of her thighs—and a stain—a stain of dried blood-mixed fluid....

The girl opened her eyes and her dark pupils shone like two deep wells. The faint glimmer of a smile floated on her face and then disappeared instantly. He eyes searched for something around the room. Then the shadow of fear clouded her face and soon turned into a look of wild unadulterated terror.

The mother raised her index finger and pressed it over her lips. 'Shh... shhh,' she hissed like a vicious snake—'Shhh...not a word...not a sound... shhh....'

From the little town, the high ranges of the Himalayas could be clearly seen to the north. In the crystal clear air of the early morning, the still higher snow-clad peaks could be seen behind the blue ridges. The golden sun rays of the morning played hide and seek on the snow-covered faces of the mountain peaks brushing them successively in gold, mauve, or purple splendour. On winter evenings, a biting cold wind blew down from the northern mountain slopes.

Her mother had forbidden her to come home during the long recesses after her examinations. She had asked her to stay back in the university campus; forced her to continue her studies after the final examination.

And she did that. First she took up some project then enrolled herself in an MPhil course. Her friends joked, 'You will turn into an old hag with all your studies. MPhil now, then you will surely start PhD and then with a headful of greying hairs you will be teaching at the university.'

Though she liked the idea, she always hastened to add, 'It is not easy to get a job at the university.'

Her mother had said, 'You stay there. Things are getting worse in our areas. Your father is seldom home. I do not know where he goes around with his politics and business. Your elder brother can come home only once a year during his annual leave and your younger brother has to look after our shop alone. I want him to move to Guwahati immediately. It has become dangerous to keep him at our place. Most nights he stays in different places. I rarely allow him to sleep at home. It is safer that way you know....'

Her mother was visiting her at her hostel. She had not been home for a long time.

'But how do you stay there alone?' she asked her mother.

'I am an old woman. What do I have to fear? I am not in any danger. There are two helpers. One is new. Her name is Bindi. You have not met her. She is a good woman. Only she talks too much. You know the other one, the middle-aged tribal woman. She comes for the day and stays from morning till night.'

'The agitation has been going on for a long time, has the situation worsened lately? Has anything new happened?'

'Anything new?' her mother thought for a long time and then said, 'Things are getting worse every day. Our tribal helper, you remember her? Don't you? You would also remember that she used to wear only a sari or mekhela sador in the past. One day she came to work in her tribal dress. She had never done that before. "What is the matter," I had asked her. "You are wearing your own dress today! Are you going somewhere? Are you visiting relatives?" Do you know what she told me? She told me that the movement leaders had asked all the tribal people to wear only their own dress. "They have forbidden us to wear your clothes!" she told me.'

Her mother had become silent; as if she was trying to recollect something. Then she said, 'That day I knew that things were turning from bad to worse. The movement, from then on, was no longer about fulfilment of tribal demands. For the agitationists it had become a movement of "them versus us."'

'But those things happened long back—those are old stories. Has anything new happened?'

'Now, in many places, the agitation leaders have asked all other people, the non-tribals to leave.'

'Where to?'

'That they have not said—they have only asked people to leave. It has not happened in our place. But who knows, it may start in our place too. Yes, it may start any time. In many places people have left their homes, their lands, and moved away. There have been rumours of looting, arson, and even killing.'

Before she left, her mother again forbade her to go home during the vacations. 'I have been asking your father to buy some land and build a house in the capital city for a long time now. We have to shift our business also. But he won't listen to me. This time I am arranging some property with the help of my brothers—your uncles. At least now, for the first time your father has not objected. I am really worried about your younger brother. He has to go to the shop quite frequently. And you know what, many of his tribal classmates and friends have disappeared. I have heard that they have gone to the forest, have gone underground. I am really afraid, you know. That's why I do not allow your younger brother to stay at home for more than a night at a time.'

She had become really worried after her mother had left and the worry and anxiety increased day by day and continued to build up. So in the first recess she got, after her mother's visit, she had packed a bag and gone home. Just outside the university campus one could get into private buses that ran from the city to her small town up north.

When she got down at her hometown, she could immediately feel a suppressed tension all around. She was not sure whether the tension was really there or she had only imagined it. Rumours floated in the air. That in some places certain people were taken down from buses and shot—women, children, everyone. Man could so easily turn into a cruel vicious animal! And such things happened more frequently with the politics of hatred around.

The new help had gone home for a few days. The tribal woman was also absent that day. After she had started wearing the tribal dress, she had become foul-tempered as well as irregular in coming to work.

It was almost summer. The days were quite hot and it became pleasant only in the evening after sunset. After the midday meal, her mother left home to attend some function somewhere. She wanted to go too, but her mother had said no. The times were not good. It was not safe for a beautiful girl to move around. Her father, as usual, had gone out on business and had been staying in some other town for the past couple of days. Mother had sent her brother to the city to look after the construction work of their new home. He would install a deep tube well there. And once that was ready they would shift to the city even if the house was not complete. Her mother would not stay in this place any longer than she could help.

Her only regret was the large amount of property they had acquired in this small town. Nobody wanted to buy that now. There was practically no price for the land and other properties in that area and there were no buyers. The movement leaders had decreed that property could only be sold to local tribal people and not to others. There was an undeclared ban on the transfer of property. Their large grocery shop would be run by a distant relative of their father—a distant nephew with shifty eyes. He had married a tribal girl and hence would be safe. That arrangement was also complete.

'There is practically no chance of getting any income from the shop in future, none at all', her mother kept saying repeatedly.

Her mother went out of the house instructing her to stay indoors and to bolt the door from inside. She said, 'One must be very careful. Trouble has also reached our town. Silently, people have started to leave the town. We shouldn't delay either.'

It was quite hot. After lunch her eyelids became heavy with slumber. After her mother had left she removed all that her mother had said from her mind. What was the use of mulling over all that? The decision to move out of town had already been taken. She too had accepted it. The house, the surrounding trees, the flowering shrubs, with which she had developed a close bond over all these years, yes, she had already been able to put them out of her mind. She had become totally indifferent to the cosy comfortable familiarity of the old sprawling house.

After her mother left, she brought out the thick half-read English novel that she had brought from the university and lay down on her brother's bed in the room outside. The large carved bed, which had belonged to her grandmother, occupied a major portion of the small space. Her eyelids felt heavy, she felt lazy to even open the book she had brought. She looked at the cover which showed a photo from the film based on the novel. The actor and actress were looking at each other's eyes in a romantic pose. She kept looking at the beautiful cover for a long time till she began to doze off....

There was a commotion somewhere—some sounds. Through her sleep haze, she thought they were the sharp cracking sounds from firecrackers. Who had let off firecrackers at noon? Somebody was shouting in the distance. What was the matter? The commotion was increasing—she raised herself from her midday stupor and tried to look out through the small curtained window near the bed. She saw nothing. She got up from the bed in her sleepy daze, opened the door, and came outside to the long wide veranda. She did not see anything in the distance. Though their house had a large compound, the main road leading to the market of the small town could be clearly seen from there. No, there was nobody, nobody could be seen on the road. She came back from the veranda and went to her bed. Occasionally, sounds of shouts, like that of children playing boisterously, floated in and then it became silent again.

She still felt sleepy. She lay comfortably on the bed with her head on the pillow and absent-mindedly gazed at the cover of the novel and again drifted off to sleep.

She heard footsteps in the front courtyard. Somebody had climbed the front steps and was walking on the veranda. Through the haze of sleep, she felt as if she was hearing the footsteps in a dream. You knew that somebody was walking, there were sounds of footfalls, but you did not actually hear sounds! You did not hear sounds in your dreams—you only thought that you did. Inside her closed lids there was a world of opaque colours and through that opaque world she heard the sound of footsteps—the sound of a door being opened and closed....

Somebody was entering through a door. A tall man, his figure framed by the open door and silhouetted against the bright light outside. Somebody was saying something—there was a faint sound of the bolt of a door being drawn....

She opened her eyes. A sleeveless yellow vest, a green patterned cloth wrapped around the waist, and a white cotton gamusa bound tightly like a belt over it! Golden skin, a head of dark hair that seemed to have a life of its own, shapely limbs, a sculpted face....

And a gun in his hand! The girl, rising like a coiled spring from the bed was pushed back by a strong hand. She was thrown back violently. She fell down on the wide bed. The boy held her down. He removed her clothes, held her tightly to himself. His mouth descended over her. A strong acrid smell of male sweat from his muscular body set her brain on fire. The taut muscles of her limbs loosened and gave way. She still thought it was a dream—a romantic dream. In the hot silent noon a golden man suddenly came in, embraced her, and gradually possessed her. She felt an unbearable heat in the lower part of her body and through the heat felt a sharp pain entering her.

By the time the golden man left her, she was unconscious.

The noon chased her around after that like a poisonous snake. How her mother overcame her initial shock and became normal she did not know. How her mother arranged a taxi that very evening and left the little town after locking up their house she did not know. Her mother never mentioned the incident afterwards.

'Nobody should know anything,' her mother had hissed like a serpent before they reached their uncle's house that night. 'Not a word to anyone, not even to your father and brothers. It will be a thing between us.' Her mother watched over her like a hawk till her next monthly cycle—and she checked it herself—not believing her daughter's words alone. She counted the days of bleeding and on the fifth day heaved a sigh of relief. Then she banished the memory of that incident forever from her mind.

She too tried to shut out that memory, but couldn't. After coming to the city, her mother started pestering her husband and brothers to find a groom for her daughter. She would pick on her daughter all the time, pestering her to get married, till she was really annoyed and declared that she would not even think about it till she completed her PhD.

Her mother gave up after sometime. In the hostel, the memory of the incident chased her around like a slimy, hissing, poisonous serpent surfacing at the most unexpected moments. And slowly a bitter broth of hatred began to brew inside her. She began to hate herself, her body, the boy with the golden skin, the acrid smell of the sweat of his body, everything. She started hating the movements that spawned ethnic violence, where for an elusive goal of ethnic purity, innocent people could be looted, raped, terrorized, and killed; houses and villages burnt. And these were all done not by criminals but by normal people, without any feeling of guilt!

Oh, how she began to hate everything. She hated herself for not being able to hate the boy sufficiently. Yes, for not being able to hate him sufficiently. Sometimes, especially in the long lazy summer afternoons during college holidays, especially when she was drowsy, before her siesta, she would suddenly feel that a door had opened somewhere. And, through that open door entered—no-no, not a golden skinned boy, but a terrifyingly beautiful green serpent. It had the colour of young foliage; golden eyes, a darting golden tongue, and golden washes on its green body. The serpent would advance towards her and she would hear its hiss. Then it would twine itself around her body which was paralyzed with terror. She would feel its breath on her mouth. She would feel its warmth—no-no, not coldness, but invigorating warmth. It would slither over her spreading the warmth all over her body and then it would go down by the side of her navel and would enter her body. And her brain would explode into a fiery flood of perfumed chemicals and her whole being would dissolve into nothingness.

Try as she might, she couldn't hate the Green Snake—couldn't throw it out of her being—and she hated herself all the more for it. A witches' brew of barren hatred welled inside her mind.

After she had registered for her doctorate in the university, she got a job in a newly-opened college. Her professor and guide had arranged it. The college was in a satellite township of the capital city, some distance away from home. She could commute daily to her college. She had to go out quite early in the morning and could only return after it became dark. After a few months she decided to stay in that small town and took a part-house near the college on rent. The house belonged to a member of the college governing body and the arrangement was quite comfortable and safe. At first her mother opposed it quite vehemently. She was very angry with her for saying no to a few marriage proposals that had come for her, but when she saw that her daughter was adamant about staying near the college, she insisted that Bindi, the maid who had come to live with them in the city, should stay with her. This she did not oppose.

She felt she was quite happy amongst the noisy young college students. But there were also moments of self-doubt when she would question herself—was she happy? She could not say no. She knew she was not unhappy but was not sure whether she was happy. And after she had taken up that job; the green serpent had nearly stopped coming to her—for a long time, she hardly heard its hiss.

And then it began to appear again. She could feel its presence lurking unseen near her. Sometimes she sensed that it was lying coiled up under her quilt, under her pillow and if she put in her hand she would be able to touch it! Touch it, and feel its invigorating warmth.

Lately, she had developed a new closeness with her younger brother. He would frequently come and stay with her for a night or two. Her little brother had grown up into a strange and beautiful man! She could sense that the girls of her college, many of whom came to her house quite frequently, were an added attraction for her brother. She was quite amused. She would watch her brother as he sat near her talking like a friend, confiding in her his intimate fears and fantasies as one would in a good friend. And she would feel happy, really happy.

One evening, while they were talking, he suddenly asked, addressing her affectionately, as usual, as his elder sister, 'Bamoni, why are you rejecting such good marriage proposals one after the other? Is that incident the cause of it?' His voice shook a little.

Incident! What incident? The clear afternoon sky suddenly filled with the rolling thunder of an impending monsoon storm! Lightning flashed, and the wind hissed like the breath of a poisonous snake threatening to blow her away.

'You are afraid that if I remain unmarried, you won't be able to marry, heh?' she regained her composure and tried to joke with him. But she could make out from his liquid eyes that he was expecting a different answer.

'No, I don't think that's the cause,' she replied slowly after some time trying to be truthful to herself as well as her brother. 'I have not taken a vow not to marry.'

Her voice trailed off. How had her brother come to know? From her mother? How much did he know? Was this the reason for his latest concern and love for his sister? Even their father, usually so uninterested, had become more concerned lately.

'I have been able to banish all memories of that incident from my mind....' she said in a whisper. 'All memories, completely....'

That golden green snake! That terrifyingly beautiful serpent! No, no, she couldn't tell anyone about that. That, that was entirely a private thing, her private serpent, her private ghost.

She could see the relief which flooded her brother's eyes after hearing her slowly transform itself into a vicious cruelty. 'He came from outside', her brother said. 'He was not from our area. He came and became a leader of the agitation in our town. And they planned to drive away all the non-tribal people from the town. And he was sent to do it with terror. Houses were burned—especially outlying houses near the forest, one or two were killed, people were threatened, terrorized. And as a part of that campaign of terror, people were humiliated, molested, raped—all these were part of a plan. If I get him—if I get him!' Her brother clenched and unclenched his fists.

No-No-No-No.... She wanted to scream out, terrified at a sudden strange foreboding that came over her.

She came to the hill station to attend a refresher course in the university. She was happy to be able to escape from the monotony of the daily drudgery in the college for a few days at least. Therefore, she did not complain as many of her colleagues did about every small feature of the course.

The hostel set aside for the participants filled up with teachers from different places. On the first day of the course they met their male colleagues for the first time. Free from the constraints of a known milieu, they talked freely amongst themselves. Most of them were nearly of the same age. There were one or two senior persons in the course and it was they, the senior ones, who had a haunted and lost look in their eyes.

During the course break they went to the canteen at the edge of the hill. The hill slope, strewn with boulders, went down steeply to a wooded grove below. There was probably a small stream amongst the woods. The gurgling sound floated up to the canteen. The hill in front was covered by a pine forest, one of the last surviving woodlands, where the wind whistled constantly through the boughs. The lecture halls were at some distance from the hostels. On the way back after the classes, the participants came together, gathered fallen pine cones and joked about the teachers.

One of the participants, a young teacher about her own age was the most energetic participant of the course. He had studied in that university and knew all the nicknames and idiosyncrasies of the teachers, and also the gossip about them. He regaled all of them with those stories. She was particularly taken in by the smart, smiling, outgoing young man and they soon became friends.

Towards the end of the course they were assigned project work. They did it together and one day, after classes were over, they stayed back to talk with their teachers about the project. When they returned, it was quite late. Everybody else had gone back.

They walked down the long pine-scented road to their hostels. After another two days the course would end and the participants would go back to their respective homes, clutching the course completion certificates and carrying a load of mixed memories which would fade fast. They were unlikely to meet up again.

On their way back, they discussed the project report they would have to submit and present the next day. He lit a cigarette elegantly and said, 'Let's take a break from academics and have a cup of tea.'

The canteen was already closed. They had to go down the slope to a small hut where a lady sold tea and biscuits. They sat on the bench, a thick wooden plank placed above some rocks, and ordered tea. The lady washed the glasses with hot water from an aluminium kettle which shone like polished silver from repeated scrubbing. She then put a saucepan with water to boil over the Primus stove.

'Let us forget about studies and projects for some time. We have not enquired about each other properly. We only know which college we have come from, nothing more, do we? Where did you teach?' he asked her. She told him. She told him she had completed her MA and MPhil and had registered for PhD too. But until then, the registration was her only concrete progress towards getting her doctorate, nothing more.

He said he had also done the same courses from this university but had not registered for a PhD. And he had completed MPhil only a year ago, though he had joined the course long ago. There was a gap, he said, and he joked that he was senior to her.

'Why was there a gap?' she asked.

'Politics,' he laughed sheepishly.

'Where are you from?'

He named a village and said that it was in the foothills of the Himalayas in Bhutan. Even today, one had to walk for more than four kilometres to reach his village.

'Where is your home?' he asked.

What should she say? In the capital city, where they were staying? Or should she name the little town up north, which they had left? It was getting dark, a light was falling. The blue flame from the primus stove hissed continuously.

She looked at him. He was watching her with expectant eyes. The blue flames of the primus stove were dancing deep inside the pupils of his eyes. She told him the name of the little town.

'Do you stay in the main town?' he asked.

'Yes, right in the centre,' she said. 'Our house is an old tin-roofed bungalow with a big compound. The compound is full of trees.'

Suddenly, she saw his eyes glowing with the light of surprise and recognition. He was looking at her intently, looking her all over and it was in that instant that she recognized him. Recognized the sharp, glittering, snakelike eyes—eyes which had turned opaque like the eyes of dead fish right at that moment. A strong smell of sweat floated in the air.

She stifled the cry that rose to her mouth and rose unsteadily from the low bench. She began to run uphill to the road and then to the girls' hostel. The evening wind had freshened, and it started to hiss amongst the pines like a serpent.

He remained sitting on the wooden plank for a long time. If she knew some charm she would have summoned the poisonous snake—the vicious black snake that used to come at first and fill her heart with poison. Let it come and spawn hatred all around—let the world burn in the fire of hate, let it give birth to a desire for revenge, and let it bring out a desire to kill, to murder a man.

She wanted to summon that hatred after she came back from the course, but, but.... She could not.

The boy got down from the bus. He looked tired and worn out, a resigned tiredness brought on by anxiety. As soon as he got down, a dusty current of air, typical of early spring rose up and swirled around him. It eddied around the bus and the other passengers, depositing a fine film of dust. Dust entered his eyes, nostrils, his mouth, giving him a gritty feeling inside. He blinked his eyes. He felt a sneeze coming on. He brought out his handkerchief and covered his nose and face.

Holi was just over. The coloured marks of hands dipped in the many-hued powders of Holi still adorned the shutters and the bamboo posts of the little shop at the bus stand. Magenta-red hands. People had rubbed lime already above the red marks in many places. He walked through the dry soft dust which layered the yard of the little public bus stand.

Ah, those days! Those days, four years ago. Those heady days of raw power, the power bestowed by a gun, the blood of youth congealed with hatred and a mind divided into Them and Us. The air was heavy with the smell of burnt houses, screams of people, and the sounds of guns bursting like firecrackers and amidst all of it, the fading memory of a hot afternoon which floated up.

'They must be made to leave this place...it belongs to us,' that was the thought. 'The leading citizens must be targeted, terrorized, their daughters humiliated—then they will leave the place. After them there will be an exodus'.

Those were the calculations of the politics of hatred.

And that hot afternoon—was it also a result of the politics of hate? He saw a boy running, running frantically! Running away from himself. He felt powerful at first. Yes, all powerful after the hot afternoon. He had a gun in his hand and a little pressure with one finger on the trigger could bring death to someone! Yes, death—the finality of death. He felt the might of youth coursing through his veins and he thought that he could fertilize the whole world with it.

Sometime after the incident, he gradually began to feel as if on that hot afternoon, some vital forces had flowed out of his body. He had felt empty inside. And after that he had lost his sexual powers for a long, long time. The pleasurable excitement of sexual arousal totally left him and gave him a very deep disturbing memory. He gradually distanced himself from the movement—from politics—and returned again to his studies—to his university.

He was quite disturbed then. At times, he felt a despairing depression and a sense of worthlessness. An unspoken, sterile guilt hung heavy around his neck.

He walked slowly on the dry dusty road. It felt dry all around as if the dry air of the early spring had sucked the sap from the world. His mouth felt dry. Dust had caked at the corner of his mouth and eyes. He lifted his eyes and his gaze fell on the parched bushes along the road. The leaves had dried up and fallen off. In some branches a few shrivelled brown leaves dangled like tattered flags. He looked at the dry branches of the roadside bushes while he walked slowly along. What were those small reddish-green things in the branches, like some gum oozing out? He thought. When he looked properly he could see that those were new leaf buds!

Ah, new leaves were budding on the dry branches—the leaf buds of early spring.

The long afternoon hung suspended in nothingness. She sat on her bed, folding her knees to her chest and holding on to them. Lots of thoughts, disjointed, mostly meaningless, floated in her mind. Lately, everything tended to become a confused jumble. She had loved to read books, novels, stories, but now she could not read at all. After a few lines she would lose track and the lines in the book would become incomprehensible. Even the print would become misty, and swim before her eyes.

It was getting quite hot, the fan ought to be switched on, she thought. But she did not move from the bed. Through the little glass panes of the window near her bed she could see the cloudless blue sky, the dust-laden leaves of the trees in the garden, the rusted iron gate at the end of the long path leading down from the veranda of the house. She felt the whole scene to be unreal, as if it was an unknown place that she had dreamed up in one of her troubled dreams.

She saw a man stopping before the closed gate. He hesitated for a moment then came to the gate and opened it slowly. Then he came in. He crossed the fragrant lemon bush near the path and stopped for a moment under the temple flower trees. Then he crossed the gardenia and the jasmine bushes. The shadows of the tall areca nut trees entwined with beetle leaf vines had fallen directly across the path. He walked over those shadows. He then lifted his head and looked at the house. And the afternoon sunrays, filtered through the leaves and branches of the trees, fell on his face.

It was precisely at that moment that she recognized him. And through the din of her own heartbeat exploding inside her chest, she could hear herself exclaiming silently—he has come! He has come. She waited for the knock on the door. As she tightly clasped her knees drawn up to her chest, she sat on the bed and waited.

Translated by Maitreya Phukan

CLOSE OF DAY WITH MISS HAVISHAM
ARUPA PATANGIA KALITA

My husband has fifteen days' leave left. We have been married for about twenty days, but most of them have sped by in visiting relatives, his as well as mine. Tickets to Puri have already been bought. After spending the day in Guwahati tomorrow, we will have to board the train the day after. My father's elder and younger sisters, my Jethai and Pehi, as well as my mother's brother, that is, my Mama, are all in Guwahati. Besides, there are Pokhila, Jonali, Bidyut, and all the others. And in addition to my husband's father's younger brother, and his father's younger sister's husband, my husband has countless friends living in Guwahati. Whom shall we visit, whom shall we leave out? My parents have repeatedly told me, 'Even if you don't go anywhere else, you must definitely visit your Borma.' How can I even think of leaving Guwahati without meeting my Borma, my father's elder brother's wife, in Panbazar?

We spent the night at my husband's father's younger brother's house. We decided to go out for the day early the next morning, right after we had had our baths. My husband calculated, 'First we shall go to your Borma's house. Since she lives in Panbazar, there's no problem, then Mama in Maligaon, Jethai in Jalukbari....'

'If we are delayed at Borma's house?'

'How long can it take? Its nine now. Ten minutes to get to Panbazar, twenty minutes in Borma's house...we'll be in Maligaon well before ten. We won't eat anything anywhere; we'll just look in on them. We two newly-married people will hang a 'DO NOT DISTURB' sign outside our door and lunch someplace.'

'If Borma is having her bath?'

He doesn't understand. My husband has been educated in England. How can I make this restive, restless man understand Borma's way of life?

I was studying in Class Eight at the time. Bordeuta—Borma's husband—had to be in Delhi for a month on some kind of government training programme. They were childless, so Bordeuta would usually take Borma along with him wherever he went. This time, however, she could not accompany him. He would leave her with us. There had been quite an upheaval in our house as soon as we had learnt that Borma was to stay a full month with us. My mother had grumbled, 'Why should people such as that demi-goddess have to stay with people like us? She has her brothers in Guwahati, why doesn't she stay there?'

Father had laughed, and said, 'Dada wants Bou to stay with us because, after all, he thinks of us as his own people.'

My father, a schoolmaster, greatly respected his elder brother, a very well-placed government official. My father had shouldered all the responsibilities of the original household in the village. We were living in the old house built by my grandfather in his day. The harvest of the outlying fields was my father's responsibility to dispose of, as he deemed fit. Since Bordeuta had already built his house in Guwahati, my father had assumed that his brother would not want a share of the paternal inheritance.

Aita, cleaning the rice, had called out, 'Where will the brother keep a sister-in-law like her, then?'

Once, Bordeuta had taken my grandmother to Guwahati for an eye operation. Later, even though my father had only gone to Guwahati to inquire after her well-being, Aita had come away with him. Her eyes had still been bandaged. We had been annoyed with her. Bordeuta's house had all the modern amenities: toilets inside the house itself, running hot and cold water in the taps. There were expensive fruits on the table, a car to take her around, and a doctor within call. Whereas here, things were as they had been during my grandfather's time. The toilet was in an outhouse, a long distance away from the main house. The door to the bathhouse was rotting with the effects of too much pond-water. Aita should have come back only after her eyes had healed completely.

Back home, Aita went to the toilet with a walking stick to help her hobble around. She ate the simple food that we normally did. In fact, she even had the dressing on her eyes removed by our local doctor. Borma and Bordeuta had tried their best to provide all the comforts to Aita, yet she had come away.

'Who can stay in that house? It's like a palace all right, but deadly silent, inside which lives that close-mouthed woman. That one does nothing but clean the house, day in and day out, far into the night. She bathes for a full hour, spends half an hour in her toilet. No visitor sets foot in that house, nor does she go out anywhere. I was there for a whole month, but I never saw her move out of the house even once.'

But what had upset my grandmother most had happened on the day after a certain incident. Not being able to find her way to the toilet, my grandmother had fumbled her way to the veranda, and urinated there.

Next day, Borma had had the veranda washed with phenyl and Dettol, complaining of the stink all the time. She had vomited twice, and not touched any food the whole day.

This is the Borma we are going to visit now. My husband is already dressed and ready to go out. 'Let's do it this way,' I say. 'I'll go to Borma's house on my own.'

He is hurt by my proposal. I change my tune immediately. 'Come along. I only suggested that I go alone because after all she's an elderly lady...I thought maybe you would mind....'

Taking the bottle of cologne, he dabs some on himself, and sprinkles some on my elaborately woven sador. 'I've seen old people living alone in England. They are always a bit eccentric. In the block of apartment houses where I had my flat, there was an old lady, Mrs Kennedy. Her husband had died and her children lived far away. She would talk to her dog the whole day long.'

But Borma, my aunt, does not speak at all!

∽

On that particular occasion, Borma's husband, my Bordeuta, had come to our house just before Borma's scheduled visit. We always looked forward to Bordeuta's visits. There would be fun and merrymaking. He would eat whatever was placed before him without any fuss. Over lunch, Bordeuta had told my father, 'Let us do up the front room a bit. Your Bou will be staying for a while. In any case, a room is required for us when we come here. Besides, who knows, maybe I'll return here when I get old, to my own place, near you.'

Within a week, the windows had been enlarged, and an attached bathroom with modern fittings was built alongside the room. The water in our pond is so clear that one can see the fish swimming in it. Bordeuta had a pump fitted to this reservoir so that there would be running water in the new bathroom. While we were yet to get over our astonishment, a truck had drawn up in front of our house and deposited a dressing table, a bedstead with a foam mattress, a carpet, a room heater, and a record player in the renovated room. Let alone the neighbours, even my mother had asked my father, 'Are they really coming here for good?' My father, too, had not been able to make out exactly what was going on.

My grandmother had laughed. 'Well, thanks to this visit of Ai-Goxani at least there's a proper guest room in the house now. He would never have spent all this money if the goddess hadn't thought of coming here.' My grandmother always referred ironically to her elder daughter-in-law as Ai-Goxani, or Mother Goddess.

My father had said irritably, 'Your filthy habits provoked Bou to say something. Why are you holding it against her even after all this time? Be sure you don't spit betel-nut juice all over the place while Bou is here. Don't even set foot in that new toilet while she's here.' He had turned to my mother and shouted, 'I'll sell off the ducks—they shit all over the place.' Ignoring what my mother and grandmother had to say on the matter, he had sold off the ducks. He had heaped endless instructions and orders on my head and my brother's.

Finally, Borma arrived. She brought with her four large suitcases. In her crisply ironed white silk mekhela-sador, she did indeed resemble a goddess. My parents had been quite flustered as they tried to make her comfortable. Before leaving, Bordeuta had placed some money in my father's hands, and said, 'Look after her.' He had sighed, and added, 'There are no children… she doesn't even go out, gadding about as I've seen my colleagues' wives do…I am the centre of her world. She is totally dependent on me. She's the daughter of such a rich man, but she never complains, nor does she ask for anything.'

'It will be okay; don't worry about Bou, Dada.' My father had not wanted to take the money. But Aita had taken it from her elder son, telling my father, 'Your Bou will need all sorts of things, where will you get the money to buy them for her?'

Borma had stayed with us for a whole month. During her visit, my father's middle sister, my Maju Pehi, had come with her two sons to stay with us for a while. Though my brother and I had obeyed my parents' instructions, who could control Pehi's small children? On one occasion, the older one had gone to Borma's toilet for a bath. He was, after all, a small boy; he had probably urinated on the floor of the bathroom as well. Borma had not had her bath that day, nor had she eaten any food. On another occasion, the younger toddler had defecated on Borma's folded sador. Seeing Borma wrapping it up in a newspaper preparatory to throwing the sador away, Pehi had snatched it from her and washed it thoroughly. But Borma did not touch the sador even then. In a loud voice, Aita had said to Pehi, 'Wear it yourself. God will see to it that a person who is so revolted by a child's natural functions will remain childless. She is fated to have a barren, empty lap.'

That afternoon, when I had gone to her room with her tea, I had not been able to look directly at Borma's beautiful, piteous face. Pehi had planned to stay for a while with us on that occasion, but my father had taken her back to her home quite soon. Indeed, Maju Pehi had not taken kindly to this.

While she was with us, Borma had stayed in her room. In the beginning, people were offended by this. Later, whenever we had visitors, they would go to Borma's room to exchange a few words with her before leaving.

∽

My husband drives us from his Khura's house in Chandmari to Panbazar. When we are near Silpukhuri, he asks, 'When did your Bordeuta die?'

'Two years ago. I was just appearing for my BA finals at the time.'

'Who does Borma stay with?'

'She lives alone.'

Everybody says that Borma is fond of me. Pehi and my father's other sisters would always say, 'Your Borma likes you because you're fair, you know!'

When Bordeuta had returned on that occasion, Borma had looked at him and sobbed aloud. She had wept like a pampered child does, with wounded pride, when his mother returns to him after having left him behind for a while. Later, Aita had commented, 'The way that one cried, one would have thought that she had been living in Hell all these days.' As she crushed areca nut and betel leaf on a mortar and pestle into a consistency that she could chew on with her toothless gums, Aita had also scolded Bordeuta, 'It's your fault. Just because she's a rich man's daughter and fair, there's no need to keep her like a doll. Sometimes you should allow her feet to touch the ground, also. '

After I had passed my Matriculation examinations, Bordeuta had invited me to stay in his house while I pursued my studies in college. But Aita had vetoed that invitation. 'She's at an impressionable age still. If she stays there, she'll pick up all those peculiar ways of that Goxani. Didn't you notice how much of the habits of that goddess she had acquired during that one month itself?'

Truly, during those days, when I had been poised between childhood and womanhood, I had been extremely keen on becoming as smooth-skinned, soft, and beautiful as Borma. I began to spend a long time in the bathroom. I asked my father to bring me the toiletries that Borma used—the same brands of soap, oil, powder, and snow. Even today, I use the same toiletries that Borma does.

Even though I had stayed in the hostel while in college, I had visited Borma weekly. She led a very slow-paced life. She always had the same indifference to externals. She would never actually initiate a conversation with me: if I said something, she would reply in monosyllables. Sometimes she would put on some music on her record player, and sit for hours on the balcony, listening to it. Her face would always remain devoid of any expression as she gazed at the sky with her large eyes. Did Borma actually listen to the music? Sometimes she would pick up a book. This would remain untouched in her hands, while Borma gazed at something else. Even if she had a piece of knitting or some embroidery in her hands, the impression one got was that the work in her hands was but an excuse. Her real job was to fret, to worry.

What did Borma think about all the time? What did she ponder on? Borma hardly ever sat quietly in one place for very long, unless she was listening to music on her record player. Besides cleaning and dusting, the chief occupation of her life was to keep Bordeuta's things tidy and in the best condition, to pander to his every need. She would re-iron even those of Bordeuta's clothes that were freshly laundered by the dhobi. Before he donned his undervests, she would cool them under a fan in summer, and warm them in the sun in winter. She would pluck out the burrs sticking to his socks with her own hands; re-polish even those of his shoes cleaned by the cobbler. She would knot his tie for him, stitch the buttons on his shirt, arrange his stock of areca nuts and betel leaves for him to take before he left for office, and cook his favourite dishes for him. When Bordeuta was at home, Borma hardly had time to breathe. When Bordeuta was in the office, or away on tour, it seemed that Borma tried to prop herself up by clutching on to music, a book, or some knitting.

Once, after Bordeuta had left for office, Borma had cut her foot on a blade lying outside the house. I had been with her at the time. It had been a rather deep cut. In spite of dabbing iodine on it and bandaging the cut up, I had not been able to stop the flow of blood. I had wanted to take her to a pharmacy to stitch up the wound. After all, their home was in Panbazar, the heart of the city. There were pharmacies and doctors galore in the neighbourhood; indeed, the hospital was but a stone's throw away. But Borma had asked me, in a weak voice, to telephone Bordeuta. She had looked ready to burst into tears. As I had looked at her piteous face, and her bleeding cut, I had felt a wave of irritation. How would this woman handle a serious emergency? She wanted to drag her husband away from his work for such a minor mishap. I had telephoned Bordeuta. Borma's tears had flowed copiously as soon as she saw him. He summoned a doctor, berated the servants for leaving the blade lying around. Free of worry, Borma had drifted off to sleep. Under Bordeuta's directions, I had taken on the responsibilities of the household. I had looked after Borma, bringing her glasses of milk and fruit juice, as well as her food.

It was the month of June, and it was very hot. I was quite tired. I had been about to fall asleep under the fan in the inner room. Bordeuta had come running in, 'Your Borma has fallen asleep only just now—she'll wake up!' I knew that Borma could not tolerate the sound of the fan. She had an air conditioner in her room.

I had been quite annoyed. I had remembered what Aita had said as she had crushed the areca nuts in her mortar. 'Just because she's a rich man's daughter and fair, there's no need to keep her like a doll. Sometimes you should allow her feet to touch the ground, also.' Bordeuta took things too far.

In my anger, I had not visited them again for a fortnight. Borma had herself come to my hostel to call me over. I had been surprised to see her in front of the hostel gates, standing in front of Bordeuta's car. Truly, the goddess herself had come down from her pedestal! Borma would have to make preparations from early in the morning if she had to go out anywhere. She would bathe, get dressed, check whether Bordeuta had a fresh change of clothes for work the next day, if not, she would have to arrange and organize the clothes, she would lock up the house, forget something...if she had to be somewhere at noon, it would be evening by the time she could leave the house; if she was scheduled to leave in the evening, it would be night before she could make it.

I had introduced Borma to my friends. A couple of them had said, 'Your Borma is beautiful, like you.' I had been quite flattered at being compared to Borma. At that time, I had not yet got over my desire to be like her.

∞

'Which way do we go now?' He slows down in front of Cotton College. At 9.30 in the morning, the Panbazar crossroad is pulsating with young people. In front of this lively, colourful scene, the heaviness in my heart vanishes. I feel energized again. We had once staged a street play on women's rights just here. Bidyut, in the character of my wayward husband, had smacked my face just there, under that tree. I had rolled on the ground, and poured a bottle of alta on my forehead. Two youths passing by on their motorcycles had wanted to beat up Bidyut. When I relate this incident to my husband, he laughs uproariously.

We turn at the bend near the Medical College hospital, and, driving past the jeweller's shop, go on for a while till we reach the green, double-storeyed house. The colour on the walls is faded. It probably hasn't been painted for a couple of years. When Bordeuta had been alive, he had had it painted annually. We get down from the car. In a small space in front are about half-a-dozen rose bushes. Bordeuta used to care for these beautiful, bi-coloured roses himself. The place used to be bright with huge blooms in a variety of colours while he had been alive. Now, the original bushes are strangled with a heavy growth of wild flowers. And even those wild plants are choking in the dense undergrowth.

The main thoroughfare is busy with the constant movement of vehicles and people. I ring the bell. Five minutes pass, ten. Nobody comes out of the house. My husband keeps pacing up and down the steps. 'There seems to be nobody at home. The windows are all shut as well.'

'No, I think she's in. There's no lock on the door.' Why are the windows shut? When Bordeuta had been alive, he would get up early and open the windows every day. 'Wait, I'll go around the back and look.'

The courtyard at the back is damp and chilly. The Marwari businessman to the east of the house had wanted to raise a seven-storey supermarket complex at one time. Bordeuta had taken him to court and had had the work stopped. The businessman had doubtless re-started work on his construction as soon as Bordeuta had died. The courtyard is covered with lichen, and there is a damp, fetid smell. The veranda is dark. In a corner lies the sack that had been Tommy's bed, as well as his bowl and chain. I had been afraid of the huge dog that had always accompanied Bordeuta, running with him, in the mornings. Is the dog running free somewhere? Tommy's chain is rusty, and his bowl is green with mold. Is the dog dead, then? There is silence all around. Only the sound of the shower in the bathroom can be heard.

From inside, Borma asks, 'Who is it?' The sound of running water stops.

'It's me, Anju, I've brought my husband along.'

'Sit down.' Once more, the sound of running water from the shower.

The drawing room is musty. It must have remained closed up for a long time. The rank smell makes me nauseous. I open the door to call my husband in. He is smoking a cigarette in the nearby paan shop. Let him finish his smoke; who knows how long Borma will take. The doorway is covered by spiders' webs. That means that it has not been opened for a long time. Does that mean, then, that Borma hasn't set foot outside the house for a long time; that nobody has come into the house? I open the windows, then close them again. The seven-storey building has shut out the sky. There is no air, nor is there any light.

Suddenly, the room becomes bright. My husband, entering the room, has switched on the light.

'Borma takes a long time to have her bath.'

'It's okay.' True, he has said it is all right, but there is impatience in his eyes and on his face. The furniture and upholstery, the walls and ceiling, all gleam in the light. There is not a speck of dust anywhere. There is a clear imprint of hardworking hands behind the cleanliness of this room. There seems to be no domestic help around. My mother had said that no hired help stayed on for very long with Borma. Twice, she had sent two girls to help Borma with her chores, but not one of them stayed on. Borma kept cleaning till midnight, and even beyond that time, every night. Not only did she herself not go to bed, she would not allow the help to go, either. Borma lunches at three o' clock, and has her dinner at one o' clock. On many occasions since my uncle had died, my parents had wanted to take Borma back to our small town with them, but she had not gone.

Several old magazines are piled neatly on the table. I proffer him one. Inside, the sound of the shower has stopped. We hear the sound of clothes being washed. It's already past ten. He gets up, saying, 'I'm going to the bookstore—I'll be back soon.' Why on earth did I have to bring him to Borma's house? I've made a big mistake. He brushes past the table as he leaves. The tablecloth falls down. I pick it up, and replace it after giving it a shake. Yes, it's the same tablecloth, almost unchanged.

Once, when Bordeuta had gone on tour, I had stayed with Borma. She had wanted some material for a tablecloth. Bordeuta, it seemed, did not know the first thing about buying such an object. Panbazar, the main shopping area of the city, thronging with people, was just on the doorstep of the house. I had forced Borma to come out with me, but I had received my just desserts for dragging her out on the streets. Borma had just not kept pace with me. She had lagged behind, and I had been forced to turn around every now and again to check where she was. The pavement had been full of large potholes. Indeed, Borma had been on the verge of tripping and falling once. Even though Borma had been born in Guwahati, and had always lived here after her marriage, she needed to be guided by a helping hand when crossing the road. Under the hot, strong sun, Borma's face had become flushed. At the draper's shop, she had begun to gasp for breath. I had chosen the material for the tablecloth myself. She had seemed to be suffering greatly. Even though I had grown up in a small town, I had become used to traipsing around the city on my own. The distance between Borma's house and the shop was so negligible that even rickshaws refused to take passengers for this small stretch. I had had no idea that this short distance could so tire out anybody. She was a person who hardly ever ventured out of her house. Just because I had been bored in her company over the last three days, just because I had tired of her silent ways during this time, I should not have dragged her out in this manner. I had taken Borma to a nearby restaurant for a drink of water. To my great surprise, she had had a cup of tea, and some sweets. Following me around as a small child follows its mother, Borma had bought biscuits and bread of her choice. She had even entered a shop that sold traditional woven mekhela sadors from Sualkuchi, and bought a couple of sadors. Smiling slightly, she had said, 'Your Bordeuta always buys the same kind of sadors.'

It was high noon on a hot summer's day. The sun was very strong. Throughout, my heart beat with fear—what if something untoward happened now? As soon as we reached home, Borma had developed a headache. She had even vomited once. Bordeuta, too, had arrived just then. In the commotion of calling a doctor and getting medicines, I had slipped away.

∞

Borma enters, moving the curtain aside. In these two years, Borma has lost a lot of weight. Her hair has greyed, and there are hollows under her cheekbones.

My husband enters, and greets Borma respectfully. Borma smiles slightly. She is as pale as the stark white clothes that she wears. The veins on her hands and feet stand out clearly.

'How are you? How is your health?'

'I'm all right.'

'I don't see Tommy around.'

'He died.'

Looking at my husband, she murmurs, 'A cup of tea?' He shakes his head vigorously. 'No, no, nothing, no tea please.'

'A glass of lemonade?'

He protests once more. He wants to escape Borma. It's quite normal for people to want to distance themselves from a woman who is as cold as a corpse. I ought not to mind. I follow Borma inside. Half-an-hour to make the lemonade. She will open the fridge, rub the handle, wash the glass, and wipe it.

Just behind the drawing room is Borma's spacious bedroom. On one side of the room is Borma's bed, on the other is a metal bed meant for invalids, with a handle by which it can be winched up or down. Below the bed is a glass. I shudder involuntarily. It seems as though Bordeuta, dead now for two years, will groan from the bed, 'Anju! Where is your Borma?' The bed of the dead patient, the bedpan, even the bottles of medicines are all scrupulously clean. It seems as though the sick man will return just now; he has merely gone to sit outside for a while. It was from this very bed that Bordeuta had been taken to Vellore for treatment. With four suitcases and two bags as luggage, Borma had prepared herself to accompany him. My father and my Peha, who had undertaken the responsibility of taking Bordeuta to Vellore, had panicked. Who would take on the additional burden of looking after Borma if she went with them? She would hardly be able to fend for herself there; she would have to be looked after at every step. So Borma had been left behind. I had stayed with her during that time. Throughout the night, she would unpack and repack her suitcases and bags, again and again. I would wake up at night, startled by the sounds of her activity.

Bordeuta did not return home again.

∞

Borma roasts some semolina. 'Borma, who does your shopping for you?'
'The store across the road home delivers everything.'
'The financial matters, the chores at the bank?'
'Bhaiti, my younger brother.'
'Don't you have any help at home?'
'No.'
My husband sits sprawled on a sofa with furrowed brow.
'Done? Let's go.' He looks at his watch.
'Borma is cooking something for you. I won't go to my Mama's house; we'll just visit the people from your side. It's already so late.'
He laughs his sunny laugh. 'Have I said anything? Why are you taking the blame upon yourself?' He comes closer, and holds my hand. I tidy up

the magazines and papers scattered on the centre table again. Sounding somewhat surprised, he says, 'These journals are all from 1990.'

I shudder again. None of them are newer than the January of two years ago. Bordeuta had been taken to Vellore in January 1990. The neatly stacked papers and magazines had stopped coming into the house from February onwards. Bordeuta had died towards the end of January, and his last rites had been conducted in February. Because my examinations had been going on at that time, I had not been able to come and attend the obsequies.

During that time, the question of inheritance of Bordeuta's property had come up. Borma's elder brother had spoken some harsh words to my father about the inheritance. People had said of Borma, 'Why should she shed tears? There are lakhs in the bank.' Throughout all this commotion, Borma had sat like a lifeless doll, with a blank face, devoid of any individual stamp of personality. I had looked on that visage once, and had been unable to face her again. After this, I had gone to Delhi for my post-graduate studies. I had got married. It's after a long time that I am meeting Borma now.

Borma takes out a platter in order to spread out the cooked semolina and cut it. She wipes the platter, and spreads a little ghee on it. I had always enjoyed seeing Borma lay out and serve Bordeuta his food. If Bordeuta were to leave for office at nine, Borma would begin to set the table from eight. She would lay out a white tablecloth, over which she would put the placemats that she herself had embroidered. She would wipe the crockery, fill up the glass with water, stand back, and examine it. She would shape the salad sometimes in the form of a fish, sometimes a lotus. She would fashion the mashed potatoes into a rabbit with eyes of pepper, and a nose made of a piece of carrot. A rose-shaped onion would bloom on top of the chop, while the tomato would be transformed into a water lily. I would watch her, and reflect that it was not food that Borma was serving Bordeuta. No, she was offering her God his ritual offerings, his oblations. She herself would just take a plate and eat very little, that too, at odd hours.

I take the tray from her hands and go to the drawing room. My husband sips the tea quietly. Borma sits gazing outside. The veins stand out clearly on her hands as they lie folded in her lap. Her beautiful eyes have sunk in their orbits, her cheeks too are hollow. Her once rosy complexion is now sallow. As a child, I had scrubbed my hands and feet endlessly, hoping that by doing so I would become like Borma. Where has that woman gone? I do not recognize this person sitting in front of me.

Borma gets up and collects the cups and saucers with trembling hands.

'Come over for a meal one day.'

'Certainly.' The sound of his young voice shatters, briefly, the quietude of the house.

'When?'

'We shall be returning from Puri on 15 April. We'll be in Guwahati for a night or two, after which we'll go straight on to Namrup. I have to join immediately after. So, Borma, we'll be able to have a meal with you around the 17th.'

'How many days from today will that be?' Borma's voice sounds very feeble.

'17 April,' says my husband.

'Wait, I'll mark it on the calendar.' Going to the wall calendar to mark the date, I get a shock. What is this? It is the calendar for 1990, and the page shows January of that year. Indeed, every calendar in the room has stopped tracking the time after January 1990. Did time really die two years ago in this dark house? Newspapers, journals, calendars—each one of them is saying, 'Time is dead in this house.' I feel a strange sensation. My throat turns dry with horror.

Taking the tray from Borma's trembling hands, I rush inside. Borma follows me in. Shall I wash up the tea things for her? No, let them be, even if I wash up, Borma will do it again.

The clock on the medicine table shows the time to be twenty minutes to nine. Bordeuta would wind up the large wall clock with its golden pendulum every day. Only after winding the clocks did he have a cup of tea and go in for his bath. Leaving behind the clocks that he wound daily with his own hands, Bordeuta had boarded the nine o' clock train for Vellore. The person who had wound the clocks had never returned. I look at the clocks once more. They are gleaming. Borma, who had always dusted these clocks daily, must have done so today as well.

There is a rustling below the white-sheeted invalid's bed. I jump involuntarily. I shiver as though I have a fever, and I break out in gooseflesh. Why am I so fearful? The electricity must have failed. The house is enveloped in an unnatural dusk. A rat climbs out of the bed-pan, and burrows under the other bed. I leap to Borma's bed, and sit with my feet drawn up. I am afraid to let my feet dangle from the bed. I get the impression that the house is stuffed with balled-up caterpillars, that slimy snakes are looped around the rooms. If I even stir from my place, they will all come crawling out.

'When did you say you will be returning? After how many days? I don't keep track of dates and the days of the week.' I am extremely startled. It takes me a while to get my breath back. 'I don't keep track of dates and the days of the week.' Where have I heard this before? Somebody whispers in my ear, 'There, there, I know nothing about time. There, there, I know nothing of the days of the week.'

Borma is staring at me. This is not Borma at all. Who, then, is she? Who is this woman sitting on the ruins of time? In this twentieth century, sitting in Panbazar, Borma is speaking the very same words uttered by Miss Havisham in Dickens' novel way back in the nineteenth century. How is that possible? Miss Havisham had been deserted on her wedding day by a cheat and a scoundrel. At that moment, time had died for her. In her tattered wedding dress, with the lace and satin in shreds, Miss Havisham had sat amidst the ruins of time before the remains of a putrid wedding cake. And here is Borma, sitting amidst the ruins of time. For her, time stopped with the death of a man. Both women are of different places, of different times. How have they become one?

Borma clasps my hand as I prepare to leave. I shiver uncontrollably at the touch of the spectral Miss Havisham. My hands are still dewy-fresh with the auspicious bridal anointments of turmeric and lentil paste. I feel that the ghoulish Miss Havisham will take my hand in her own dry ones, and place it on her breast. She will ask me in her whispery voice, 'Do you know where you have placed your hand?'

'Yes, I know.'

'Where have you placed your hand?'

'On your heart.'

Like an apparition, Miss Havisham will say, 'Broken'.

Translated by Mitra Phukan

THE JOURNEY
KULADHAR SAIKIA

Perhaps there is nothing strange, nothing strange at all about the way I have cursed under my breath. My situation has been reduced to such a precarious one that it is no longer possible for me to sing happy notes or chant mantras. Meanwhile, instead of rushing forward through the sudden rain and storm, I have cleverly placed myself beneath the umbrella-like circular shed of a traffic point. This must surely be an indication of my farsightedness, for had I not paused here a while, I would have been mercilessly drenched on this long road without any refuge of my unfinished sojourn; and being wrapped in darkness, I may have even lost my direction. So maybe there is nothing wrong in saying that this timely action on my part is, after all, a reflection of my wisdom.

The blowing wind, the splashes of the slanting rain, the croaking of the frogs here and there, and the dying sound of thunder—all these are my companions now. A little distance away from me, a skinny mongrel has been sitting for a while now. For it, I must be an unwelcome intruder. Its terrified eyes have been trying to convey that my entry into its occasional shelter-turned-domain has brought about an unknown fear—the fear of being ousted from its own territory.

I need to pull apart the veil of darkness and peer at that part of me where the shoe has been hurting me for long. A thorn has found its place in my foot without my knowledge. It takes delight in its nagging pain and wishes to state that I cannot forget its existence; there is little hope of relief as my searching eyes have so far failed to locate it. I can now barely see my fingers or the sole of my foot but a while ago, everything—the road, the houses, the entire area—had been flooded in light. Moreover, brisk human activities had kept the white uniformed man, standing under the shed, immensely busy. But now only silence prevails—the clamour, the mad rush of the people can no longer be felt. The weary town has fallen into a deep slumber. The storm has taken its toll on the powerful transformer and now darkness, terrifying darkness prevails.

I tell myself that there is no need to despair at this seemingly endless state of calamities around me and at once, by putting a 'ROAD CLOSE' sign, I try to divert the direction of my racing thoughts. I feel an affinity with the road that lies to the left of where I sit now. This is the way that leads me to and from my workplace. Perhaps, had this road not led to the company where I have been employed for a while now, had I not been selected from amongst the scores of men aimlessly moving about, things would have been terribly different—I would have been asked to vacate my rented room with the result that I would have then had to bundle up all of my belongings (including the certificates earned in college and university) and finally return to my native village. I would have had to wind up that chapter of my life where I had engraved my day-to-day experience and leave behind my friends residing in a long line of rented rooms resembling a chain of railway coaches. These pages of my life also speak of the beginning and the end of my relationship with Anupama; they also remind me of my friends, Nandan and Prakash, who left me behind to languish alone in this God-forsaken place. All these experiences must surely be associated with the road to my left where a couple of days back I had suddenly come across Anupama after three long years and I had asked her:

'Do you remember that river burdened with the stinking, murky water through which flows the entire city's waste, pollutants, and chemical effluents?—What was the name of the red flower that was floating over the sluggish water, an oleander, a hibiscus?'

Anupama had peered through her gold-rimmed spectacles and given a very definitive reply, 'It was a bunch of gulmohar!'

'Look at the disparity! The sanctity of the gulmohar over the defiled water! Can a bunch of flowers be responsible for purifying the filthy water or is the impure water responsible for tainting the flower's freshness?'

'You can look at it both ways....'

'You are right. Actually, it is the way we look at things that matters—how the visual inputs strike our nervous system. What is more important is how exactly psychology analyses our situation, in what background and in what context. If we take the contaminated water of this river into account....'

'We are meeting after three long years; don't you have anything else to ask me? Don't you want to know about Nandan, about our marriage, how we're faring together, if everything is fine between us...?'

'I presume everything is fine. Didn't you abruptly end our relationship of five years to marry Nandan, who lived in the room next to mine, because you yearned for commitment, for security in life...? So, I assume everything must be fine.'

'You are such a naive person, there is so much of negativity in you...

your stories, poems, everything. There was that line you had written about a man's insecurity, about his fear of losing his identity, of being ousted from his own territory…the relentless struggle of self-preservation….'

'You still remember that after all these years!…. Anyway, where are you all now? Nandan? Your children and your family? Yes…you had planned to work in the city's slum areas, to bring back the smiles on the faces of the ailing children who would no longer be required to toil, to break the rocks of the hills, to trace their wasted childhood in heaps of refuse. You had so much you wanted to do—and to have suddenly met you today. So—'

'None of that happened you know.'

'What do you mean?'

'These things are no longer feasible now.'

'Maybe there is something else you plan to do…?'

Through the window of a nearby car, the cherubic face of a little kid whose nose-eyes-ears bore the genetic impression of Anupama, drew my attention. With soft petal-like fingers, the child was carving some undefined geometric patterns on the windowpane—

'Yours?'

'Yes.'

'What's her name?'

'Prastuti'—the initiation.

'Beautiful.'

'After a story of yours. You may not remember, but it offered a very attractive proposition. You had written that the whole process of initiating the path of our lives takes up all our days. This is one of the physical realities of life. And probably in the concluding line of the story, you had expressed your doubt whether, without any reference point, it would ever be possible for us to locate the position of our lives in this vast universe and in eternity. I could not exactly perceive all of that then, but nevertheless, your line of thinking did attract me….'

Inside the car, Anupama's daughter, Prastuti, was trying to absorb the brisk activities around her. The excitement was unlimited, the experience varied—the tong-tong sound of the horse-drawn cart, the ring of the rickshaw's bell, the echo of the distorted footsteps of the frenzied populace— all these were selectively stored in some corner of her mind.

'My address is still the same, you know. You can meet me on this road itself, as I cross it daily at regular hours, which of course, may or may not be convenient for you.'

Anupama did let me know that they would remain here only for a couple of days more. For Nandan, who had jumped into the fray; for whom life was meant to be a soaring flight, official leave was something that he could hardly afford. The world, according to her, had become such a small place that there was no reason why we should not run into each other again. With these words, she soon drove away with Prastuti. And I remained here, rooted to an impaired section of the road along which flows the murky river water. The bunch of gulmohar flowers which had been floating along the surface of the water had stopped midway and I suddenly realized that it was only a piece of red plastic. If Anupama had been here, we would have had a good laugh over the comic situation arising out of this error in vision. She would have probably spoken about our tendency to misinterpret situations, our inability to distinguish between reality and illusion due to the absence of an absolute power within us to analyze the different visual inputs that crowd upon us—thus illustrating the eminent psychologist Kurt Lewin's field theory that for the entire gamut of our decisions, the ground or field has a very important role to play....

'You have had a long journey on the road that lies to the left—your wonderful reunion with Anupama, the words that you have exchanged... all these must be giving you now a kind of nostalgic pleasure. For you, all the roads forking out from this point have no significance, except, the long straight road moving endlessly along the stinky river—the road where you have taken your journey so far.'

'From this crossroad I can move forward in any direction, as all the four roads are familiar to me. I know the elevation; I know where and how much each road turns. The trees, the shops, and the houses lying on both sides of the road are known to me—there is nothing about these roads that I don't know. It could be that the roads move forward because I too do so.'

'But what about the road on the right? Have you ever tried that?'

I do not exactly enjoy being quizzed by the dog in this manner. I know it was taking advantage of my solitariness and hurling missiles of questions at me. It wants to assess my geographical knowledge of this place; the depth of my relationship with my own soil. In the darkness I put my hand forward and from the hand that manages to touch the furry animal, I have come to know that it has remained rooted to the same spot.

I take the mucky road on the right, move forward, and finally sit on the steps which are there on the wide bank of the river. The water of the river brushes against my feet and fresh waves come every moment and wash that part of the sole of my foot where the thorn continues to hurt. I try to recall that evening when I had met Parag here for the last time....

'Why don't you go back home?' I had asked him in a rather patronizing tone.

'I cannot.'

'But why?'

'All the doors are closed for me.'

'Put your poetry aside and explain to them in simple terms what you really intend to do. How long can you go on like this?'

'I am the prodigal son of the family and there is no return for me. Do you want to see the advertisement they had put up in the newspapers? Here....'

'Can you really turn away from home? Return and you will be welcomed back to the fold. Your own people will never allow you to take the path of destruction, to go to the dogs....'

'My father has conveyed through Bapukan that they will not accept even my dead body if asked to do so.'

'These are just senseless utterances. Can Ananda Uncle ever forget the time when you were born, those delightful childish gurgles, the first words you had lisped, the catfish curry that was cooked for you? You should think more deeply. You simply cannot look at things so dispassionately. Think about the pathetic plight of your mother, how grief-stricken she must be, how many sleepless nights she must have passed pining for her only son. Think about that....'

'My decision is final; there is no question of looking back. I have come away from everyone—my own people, from Rashmi, and from all of you. This escape, the endless journey, the long sleepless nights have all become a part of my being, the very essence of my living. You will never understand.'

'Do you really think that you can achieve something with the thing that you have tucked in your trousers?'

'Not exactly.'

'Then why?'

'Have my plans ever materialized? You can presume that this will be my companion in one such mission. After all, failure has always been a part of me....'

The deliberate scent of the burning of incense sticks from the crematorium nearby struck our nostrils and we turned our eyes that way.

Amidst the mad rush of the people, amidst the clamour of the busy city, here was an area that spoke only of stillness and solitude. A kind of emptiness shrouded the peace and I said—

'Do you think this is the finishing point, the end of life's journey? Or are you foolish enough to be convinced that there will be others who will take over your incomplete mission from here onwards?'

'You can keep aside these sorts of questions for the literary types like yourself.'

'Since you have not cut yourself off completely from the village, why don't you get a job in the local school? That way you may even derive the satisfaction of initiating some change....'

'Ha! Ha! Ha!'

'I can feel the sarcasm in your laughter. So, you must be amused at my seemingly clever way of dumping on you the work that I cannot carry out myself—'

'How long has it been since you visited the village?'

'It has been quite some time, but then I am always in touch and when Dharani and others come here, they always make it a point to meet me.'

'Let's leave all that. What about Anupama? Have you met her? Or have you wiped her off completely from your mind?'

The day both of us parted from each other, Parag walked into the darkness and became a part of it, whereas, it was along the street lights that I found my way. There was a terrible pain somewhere in that part of me where the thorn had hurt me resolutely. My limping made a very ugly sight. Who knows I may have even looked like a horse with entwined forelegs or a skinny dog which had hurt it legs, limping its way through....

The dog is gradually coming closer to me; perhaps the damp weather following the heavy rains is making it search for warmth. Unknowingly, even I am being drawn towards it. A kind of togetherness between us is gradually taking shape. Our similar situation has kindled a bond between us and I decide to recount before it my last meeting with Parag—

I begin—I met Parag again on this road to my right. I followed him to the river bank soundlessly and without any inhibition like an entranced man. At that moment of our journey there was no exchange of words, only the whisperings of the blowing wind and the moving vehicles reached our ears. Parag was moving forward with four other men maintaining an equal distance from me. He was made to lie on the deserted area near the river bank, and soon he turned into a ball of blazing fire. The deliberate scent of incense sticks engulfed the entire crematorium. I watched dispassionately at the finishing line of a journey of life. The hired pall-bearers soon departed whispering among themselves about the bizarre situation—the headless body, unnatural death, and absence of family members at the funeral. Till the end, Parag remained an alien—and I returned with the unbearable pain in my foot looking like a limping dog—

The rain falls even more heavily and the undeterred flow of water drenches the lower portion of my body. At one point, I lift up my legs to sit like Buddha in meditation on the concrete floor of the traffic shed. The consumption of cheap liquor has completely numbed my senses and I am yet to come out of its intoxicating spell. I may even throw up any moment as I have consumed more than my share and the liquor having entered my intestines seems to fill the pot and sets my blood pulsating. I realize that the road behind me leads to Hasina's shop. I have been regularly moving on this road and all the excitement that surfaces on my evening stroll rushes forward in this direction. I have been making new friends there, where gambling sessions of cards and dice are carried out to the rhythm of cheap music. Through the dim light of various shades, we lift the glasses to our lips—I may even ask that short-haired girl her name as well as that of her dear one; I may even want to know the name of her village, but there is hardly any need for that—

And when somebody lets me know that a police raid is on, I make a quick departure through the back door to the railway track and finally take shelter in a deserted coach—at last some sense of security—while the railway station continues to buzz with various activities. I leave behind all these and run through the lanes of the slumbering city. The deserted street moves along with me. I turn to the right, change my direction to the left with the tar-coated street matching its steps with mine. Its length matching with the length of my journey and its change of direction being controlled by mine, my driving force becomes its life force. They all move along my course—the wide road, the pavement, and even the stinky, murky water flowing under it. I run faster and there stands right in the middle of the road, the traffic point blocking my way and I pause...somewhere the transformer bursts and this is instantly followed by power failure—

And now I am steeped in darkness and except for the dog sitting near me, I have no other companion. I can move on the road lying in front of me, I can even sit on the edge of the big pond nearby and at the break of dawn wash my body and mind to gear up for another monotonous day, which will have to bear the burden of my mechanical routine activities.

I decide not to take the road in front of me, as moving with me it will only arrive at my doorstep and from where there will be no moving further. The rains have visibly receded. The raindrops have become smaller and the wind too has lost its fervour now. I abandon my posture of meditation and stand up. The pain in my foot, which seemed to have subsided, surfaces once again and in utter frustration, I take off my shoes and fling them away making them land on the concrete road with a thud. I emerge from the traffic shed to step on the public road and move towards the railway station—

I wish to board any waiting train and move to whatever destination it would take me to at its own pace. The entire area is now plunged in darkness and I begin to walk—

I can feel the skinny mongrel following me. The communion between us leads it to follow my footsteps, my whole body reeking of cheap liquor—

The road is very familiar to me; I know all its distinctive features and even in this state of complete darkness I can locate them. I can feel the pain in my foot gradually ease away. I stumble on the uneven road, frequently slip over fallen leaves, rise at once, and continue to move forward in this familiar road of mine—

'Where are you going?'

'To the railway station.'

'Why?'

'Because I wish to, because there is a long journey ahead.'

'Are you moving towards the finishing line?'

The dog's condescending attitude irks me. Suddenly, electricity is restored and the whole area is flooded with light. The sudden, unexpected light almost blinds me and to my dismay I realize that the road along which I have been moving has entered my own doorway. It dawns on me that by drifting without a sense of direction I have landed not at the railway station but at my own doorsteps.

The pain in my thorn-pricked foot has become acute and unbearable. I turn to the dog that has been following me and bark at it:

'Bow, Bow, Bow.'

'Bow, Bow, Bow.'

'Bow, Bow, Bow, Bow....'

I limp and limp and drag myself to the familiar house unwillingly, irresolutely.

Translated by Arunabha Bhuyan

AN INCOMPLETE STORY
RITA CHOWDHURY

I cannot say anything about her, though I wish to. A long time ago, I had begun to write, but after writing some lines, I had stopped. I felt that I should leave it aside. My pen was not yet ready to bring out the sufferings of that woman.

After many days, I have started writing again. I am still not sure whether my pen is willing to write.

Words are not enough to express the sufferings of a woman.

At least for me.

I used to meet her only at long intervals, that too, when I visited my aunt's home. When I met her last, she had reached the autumn of her life.

She was my aunt's sister-in-law.

While looking carefully at the elderly woman, with very short grey hair, that looked almost as though it had been shaved, it was apparent that she was once very beautiful.

I don't remember exactly what she was wearing.

Perhaps she was wearing a mekhela, a longish one, which almost reached her toes. She had tucked part of it into the upper portion of her body and the rest was draped around her in pleats. Whenever she went out, she also had an aaguran, a wrap, wrapped around her, with detailed weaves like her mekhela.

Grave anguish was visible on her mature face.

'It's a matter of the rules of the Mouzadar's house, Aai. It's a matter of the customs of the Mouzadar's household.' This, she would often say in her conversation.

It is my passion to read people. I had this passion during the early days of my teenage and youth as well, but it was not as strong as it is now. There was a great desire to know the unexplained and what I could not understand was my unusual attraction towards her.

Mouzadar's house. The house of rich and influential people. It was the time, when the influence of the Mouzadar was on the decline. There were two large ponds, one at the front and the other at the rear, which seemed quite huge to my young eyes; a traditional Axomiya house of bamboo whose shoots and offshoots had gone into so many places that their ends could not be seen; a big storehouse; a telephone; an Ambassador car; many male and female workers; a group of young men reading and writing; a large kitchen and a dining room....

Just like a fantasy.

The entry of a small family to this large house, surrounded by a peaceful environment, opened the door to another world. If I had not met her and had not been so attached to her, I would have been overpowered by an inferiority complex.

My uncle did not look like my uncle; rather, he looked like a distant relative. Others too looked like they were from elite families, with whom it was difficult to make contact.

One day, away from this large and busy house, when the elder sisters and brothers and family members were engaged in conversations, away from their arrogance, I was engrossed in playing the game—ekka-dukki, hopscotch, beneath the shadow of a tree, beside the storehouse. The gheela was lying beyond the baseline and I was wondering what I should do, when suddenly, my aunt came and picked up the gheela and threw it near me and said, 'Come here, people of the Mouzadar's house do not play gheela.'

I was so involved with the game that I was not even interested in listening to her. I picked up the gheela slowly, and murmured, 'Who are you? I am not from the Mouzadar's household. I will play.'

'I am your aunt. I am your aunt's sister-in-law....'

I had not seen my aunt. She had passed away, a long time ago. However, I have seen her portrait. A tall lady, wearing a sari, adorned with a brooch pin.

My aunt was like an earthen lamp in the light of the sun.

'What shall I call you?'

'Aunt. You can call me Aunt.'

After a while, she said softly, 'Do you know, I used to play gheela a lot.'

'But members of the Mouzadar's family do not play gheela.'

The lady smiled. Only for a moment. And during that instant, curiosity arose in me.

'I used to play gheela, all alone behind the storehouse. Later, I got married. I was even younger than you.'

'Really? You got married in your childhood? That too, when you were younger than me?'

'Yes, at a very young age.'

'So how did you come here?'

'It's a matter of the rules of the Mouzadar's house, Aai. It's a matter of the customs of the Mouzadar's house.'

'Please tell me, how did you come here?'

'What will you do after you know? It's all over. And that's how it is supposed to be. Why not? As you sow, so shall you reap. Look there, it's a Baya's nest.'

Earlier too, the wonderful nests of the Baya birds had captivated me. Aunt said, 'I had told your aunt so many times not to take out the chicks from the nest. But she did not listen.'

'Why?' I shuddered. I threw the gheela aside and went to her.

'To eat fried Baya chicks.'

'Issh! Was there nothing else to eat?'

'It's a matter of the rules of the Mouzadar's house, Aai. It's a matter of the customs of the Mouzadar's house! Important matters, significant matters.'

My aunt looked unhappy.

I couldn't understand a thing. But I wished to know more. I did not like people who ate fried Baya chicks. In fact, I adored the woman who was fond of playing the gheela.

I was at ease with her.

I could relate to her.

She was my uncle's sister, but I was closer to her than I was to my uncle.

My aunt was no more. Many years had passed since her death. For the motherless children, this lady was like a mother figure.

But no one cared for this helpless mother.

Who would? She had no property at all in her name.

At the tender age of eight, she had been married off. She was to be sent to her in-laws' house, after she had reached puberty. But, before she could be sent, she became a widow.

A woman who became a widow at a young age, a woman who had no means of earning, a woman who depended on others...there was nobody who would value her. I began to take an interest in her. Gradually, I realized that she was not treated with respect at the Mouzadar's house.

She lived there in that huge house like a discarded object.

Undesirable. But she was useful.

I could not figure out why. What I could understand was that there must be some reason that the people of that house needed her.

No one gave her any importance. Even if she wished to say something, nobody listened to her. Nonetheless, even my immature mind could read what was going on in her mind. Yet, all the members of the family, especially women, competed with one another, insolently, to win the heart of this insignificant woman.

I felt very bad. This was perhaps the reason why I spent more time with her.

Everybody noticed my proximity to my aunt. With visible displeasure, and sarcastic laughter, they tried to keep me away from her.

I did not know why they wanted to keep me away from her.

It was only after a long time that I could understand. Due to that awareness, even today, there is a lot of anguish and grief deep within me for this insignificant woman who had no desire to say anything.

∞

After an interval of many days, when I visited my aunt's home again, she could not be seen anywhere. Unlike other days, she did not come out.

'Where is my aunt?'

'She is sleeping. She is unwell.'

'What has happened to her?'

'Don't know.'

'Why doesn't anybody know?'

Babuji and the other people know about it, said one of my elder cousins, indifferently. This was typical of the arrogant indifference of the Mouzadar's household.

Without saying anything, I went inside my aunt's room.

I was shocked to see the dark, filthy, stinking room.

In the feeble light coming from the skylight over the closed window, I discovered my aunt sitting on a broken bamboo chair.

She was so grief-stricken that she did not hear me come in. I stood beside her. She looked at me. For some time, she kept staring at me and then asked, 'Nobody comes inside this room. Why have you come here?'

'Why can't I?'

'You can come, Aai. It's a matter of the customs of the Mouzadar's household. But I am not the Mouzadar.'

'Why do you always talk about the Mouzadar's household? You are also part of the Mouzadar's household.'

'I am from the Mouzadar's household. The servants also live here in the Mouzadar's house, Aai. I am a servant.'

'Why are you saying this? It doesn't feel good.'

'I know that you feel bad. You are a kind and compassionate girl.'

'What's the matter with you aunt? Everybody is saying that you are unwell.'

'What else can they say?'

'Then are you not ill, aunt?'

She did not say anything.

I was not a writer yet. However, I did write poetry. Meanwhile, the seeds of a writer were sown within me.

I took her in my arms.

'Please tell me, aunt.'

Aunt had withered away. In that dark room, crushed by the indifferent attitude of the Mouzadar's household, she opened the door to her inner self.

She got up from her chair and pulled out a trunk which was lying underneath her bed. An old, colourless, and broken trunk. She took out a mesh bag from it. Inside this bag was a bundle of torn pieces of paper wrapped in an old cloth.

'See, it's a matter of the Mouzadar's house.'

'What is it, aunt?'

'Have a look. Have a look, for once.'

There was a packet of torn pages from a book. On these faded pages, she placed her wrinkled hands.

'I do not understand, aunt.'

She was silent for a while. Then she opened up her past to me.

A little girl was standing in front of me. At midnight, the eight-year-old girl wearing bridal clothes was being carried by a man to the sacred fire.

The bride, though fast asleep, was made to sit on a small wooden stool. She kept slumping down again and again, but somebody from behind supported her, again and again.

The unbearable night filled with smoke from the sacred fire; new clothes; helplessly weighed down by jewellery, hunger, sleep; the sound of a flute, drums, ululations, and wedding songs, somehow passed.

She had a vague memory of an unknown man wearing a bridegroom's ornamental headgear and vermilion, who changed her into a married woman.

A few months later, the house was filled with the sounds of wailing. Somebody removed her jewellery, somebody removed the vermilion from her forehead, and somebody made her wear a pair of white clothes.

She had become a widow.

Even before she reached her springtime, she had lost all that she was entitled to in life. In the Mouzadar's house, her fate was sealed.

The Mouzadar was an illustrious and influential man.

There were many people in this large joint family. Although the father did not show any affection for his daughter who was a widow and deprived of the right to happiness, in his heart, he had great love and affection for her. That was why she was gradually allowed to wear coloured clothes and jewellery, and could lead her life just like any other unmarried woman.

The Mouzadar's concern for his daughter led him to consider marrying her to a poor boy, who had been living under his guardianship in a room in a row of houses near the large premises.

The boy was very smart but he was not good at studies. He had never visited the house.

A small portion of his room could be seen beside the pond at the rear. When the girl stood there, he would come out of his room and stand in front of the house. She would then bow her head and would go back without looking up. This is how they looked at each other.

Both of them were aware of the proposal. The young woman's life was enlivened by a wonderful experience.

My aunt had fallen in love.

She did not speak to him.

In fact, she did not find any opportunity to speak to him.

There was nothing, except looking at each other.

Arrangements were being made for the marriage. However, at this time, while the arrangements were underway, the boy broke the rules.

He went to the banks of the pond.

After a few quiet moments, the boy gave her a book in which he had written her name and his wish to present her a gift.

Keeping the book close to her chest and absorbed in her dream, she reached home and encountered her father.

"'Call me Mouzadar, not Babu.'"

After instructing my sister-in-law along with Jetuki to take the book from my hands, he sat in the backyard, smoking his hookah.

"I fixed the marriage. I fixed the marriage! How dare they get ahead of themselves? This is not done. Stop the marriage. Let her go. Let her go, now."

I heard Babu saying all this to my mother. I saw how he tore the pages of the book into pieces. The house of the Mouzadar was silenced by the voice of a roaring tiger.

The boy was thrown out. They did not think about us, not even for a while. At the time of his departure, I did not get a chance to see him even once.'

In that desolate darkness, my aunt's pain-soaked voice was telling me the story of the times when egoistic masculinity was at its destructive best.

'What happened after that, aunt?'

'What could I do, Aai? Who can dare do anything in the Mouzadar's household?'

My aunt did not do anything. She only cut her waist-length hair short. She removed her jewellery and chose the clothes of a widow.

She had to pay a price. She lost her life. Still, she was useful. I had seen how important she was, when I stayed there. A number of women came to the room and before the eyes of a woman on her deathbed, they took out the jewellery from her trunk. In front of her, they fought with each other, pulled and pushed each other and divided her jewellery amongst themselves.

What was her name?

Till today, I do not know.

Translated by Surekha Sachdeva

HE RETURNS
MANOJ GOSWAMI

1988

(One)

Barman lifted the receiver off its cradle. At the other end was Deputy Inspector General Hara Dutta. Every one of the tinny words he uttered was loaded with tension and excitement.

'Yes, Sir,' Superintendent of Police Barman responded. In a very obsequious and cautious tone he updated, 'Sir, I have made all the arrangements as per your instructions. Two inspectors have been stationed at Chaukidingi outpost. I myself am going on an inspection right now. Red alert has been flashed to all the police stations. And Sir, I have just received the latest intelligence input.'

More instructions followed, terse and brief, and the telephone cable seemed to tremble with the urgency of the message it carried. Barman knew the facts only too well. The man was a dangerous character, the top leader of an insurgent group. He had been involved in a series of political assassinations. After several bank robberies and anti-national activities, he was captured seven years ago after much effort; but had soon slipped out of police custody. Because the police and the intelligence agencies upped their ante, he once again broke through the police dragnet and crossed the borders of the country. Many members of the terrorist outfit had already been arrested, some had become inactive and some others came over-ground and were now cooperating with the government. In plain words, their backbone had been broken. It was perhaps because of these developments that he was coming back. The feedback was that he had undergone training in the operation of latest weaponry, so he was now capable of inflicting serious damage. Who knew, he might even be carrying a large cache of sophisticated arms.

'Yes, Sir,' Barman's response was smart.

Ananta Barman had become a superintendant of police at a fairly young age, superseding many of his seniors. He knew the tricks of building a career. He had the devotion of a hound to its master, the swiftness of a hyena, the alertness of a hare, the daring aggression of a wolf; a schemer with limitless ambition. He sought to rise further to a very high level. So he needed this prize catch. He was ready to take some risks for it. Barman knew very well that it was one of those opportune moments that carried a bagful of promises; promises of awards and promotions. It would be a prize catch. He valued his career prospects, yes he did.

'Thank you, Sir!' Barman hung up. Droplets of sweat glistened on his face.

(Two)

The chief editor seemed to be satisfied with the layout of the first page. He took off his glasses, thought for a moment and said, 'Yes, the headline is fine—"Samiron Barua is on his Way." Wah! It will sell. But we need a photo of his, here.'

'But Sir, there was no way we could manage a photo. Goswami and Lahkar tried their best. Even the police files don't have one,' the Staff Reporter explained. The chief editor lit his cigarette, a new one from a fresh pack.

'All right then. Goswami, you keep in touch with the police station. Let Lahkar keep trying his sources. Make daily box items of whatever information you get from the sources. If he is arrested, the first photograph should be in our paper. We will be informing our readers about his movements. Do remember, it is Samiron Barua—the very name sells.'

The teleprinter was spewing out words in the next room, bits and pieces of news from various places. The sounds of vehicles honking on the street below also reached their room. A telephone rang in another room. The sub-editor and Goswami hurried there.

Lahkar pulled his chair a little closer to the editor's table. He looked around carefully and then said, 'How about something different, Sir? As far as I can see, there is hardly any hope of meeting the man. The police haven't found any trace either. So, I mean…can we go ahead with a fake interview?'

The editor groped for his ashtray, his eyes remaining glued to Lahkar. 'You mean, one of us is taken blindfolded to a hideout used by these insurgents. There we meet our man, speak to him about his future plans, his experiences across the border, his views on the present government…?'

'We can also give a hazy photo of that interview to go with the article,' Lahkar added enthusiastically.

The editor stubbed out his cigarette. His face showed graveness born of long years in the field of journalism, 'No, no, no, don't do anything like that. That will cause trouble, Lahkar. Police interrogations, cross-examinations... and if later it leaks out that it was all a cooked-up interview...the paper's image will take a battering, all for nothing.'

(Three)

Neela was combing her hair, the huge dressing-table mirror before her. It was a calm afternoon, one that lulled. A Cliff Richard number was playing softly on the tape recorder. The tape on the cassette completed its rotations. The servant boy was out for a matinee show. Her husband, Neelam Mahanta, generally did not return before four-thirty.

The emptiness of their swanky villa was getting to her even as she massaged face cream on her cheeks. From the window, she could see the afternoon street; deserted, except for the rare vehicle that sped by. She got up abruptly and flung herself onto the bed. The lazy moments of the afternoon hours dripped off the wall clock. The curtains rustled in the light breeze.

Just then the telephone rang. Neela sprang up at once. She was too frightened to even look at it. What should she do? Pick up the receiver? The telephone kept ringing, as if the whole house was shaken by the persistent ringing.

She approached the instrument hesitantly. She felt a chill run through her being. As she stretched out her trembling hand to pick up the receiver, she thought, what if it's him at the other end? What if it's his voice! That deep, grave, and manly voice?

'Hello?' She could hardly recognize her own voice.

'What's up, Neela? Aren't you well?'

Ohhhh.... It was her husband. The racing heartbeats hadn't been quelled yet. She took a few more seconds to regain her composure.

'Neela? Is something wrong?'

'No, nothing. I had dozed off, that's all.'

'How about a movie this evening? They are screening a good Spielberg film. Get dressed. I'll be there in fifteen minutes. And we have to go to Bhatta's place this evening, for his son's birthday party, right?'

Neela shut her eyes. She tried to immerse herself in the comforting tones of Neelam's voice. It seemed to be the only possible refuge.

'Not today,' she said. 'This Anil has also gone off somewhere. See if you can come home a little early. I'm feeling quite lonely today.'

Neela walked through the large room. The carpet beneath her feet was soft and thick. There was expensive furniture all around. In one corner, the refrigerator stood like a huge block of ice. In the Belgian mirror she saw the image of the latest TV set. Neela drew the colourful curtain of the window. She could see the garage beyond the lush green lawn from where her husband, only a few hours ago, had driven the blood-red Maruti to his company office. Her heart started racing again. Would she be able to carry on amidst this cosy comfort without a worry, she wondered. Would he allow her to loll in this luxury without any tension? Who knew, on one such lazy afternoon the doorbell would ring, she would open the door, and then she would find him waiting there.

'How are you, Neelie?' he would ask, that cruel, slightly enigmatic smile on his face. Hair unkempt, a thick beard masking his face, clothes soiled; he might appear thin, the two lean hands, hardened by many acts of vengeance, hanging loosely by his frame. Perhaps he would advance a couple of steps, looking around disdainfully at the opulent decor of the room. Perhaps he would look her straight in the face for a few moments, and say in a languid tone, 'Come back, Neelie. Come back to me.'

Neela shuddered. One day, he would certainly come back to her. That was certain. He would never forget her. She also knew he brooked no barriers; that he held society in utter contempt, that he was impassive even in the face of death. And now, after having lived for seven years in the jungles among wild animals and in the company of a band of wrathful rebels, he must have become all the more reckless. She felt disgusted with herself. What a shame! What an ill-starred moment it was when she had first met him ten years ago. Why did that feeling of affinity grow in her mind, leading her to spend so many intimate moments with him? Love... the very word repulsed her now. But it was only because of that love that he would return to her. No, she had never been in love with Neelam, yet, she has been living a secure life in the comfort of his arms, amidst these possessions—fridge, TV, car, swanky house.

Now he was returning. This comforting existence of hers was now threatened by the dreadful memory of her relationship with him, a relationship which they had called love. Her cheek against the grille, Neela stared out of the window. Yes, Samiron Barua was on his way....

(Four)

Someone had opened a fresh bottle of whisky, a glass fell on the floor with the careless swipe of someone's hand, there was the glugging sound of liquid being poured, and a voice could be heard singing, 'It's been a hard day's night, I should be sleeping like a...' very off-key. It was a dimly-lit room filled with cigarette smoke. There were a few scattered chairs, a table, and a cot. There they sat, like some shadowy figures—Bipul, Ajit, Dool, Bagen, and Rafiul.

Ajit got up and opened the window, letting the night breeze into the stuffy room. Turning, he recited in a solemn voice:

> We drink the whole night through,
> A cocktail of darkness and drink
> For we are the ones
> To see a new morning in...

Perhaps these were a few lines from one of his poems. He was considered to be one of the front-ranking young poets.

'Shut up, you fool!' Bagen snapped in irritation. 'This'—an obscene gesture followed—'is what I think of your poetry.'

The room seemed to rock with the guffaws of a bibulous Dool. 'Why do you say that, partner? It's through such poems that he makes such a name, receives gamosas of felicitation, gets mobbed by beautiful girls seeking autographs. And God knows how many beautiful chicks this rascal has....' A groggy Dool struggled to complete his sentence.

'What good does my poetry do?' Ajit asked somberly. 'Damn it, every bloody word in my poems rises to mock me. I tried so hard for the Publicity Officer's post, showed so many issues of magazines with my published poems to the Interview Board. All came to nothing.... Some guys came from somewhere and took the jobs.'

A motorcycle stopped outside. They knew it was Ishwar. He was leaving for the US to take admission in an American university on an overseas scholarship.... He was treating them to drinks this evening.

'Hello,' Ishwar greeted them as he entered.

'Are you leaving us, young man?' someone asked.

'Sure, I'm leaving you!' declared Ishwar, taking a swig of his drink. 'You guys must come to the airport in the morning. You must, for sure.'

Rafiul walked unsteadily towards him. He put a hand on Ishwar's shoulder, 'And what will you send us from America, bhai? Some good brand of liquor, pictures of sunbathing American blondes, some hot porn...?'

'A lot of colourful rubbish,' finished Ajit.

'Promise, do promise, you bloody... shouted Bipul.

'I promise,' Ishwar smiled wanly as he put his empty glass on the table.

'Go, you bloody bastard, all of you get lost,' Dool said, 'And when you come back after five years, you'll find everything changed here. A quintal of rice for twenty bucks, this bottle of whisky of hundred and twenty-five rupees today will sell at thirty maximum, fags will be free, and girls queuing up to marry loafers like us, money floating around like fallen leaves.... A real Ramrajya. Because we have heard that....'

'Well, I'll make a move now, have to drop in at many other places, I haven't even been to Neelie's yet. I'll meet you guys at the airport in the morning.' Ishwar took his leave in a very stylish manner.

'Goodbye, young man. Wish you all the best,' someone said from a dark corner. 'We've had some fun at your expense, but forget that. You too were no less. You too talked about revolution, about changing the system. We do not hold on to those any more. Remember you said, "They should be shot, hanged from the nearest telegraph post," that's what you said about all black marketeers, corrupt officials, MLAs, deceitful girlfriends....'

Ishwar smiled thinly, 'I have shut the door on yesterday and thrown the key away. Good night.'

He walked out. They could hear the motorcycle revving up and then its sound fading into the distance. '*Lie back in someone's arms*,' Bagen sang in a creaky voice. In the darkness, he got up and made his way unsteadily towards the open window.

'Okay then, you fools!' Dool suddenly shouted, 'All right! We'll shoot them. We'll hang them all...these black marketeers, ministers, MLAs, corrupt officials, unfaithful girlfriends.' He crawled on all four towards the centre of the room. They could now see that he only had his underpants on. Completely sozzled, he turned towards Ajit and the others.

'Don't you worry, brothers,' he drawled. 'Everything will be fine. We'll take up sten guns and grenades.... Oh, you want to know who'll give us arms? Don't worry. You know our Samiron Barua is on his way back. He'll lead us to heaven.' Dool was about to break into roaring laughter. But he suddenly stopped and threw up uncontrollably on the floor.

(Five)

The flickering flame of the kerosene lamp failed to light up the veranda. In that dim light, the woman holding the lamp seemed even more emaciated.

The man opened the gate and came in; without a word he crossed the threshold. The lamp followed him till he stopped. He took his shirt off and threw it on the bed. His face showed his exhaustion; hair tousled. With a distraught expression he sank onto the bed.

'It seems he's come back. Everyone says so.' The flame of the lamp flickered; so did his shadow. 'Why has he come back at all?' he murmured, as if carrying on a monologue. 'He's been dead for a long time for me. Did he ever send a paisa to me, his old father? His three sisters are to be married off. Will it be possible after he returns like this?' His voice turned moist with long suppressed emotions and hurt feelings. 'Why did he not die instead? All those animals in the wilderness…bombs and bullets…could none of those finish him off?'

The woman clutched the lamp. A deafening silence followed. 'I knew he would return one day.' At last she spoke a few words in her feeble voice.

(Six)

On the huge, elegant table lay some newspapers and magazines, a packet of cigarettes, an ashtray, two platefuls of cashew nuts, and a few glasses of soft drinks. Five men were seated around it. 'So Phukanda, you must know Samiron Barua pretty well?' The burly one asked after some hesitation.

'Yeah, I know him. I know him well,' answered the old man. He was a veteran politician of the state, one of the senior-most. He sat leaning back on his sofa. Silver-framed glasses were perched on his nose. Two golden buttons glinted on his kurta. His walking stick was propped against the table at his side. 'His father and I were in jail together. We were friends. After Independence, I became a Minister and we completely lost touch—I don't know where he vanished. He was a very touchy man by nature; had a very strong sense of self-respect. He was simply not one to be in politics. Many years later, I met him once in a village where I was to address a meeting. He was the Headmaster of the school there. "How are you doing, Phukan?"

He had asked me directly and introduced the small boy by his side as his son, Samiron Barua. The lad greeted me with a namaskar, addressed me as Khura, his father's younger brother. That evening, I had tea at their house. Yes. Of course I know him.'

'Then why don't you tell him, Phukanda? Tell him that our party will be the best platform from which to counter the present government?' One from the group asked excitedly.

The old man's lips puckered into a faint smile.

'You must get hold of him by whatever means possible. We'll get you all the information about him. Phukanda, you know that this is a golden opportunity for our party to come to the political centre stage. If we miss this, there's no hope left.'

'Ah, I can manage that. Only, it will need some histrionics and some deceit. And I can do that much,' the old man declared. He picked up his walking stick and fiddled with it for some time. 'I've taken myself to a very distant horizon. Today, I dwell in a world where I do not hear my own shout. I do not feel the need to keep track of myself.'

'The oldie must have had a bit too much,' one of them whispered.

'I will definitely speak to him. When I meet him, I will put my hand on his shoulder very affectionately and in a voice dripping with emotion and sympathy, I will say, "Sameer, you must return to a normal life. What will you achieve from all this? The path you have chosen is not the one for someone from our part of the world. Give it up, son. Come with me. Come and work with our party. Try to do something for the people, Sameer, stay with me. You know how long your father and I have...."'

(Seven)

He had reached the cinema theatre at the crossroads; a huge, new theatre; fresh paint still shining on its walls. Samiron recalled this was where their teacher Kusha's house had once stood. But where did the family go? How audaciously this swanky cinema hall existed in the place now!

After many years, he had entered the city again, two days ago.... There were massive changes everywhere. He did not see a single familiar face on the streets. No warm hello from anyone, no pleasantries exchanged. There had been a huge banyan tree at this very corner. It had probably been cut down.

Shops and buildings had mushroomed everywhere. The roads were crowded now, many more cars and buses. The horns of the speeding vehicles, the shouts of the handymen all added to the constant din around.

Samiron went gingerly into a nearby tea stall. There was a thin crowd inside. He sat on a corner table with a cup of tea and kept a watchful eye on the entrance. He hadn't gone to any hotel to spend the last couple of nights he had been here. His own home was out of question. Nor could he muster up the courage to stay with any friend or relative. He had come to know that the police had sniffed out his presence in the city. He had barely managed to escape the police cordon at Chowkidingi. At the Lumding railway station too, he had noticed several suspicious characters, possibly from the Intelligence Branch.

Two fire trucks sped past with screaming sirens. He was startled and looked furtively around. Nothing; nobody was curious. The clatter of the utensils, the manager's harsh orders, a Hindi film song coming from a tape recorder; everything was progressing amidst this normal din. Samiron placed the emptied cup on the table.

So he had returned. He had returned empty-handed. The little money that he had was almost exhausted. He had managed to secure some ammunition which should reach here in the next couple of months, but this hinged entirely on trust. And these days, he was increasingly beginning to doubt whether it had been wise to depend on this thing called trust all these years. Most of his old comrades had drifted away. Pinaki Mahanta was in a cushy job; Dwipen Phukan was a prosperous contractor; Ramen had become an MLA, and he had seen a minister's car parked outside the home of his best friend, Dwigen, a couple of nights ago. What was he to do now? Where could he go? He hobbled around like a man mesmerized.

A marriage party passed by. There were those cars decorated with cascading flowers and bright lights; a hired band played loud music with clarinets and drums. A group of young men danced along, enjoying themselves to the fullest. A happy clamour filled the street. Samiron passed a group of young men aimlessly loitering outside a paan shop. They shouted near-obscene remarks to a bevy of girls passing by.

A crowd shuffled and strained to watch a cricket match on the TV inside the showcase of a shop.

'Another wicket fell! Ravi Shastri is bowling really well!' someone commented spiritedly.

He, Samiron Barua, kept walking through all this. He was exhausted, impecunious, and forlorn. People swarmed the street outside a cinema hall.

A show must have just ended. On the wall in front were garish hoardings: a Bollywood hero in a 'romantic' pose, lifting the heroine on his shoulders; of a cigarette brand, another one of a 'Musical Nite' taking place in the city shortly, then that one on birth control. On the top of the clothing store of Ramlal Sevadutt there was a big billboard advertising underwear with pictures of a man and a woman, practically nude. The city dwellers passed by nonchalantly below.

Suddenly, Samiron was startled by a loud cacophony. Two busloads of youngsters passed by. The loudspeakers behind the bus amplified their screams. Perhaps it was a picnic party.

He trudged on wearily away from the uproar. Near a salon a man was selling groundnuts. He stopped by and bought nuts for two rupees. A furtive glance around—no, nobody was watching him. He stood in front of the barber shop and assuming a very casual expression on his face, started shelling the groundnuts and popping them into his mouth. On and off, he was assailed by gusts of sound, of dust, and by flashes of passing vehicles. On the hoarding at a distance, the halogen light kept flashing on and off. He caught sight of his face in the salon's mirror—clean-shaven, longish hair, bespectacled. He appeared gaunt and tired; the cheekbones showed. Has he become a little hunched lately?

For whom had he returned? Why had he stayed away so long in the wilderness of alien lands braving wild animals and ruthless men? What had forced him to bury the many colourful dreams of his youth? For whom? He thought, don't these people around ever yearn, just once, for anything? He had once thought that people in society kept counting their moments of suffering in an endless saga of disquiet, just like distressed passengers trapped in a train accident. But no, nobody is waiting, no one is suffering. It is a smooth flow. All around he saw happy celebration, there is money, there is mirth. Does anyone need him at all? If he stood at that street corner and shouted, 'Hey, here, here I am, Samiron Barua!' would anyone rush to him other than the police?

'Should I give you some more?' The old groundnut seller asked him. With his shaky hands he was roasting the nuts on a dilapidated kerosene stove on the pushcart. The aroma of roasted nuts wafted in the breeze. The flame of the stove quivered and the cold air around could not be warded off by the heat of that flickering flame. Samiron bought some more.

'Did you sell enough today?' he asked as he took the small paper bag from him.

The old man beamed a toothless smile. 'Just seeing the day through.' he said. 'It's the same every day.'

Samiron continued to stand there confused, shelling the groundnuts one after the other. Should he go back to where he had come from? Or to his mother? Should he surrender to the police? Or should he go to some distant city, begin life afresh, lead the law-abiding, normal, secure life of a citizen?

Samiron walked slowly on. The city was still bustling with life, throbbing restively with many emotions. There was the typical hubbub around. There was the very mechanical illumination of the glow-signs with their advertisements, the yellow light of the halogen lamps. Samiron took the last nut out of the packet. He was about to throw the wrapping away when something on that scrap of newspaper caught his eye. Printed on it in bold letters was the headline—

SAMIRON BARUA RETURNS!

He shivered to the core of his being. With a bewildered expression, he stood still with the piece of newspaper in his hand.

An endless stream of vehicles and people kept flowing along the city streets. There was laughter, gaiety, and music all around. A bevy of young girls in colourful dresses went past, followed by a few ladies. A group of children went past next. The clique of boisterous youngsters at the paan shop had dispersed; he could see the young men coming along the road. A few senior citizens were walking leisurely on the pavement. He let go of the scrap of newspaper in his hand.

SAMIRON BARUA RETURNS—this enduring bit of news wafted about in the dry wind and disappeared in the busy crowds of the city.

Translated by Amritjyoti Mahanta

NO MAN'S LAND

ANURADHA SARMA PUJARI

The air in this remote town is all charged up. People are talking about the football match even when they are shopping for their daily quota of rice, oil, vegetables, and eggs.

I have been around in this town for less than a month. The first day I set foot here, I felt I had come to some place outside India, a place at the back of beyond. After crossing the lofty mountain range, where the peaks, kissed by the feathery clouds and playfully hugged by the waterfalls create a mesmerizing picture, the meandering narrow road led me to this place called Dauki.

Situated on the border of Meghalaya and Bangladesh, this happens to be the last Indian town in these parts. For the last two years, I have been associated with this organization for conducting a demographic survey of the bordering towns. I do not know what the outcome of the survey would be but I am enjoying myself. I have begun to understand that people cannot be bound by any man-made boundary.

This small town is actually a modernized village. There is a church, a football field, a school, and numerous food joints and shops. In these shops one finds 'Made in Bangladesh' potato chips, Dhaka's Khan Namkeen packets, and even cakes and biscuits that are cheaper than the Indian ones. In the summer heat, one can quench one's thirst with small juice bottles from Bangladesh. I went looking for an electrical shop to repair my iron and I found one near the football field. While the electrician was mending my iron, I watched the game the local guys were playing. It was then that he said, 'There will be a big match. Bangladesh versus India. We are all waiting for it.'

I paid the Bengali electrician and walked out. Passing by those tea stalls, I thought of having a cup of tea in one of those kiosks, rather than going back home to make it myself. Though the Jaintia community is the largest here, there are quite a few Bengalis, Biharis, Hindus, Muslims, and Jains. Most of the Christians are Khasis, who stayed back here for business. The main road is perpetually lined with trucks carrying coal and Army convoys. Any newcomer would feel that the region is on the brink of a war. Even the locals seem to be worried.

I went inside a tea stall. The wooden bench had seen better times.

One could make out that it was once painted blue. Though it is called a tea stall, it serves rice and roti round the clock. Three Army jawans were having roti and subzi. A huge Shaktiman truck which carried rations for the Army was parked outside. They were speaking in Hindi and the topic was the forthcoming football match.

'I was told yesterday that Abbas is right-in. I wonder who will be the goalkeeper. But whoever it is, nobody can match up to our Randheer. However, our forward is weak. Thapa would have been the best choice. But he is on duty on the Rani border. They could have brought him here for a day....' While the two youngish-looking jawans were talking non-stop about the match, the lanky middle-aged one was quietly eating roti-subzi, pickles, and damp jalebis. Though the jalebis were so cold that even the sweet syrup had crystallized back into sugar form, he was savouring every bit of it, nodding his head in ecstasy. Except for calling out to the slim and fair Jaintia girl with 'Give me rotis' or 'Give me chillies', he didn't take part in the discussion at all.

The girl asked me what I would like to have with tea. In the glass showcase there were biscuits, jalebis, and cupcakes. I didn't feel like having any of them, but it is always nice to nibble something with a cup of tea. As I couldn't make up my mind, the girl offered, 'Have one of those cakes. They are fresh.'

'From Bangladesh?'

'Yes. Quite tasty.'

I nodded. She brought me a triangular piece that reminded me of a sandwich. Placing the plate in front of me, she said, 'On the day of the match, men from Shillong will come here to make samosas and kachoris. The trucks will be banned on the road that day. People from Cherrapunji, too, will come for the match.'

These tea stall owners get most of their business from the drivers and handymen of the hundreds of trucks that cross the Meghalaya border to go to Bangladesh. At the checkpost, the handymen get down. Only the driver is allowed to drive up to the demarcated coal depot and drive the empty truck back. The drivers and the handymen are familiar with the jawans. However, most drivers hand over their vehicles to their handymen to cross the checkposts and they rest at these tea stalls, have tea, and flirt with the women.

'Are you from this side or that side?' the Jaintia girl asked me in Hindi. 'I am from this country. Why?' 'You are new here. There is a lot of checking these days. Last month, a boy came here for a meal. Immediately after that the Army raided the shop. They harassed us too. The boy was in the rest house. The Army caught him. They recovered arms and ammunition. He had crossed the border in one of those trucks carrying coals. Such incidents keep happening. They do not usually get caught. Hopefully, the match will be over without any hitch. My relatives will also come to watch the game.'

'How come you have relatives there?' I was surprised.

'My father was from Sylhet. He married my mom and stayed back. He died two years ago.'

She explained briefly and walked up to the stove to pour tea. Plenty of Bangladeshi men marry Khasi and Jaintia girls and occupy land and property here. To avoid that, the elderly people of the bordering villages now keep a strict vigil over their girls so that the Bangladeshis cannot seduce them. This is the only way for a Bangladeshi man to settle down this side of the border. I have heard a lot of scandalous stories during my short tenure here. Bangladeshi people easily cross the Tamabil border and sell their rasgullas here. Sometimes, they even stay back. It's only when one crosses the border via the No Man's Land that one has to produce one's passport. Otherwise, they do not have to pay tax on their merchandise. It is more like neighbours exchanging a fruit or a vegetable from their kitchen garden or exchanging pleasantries from their balconies.

Lily Marbaniang was sitting with three hilsa fish, imported from Bangladesh. Other than those, she had a few katla fish too. In the direct heat of the sun, her pink face had turned red, so much like the gills of the fish laid out in front of her. The flies hovering over the fish were troubling her too. She didn't bother much about those sitting on her wrap-around skirt but she got irritated at those buzzing in her face.

Sylvia, who was sitting close by looked at her and yawned. 'Haven't seen that Major for some time. Had he been around, your fish would have been sold out by now.'

The statement was directed at Lily. 'You have already sold two hilsas. I am yet to see a buyer. Looks like I will have to wait for those Biharis who come for a bargain at closing time,' she continued.

Lily was getting used to Sylvia's barbed comments but today she lost her cool. She had hardly eaten anything the whole day. Robin, the chaiwallah, had come with his trolley twice to ask her if she would like to have tea and cake. But she was waiting for the coal trucks, because that meant business. Now, it was almost afternoon. Her stomach was growling. She slapped the hardboard fan near the fish and looked at Sylvia and said, 'Old lady! Are you getting so desperate because the Biharis are not around for you to flirt with, that you are taking out that frustration on me?'

Sylvia opened her betel nut-filled mouth to reveal her nicotine-stained teeth. 'You are a fine one to talk. Should I tell Simon about you? We have to pay 20 per cent tax on the fish we buy. You get it without paying anything. How?'

Lily kept quiet. Sylvia knew where to hit.

Lily covered the fish with the black polythene sheet, put two bricks on either side and got up. She went up to Robin's tea trolley and asked him for a cup of tea. 'I don't want these cakes. All right, you have a few onion pakoras there. Give me those.'

'These are from the morning lot. They have gone stale. Have a bun. It's much more filling.'

When I came here, the first thing I had learnt was the popularity of Robin's tea. I got myself a cup of tea and a packet of made-in-Dhaka Khan namkeen and parked myself on the bench under the peepal tree. As I was flipping through my notebook to check out the must-do list, Lily with her cup of tea and bun sat next to me and started eating without looking at anyone. I was enjoying the fight between her and Sylvia. She smelt of raw fish. Her cheeks were red. She had a pair of green slippers on and, without being conscious, she was swinging her well-rounded thighs to and fro. She looked like a wild lily in this dry, lifeless place. Small wonder that she evoked jealousy among Sylvia and her kind.

Still oblivious to her surroundings, she got up, scratched her hip and glanced at some faraway object. Robin looked at her and commented, 'Maybe today the Major will turn up. Saw him leaving for some place a couple of days back.'

Lily gave him a killer look. 'You men just have a one-track mind. If he buys fish from me, he drinks tea at your stall too. But no, no one takes it in that sense.' Lily kept the cup on the wooden plank with a thud and told the boy, 'Add it to my account.'

'Why? The owner of Ghosh Hotel himself bought two hilsas from you this morning. Fish which you bought without paying any tax! So much profit, why can't you pay for a cup of tea?' Robin charged her.

In anger, Lily's small slanted eyes narrowed down to two slits. She put her hand inside her clothes, and fished out a small pouch from near her breast. She peeled a hundred-rupee note from the bunch and thrust it into

Robin's hand. Even before Robin could pocket it, Lily asked him rudely, 'How much more do I owe you?'

'Seventy rupees and sixty paisa. In fact, I have to return the change.'

'You beggar, you insulted me for just seventy rupees?'

'Don't get me wrong. I tease you only because you are so pretty. I know you don't give a damn about that Major, it's him who tries to be close to you on the pretext of buying fish! Why do you have to react to Sylvia's comments? We all know what this middle-aged woman was in her heydays. Don't we know that she looks at you as her rival?' Robin whispered all this to Lily, careful not to let the words fall into Sylvia's ears. But I could hear them clearly.

Lily went back to her original position. I too got up to pay Robin.

'Will you come to watch the match?' In these last few days, Robin had become friendly with me.

'Of course! I'll never miss this one!'

'They have a few good players. Rumour has it that all the hotshot Army officers from both countries will come to watch this one. But even without a friendly match, those people are civil to us. We take cake, biscuit, puffed rice on credit. They too take back rice, kerosene oil. This divide is meaningless. If the law is so strict, they should stop our animals, our birds from crossing over. Like the cows and the goats, people too come and go. The Army harasses some people, some they allow to go scot free. In a few cases they even turn a blind eye. I do not understand.'

Robin came a little closer to me, 'Lily too goes to Tamabil to get her fish. But she takes a different route. The Major knows about it. But he simply ignores it just because she is so beautiful. He, in fact, buys fish only from her. Lily's husband was jailed twice on charges of smuggling opium. But both times he was out in no time because of lack of evidence. He has been missing for the past two months. Lily can no longer depend on him. That's why she has started this business. She has earned a bad reputation though.'

Quietly, I paid him and headed towards the bus stop. Given a chance, Robin would go on gossiping about Lily. And such talk spreads like forest fire. I looked at Lily. She was busily shooing off the flies. As she sat there carelessly, her skirt parted, giving a glimpse of her thighs. Her eyes were pale like those of a dead fish. Perhaps it was because she was worried about her husband! A bus arrived. The passengers inside were packed like sardines. Even so, the conductor shouted, 'Tamabil, Tamabil, empty bus'.

Just then a jeep halted there. Two men got down and walked up to the drain near the road to answer nature's call. They were talking in Assamese. There was a public toilet nearby. Perhaps they did not know about it. Newcomers, perhaps. I asked the one who was stretching himself near the jeep, 'Where are you from?' Sometimes a simple question brings a solution to many complicated situations. That's exactly how it happened with me. They turned out to be a team of engineers and geologists studying the currents and direction of the river water for some irrigation project. Quite suave and fun-loving people! They didn't just give me a lift, but entrusted me with the responsibility of showing them around the border. I obliged.

The middle-aged engineer in a green t-shirt and a pair of corduroy pants talked to one of the jawans and kept his foot on the No Man's Land. Waving his hands frantically, he called out for me. As soon as I reached him, he shouted with joy, 'This No Man's Land is the holiest land on earth. This is where the earth is independent in the truest sense of the word. Today, this planet is tamed by the human race, which was not the case some forty-five thousand crore years ago. The animals, the trees lost their freedom at the altar of civilization. But do these trees know which village in India they belong to? Their address? Does this river which flows through this state know that one part of it falls in India and the other in Bangladesh? But it has added a serene beauty to this border area of which one can only dream. The road to Tamabil unites both countries in more ways than one. The trees on this road have their roots in Bangladesh but their trunks and branches fall in Indian territory. The vines cross over the border without any hesitation. The rows of betel nut trees out there look up to the Indian sky. The pebbles which get carried away from here by the river are collected by Bangladeshi labourers on the other side. These then get sold in Bangladeshi markets. Do these pebbles know where they come from and where they go?'

'Don't be afraid. You can come over to this side,' said the border security guy, putting a full stop to my train of thought. The smiling man had a name—Riyaz Ahmed. When they saw us hesitating, the others joined him. 'We are coming to play the match, don't you know?' they asked with such zeal, it was as though they believed that this particular match would erase the India–Bangladesh border once and for all. And after that there would never be any question about the political territory of Bangladesh. Only two days more! After that both countries would merge into one, courtesy this friendly football match!

Riyaz, still with his winsome smile intact, came a step forward. 'Your Colonel was here yesterday. Had a cup of tea in our camp. Why are you so scared of stepping into our country? Look, what is written over here,' Riyaz pointed at the signboard on his side. It read, 'Welcome to Bangladesh. Wherever you are is your own country.' However, the Indian security man was not buying this. He shouted at us, 'Enough, come back now.' I looked at Riyaz and said, 'We will come to your country someday with a permit. We will come to see the match. Best of luck.'

Riyaz was, perhaps, getting to be a bit reckless. He came up to the No Man's Land and shook our hands. Smiling that beautiful smile, he said, 'You always speak the truth when you are standing on this zero land. People should actually think from a zero perspective. Then no one would be biased. Religion, caste, country, border—everything merges into one to become one big football. Even the images the astronauts took from space shows the world as a big round football.'

Lost for words, I kept looking at Riyaz. In that uniform with its camouflage prints, and the cap which covered his forehead, his eyes shone like two bright stars. A few moments with this Army man liberated my soul. The engineer in our team held Riyaz's hand and said, 'Damn this political boundary. You are my brother.'

Even as we walked back, we kept looking over our shoulders and waved. The engineer said, 'Had Bergman or Antonioni seen this moment, from which angle would he have captured it?' Maybe he was just trying to show off his knowledge on filmmaking.

'I can speak for Ritwik Ghatak. He himself was an immigrant and he captured the pain of Partition through his camera,' I said quietly.

Suddenly, I spotted Lily walking on the road that was parallel to the border. She seemed to be in a hurry. She was walking fast without looking anywhere. I had seen Lily at Dauki only two hours ago. Why would she abandon her business for the day and come to this place? Maybe she was looking for that Major. The BSF jawans saw her but they did not object. These things are normal. They recognize the people living in the border areas. It's okay for a person living here to share a cigarette with someone across the border or invite him to sit under a tree and share his domestic problems. They do not object to such things. My companions and I parted company. They had to get back to their work station and I did not want to take any more favours from them.

So I decided to catch a bus back. It would hardly take me twenty minutes. I threw a last glance in the direction of Lily. She had disappeared from view. Maybe her house was somewhere here. But what had happened to her fish, I wondered. Maybe she gave them to Sylvia to sell. But Sylvia was having difficulty selling her own. And again these two did not get along. So where did she keep her fish? Why on earth am I bothering about Lily and her fish, I rebuked myself. I better think about the work I have to do. One should be detached, like a zero. I should keep that nuance of the No Man's Land within me.

Suddenly, I remembered Riyaz. I had never met such a romantic and philosophical jawan before. They say a huge number of highly educated men join the Army as there are hardly any career options available in Bangladesh. This football match between the BSF jawans of both the countries would surely be fun. Truly India and Bangladesh became one that day. As if it was not just a local match but the World Cup final. The excitement in and around the field was palpable. There were more than two hundred people from Bangladesh to support their team.

Riyaz was the left-in. Whenever Riyaz manoeuvered the ball, I yelled—Riyaz, Riyaz! 'I hope I am not betraying my own country by supporting Riyaz,' I thought for a second. But then it was a match, a friendly match, a match that washed away the feelings of enmity from our minds. In fact, we should support them and they should cheer our players and set an example—no, I did not suffer from any guilt pangs. For that moment, I became a bird, a tree, a turbulent river, a fountain of joy in the No Man's Land.

India beat Bangladesh 4–0. After the match, there was a feast for players and jawans of both the countries. The Bangladeshi visitors went back. The place wore an unusually calm look after months of excitement. I had to go to Shillong to submit my reports at the head office. After two days, I came back. I headed towards that Jaintia girl's tea stall. This time she offered me a new kind of biscuit—a creamy chocolate layer between two wafers.

'Bangladesh?' I asked her pointing at the biscuit.

'A new biscuit dealer had come on the day of the match. He gave us these. If they sell, he will bring more.'

'Did your relatives come?' I asked.

A little shadow crossed her face. 'They could not,' she replied.

Lines of trucks carrying coal were rushing towards the border. There were new faces in these stalls. Some exchanged takas in these stalls. Nobody asked them questions. Who wants to bother about such things? That's solely these security guards' headache. I walked towards the fish market. I thought of buying a fish from Lily. Just for those sad, lonely eyes.

But Lily was not around. Sylvia was happy, doing roaring business in Lily's absence. Even Robin's tea trolley was surrounded by customers. I waited for Robin to be free. On the first opportunity, I spoke to him, 'Lily is not selling fish today. I wanted to buy a hilsa.'

Robin was pouring water into his kettle. Without looking at me, he replied, 'How will she come? She was shot at. Don't you know? Everybody here knows about it.'

I felt slighted. 'I don't know. I was away in Shillong for two days,' I said.

Robin started mixing milk powder and sugar with a spoon. With a smirk, he continued, 'Those many supporters who came from Bangladesh on the day of the match, not all of them went back. One of them was left behind. There was a problem at the checkpost because of that missing number. Next day, in the wee hours, two figures tried to sneak into Bangladesh and the Army fired at them. Both were together under one large wrap. They could not get past the No Man's Land. Both fell on the ground. Those two turned out to be Lily and the missing Bangladeshi man. He had spent the night with her. The Major kicked her with his boots very badly despite the fact that she was bleeding from the shot in her arms. Nobody knows whether she wanted to go with that Bangladeshi or was just helping him to go back. Everyone thought Lily frequented Tamabil to meet the Major. Nobody knew about this Bangladeshi man. The jawans injured him badly too. God only knows what will happen to Lily.'

'Where is she now?' I couldn't help but ask.

'In the hospital, where else? There was a fight between the two armies at the border. The chief commander of that side got so wild that he wanted to shoot her dead. The man's name is Riyaz. He came here to play in that match. The Bangladeshi took a bullet in one of his legs. After many meetings between both the security forces, it was decided to send that man back to his country. Lily will be punished. The Major is still mad at her.'

Walking slowly, I left that place. Sylvia's voice came from behind, 'Fresh fish. Buy one. There are hardly any left.'

Poor Lily! She had understood the meaning of zero, without being taught.

Translated by Parbina Rashid

BAK: THE WATER SPIRIT
IMRAN HUSSAIN

And neatly folding the fishing net into halves and making two handfuls of it, Haren advanced to unfurl the net, only to stop short in his tracks. Down the ribbony village alley, which seemed now to be floating in a mass of fog, he was coming this way. A peculiar manner of walking and his crooked and grotesque posture made it easy to recognize him even from a distance. In the flickering moonlight that filtered down through the slender leaves of the thin bamboo grove, his dew-wet ugly body shone with an eerie brightness. His human form seemed imbued with a strange ghostliness.

The gathering fog lingering over the water, the rustling sound of the wind blowing across the bamboo grove, and the hazy, striped moonlight all combined to give the shores of the lake a magical hue. Quite fearsome even in daylight, now, in the foggy moonlight, the place seemed even more haunted and mysterious. Now, the familiar paths, trees and shrubs, and the boats of various sizes which were kept hull-up on the bank of the lake, all seemed strange and unfamiliar.

The river was not a great distance away. In fact, a part of the lake even flowed into the Kolong. Yet, for the surrounding Kaiberta, Kalita, and Lalung villages, this lake was a lifeline. The simple lives of the people of different ethnicities who lived in these villages centred on this lake. The whole day long the western side of the lake resounded with the cheery voices of the village maidens and youths, as they bathed or fetched water or swam in the lake. Moreover, the village fishermen with their large and small boats were to be seen unfurling their large or small nets almost all over the lake during the day. But everybody feared this north-eastern side of the lake, especially where it touched the edge of the cremation ground. Here, a gigantic old elephant apple tree, an Ou, stood with its numerous branches spread menacingly. Even the Sylheti fishermen who worked for the fish merchants gathered up their nets and did not venture out in that direction.

The elders of the village said the place was haunted. It was here that, coming to fish on a bright full moon night, Ratneswar Bora had seen a boat of gold floating on the lake. Frightened out of his wits, he had somehow managed to reach home. He lost consciousness when he was at the bamboo shafts that were the gateway to his home. When he came to, his body was burning with fever. He began to mutter strange things about a boat of gold with oars of silver, of treasure buried under the Ou tree and much else. People said that Ratneswar would not have survived the ordeal had not his older brother, Suren, gone to Rajamayong that very day to get charmed oil from a renowned faith healer.

Ratneswar, then a strapping youth, was an old man now, his hair and beard grown grey, his face lined with wrinkles. But he never tired of recounting his experience as vividly as if it had occurred only the other day. For many years after that, people, out of fear, had avoided going to that area until it took on an abandoned and deserted look.

But unable to fulfil the needs of his newly-wedded wife with the proceeds that he gathered from petty thievery, Hebang had once tried to dig beneath the Ou tree. No pot of riches was unearthed. But it was said that he did find a few gold coins. However, he did not live to enjoy them. That very night he began to vomit blood, and died, leaving his new bride to wear a widow's clothes.

But for the people of the lakeside, the most astounding occurrence was that of the water spirit killing Tikheroo. He then shape-shifted to Tikheroo's form, and came to live with Padumi, Tikheroo's young and beautiful wife. Till today the spirit would have been slave to Haren Mahaldar, the lessee of the lake, and would have guarded the lake for him, had he not escaped after tricking Tikheroo's mother into giving him back his magical pouch which had been kept safe within a casket full of mustard seeds.

Back in those days, when the spirit was slave to Haren, the Mahaldar's house had overflowed with cash and kind. But Haren's luck seemed to have fled along with the spirit. His state deteriorated and he took to smoking opium, drinking, and gambling the whole day, which took a great toll on his health and money. So much so that Haren, who used to provide fish for the entire village on festival days from his own lake now took to fishing furtively on the lakes of others.

Bak, the water spirit is gone; seven years have gone by since beautiful Padumi's death. But their son Garoi remains. The villagers say that he too is Bak's spirit, being the son of a Bak. Otherwise why would he roam along the side of the lake incessantly, day in and day out?

For the past six or seven years, Haren had lived on what little he earned by fishing secretly on this north-eastern part of the lake. Here he could fish undisturbed. Only a few stray jackals came here sometimes. But for the past year, Garoi's mysterious presence in this area had caused him a lot of trouble. On the dark moonless nights of the dark phase of the moon, namely, the Krishnapakshya, Haren avoided coming to this part of the lake and unfurled his net somewhere in the vicinity of the village itself. But on the moonlit nights of the Suklapakshya, the bright phase of the moon, fearing that he would be caught poaching by the keepers of the Morigonya Mahaldar's lake, he ventured out on the lonely, deserted stretch by the Ou tree. Hiding his net just before dawn near some bushes, he would hurry home down the narrow alley. But now, fearing a meeting with Garoi on the way back, he took a roundabout way through the undergrowth of small bushes and shrubs. Frequently, Garoi would come this way with the steady, heavy stride of one walking in his sleep. He would stand by the Ou tree staring down at the glittering waters of the lake. Haren thought about it but could not understand why Garoi should behave in this way. Haren was his nearest neighbour; the lad had literally grown up in his backyard. Yet Haren hadn't a clue as to why the boy was behaving so strangely these days.

Garoi's behaviour had given rise to many a rumour in the village. Each one had something different to say. Nitai, the fisherman from Sylhet and Mayarani, Paran's mother, whispered: It's the call of the darkness, the call of the spirit; he is lured by the water spirit.

Some days ago an LMP doctor from a nearby tea estate had come to visit the village head. He brought up the subject of sleepwalkers and related how certain people were prone to walking in their sleep without being aware that they were doing so. The villagers, of course, saw no truth in such things, which seemed improbable to them. Whosoever believed in a man walking in his sleep would also believe in hair sprouting on a frog's back. They knew otherwise. They knew that the water spirit called Garoi to the lakeside on moonlit nights. Sitting beside the Ou tree, father and son would devour raw fish throughout the night and when day dawned, the spirit sent his son back home. Some of them had even seen Garoi following the spirit to the lakeside. Amongst them Heremba had given such a vivid description of both father and son that most villagers had stopped going outdoors at night even to answer the call of nature. On the last Ekadasi, the eleventh night of the lunar cycle, Heremba came out from the opium den. He came out to urinate and saw Garoi walking behind a tall shadowy figure towards the lake. He even recalled seeing Garoi holding on to the fishing net hanging from the shoulder of the mysterious figure. Gravely the village folk remarked, why shouldn't he? He was the water spirit's son, after all.

No matter whosoever said so, old Pabhoi, Garoi's grandmother, refused to believe in such wild tales. Deaf though she was, if she came to know of anyone speaking of such things, she rebuked them soundly, and cursed them thoroughly. She would cry out loud for all to hear, 'Garoi is my grandson. My Tikheroo's son. Which whore's son says that he is the spirit's offspring. Bring him to me and see if I do not beat him black and blue with my mekhela. May the gourds in such an evil speaker's garden turn bitter...may his face fester with sores, the bastard.'

As a matter of fact, old Pabhoi could hardly bring herself to believe that her son Tikheroo was no more and that he had not returned after that fateful fishing expedition. How was she to believe it? Didn't she know that in all the villages surrounding that lake her Tikheroo had been the best swimmer in all Morigaon? None but he dared to swim across the entire length of the lake at one go. Did he not remain underwater for the whole day fixing a trap of bushes and shrubs to ensnare the fish? The lake was his second home, why would any spirit of the lake want to kill him? Those who had seen him even once could not erase his memory from their minds. He was amazingly adept at catching fish. Not only the small puthi, khalihana, but also the large rohu and barali fish seemed to just flow into his net. At the time of the festival of Magh Bihu, when the whole village descended on the lake with their fishing nets and tools, it was always Tikheroo who made away with the biggest catch. On other days, Tikheroo used to sell his fish either at the Hindu village nearby or at the village market, but on such festive days he always distributed his catch among the villagers.

But the villagers could not enjoy his generosity for long. Soon the government levied a tax on the lake that was so loved by the villagers. They came to know that the lake was to be auctioned off. The people of the village raised a hue and cry. But it was all in vain as the richer section of the villagers, hoping to become Mahaldars themselves, turned deaf ears to the entreaties of the village folk. And one day, the lake was indeed auctioned off. To everyone's surprise, Tikheroo's cousin Haren, who spent his days fighting and quarrelling and his nights smoking opium, became the new Mahaldar of the lake almost overnight.

Of course, he did not become the sole owner. With him were two other fish merchants from Morigaon who became co-owners of the large lake. But Haren was the most fortunate among them for he got the best portion of the lake to himself. He got the most productive north-eastern part with their village at one end and the Ou tree near the cremation grounds of the village, at the other end.

From the next day itself, Haren stopped the villagers from fishing in the lake. Defying his orders a few villagers did venture out to the lake, but Haren, flaring up like an angry water snake, rushed out at them. Soon, there was a great uproar. The quarrel would have gone out of hand had the village head not explained the government rules and regulations to the simple villagers.

About three days after that, the quiet surface of the lake was invaded by fishermen from Sylhet and Bihar. Among them, the villagers were surprised to see Tikheroo. He stood out in their midst, tall and dark as a sol fish.

Tikheroo's presence among the strangers came as a surprise to the villagers. All knew of the feud between the families of Haren and Tikheroo. The two families, though closely related, were not even on talking terms. Even if her family had to go hungry for days, Pabhoi never took a step towards Haren's house. Things had been much better when her husband Betharam had been alive. But, unfortunately, he contracted tuberculosis early in life, and the disease killed him. Upon his death his younger brother Paniram, Haren's father, drove poor, widowed Pabhoi with her infant son Tikheroo, out of their home. Everyone in the village knew of the great hardships Pabhoi had to face in order to bring up her son. Anyway, the villagers were rather pleased to see their own Tikheroo in the lake among the unfamiliar fishermen. But gradually, he became an object of envy for the other fishermen whose entry was banned on the lake, and whose only source of livelihood was thus taken away from them. Their once loved Tikheroo became like an underwater thorn for them. The fact that he was Haren's kin now surfaced in their minds as a dead body surfaces in water.

Actually it was not for any feelings of kinship that Haren had engaged Tikheroo. Opium-fuddled as his mind was, nonetheless, he was aware of Tikheroo's great dexterity in fishing. He knew full well that someone like Tikheroo would be an asset to him in the business. So, the night before formally starting to fish in the lake, Haren came to his aunt, Pabhoi, and fell at her feet imploring her to forget old feuds. The elders of the family were now no more. What good would it do to remember old quarrels, he reasoned. His wife was a sickly woman, he said, and entreated his aunt to return home once again to take up the reins of the house in her able hands. Such requests could not move old Pabhoi but when Haren whom she had brought up, who she had carried piggyback many a time, started weeping a sea of tears, old Pabhoi found herself unable to resist any longer. That very night, along with Haren, Tikheroo and his mother made their way back to their ancestral home and began to stay in the same compound.

The next day, fishing was formally begun on the lake by Haren's men, after holding a puja to appease and worship the god of the lake. At the crack of dawn, a huge barali fish, caught in Tikheroo's net was chosen and its forehead dotted with vermilion. The fish was then released back into the water. A few fishermen made offerings of milk and salt while those from Sylhet arranged their own puja of Gangadevi.

From that day, fishing began in earnest on the lake. Tikheroo not only competed with the Bihari and Sylheti fishermen to catch more fish but also taught them many new tricks of the trade. The skilled fishermen, among them, were a little condescending at first but after a week or so they too acknowledged his sheer mastery. Initially, Haren found it a little difficult to understand this new business, but due to Tikheroo's honesty and skill, he made better profits than his partners. Hoping to make even more profit without putting in any effort of his own, Haren not only allowed Tikheroo to put up a house for himself in his own backyard but also handed over the running of the business to him, putting him in charge of the fishermen as well as the lake.

By the turn of the year, Haren was able to buy many plots of land in and around the village. Soon his granaries overflowed with paddy and his fishing business spread to Morigaon, Jagiroad, and as far as Guwahati. The newly-rich Haren changed a lot in manners and appearance. He now began to wear a long dhoti and kurta like the clerks of the nearby tea gardens. To avoid the company of his old cronies and fishermen friends, he stopped frequenting the opium den. His very look changed and so did his manners as he put on airs like he was the great merchant, Bhola Saud, himself.

On the other hand, Tikheroo's health deteriorated due to excessive labour. He spent most part of the day under water and perhaps due to this, became a little hard of hearing. His throat too began to trouble him all the time. Yet, his zest for work did not diminish. Even when ill, he would fish from dawn to dusk tirelessly.

Near the lake was a tongi ghar, a small bamboo hut on stilts, used by the Mahaldar's men to guard the lake at night. It was here that Tikheroo loved to spend most nights, with the fish spread out around him even after the rest of the fishermen had gone back to their villages for the night.

Many a time, on an empty stomach, Tikheroo would lie awake far into the night, the stench of raw fish around him, till dawn. The very little time that he stayed at home, he remained silent and unobtrusive. Most of his time at home was spent in the open space behind his hut mending and repairing old nets owned by the Mahaldar or in weaving a new one. His being or not being at home, made little difference to his mother, now weakened by age and severe ailments. Pabhoi had her hands full with running her own house and pitching in to help at Haren's whenever his sickly wife found it too much to manage. She had long given up the hope of a daughter-in-law coming to aid her in her old age and gave all her love to Haren's wife.

Tikheroo was now almost two score years of age. No amount of coaxing or cajoling could make him agree to a marriage. But one day, to the immense surprise of the villagers, Tikheroo arrived home with a young bride in tow, a girl from Mayong, as comely as a mermaid.

About four years earlier, Haren's wife, Seuti, had given birth to a son. But it was a tadpole-like premature, still-born child. She showed no signs of motherhood after that. They had consulted renowned faith healers but to no avail. Haren's infertile wife became sicker as the days passed. Despite his immense wealth, Haren remained constantly disturbed by the fact that he was childless. During the day he busied himself with his business but at night, when his ragged and wretched wife settled down to sleep beside him, he was extremely disturbed, as his nagging worries seemed to return and their bed seemed to droop under the weight of their sighs. That was why Haren had sent Tikheroo to Mayong in search of a cure. Tikheroo, who was to return a day after, came back after spending three days in Mayong. The old faith healer sent a cure of potherbs mixed with the flesh and blood of a rhino for Haren. Along with the cure he also sent his beautiful young daughter as a bride for Tikheroo.

That evening, when Tikheroo's young bride alighted softly from the covered bullock cart, the whole place seemed to fill with the fragrance of turmeric and black pulses used for the ritual wedding bath of the bride, and that of lotus.

After evading the subject of marriage for so long, the sight of Padumi must have made him readily agree to marry. But how long did he enjoy the bliss of his married life? Barely two years after his marriage, Tikheroo left home one night to fish and never returned. Padumi saw him for the last time that evening as she lighted the lamp near the tulsi plant in their front yard. In the fading evening light she saw her husband standing in front of their granary talking to his mother. Even in that dim light she could make out that he was dripping wet. The net that hung from his shoulders was drenched and his clothes were dripping wet. As she glanced at him, some strange foreboding seemed to cross her mind. That evening, without even bidding goodbye to Padumi, Tikheroo left to go fishing.

When there was no sight of Tikheroo even three days after that, a worried Pabhoi informed the villagers of his disappearance. They came and gathered in their courtyard. As the crowds swelled, Padumi drifted in and out of consciousness several times. Their house and courtyard filled with people and it was then that Haren, with utmost reluctance, revealed the truth.

What he had to disclose seemed like some fairy tale to them. A nightmarish, fantastic, unbelievable tale. He said that it was around three months ago that on hearing the sound of fishing near the Ou tree, he and Tikheroo had made their way there. On reaching the place, they found no one and hence, gathering courage, they proceeded to the cremation ground. Again finding no one there, Tikheroo decided to do some fishing on his own. His net was in the boat. Chanting certain hymns he unfurled it and in no time had a good catch. After some time, feeling an urge to urinate, he paddled the boat towards the bank. Returning a little later, he settled down at one end of the boat. Thinking that Tikheroo must be tired after his bout of fishing, Haren himself began to row the boat. After crossing the Ou tree, Haren noticed a reduction in the quantity of fish in the boat. At that instant he also heard the sound of someone swallowing. Turning his face slightly, he saw clearly by the light of the moon that Tikheroo was devouring the raw fish kept in the boat.

Haren at once understood what must have happened. Having strangled and killed Tikheroo and taking his shape, the spirit was now on the boat, a spitting image of Tikheroo himself. Seeing that the spirit was busy eating, Haren hurriedly rowed ashore and after having grabbed the magic pouch of the spirit, made his way to the granary in their house. Immediately throwing the pouch into a big casket full of mustard seeds, Haren began to tremble with fear when he heard the sound of someone crying outside. Peeping out through the slits in the bamboo wall, he saw the water spirit weeping piteously and asking for his pouch saying that he was powerless without it. Haren did not return the pouch. So the water spirit, unable to change back to his own form had remained as Tikheroo in their house for the last three months. Haren too remained silent, not knowing how to reveal the truth to the young bride. On the previous evening, saying that

Haren wanted the pouch, the spirit made Pabhoi bring it for him from the mustard-seeds casket and thus got a chance to run away by taking the magical pouch with him.

On hearing Haren's tale, old Pabhoi broke down into heart-rending cries mourning the loss of her son. Padumi's wails floated in the air like the sad notes of a flute. The villagers, on hearing them, joined in. The very air seemed to be filled by Padumi's anguished cries. Her sobs seemed to move the waves of the lake to turbulence. The cries and moans of the villagers seemed to be echoed by the clouds themselves until the sounds of mourning blended with the sound of the terrible storm and heavy downpour which followed soon after.

Amidst the crowd of mourners in the house and the sound of the storm outside, no one noticed that Padumi had slipped out and run like one possessed in the direction of the lake. As the sound of the storm subsided along with the sound of the mourning, old Pabhoi noticed Padumi's absence and started running towards the lake. Not knowing what the matter was, the villagers too followed her and came to the bank. Here they saw Padumi sitting on the bank, gazing down at the water like one in a trance. Thousands of dead fish were afloat in the water.

From that day onwards, luck seemed to forsake Haren as his fishermen hauled up dead fish and snail shells day after day. Thinking that someone had cast an evil eye on the lake, Haren sent for a quack from Pabakathi. But the quack who descended on the lake with provisions of food and water and his hubble-bubble, could not unearth anything even after three days of mumbo-jumbo directed towards the depths of the lake.

Seven months later, after a night of excruciating labour, Padumi gave birth to a boy-child. Purple-hued like a water hyacinth, the baby was an ugly one. That night too, a storm raged overhead followed by rain. In that rain, multitudes of garoi fish rained down from the sky, not dead but alive. On the day of his birth, since their courtyard was covered with a large number of Garoi fish, people took to calling the baby Garoi. Of course, Padumi had chosen a fine name for her son and used only that name. She had named him after some flower. Like Padumi, Haren's wife Seuti also called him by his proper name. Unlike others, Seuti was not repulsed by his ugliness. She extended her skinny fingers towards the baby and gently stroked the throbbing chest of the child. But neither Padumi nor Seuti lived long to call him by his actual name. Within a year of his birth, Seuti grew even more emaciated and passed away. Padumi, on the other hand, bloated to an immense size and died leaving her three-year-old son behind to be cared for by Pabhoi. Anyone seeing her at the time of her death would hardly believe that she was once so slim and pretty. It is said that back in Mayong, her father had some old enmity with another faith healer and this man took his revenge by making Padumi swell up like a pot.

Padumi died a painful death due to her illness, but till the time of her death, as long as she could, she continued to look after her son and mother-in-law, and perform her household chores. But Pabhoi could not accept the fact that her daughter-in-law was cohabiting with the water spirit. Moreover, how could she accept the spirit's son as her own flesh and blood? In the beginning she had tried to coax Padumi into aborting the child but Padumi had been adamant. Secretly, she had mixed pot herbs in Padumi's food to get the child aborted but in spite of all this Garoi was born. Without Pabhoi's assistance, Padumi gave birth to her son. Pabhoi never took the child in her lap but the child survived and was soon running around not needing to be carried about at all. Yet, at the age of three when he was orphaned, old Pabhoi's stone-like heart melted with grief. To the surprise of the large crowd at her doorstep, she gathered the child and held him to her breast wailing, 'Do not cry my grandson, I, your grandmother am still alive.' Under her care, gradually, Garoi's purplish-black complexion began to lighten until it almost resembled her wheatish one.

As a child, Garoi, like the others of his age, spent his time flying kites or searching for wild cats among the tall grass of the surrounding fields. His large eyes, rough skin, and hunched back did not deter the other children from playing with him. They neither feared nor hated him. His peculiar stature, in fact, made him all the more attractive to them. They felt drawn to him because of his odd posture, lisping words, and innocent smile. He was never angry if anyone called him the spirit's son. Instead, he would clap his hands and laugh aloud strangely, making a peculiar sound like a hiccup. Whenever he was happy he laughed in that way.

Though unnatural in looks, in manners, he was completely normal. As he grew up, he came to realize the import of many things. When he herded the village head's cows along with the other men, he came to know and understand much. Now he fully understood the true meaning of many a comment made by the villagers in passing. Now, when the youngsters pointed to him shouting, 'The spirit's son! The water spirit's son!' instead of laughing at them, he began to throw stones in their direction. Day by day he grew more morose and angry. His friends too did not escape his anger. Even simple jokes provoked him and he lunged at them, stick in hand. Now the only person who could still claim some intimacy with him was the village headman's son Dhaniram. Though Garoi was a working-class person, Dhaniram affectionately called him his 'friend'.

Garoi too meticulously carried out whatever was asked of him by Dhaniram. Every morning, after leading out the cows to graze, Garoi came to Dhaniram and spent most of the day with him. He remained with Dhaniram, like a shadow, all day long. Dhaniram himself was quite fond of the boy. But one day, he also passed a demeaning comment about Garoi's birth. Many indirect comments had reached Garoi's ears but till then, none had dared to speak directly to him on this matter. And it was thus that the truth dawned on him. This time without retorting or getting angry, Garoi kept staring at Dhaniram with a mute and hurt look in his eyes. For a long time he remained sitting like one thunderstruck. Suddenly, like a pebble released from a sling, he ran home without a word to anyone.

That night, it was only after a lot of cajoling that old Pabhoi could persuade Garoi to come into the kitchen for his meal. She lovingly served him his favorite curry of sol fish cooked with radish and smoked fish with a pinch of salt and mustard oil. Noticing that even the aroma of his favourite dish aroused no enthusiasm in him she remarked, 'These are all man-made stories boy, all wild tales. These simple villagers may believe in such concoctions but I don't. No matter what people may say, I know you are my grandson, my Tikheroo's son. Your mother Padumi was as comely as a mermaid. From far off Mayong, your father had brought your mother as a bride. Would you like to hear about it? Have your meal and then I shall tell you of their marriage.'

'As comely as a mermaid was your mother'—this oft-heard line gave a strange pleasure to Garoi. Several times, on other occasions, Garoi had heard of his mother's exquisite beauty. Sometimes, peering at his own ugly reflection on the still waters of the lake, he tried to recollect his mother's face. Somehow, he could never fully reconstruct that long-forgotten face. Only like some haunting melody heard from afar, like the fading notes of a lullaby sung by a mother to her child, hazy and indistinct, the figure of a faceless woman formed in his mind's eye.

Yet, he did have a distinct recollection of one event from his early childhood. One day, leaving him to play by the lakeside, his mother was washing clothes when, engrossed in his play, he slipped and fell right into the lake. Sick as she was, Padumi too jumped into the lake and it was quite a while before she found him and swam ashore with him safe in her arms. People said that the water spirit had tried to take back his son. It was only because the mother went to ask for the child that the spirit returned it. Garoi's short life had almost come to an end at that time. Fearing a recurrence, Padumi made an offering of his navel cord that she had preserved since his birth, a few matchsticks, and an egg to the lake praying for the long life of her son. He never learnt to swim like the other boys of his age. That incident had instilled a deep fear of water in his mind and he never attempted to learn.

That night, holding Garoi in the circle of her arms, close to her breast, old Pabhoi began to speak of her son Tikheroo. Like a small boat left adrift, Garoi floated in the waves of old Pabhoi's tale. Till late into the night, Pabhoi continued her story until, unknowingly, she drifted off to sleep. But Garoi lay awake. With eyes wide open, he peered into his grandmother's face trying to trace in that face the face of his father.

A long time after that, the moonlight crept in stealthily perhaps right into the recesses of old Pabhoi's mind. Her thin angular body, now curved in sleep, straightened a little. The air in her throat blending with the saliva in her mouth came out like a tortured groan and suddenly in her sleep, like a gushing water spout, words gushed out of her mouth....

'How many times had I forbidden her to go to the lakeside all by herself? With beauty like hers, something was bound to go wrong. Did she listen to me then? Did she? She was ashamed, she felt shy to bathe together with the other women of the village. She had to go alone. My worst fears came true...the water spirit was enamored of her looks. He killed my son to live with her. He too ran away taking the magic pouch with him. What do I do with this boy now? Whatever do I do with him?'

What she muttered now was a total reversal of all the tales she had told him in her waking hours. With a sinking heart he heard his grandmother too reiterate the fact that he was indeed the water spirit's son. No wonder the women of the village mocked him, and the children pointing their fingers at him shouted 'The spirit's son, the Bak's son.' He was truly the spirit's son then. Then where was his father? Where did he live? Was it in the depths of the lake or in the marsh near the cremation ground? Where?

Leaving his bed, Garoi went looking for his father; right up to the lakeside. Wandering to and fro he grew tired and stood by the Ou tree. There, sitting in the dark, a few yards away, was Haren. With his net unfurled Haren sat, drifting in and out of sleep. The sight of Garoi at the foot of the Ou tree sent a chill of fear through Haren. He was, by nature, a fearless man but now he felt a strange fear. He did not believe in any ghost or spirit, but today, the sight of Garoi in the light of the moon made his heart beat faster. He thought the shadowy figure to be that of some spirit. From that time onwards, Haren frequently spied Garoi wandering restlessly by the lakeside on moonlit nights when he came this way to fish. He did not know whether Garoi came this way on dark, moonless nights too.

One night, apprehending that Garoi would disturb his fishing, Haren came to the lakeside earlier than usual. But the net on his shoulders did not touch the water that night. As Haren glanced at the bright full moon reflected on the waters of the lake, he was suddenly reminded of Padumi. Indeed, her beauty had been like that of the full moon, bright and ethereal. Like a sweet fragrance floating in from a distance, the memory of a day, eleven years ago, came to Haren's mind.

That day, Tikheroo was away from home and so Haren himself had to spend the night guarding the fish in the tongi ghar. At the crack of dawn, he sent out fish to Morigaon and Jagiroad and started on his way home. Taking a shortcut instead of the road, he was advancing down the lakeside and had not yet reached the bathing place of the village maidens when a sudden sound in the water attracted his attention. Peering down into the water he saw Padumi swimming with strong back strokes, her face up towards the sky. Through her wet clinging clothes, her dark-hued body was clearly visible. She had been married for almost a year now. Right behind Haren's house was their small hut. Yet, in the course of that year, Haren had seen her at close range only once and on that day he had jokingly remarked to his sister-in-law, 'What charmed betel nut have you fed my brother?' He remembered that instead of retorting, Padumi had blushed red, veiling her face even further. A bashful girl, she always ran indoors at the sight of Haren after that. The name, Padumi, always conjured up the image of a pure and innocent face for Haren. But that day, the sight of her in the water had made Haren stop in his tracks. Among the lotuses of the lake she too seemed like a lotus as she floated leisurely. But soon, turning in the water like a fish, she took a deep dive to the depths of the lake emerging a long time later at the side of the lake among the small waves. Once again she floated, breast upwards. The soft morning light made visible her conch-like breasts, the deep whirlpool of her navel, and her narrow waist, like the neck of a bamboo creel. And playing in and out of the wave-like contours of her silky smooth body were hundreds of tiny fish.

For a long time, Padumi remained in the water. Using her legs like a mermaid's fins she swam in the water almost setting it afire with the unearthly glow of her beauty. That day, it was not only the waters of the lake that was set on fire. The same fire was lit in Haren's heart too. Jealousy and passion raged in Haren. After burning in that heat for quite some time, on a rain-drenched night, he had satiated his passion. Asking Tikheroo to remain in the tongi ghar, Haren entered the ramshackle hut where Padumi slept like one dead. Haren lay down by her side. At that time a fragrance like that of a lotus seemed to be wafting out of her body. In that heady fragrance he invaded her body slithering in like an eel. Outside, the monsoon raged incessantly and the fishes in the lake moved upstream in shoals.

Tired from her day's work, Padumi slept soundly. She was used to Tikheroo coming in late at night, sometimes even after midnight. That night, taking Haren to be her husband, she lay unsuspectingly, drowsy, half-asleep and would have drifted back into the river of deep sleep, had she not become conscious of a strange hardness and unfamiliarity of touch. In her sleep-benumbed state too she was conscious of a weight upon her breast and tried desperately to push it off but failed. A dark strong hand came down on Padumi's open mouth before she could scream. The bolting rain outside flooded the lake drowning her groans.

Padumi was innocent. Despite all that had happened she was innocent. In spite of everything, the thought that someone other than her husband had touched her did not arise in her mind even once. Thinking that it was some evil spirit, she got up, took a bit of mustard oil and invoked a charm to ward off the evil eye. Once again she lay down but sleep evaded her for a long time and it was only early in the morning that she drifted into an uneasy slumber. Her sleep was disturbed by strange dreams. She dreamt that Tikheroo's body had bloated up like that of a pregnant woman and someone was whispering that he was expecting a son.

That was not the only time. On another night as well, smearing himself with raw fish, Haren came to Padumi's hut to drown once again in the lotus-like fragrance of her body.

As these thoughts came to Haren's mind, even in the freezing cold, Haren felt warm. A slow smile flickered on his lips. He wanted to keep thinking such thoughts but the eerie screech of some night bird startled him out of his reverie. It was getting late and he hadn't caught any fish yet. Hurriedly, lowering his old worn-out net from his shoulders and neatly folding and making two handfuls of it, Haren advanced to unfurl the net only to stop short in his tracks. Down the ribbon-like village alley which seemed now to be floating in a mass of fog, Garoi was coming that way. On seeing him coming much earlier than his usual time, an irritated Haren started folding up his net. Gathering his bamboo scoop, creel, and small bamboo basket and tying them to his waist, he was starting down the shortcut when he noticed that Garoi seemed to be walking almost at a snail's pace, very slow but steady. It took him a long time to reach the Ou tree. What's wrong with the boy? Curious, Haren tiptoed carefully over the dew-wet fallen leaves and advanced towards Garoi. To his utter amazement, he saw that even in this numbing cold, Garoi was naked, completely naked!

That afternoon, Garoi had been sitting gloomily under a mango tree thinking of his mother. Suddenly, the village head's milky white cow which he had helped to tend along with Dhaniram came that way. Stopping near him she started to lick him. Having left the village head's service now, he was always saddened to see these cows. Unmindfully, he began to stroke the white cow. Dhaniram, with a few other cowherds, were watching from a distance. All of a sudden, as a mischievous thought struck him, he blurted out in his high-pitched voice, 'You see, that is how the water spirit must have fondled your mother.'

Each word uttered by Dhaniram pierced the depths of Garoi's soul like the pricks of a thorny fish and made him feel like a magur fish cut and salted alive. Yet he sat unheeding, still stroking the white cow. But when he heard more inciting comments, his normally subdued but hot temper was ignited. Suddenly, running at great speed towards Dhaniram, he dealt him a blow on his right arm with the stick he held in his hand, then another and another till he had hit Dhaniram good and proper.

Seeing him attack Dhaniram, the rest of the cowherds surrounded him. On hearing the commotion, the village head's farm labourers also ran that way. Without stopping to listen to Garoi they all started raining blows on him. Unable to ward off their blows, he fell to the ground almost unconscious and began drooling at the mouth. Someone even pulled off the loincloth he wore tied around his waist. As he lay in their midst in his rough, ugly nakedness, they formed a circle around him laughing with a sort of unholy glee.

As he lay unable to move, Dhaniram came to check if there was life left in the bloody and battered body. When he moved closer, Dhaniram seemed to get the smell of raw fish. One by one, following Dhaniram, the rest of the cowherds too moved close and all of them found him smelling of raw fish. Now there remained no doubt in their minds that he was the son of the 'Bak,' the water spirit. After a while, on seeing him move, the men ran homewards all chanting in tune, 'Garoi, the spirit's son, Garoi, the spirit's son.' Before running off, Dhaniram flung Garoi's loincloth, out of reach, on to a high branch of a mango tree.

On moonlit nights, Haren was accustomed to seeing Garoi wandering about the lakeside near the Ou tree. That was nothing new for him. But the sight of Garoi now, naked and injured, with deep welts running down his back was an unnerving sight for him. It looked as if someone had made cuts on a live fish before frying it. A shiver shook Haren's whole frame as he caught sight of Garoi's wounds. His face was badly swollen and the blood had dried in streaks under his nose. He seemed to look even uglier today. Who would say that it was in beautiful Padumi's womb that this ugly child had taken form, grown hands, grown feet....

'Pitai!'

Suddenly, breaking the silence of the night, the piteous cry for his father rang out. For an instant it seemed as if the soft waves of the lake, the wind blowing over that lake, and the delicate bamboo leaves fluttering in that wind had all been stilled by that cry. Looking down into the depths of the water, Garoi was calling out, 'Pitai...!'

At once realizing the reason behind Garoi's strange wanderings, Haren felt apprehensive. Father! Who was his father? People said he was the spirit's son. When they said that, he felt a strange mirth. On the other hand, old Pabhoi claimed that Garoi was her Tikheroo's son. But how could Garoi be Tikheroo's son? A few days after Garoi's birth, the doctor from the nearby garden had secretly told him of Tikheroo's problem. After trying many remedies, Tikheroo had come to the doctor for a cure but the doctor had not been able to help him. The doctor stated that Tikheroo was incapable of becoming a father.

With much hope in his heart, Haren had rowed the boat to the lonely stretch of the lake. He had then hit Tikheroo behind the head with the oar. After writhing in agony for a while, Tikheroo's body had become still at the bottom of the boat. Binding the body with an old net, Haren had buried it in the marshes near the cremation ground. But after killing Tikheroo, Haren could not approach Padumi again. Her husband's death not only took a toll on her beauty but also stole away sleep from her eyes forever. On hearing of Tikheroo's death from Haren, Padumi had not believed it at first. But, when braving the storm she had run to the lakeside only to see thousands of fish floating on the lake surface, she had stood still, shocked. She could never again shut those eyes that she had then opened wide in terror and agony.

Though he failed to make her his own, the sight of her swelling belly nevertheless filled him with a kind of joy. Maybe not in his wedded wife but still his child was taking form inside Padumi.

'Pitai!' Advancing a few steps from under the tree to the lakeside, Garoi once again cried out. Like the moaning notes of a flute, his heart-rending cry gave a twist to Haren's heart. The fount of love so long lying dried up in Haren suddenly seemed to well up with Garoi's soulful cry. About to call out, Haren stopped himself. Instead of his voice, a deep sigh escaped him.

Standing dangerously close to the steep bank of the lake, Garoi repeated his cry in a barely audible voice. Each moment seemed to pass slowly as if unsure of itself. Suddenly, with one last shuddering call which seemed to rend both the air and the water, Garoi jumped into the lake. On seeing Garoi jump in, Haren too ran that way. Looking down, he saw a well of darkness in the moonlit water. A great many waves were circling that bit of darkness. Haren was aware that this part of the lake was deep. It was a part washed by such strong waves that a full-grown elephant with its rider would not get a footing there. It was here that the boy had jumped in.

Throwing down his net, Haren too jumped into the dark depths of the lake. The surface of the lake was washed with faint moonlight but the depths were dark, and getting darker. In those dark depths, mauled by the waves, Haren desperately searched for the boy, groping here and there. But there was no trace of Garoi. Still, as long as he was able to hold his breath, he searched for his son in that village of sleeping fish, crushing under his weight their numerous homes with its surrounding greenery of underwater plants. He even lay quietly on the bed of the lake trying to catch the sound of the thrashing of an arm or leg of his son. But no, nothing, no sound came to his ears. All he seemed to hear in the water were the deep sighs of the orphaned fish.

Disappointed, Haren ascended to the surface for a breath of air. Even before he could reach the surface, a pair of hands grabbed his legs. Haren found himself unable to escape that strong mysterious grasp. The more he tried, the more strongly those hands held him. In desperation and fear, he shouted out. His breathless, agonized scream only raised a few bubbles in the water.

Feeling that his long wait for his father had ended at last in the dark depths of the water, Garoi held him to his breast in such a strong embrace that Haren was stilled.

And then the mirthful fish swam around the embracing figures of father and son, as, naked and stiff, they whirled round and round, descending further and further into the depths of the lake.

Translated by Mitali Goswami

PROVIDENCE

MONIKUNTALA BHATTACHARJYA

Kshetrapal sahib, the retired Army officer looked extremely tired today. It seemed as though he was drenched in water, his eyes dim and vague.

'The press party is scheduled to arrive at ten,' he said, without looking at me. We had cups of steaming tea in our hands, green tea. Seated on the veranda, I was eager to enjoy the assemblage of colours laid out by the sun upon the green lawn in front.

Kshetrapal sahib sighed deeply. He had not been at home when I arrived yesterday. Later, he had been overjoyed to find me here. He showed his curiosity about a girl named Varsa who, at one time, was involved in journalism with me. He asked me quite a few questions about her.

But the more the hours passed, the more he seemed to dry up. The deep desire to meet him at close quarters that I had carried in my heart for a long time seemed to recede. No, no, I realized, this was not the man that I had imagined from his letters and telephonic talks. Like the red corpuscles of blood thickening in the veins as the night advanced, the colour of his blood seemed to grow greenish. Someone seemed to be thrashing the obstinate child in him to exhaustion.

This was the man about whom I had heard so much from my grandfather since my childhood. My grandfather had been a senior officer of the Indian Army. Strong and stout with well-built arms, he had met Kshetrapal as a Major in Lucknow. He had taken to him more as a brother than as a subordinate officer and had treated him very much like a close relative. But why? Several times I had asked him this question. In reply, he had only rolled his moustache and smiled. But one day he had said softly, 'There is an obdurate child in Kshetrapal. His buoyant spirit charms me. His presence cheers me up.'

Grandfather then had grown absent-minded. He kept quiet for a while. He seemed to be reminiscing over some bygone days. I had said 'Both of you live in the same country. Why don't you meet someday?'

Grandfather had not replied. I presumed that their relationship was not too cordial any more. But I wasn't sure, for on all festive occasions, Kshetrapal sahib kept up his contact with my grandfather. He used to send him cards and messages as before. Grandfather preserved them carefully within the pages of a special diary. But this particular diary, once so precious to him, he had himself consigned to flames in the later years of his life.

One Magh morning, we were warming ourselves by the fireside when suddenly, grandfather had showed up and we were caught unawares when he flung that precious diary into the flames. He stood there, intently looking at the flames and stirring the embers with a stick until the treasured piece was totally reduced to ashes.

Grandfather's temper was different from that of anyone else in the family. We were stunned by his action, our mouths agape, and eyes wide open. The letters from Kshetrapal that had been kept inside the diary were also burnt to ashes.

A little while later grandfather went inside. We heard the door of his room close. The sound of the opening of the cork of a wine bottle reached our ears. And then the gurgling sound of wine being poured into his glass.

A little later he grew hysterical. He shouted, 'Kshetrapal is dead, dead and gone is Kshetrapal. A single hair has stuck to his tongue. He is dead, dead indeed is he.'

He was just saying things that were mysterious to us. It is only natural for a drunken man to utter such nonsense, we knew. But in the case of our grandfather we couldn't accept it as such.

Since then grandfather had developed a phobia. It was about a hair, a single strand of hair. Awake or asleep, he began to talk about a hair. While taking his meal, he would suddenly discover an unseen strand of hair. It would feel as though a hair was stuck to his tongue. Even when he was speaking, he felt the same thing. Sometimes he would stand before the mirror, and start looking for the mysterious hair upon his person. Towards the end, his condition became pathetic. He underwent psychiatric treatment. He was totally obsessed with that single hair.

And then, alas! One day, grandfather, my dear grandfather, hanged himself from a ceiling fan. In the suicide note addressed to me he had written, 'The single strand of hair that got stuck on Kshetrapal's tongue didn't allow me to live in peace. Burn it to ashes if you can.'

After a long search, I managed to get Kshetrapal sahib's address. The members of my family, however, did not like it at all. Yet, I thought of establishing contact with him, because my heart longed to meet him.

We started talking over the phone. I told him about my grandfather's condition during his last days. I told him, 'I do not know why he fancied a hair getting stuck on his tongue and how that was related to you. I would like to have an answer. If you give me an appointment I shall have a chance to learn certain things about my grandfather.'

Kshetrapal sahib invited me to his place. He said, 'I shall be going shortly to Pakistan. You can come after my return. It is now 2001; the year is about to close. Let it close; it's better that you come in the New Year. We are new people; we shall talk in a new fashion. What do you say?'

The man was amused at his own words. He laughed aloud.

We started talking on the phone. He often told me various stories about Indian soldiers. These witty accounts made him excited. He said, 'Do you know what Sir Jasper Nicolls said about us?'

'No, I don't. I'll trouble you to let me know.'

'All right then. Nicolls sahib said that it was easier to control five thousand Indian soldiers than one thousand Europeans. The real reason for this is that the Indian soldiers are quite honest and simple, ever prepared to sacrifice themselves for their country. Sir Thomas Rainel, who was major-general at that time, observed that Indian soldiers were loyal and patient. They believed in and were inspired by an auspicious power such as God.'

'Do you possibly remember the year when he so observed?'

'That was in 1832. That was the time when the Commons Select Committee was formed to make enquiries about India. Would you believe, once it so happened to me....'

He would often ring me up. Sometimes he would say, 'Just to remind you, hope you haven't forgotten; we meet at the very beginning of the New Year.'

He considered me as a very young friend. That's why I developed a friendship with a person senior to my father. As a token of friendship he sent me various gifts. Among them, a golden bookmark, a paper knife made of walnut, and a Parker pen with a golden nib were the most precious ones.

∽

The New Year arrived. The entire world welcomed it with great gusto. Meanwhile, Kshetrapal sahib returned from Pakistan. He rang me up but his voice sounded depressed. 'The next seven days will be for me days of privacy,' he said.

'What do you mean by that?'

'I want to keep the coming week exclusively for myself,' he said.

We did not talk of anything else. My sixth sense told me that for some important reason he wanted to be in seclusion for the next seven days.

I was very uneasy those next seven days. I wanted to fill the time with prayers for my friend. I wondered why my grandfather often implicated this friend of mine with the unseen strand of hair he thought was stuck on his tongue.

Meanwhile, I rummaged once again through grandfather's remaining diaries preserved in his trunks and pored over the pages. That was the year 1971. At one place, in his neat hand he wrote the painful lines, 'Today Second Lieutenant, Arun Kshetrapal, fell in the battle on the border. The twenty-one-year-old son of my colleague, Madanlal Kshetrapal, today becomes a martyr. Madanlal, my friend, more like a brother to me, and so close to my heart, oh how painful!'

I jumped up in surprise. Kshetrapal sahib's son was also a soldier! He's a martyr's father!

I read further. But there was nothing more of it, except the inscription, 'Victory of Mother India.'

At long last, the anxious waiting was over. Kshetrapal sahib called me to his place.

And now I was at my friend's house. The walls of his drawing room were adorned with large wall paintings of his martyred son.

Seeing me pause in front of a picture, he came and stood very close to me, and said, 'My son, Second Lieutenant Arun Kshetrapal. At the age of just twenty-one he was honoured with the Paramvir Chakra. This is my son's picture.... My son's picture.'

We sat face to face until the late hours. He enchanted me with many an account of the war front. He told me about his forefathers. He said, 'That was 1849. My ancestor was a Sikh soldier. He fought against the British in the Second Anglo–Sikh War, at Chillianwallah. My father was also in the Indian Army. That was the time of World War I. After that, he joined the Punjab Civil Services. And about me, well, you know my case.'

With his eyes fixed upon mine, Brigadier-like, he smiled with pride. I continued to stare at him. He resumed his story, 'Our forefathers were from West Punjab. That is now in Pakistan. We became refugees in 1947.'

Kshetrapal sahib's drinks began to make him open up. So it happens. When a person wants to go back to his past, he fails to discover the people who lived then. Many were lost in the bosom of death. In such a situation, a person's yearning to return to his past seeks a lantern, seeks a staff.

Yes, it so happens.

Today, with Kshetrapal sahib, the coloured glass took the form of that lantern, or the staff. A night bird settled on the wood rose in the corner of the lawn with a thud.

I quietly rose to leave. He lifted his eyes, and with due courtesy wished me 'Good Night.'

∽

We were now sitting on the front veranda of Kshetrapal sahib's bungalow, with cups of green tea in hand. I looked at him, and thought that perhaps he had been sitting there all alone after I had left him the previous night.

Who knew?

Did he himself know?

My impression was that he had passed a sleepless night, weeping throughout.

Once more I looked at his face. In the morning sun, the lines showed up. His eyelids were swollen. No doubt he must have wept.

Maybe so. The frolicsome child that I had discovered in him when I had first come to know him, seemed to have vanished. He was completely without cheer. After his return from Pakistan, a vague depression of spirits seemed to have seized him.

'The press party is to arrive at ten,' he said.

I replied softly. 'But I have to leave a little before ten for Gafur Market. I have some business there.'

'Wait a bit. My driver will report only after ten.'

'Thank you. But that is not necessary. It's only a short distance. I shall hire a taxi,' I said and quietly left his place before the press party arrived.

In the afternoon, we went out on foot. We sat in a nearby coffee house face to face. He asked me,

'You must have loved your grandfather very much, I believe.'

'Yes, very much indeed.'

'How much?'

A strange question to ask. What standard is there to measure how much a person loves another? Can one's feelings be measured? Yet I said, 'The news of the death of some of grandfather's friends could rob me of my sleep at night. I couldn't imagine that he too would die one day. I loved him so much.'

'But you are still alive!'

'Very much, indeed!'

'Actually, death is not a deep gorge for you to jump into along with the dead, or to lift them up. Not everything comes to an end. The person continues to live even after that.'

Some youth festival was going on nearby. The coffee bar became crowded with young men and women. He changed the tenor of our talk, and asked me, 'What are you writing now? Anything new?'

'I haven't started yet. I plan to write a story with my grandfather as the main character. I am thinking of writing the story of a man who had overthrown a battle tank but in his last days yielded to a single hair. That's the story I have in mind.'

He didn't ask me anything further.

In the evening we sat again in the drawing room. Today, he arranged for drinks for me too. We began to talk. On the wall in front of us was the big oil painting of his martyred son. Directing my gaze in that direction, I asked him, though reluctantly, 'At the time your son was born, did you think that your son, too, would join the armed forces one day?'

'Of course. Not after he was born, even before his birth I had decided the matter for him. He was born in 1950 in Pune. He joined the Defence Academy there in 1967. Thereafter, he joined the Military Academy in Dehradun. After a year, in October 1971, he joined a course for young officers and on 16 December, can you believe it, he went in to battle! Yes, 16 December 1971. That was the day. My son became a martyr for Mother India. My son, decorated with the Paramvir Chakra. He had joined the services as second lieutenant only three days ago. My son, Second Lieutenant Arun Kshetrapal, became a martyr at the age of just twenty-one.'

Kshetrapal sahib was overwhelmed by emotions. His voice became muffled. He sighed deeply and with downcast eyes poured a large peg into his glass.

His eyes looked like a lake.

I was helpless. What could I do? Could I possibly change the topic? But he looked eager to say more. He cast a glance at the plate of fried cashew nuts by his side, and began to speak again, 'At Jarpal of the Sharkargarh sector, the number of our soldiers was negligible in comparison to Pakistani soldiers. The squadron commander sought additional support. As soon as he heard the radio messages, my son became deeply excited.

'At that time, your grandfather also encouraged him greatly to go to battle. But after his death he secretly suffered in repentance. But listen....'

He continued to tell stories of the battlefield. He narrated the incidents in such a manner as though he was an eye witness to the military skills of his son. Yes, the twenty-one-year-old young second lieutenant advanced with his troops and captured several Pakistani soldiers on the bank of the Basantar river. Then he advanced in his own tank, and smashed enemy tanks to smithereens. An incredible feat indeed!

In the process, eleven Pakistani tanks were destroyed. Meanwhile, his tank was engulfed by flames. He was sternly instructed to abandon his tank. But the young man continued to fight frenziedly. Even in his wounded condition, he destroyed another tank. He had managed to damage four enemy tanks! But then his tank was surrounded by enemy soldiers. Whack! Whack! They struck at the burning tank from all sides. And then a terrible dying scream! They hit him with gun barrels as he was desperately trying to fight and save himself. Even then he was repeatedly thrashed. Growing wild in their jubilation, they talked of taking him a prisoner. But then Abhimanyu met his end.

Kshetrapal sahib heaved a heavy sigh. But now, in place of the deep shades of depression, an extraordinary glow of glory shone on his face.

For the first time in my life, I poured out a second peg for myself. The coloured drink radiated the glow of the lower part of the glass. I was feeling heavy in my heart.

'That's enough. Take a small peg. You are not accustomed to it. Am I right?' said Kshetrapal sahib. His words sounded like a soliloquy. The tone was easy. That gave me a sort of breather. He resumed his talk, 'Your grandfather was fastidious in his choice of food. I believe you are aware of it. It's good to have taste. But sometimes it lands people into trouble as well. In this matter he envied me.'

'Envy you say? My grandfather envied you?'

'Aha! Why shouldn't he? I can eat anything considered to be nutritious. I need just a pinch of salt. Would you believe that I am still in a position to digest pebbles? I could eat even raw meat laced with salt.'

'Raw meat laced with salt? Can you eat it now?'

'As a matter of fact, I haven't eaten it for several years now. Once, in the very presence of your grandfather, I had thrown up profusely. Do you know why? Because I didn't check the piece of meat. The hair of a goat was stuck there. That somehow got caught on my tongue.'

I became excited the moment I heard him say so. The mystery of my grandfather's unseen hair was going to be resolved, I thought. Just at that moment he said, 'Can you believe it, at that hour, my son had become a martyr on the front! You won't believe it, but this time I met the killer in Pakistan!'

Hearing this, I jumped up.

He looked at me and said, 'His name is Brigadier K. M. Nasir. We were seated at the dinner table. He was talking about the India-Pakistan war of 1971. He had seen with his own eyes the spectacle of a wounded Indian soldier single-handedly smashing four enemy tanks. Though they had wanted to capture him alive, he died on receiving a blow. He said that he hadn't ever seen a single soldier fighting so heroically anywhere else. With great respect he uttered his name. On hearing the name, I had turned into a statue. He asked, "Why have you grown so passive?" I had no words in reply. I said "I am the father of the martyr whose heroism you have been telling us about. Yes, I am the father of Second Lieutenant Arun Kshetrapal."'

'Then?'

'Nothing after that. We are soldiers, after all. We know, at the time of action, we have a single aim, that is to overpower the enemy. The media then surrounded us. Nasir said, "During action, we see no one's face, only the tanks."'

He swallowed the last drops of the glass. I asked him softly,

'And you? What did you say?'

'This morning at ten o'clock, the press people had come. What is there to say? We soldiers know what a battle means. I reported to them what Nasir had told me. Anyway, leave it, leave it I say.'

He began to pour drinks into the glass. I saw a colourful glow coming out of the bottom of the glass.

All was clear now. The reason why the man had looked depressed after his return from Pakistan was all clear now. I understood why he wanted to be by himself for several days. I could now see why he seemed to me to be sobbing last night.

He picked up his glass and looked straight into my eyes. I too looked into his eyes.

A pair of drunken eyes.... The lids swollen because of ceaseless weeping last night. Yes, Kshetrapal sahib was drunk. But his voice was still sober. His insobriety couldn't affect his voice. He began to speak, 'I believe in the Lord in Heaven. You too perhaps do. I'll tell you about a strange coincidence. At the time when my son fell in the battlefield, I vomited myself to exhaustion. God himself came in the form of a hair and God himself stuck onto my tongue. He prevented me from taking any food. You surely know, perhaps you know...you know.... Can a father put anything on his tongue at the time of his son's death? Even a drop of water? You perhaps know…surely you know…you know a lot of things…you must know this too that God Himself had come in the form of a hair—well, even your grandfather believed it…you too believe it, I know.'

The man's talk was becoming incoherent. He reclined on the sofa and began to sing the national anthem ramblingly. I put the glass in my hand on the table and returned to my room. The chirpings of a night bird came floating from the distance. Like last night, the bird had perched on the wood rose.

I closed the door of the room. I now had the clue to the mystery of my grandfather's obsession with an unseen hair.

Translated by Prafulla Kotoky

A TALE OF THIRDNESS
MOUSHUMI KANDALI

Sometimes when you are reading a story, doesn't it suddenly feel as if you have met it somewhere? In one of life's half-known alleys—in a bend in time. To tell you the truth, even stories have reincarnations. Or else why do we sometimes feel as if the ancient soul of an old story has entered the body of another perception and a new story is born. The differences lie only in the change in costume with respect to time, and a dab of paint in the wings of sensitivity. Sometimes…sometimes a story leads you by the hand to another story…to a living story, filled with heartbeats and blood that pulses in an incredible empire of veins…. I have just now hugged such a living story, dropped farewell kisses on his brow and hands, and descended a flight of stairs. And like the giant, sober trucks driving solemnly on the highway, have slung on my back, the warm board with the legend in red, Rab kasam phir milenge….

The story which had led me by hand to the living story was one of my favourites—Joao Guimaraes Rosa's 'The Third Bank of the River.' But, at our first meeting, I had found my favourite story strange and unfamiliar. As if I had read it in a twilight of mystery. And when I was reading it, did I ever think in my wildest dreams that it would lead me by hand to my living story; that walking on its bridge I would one day touch him with deep longing—the living story, with warm blood pulsing in his incredible, blue-veined empire. When we had shared a few drinks and chatted about numerous things dear to us, we had also talked about that favourite story of ours. Yes—that story was his favourite too. When we talked about the story, we seemed to smell the salty body of the man, rowing to the third bank of the river on a boat of mimosa wood. On afternoons heated like the sands of the desert, through tunnels of nights as chilly as the polar snow, melting in the lava of the sun, ripped by the whiplashes of the rain—as he traced circular paths on the river's bosom, night and day, day and night, year after year, on his way to the third bank, we seemed to hear his breath in the wind—cold, moist, and heavy. Of course, to me the breathing seemed to belong to somebody else. To one of my other beings. But what about him? When he listened to the man exhaling, he seemed to hear himself breathing. Perhaps the breath of his fate was mingled in that exhalation— like the breath of the wind and cloud mingling with that of the storm.

At that time, that particular area in the city was prone to frequent load shedding. The lights would go out without any warning and then come on again. When they blazed to life, the lights would cruelly shatter some moments pregnant with meaning, about to acquire a certain depth in the darkness. In such moments, oscillating between light and darkness, his face would look like the digital conversion of Tutankhamen's death mask. Was it a face or death-in-wings? Faces change according to variations in context. And we have to wait for life to teach us this simple, common truth, practically known to everybody. Death-in-wings flickering across Tutankhamen's solitary face—that however was obscured by the blinding sunshine of another face, hard and intense. The blend of bitter time and harsh reality had sown on his tongue a thick growth of yeast, and when I saw him for the first time, he had puked anger without restraint with that yeasty tongue. Belched fumes of disgust. That was a different face!

He stood there, a bust of chiselled solid granite, leaning against the podium in the conference hall. Presenting his taxonomy of intellectuals, in the national seminar on 'The Role of the Intellectual in Civil Society'... *The Compradors, The Lumpen Elites, The Cynicals, The Feudals, The Pragmatics*... as the terms flew thick and fast, we were on the verge of an uproar, when he stopped abruptly, this crazy professor...a sudden dramatic silence, a few moments of still pause and his thundering...with upraised hands and a dark smile of contempt—'My dear academons! My dearest pedants-theorists-academons—let us steal a moment out of this endless endeavour of creating a garbage dump out of theory waste for the country's progress in the temperate, dazzling interiors of this star-studded, luxurious building, let us stop grinning foolishly, and for once, at least once, spit on ourselves and beg forgiveness for this noise pollution—in Father Jesus style, let's beg the God-like public with folded hands—forgive us, for we know not what we do.'

'Oh, you were quite sozzled that day, weren't you? You stank like wet clothes kept in the house for a long time and there was so much bitterness in your voice. I heard that you attend those seminars only so that you can get drunk. How unkempt and ruthless you had looked that afternoon. Like the summer sun, spitting venom on the streets painted with coal tar. Yet in the evening, your face had glowed with the light of a thousand stars—on stage you turned translucent, pure, and luminous, like crystal. You had transformed into a seductress to the melody of the Raga Desakshi. Wonderful! I saw a braid flow out of your head, two breasts bloom on your masculine chest, breasts firming in eager anticipation of touch. You danced with abandon to that ashtapadi of Jaydev—Ratisukhasar—and then in the wonderful blaze of lights on the stage, you had generated such an incredible cubic phenomenon—three doors on three sides—on the right, the door of the known, on the left, the door of the unknown, and in between, there was another door—the door of perception—you had advanced, slowly, to the third door in the middle—on you walked—oh, that was the first time I had seen you—and on the same day, I had seen two of your faces....'

As he listened to me, he hurled the dazzling white ping pong ball he had been fiddling with into the air. The ball flew through the open ventilator and vanished into the darkness outside. Gazing after the ball that had suddenly dissolved in the darkness, he replied, 'One day you will see my third face....'

Third! Third again! Third–third–third—why was he so obsessed with the third number—the number three? He preferred a hotel room with the number 3. He was fond of cubism. His favourite story was 'The Third Bank of the River.' Shiva's third eye. The three-dimensional representation—the reality of the third world—politics, economics, sociology. He liked all the legends of the third hell. His obsession with the third—perhaps that was his fate? Fate? How it digs into our life, time and again, in spite of being clawed away by the nails of reason, much like a tick digging into a bull's back. At least once in life we sing—*Athir dhan jan, jibon-joubon athir ei sansar.* Riches and men are evanescent, so are life, youth, and this world. And then we shrug off the thought and return to our regular cycle of life, like birds shaking off water impatiently from their wings—now that is fate! In spite of our endless craving for a self-imposed exile on a deserted island, miles away from the sea of people, we return to the world of men, time and again. Yet, it is we, who hold fate responsible and incarcerate beings in physical definitions, construct every stereotype. And such lives, fidgeting like unruly cows tethered to the posts of stereotypes, take to wearing Tutankhamun's death masks. Death that stalks them from the wings throughout the conscious hours; but the will-to-live spreads its tentacles over their souls like the yellow dodder vines.

Yes! Those will–to-live veins burgeon on the wings of death...like a dodder vine, spreading its infinite web of tentacles, soaring up with a hundred yellow hoods. I don't know if Maitreyi had ever seen a dodder vine, that yellow creeper with a thousand coiling arms. I don't know if she ever saw a tree killed by its serpentine embrace and many-hooded bites.

But perhaps she could hear the hushed cries of that silent tree!

What a sensitive, empathetic woman she was! Tall, dark, and with chiselled features. She was the accompanying vocalist in all his dance recitals. Maitreyi would walk to the Professor's colony carrying her tanpura, her long hair in a black braid swaying on her back. Climbing up those steps, she would sit in his study and sing a raga. Very often, there would be an evening musical mehfil in his hall. Even the Ramlila singers of the Harijan basti were invited.... Kabir's doha in Mangeshbhai's melodious voice would waft in the air, 'Chadaria jhini re jhini....'

But Maitreyi's renditions were so different, so solemn! As if they resonated from deep down the navel, from a fathomless darkness. As if an unknown insect sang in the midst of a vast thick rainforest, a mysterious, melancholic song. It was in Maitreyi's soulful rendering of the Deshakshi Raga that night, that I saw him transforming into an Abhisarika nayika waiting for her loved one.

Ah! I remember that night! That special dinner in Maitreyi's honour. Her gait had become slower and cautious. Holding her swollen belly, she slowly climbed the staircases, panting, and sat in the rocking chair. It had now become really difficult for her to sit on the floor and sing. I told her that had she been in our place now, the women would have fed her panchamrit, the five sacred nectars; people would have invited her to meals serving the foods that she craved for. For now she was dwehridini, as the shastras say, someone with two throbbing hearts....

On hearing me, he had announced, 'Well, we will have that ceremony here, you give me a list of your favourite foods, O one with two hearts, today I shall cook for you with my own hands.' Later, after offering her the sherbat specially made for her, we had opened a bottle of whiskey for ourselves. That night, as Maitreyi rocked gently in the armchair, lost in the strains of Carnatic music, he had suddenly embraced her swollen belly. Maitreyi, eight months with child, was astounded. She had been unable to utter a single word, her eyes could only widen in amazement. Putting his ear to her womb, he had muttered inaudibly, 'I too want to conceive—do you know whom I want to mother? Akka—Akka Mahadevi!'

We all knew about his strange love for Akka Mahadevi. We had heard him narrate the unusual story of that medieval saint–poet several times. This spirited Veerashaivite poet, who had passed away when she was only twenty, had stood before a gathering of men, and shedding all her clothes, had thundered, 'Is there a real man here, before whom I would blush with feminine shame? These are all inanimate, lifeless objects—what shame does one feel before inanimate objects?' He had fallen in love with this five-hundred-year old woman, but surprisingly, that day, he had insisted, thickly—'I want Mahadevi to seed in my womb. I want to feel her grow in my womb.'

When she was about to leave, Maitreyi had held my hands tight and asked, 'What sort of fire is this? Do you see it?'

True, it was fire. But, blowing through the funnels of flesh and blood, fate had not just lit this fire in his body. In the smoke leaping from that fire, his soul had burnt too. And far more intense than the fire within was the malicious smoke-ridden fire outside; it chased him endlessly to destroy him, and choked his skies with poisonous vapour. On the streets and in the alleys, whispers mocked him—the examiner on the interview board did not see his certificates and numerous research papers—he only saw the silver bangles on his hands and the ring in his ear. Unlocking his door, he had seen his books and furniture scattered and excrement on the floor. There were missiles of anonymous letters in his letterboxes threatening severe punishment for his crime of corrupting our pure pristine culture.

That was the time when Sanjay had started living with him. How happy he had looked on those days! So calm! Like a patch of sky reflected in the still waters of a lake. As if the blue of the sky and the blue of the water merged, melted, and multiplied into an infinite sea of blueness. Everything around him seemed to exude happiness. The cumin-cardamom scented kitchen air; towels, vests, and bedsheets on the clothesline flapping in the breeze eagerly waiting to be soiled again.

But a time came when Sanjay too had to leave. One day Sanjay's father had visited him. This incense-and-match factory owner had pleaded with him with folded hands to free his only son and heir, and enable him to perform the sacred duty of perpetuating his family line. That very day, ushering Sanjay on the path of freedom, he had puffed cigarette after cigarette on the bench in the railway station, grinding the night into ash. The night was almost half-burnt, when he had heard strains of the khanjuri and mridang floating from the Ramlila in the Harijan basti. Gradually, as if in a trance, he had followed the railway line towards the Ramlila. As he picked his way through piles of plastic—scraps of paper-sacks-bottles-discarded iron—through the haze created by the drunken scent of poppy-mingled bhang that elbowed aside the raw stench disgorged by the sewage plant drain, he had felt something penetrate the small of his back, right through his spine. Something sharp, cold, and piercing.

Later, with what glee had he narrated that experience! How he had crawled on, after the invisible assailant had stabbed him, snatched his wallet, watch, silver bangles and earrings, and had thrown him on one side of the railway line. How, inspite of his body growing cold and his uncontrollable shivering, the mridang continued to reverberate inside his head—ta jhum ta jhum...that smell from the Ganga ghat had assailed his nostrils—corpses lifted on pyres—was that poppy-mixed bhang or Afghan charas—that strange odour, mixed with the scent of gutimali flowers, that wafted all around!

That odour had been his inseparable companion in the two years he had spent in exile on a damp, cold floor of a shack on the Ganga ghat. His exile had started on the day that Chitra deserted him. Chitra—whom his family had welcomed, against his wishes, with Vedic chants and the homa fire. Chitra had left and to punish himself, he had chosen the self-imposed exile. Throughout the exile, his companion had been that strange odour! As strange as the manner in which Chitra had left him. One evening, back home from work, he had discovered that the house was empty. Totally empty. Barring his clothes on the hangers, books and terracotta images on the floor. The neighbourhood dhobi, sitting on the steps, told him that Maiji had gifted him all their furniture—everything she had brought with her—beds, chairs, tables, shelves, and almirahs—and had gone away somewhere....

When we had shared drinks and talked about things dear to us, he had asked me over and over again, 'I had never invited Chitra into this barren relationship. Never! But I know I am responsible for this terrible accident in her life—and I can never forgive myself for this. But tell me, don't you think she should have at least told me that she was leaving? Why did she not bother to say goodbye.... In the time that we spent together, I'd never hurt her! Looked after her like my own sister...when she had fallen ill, I had made turmeric paste for her. I had sat by her bedside and read Mahadevi's poems to her throughout the night.... How beautifully I had drawn a lattice print on the ends of her sari.... To tell you the truth, the night when the homa fire had burnt, secretly and surreptitiously, I had carved a boat of mimosa wood.... On my wedding night, when I stretched out my hand to Chitra, I had heard that man's breath in the wind—the breath of the man rowing his boat of mimosa wood to the third bank of the river....'

Talking to me or perhaps to himself, he had risen unsteadily to his feet. He had opened that huge mahogany almirah, had come back to me with something clenched in his fist and had forced it into my hand. On my palm rested a coin of clay, modelled on the ancient seals of Mohenjo-Daro and Harappa. A coiled blue snake had been carved into the coin. A snake, swallowing its own tail!

'Here, this is my seal. When you show it at my doorstep, my doors will automatically open for you. Ha, Ha, Ha!'

When I had descended the stairs, clutching that clay seal he had so painstakingly made—I had left behind a living story, to reign in a vast empire of solitude. I could not help feeling that this living story was one of the most beautiful I had ever read. And like all beautiful stories, his face had grown to resemble Tutankhamen's death mask. And like all beautiful stories, it was achingly sad. Tragic. Yet so luminous! Just like our favourite story.

While the hero of our story rowed his boat to the river's third bank, tracing circular routes on the river's bosom, year after year—melting in the sun's lava—ripped by the rain's lashes—his last offspring sat in the solitude of distant rocks, his gaze riveted on his father. He was not a companion on his father's journey, but he saved food for him in the cracks of rocks and a robe for him to wear, and told the trees, rocks, and men on the banks, 'There—the man rowing in solitude on the waters—he is my father.'

That day when I had descended the stairs, leaving him to reign in his empire of solitude, I had left with a pang. But today, though I have hugged my living story again, kissed him goodbye on his brow and hands and descended the stairs—I do not feel any pang. Because, though I have left him in his empire of solitude, he is not alone anymore. His child sleeps sound in his lap. It is to witness this auspicious moment that I have hurried to his side from such a distance. After a long time, like the evening of our first meeting, I saw waves of light play on his face, as if a thousand stars shone on him—and he seemed translucent, pure, luminous—once again, I saw two breasts bloom on his masculine chest, two firm and full breasts, bowed with the weight of milk. Oh, how uselessly are we trapped in our stereotyped definitions—we think motherhood is only for women. But motherhood is only a concept—who says it is defined by gender, physicality? One does not require a womb to be a mother—all one needs is a womb of sensitivity and emotion. That is why that scrap of life sleeps sound in his lap—born to him—Mahadevi grows in his womb of emotion. Remember—a few days earlier, custodians of one religion had smashed with hammers the monument of another religion—and flames of hatred had burnt all over the country—rows of houses had perished in those flames, charring bodies and souls and brains throbbing with life.... From the remains of such a fire, he had rescued his Mahadevi. Amidst piles of corpses, dust and smoke billowing from burning houses, waving her hands and feet, the tiny life had lain gurgling.

One day, when that tiny life would spread her wings to fly, would she understand him—his form of motherhood? I don't know. Perhaps she would. Perhaps not. In the shadow of his complex, lonely course of life, her path would perhaps be somewhat complex, disturbed too. Or perhaps not. Who knows? I am aware, that like our contemporary stories filled with numerous questions and the uncertainty of multiple possibilities—their wills and wonts, this will or that, perhaps will not or perhaps will—the conclusion of my living story, humming to little Mahadevi in his lap, might be misted in uncertainty. And this anarchy of uncertainty is not always preferable, though it might be truthful and sometimes self-fulfilling. No, it isn't. Sometimes in life, one wants to embrace the surety of ancient classical beliefs and the certainty offered by the old tales. In the same way as it is a sin to think of a loved one's death, it is sinful to conceive of uncertainty and anarchy in a loved one's course of life. So I will accept as the conclusion of my favourite story the classic certainty of the 'happy endings' of the traditional narratives. And blissfully imagine that—one day, one day Mahadevi will tell the people around her—pour her heart out to the trees and earth and wind—

You see that man—rowing in solitude on those deep waters—he is my mother....

Translated by Atreyee Gohain

ACKNOWLEDGEMENTS

I'm grateful to Aleph Book Company, for providing this space for literature in translation from different languages. Twenty-five highly regarded stories originally written in Assamese will now travel, in translation, through this volume, to a much wider readership.

To Pallavi Goswami, of Aleph Book Company, for handholding me throughout the more than two years it took to complete this project; for acting as intermediary and for putting across my point of view to the publishers, on various occasions. For being always empathetic to the story and for letting me decide on so many matters, large and small over the course of these many months that we worked on the texts together. For those endless edits that regularly went back and forth between us. For the quick WhatsApp questions, the longer emails, and the long telephonic conversations about the work in progress. For her eagle-eyed spotting of typos which had gone past me. And not the least, for the good humour and cheeriness with which the whole project was laced, which lit up the dreary, scary hours of being curfew-bound at home in these pandemic times, before screens of different kinds.

To the translators who agreed without any qualms to work on the stories I gave them. Some already had the translations, and were ready to hand them over to me, unquestioningly, for inclusion in this volume. Their trust in me was moving indeed. And through all the edits that they discussed with me, they showed, reassuringly, that they, like me, only had the best interests of the story, and how it read, at heart. I really value that. It made the whole journey so much easier.

And, of course, the authors, or their heirs, who unhesitatingly agreed to have their stories in translation in a volume of this kind.

To all the different people I consulted, too numerous to be mentioned here, before I actually started the hunt for the stories and translators, with whom I discussed what could be regarded as some of the best stories of my language, and theirs, and who were the authors who just could not be left out of a collection of this kind—thank you. In most cases, happily, our views came together.

And last, but certainly not least, to my tech support, Rupam Phukan, without whom this technophobe would have been completely at sea through the duration of this project. Thank you for smoothening the various glitches that happened along the way!

Grateful acknowledgement is made to the following copyright holders for permission to reprint copyrighted material in this volume. While every effort has been made to locate and contact copyright holders and obtain permission, this has not always been possible; any inadvertent omissions brought to our notice will be remedied in future editions.

'Patmugi' by Lakhminath Bezbaroa was first published in the journal *Banhi*; translation included with permission of Mitra Phukan.

'Aghoni Bai' by Birinchi Kumar Barua. Story included with permission of Birinchi Kumar Barua Memorial Trust; translation included with permission of Mitra Phukan.

'Bhulor Boli' by Syed Abdul Malik. Story included with permission of Syed Kamil Hayat; translation 'Mistaken Identity' included with permission of Syed Nazim Hussain.

'Miyah Mansur' by Birendra Kumar Bhattacharyya. Story included with permission of Binita Bhattacharyya; translation included with permission of Arunabha Bhuyan.

'Kathonibari Ghat' by Mahim Bora. Story included with permission of Amitabh Bora (with the exception of films, short films, Web series, TV films, and TV serials); translation included with permission of Jiban Goswami.

'Torua Kodom' by Sheelabhadra. Story included with permission of Nalini Dutta Choudhury; translation 'Sweet Acacia' included with permission of Maitreyee Siddhanta Chakravarty.

'Oxanto Electron' by Saurav Kumar Chaliha was written in the year 1950 and was first published in two editions of the journal *Ramdhenu* in 1952; translation 'The Restless Electron' included with permission of Jiban Goswami.

'Ismael Sheikhor Xondhanot' by Homen Borgohain. Story included with permission of Pradipta Borgohain; translation 'Looking for Ismael Sheikh' included with permission of Pradipta Borgohain.

'Endur' by Bhabendra Nath Saikia. Story included with permission of Ms Preeti Saikia; translation 'Rats' included with permission of Gayatri Bhattacharyya.

'Joi Porajoy' by Nirupama Bargohain. Story included with permission of author; translation 'The Victorious Woman' included with permission of Pradipta Borgohain.

'Sanskar' by Mamoni Raisom Goswami. Story included with permission of South East Asia Ramayana Research Centre; translation 'Values' included with permission of Gayatri Bhattacharyya.

'Mojiyat Tej' by Apurba Sarma. Story included with permission of author; translation 'Blood on the Floor' included with permission of Maitreyee Siddhanta Chakravarty.

'Bondiyar' by Harekrishna Deka. Story included with permission of author; translation 'The Captive' included with permission of Mitra Phukan.

'Arpitar Erati' by Debabrata Das. Story included with permission of author; translation 'A Night with Arpita' included with permission of Meenaxi Barkotoki.

'Mrigoya' by Purobi Bormudoi. Story included with permission of Ananda Bormudoi; translation 'The Hunt' included with permission of Mitra Phukan.

'Jatra' by Yeshe Dorjee Thongchi. Story included with permission of author; translation 'Journey' included with permission of Surajit Borooah.

'Edal Xeujia Xaap' by Dhrubajyoti Borah. Story included with permission of author; translation 'The Green Serpent' included with permission of author, writing under a pen name.

'Miss Havishamor Abeli' by Arupa Patangia Kalita. Story included with permission of author; translation 'Close of Day with Miss Havisham' included with permission of Mitra Phukan.

'Yatra' by Kuladhar Saikia. Story included with permission of author; translation 'The Journey' included with permission of Arunabha Bhuyan.

'Eta Adha Lekha Golpo' by Rita Chowdhury. Story included with permission of author; translation 'An Incomplete Story' included with permission of Surekha Sachdeva.

'Samiron Barua Ahi Asey' by Manoj Goswami. Story included with permission of author; translation 'He Returns' included with permission of Amritjyoti Mahanta.

'No Man's Land' by Anuradha Sarma Pujari. Story included with permission of author; translation included with permission of Parbina Rashid.

'Bak' by Imran Hussain. Story included with permission of author; translation 'Bak: The Water Spirit' included with permission of Mitali Goswami.

'Bidhata' by Monikuntala Bhattacharjya. Story included with permission of author; translation 'Providence' included with permission of Manas Pratim Kotoky.

'Tritiyottor Golpo' by Moushumi Kandali. Story included with permission of author; translation 'A Tale of Thirdness' included with permission of Atreyee Gohain.

NOTES ON THE AUTHORS

LAKHMINATH BEZBAROA (1864–1938) is considered to be one of the stalwarts of Assamese literature. A writer of fiction, playwright, lyricist, and satirist, his works have been instrumental in giving a new direction and vigour to Assamese literature. He is known as 'Roxoraj', in acknowledgement of his inimitable sense of humour in many of his works, and 'Sahityarathi', one who gave a new direction to literature. The emotive lyrics of Assam's state anthem 'O Mur Apunar Dex' have been penned by him. His stories and plays show his deep understanding of human nature and also his desire to eradicate the injustices of society, especially towards women. They are couched in simple language, and depict, usually, ordinary men and women, and their lives, with all their challenges and triumphs. 'Patmugi' is one of his best-known short stories.

BIRINCHI KUMAR BARUA (1908–1964), a Sahitya Akademi awardee, was an internationally renowned scholar, a novelist, short story writer, historian, linguist, folklorist, administrator, and academic, who was also closely involved in the setting up of Gauhati University. His works have helped build several aspects of life and letters of twentieth-century Assam. His 'A Cultural History of Assam' is a scholarly and very well-researched treatise. Among his well-known books are *Jibonor Batot, Xeuji Pator Kahini,* and *A History of Assamese Literature,* considered to be milestones of Assamese literature. In his fiction, he delves into the lives of ordinary people, with compassion and understanding, and an awareness of the vicissitudes of life with which they have to grapple with, on many occasions.

SYED ABDUL MALIK (1919–2000), an academic and writer, a Sahitya Akademi awardee, Padma Shri and Padma Bhushan awardee, recipient of the Srimanta Sankardev Award, is one of the best-known fiction writers of Assam. His stories have a variety of settings and show a deep understanding of character. His short fictions, in particular, show his skill as a storyteller. His large body of work includes novels, short stories, and plays. It is acknowledged that his contribution to the growth of Assamese literature is immense. Among his best-known works is the novel *Aghari Atmar Kahini* besides numerous short story collections. *Asomiya Jikir Aru Jari* is a monumental research work based on the life of the peer Ajan Fakir.

BIRENDRA KUMAR BHATTACHARYYA (1924–1997) was Assam's first Jnanpith awardee. A recipient of numerous awards including the Sahitya Akademi Award, he was also a journalist, and considered to be a pathbreaker in Assamese letters. He also headed the prestigious Asom Sahitya Sabha as its President for a term. As editor of the iconic journal *Ramdhenu*, he is credited with establishing it as a magazine known for its excellence, and for nurturing many literary talents who later became stalwarts in their literary fields themselves. He was also a teacher. His best-known works are the novels *Mrityunjay, Kobor Aru Phool,* and *Yaruingam*, though he has to his credit a total of fifteen novels, and several volumes of short stories, besides travelogues, lyrics, and collections of essays and other works. His novels and short stories are imbued with humanity and compassion for the human condition, and his writings are known for realistic characters who emerge triumphant in the face of extremely adverse circumstances dictated by history, society, and political events.

MAHIM BORA (1924–2016) was the recipient of numerous awards, notably the Padma Shri, the Sahitya Akademi Award, the Chhaganlal Jain Award, the Assam Valley Literary Award, and the Assam Publication Board Literary Award. The Asom Sahitya Sabha conferred its highest honorary title, Sahityacharrya on him. He was also its President for a term. A college teacher by profession, his fiction is notable for his compassionate observations of rural life and character. Besides numerous short stories and novels, he also wrote radio plays and poetry. His works include eight short story collections, two collections of essays, four novels, of which *Edhani Mahir Hanhi* is hugely popular.

SHEELABHADRA (1924–2008), the pen name of academic and writer Rebati Mohan Dutta Choudhury, was a Sahitya Akademi awardee, and also a recipient of the Assam Valley Literary Award, the Bharatiya Bhasha Parishad Award, the Assam Publication Board Award, among other awards. His short stories, in particular, have endeared him to the people. A Professor of Mathematics in Assam Engineering College, Guwahati, in his numerous short stories, he created a fictional town in western Assam, which he named Madhupur, using the unique language and characters that formed part of his own life. His characters were often drawn from observed life around him and from the working classes. Among his important works are *Madhupur Bohudur*, *Madhupur aru Tarangini*, and *Agomonir Ghat*, in a large collection of novels and short stories.

SAURAV KUMAR CHALIHA (1930–2011) was the pen name of academic and writer Surendra Nath Medhi. A teacher of Physics at the Assam Engineering College, Guwahati, his works are credited with giving a new direction to Assamese fiction, especially short stories. A Sahitya Akademi awardee, he was also a recipient of the Assam Valley Literary Award. The story 'Oxanto Electron', written in 1950 when he was very young, created waves when it first appeared, and has influenced many writers. He wrote for literary journals and periodicals such as *Banhi*, *Ramdhenu*, *Dainik Asom*, and so on. His stories were compiled into several collections, some of which are *Ehat Daba* and *Oxanto Electron*.

HOMEN BORGOHAIN (1932–2021) was one of the most highly regarded writers, thinkers, and journalists of Assam. A Sahitya Akademi awardee for his novel *Pita Putra*, he, however, returned it in 2015 in protest against the Dadri lynching. His other important awards include the Assam Valley Literary Award for fiction. He was a civil servant for a while, before he turned to journalism. He was a print as well as an electronic journalist with his immensely popular weekly talk show 'Kotha Barta' which was aired for many years. His published works include thirteen novels and novellas, five short story collections, fifty volumes of non-fiction, and a volume of poetry. Famously, his book *Halodhiya Soraiye Baodhan Khai* was made into a National Award-winning film by Jahnu Barua. An ex-President of the prestigious Asom Sahitya Sabha, he has been the editor of several well-known journals and newspapers. His works often depict the underbelly of urban life and reveal the complexities of human nature and existence.

BHABENDRA NATH SAIKIA (1932–2003) filmmaker, playwright, and writer, was a recipient of the Sahitya Akademi Award for fiction. He was also a Padma Shri awardee, as well as a recipient of seven Rajat Kamal awards for his films, several of which are based on his own stories. Besides this, he was a recipient of the Srimanta Sankardeva Award and the Assam Valley Literary Award. A teacher of Physics at Gauhati University, he was also a member of the Sangeet Natak Akademi, New Delhi. He was the founder-editor of the acclaimed fortnightly *Prantik* and also the children's magazine *Xophura*. He was also very actively associated with the stage and theatre, and has written a large number of plays both for radio and the stage. Among his works are three novels, eleven short story collections, twenty-eight plays, several books for children, and collections of essays. His short stories are known for their delineation of character and their psychological motivations, as well as their powers of observation and plotting.

NIRUPAMA BARGOHAIN (1932) journalist and writer, a Sahitya Akademi awardee, is also the recipient of, among other awards, the prestigious Assam Valley Literary Award. She has more than a dozen novels and short story collections to her credit. She was associated for several years with the journal *Saptahik Nilachal*, and the unflinching honesty of her writings in the difficult times of insurgency was remarkable. Her fiction is marked by her commitment to humanistic and feminist values. Her finest work is acknowledged to be the novel *Abhiyatri*, based on the life and work of the fiery feminist and activist Chandraprabha Saikiani. She has since returned her Akademi award in protest against rising intolerance in society.

MAMONI RAISOM GOSWAMI (1942–2011), also known as Indira Goswami, is a Jnanpith awardee, a Sahitya Akademi awardee, and a noted Ramayan scholar whose work was recognized and lauded worldwide. She was an academic, novelist, and short story writer whose fictional works are imbued with compassion, a sense of history, and anger against social injustices and inhuman practices against both men and women. Though awarded a Padma Shri, she declined the award. She was also the recipient of the Principal Prince Claus Laureate Award of the Netherlands, the monetary component of which she donated to charitable causes. Among the numerous awards she received were the Kamal Kumari Award, the Mahiyoshi Joymoti Award, the Katha National Award, honorary D.Litt degree from Rabindra Bharati University, West Bengal, and other universities, The International Tulsi Award, and also the highest civilian award of the Government of Assam, the Assam Ratna. She was also an activist, and a mediator between the armed militant group United Liberation Front of Assam and the Government of India. Her popular novels are *Chenabor Srot* (The Chenab's Current), *Neelkanthi Braja* (The Blue Necked God), *Mamore Dhora Torowal* (The Rusted Sword), *Dontal Hatir Uiyey Khowa Howdah* (The Termite Ridden Howdah of the Tusker), *Tej aru Dhulirey Dhuxorito Prishtha* (Pages Stained with Blood and Dust), *Thengphakhri Tehsildaror Tamor Tarowal* (The Bronze

Sword of Thengphakhri Tehsildar) as also several collections of short stories and autobiographical works.

APURBA SARMA (1943) is a Sahitya Akademi awardee for fiction, for his collection of short fiction, *Baghe Tapur Rati*. He is also an acclaimed film critic and journalist. Besides the Assam Valley Literary Award, he is also the recipient of the Swarna Kamal for the Best Book on Cinema. He has been a jury member for the National Film Awards on several occasions. Working as a teacher and having retired as Principal of Nowgong Girls' College, he was also editor of the popular Assamese daily *Ajir Asom*. Among his books are six anthologies of short fiction in Assamese and the acclaimed *Axomiya Chalachitrar Sa-Pohor* (Light and Shade in Assamese Cinema), besides many writings on films in journals.

HAREKRISHNA DEKA (1943) is considered to be one of the foremost Assamese writers today, known for his novel experiments in modern and postmodern Assamese literature during the last half century. He has a versatile pen and has distinguished himself in poetry, fiction, and literary criticism. His fictions broke new ground in both form and content. He has also been writing on various socio-political issues. Belonging to the Indian Police Service, he retired from service as the Director General of Police. After retirement, he briefly edited the Guwahati-based daily *The Sentinel* and then became the editor of the prestigious Assamese magazine *Gariyoshi* till his retirement. He has more than thirty books to his credit. Among the awards he has received are the Sahitya Akademi Award, the Katha Short Story Award, the Assam Valley Literary Award, in 2010, for his overall contribution to Assamese literature, and the Padmanath Bidyabinod Literary Award, in 2015, for his contribution to Assamese poetry.

DEBABRATA DAS (1950) began authoring short stories in the 1970s and gained popularity as the harbinger of non-traditional ways of telling stories. He has also written popular novels, novellas, newspaper columns, and articles. His acclaimed column 'Hiyar Pokhilabor' (Butterflies from my Heart) in the Assamese weekly *Sadin* ran for twelve years. His *Dhuuxaratar Kabya* is recognized as the first post-modern novel in Assamese. Recipient of the Tagore Literature Award from Sahitya Akademi in 2011, Debabrata Das has written a total of twenty-nine books so far, of which seven are short story collections.

PUROBI BORMUDOI (1950–2019) a Sahitya Akademi awardee, was also the recipient of several other prestigious awards, such as the Prabina Saikia Award, Chhaganlal Jain Literary Award, and the Basanti Devi Award. Her works include a large number of short stories and novels. Some of her well-known works of longer fiction are *Santanukulanandan, Gajraj, Prem Aru Banditwa, Baghsaal, Baghjal Aru Manuh,* and *Rupowali Noi, Sonowali Ghat.* Her works are suffused with compassion for people as well as animals and a great deal of environmental awareness.

YESHE DORJEE THONGCHI (1952) is an Arunachali bureaucrat and writer who writes in Assamese, his mother tongue being Sherdukpen. He has several works of fiction, poetry, and plays to his credit. His works show the swiftly changing rural world of the villages of Arunachal Pradesh. He is the recipient of the Sahitya Akademi Award, the Bhasha Bharati Award, the Bhupen Hazarika Award, the Assam Valley Literary Award, and the Sukapha Award. His works in Assamese are also important as a symbol of harmony. Among his important works are the novels *Sonam, Mouna Oth,* and *Mukhor Hridoy.* He has eight novels to his credit, as well as several short story collections, and a history of his community titled *Sherdukpen Jonojatir Itibrittya.*

DHRUBAJYOTI BORAH (1955) is a medical doctor, writer, and critic, a Sahitya Akademi awardee, an Ambikagiri Raichoudhury awardee of the Asom Sahitya Sabha, and an ex-President of the Asom Sahitya Sabha. He is currently the editor of the literary journal *Gariyoshi.* His is a major voice in contemporary Assamese literature. His works have been critically acclaimed, dealing often with history and social issues, and have been widely translated. His best-known works are the novels *Kalantarar Gadya, Katha Ratnakar,* and *Tejor Andhar.* Among his works are eight novels, as well as important non-fictional works and studies. These include a study of the Moamoria Rebellion of Assam, as well as studies on the development of the Assamese language, besides other historical studies. Through sensitively conceptualized characters and deftly handled situations, he paints his fictions with broad brush strokes that also delve into the minutae of lived life.

ARUPA PATANGIA KALITA (1956) is a Sahitya Akademi awardee, and is well known for her sensitive fiction, both short stories and novels, focusing especially on women, insurgency, and the effects of violence. She taught in Tangla College for many years till her retirement in 2016 as Head of the Department of English. A few years ago, she declined the prestigious Basanti Devi Award from the Asom Sahitya Sabha, on grounds of it being a 'woman only' category. She has more than ten novels (including *Ayananta* and *Felanee*) and short story collections to her credit. Among her other awards are the Bharatiya Bhasha Parishad Award, the Assam Valley Literary Award, the Prabina Saikia Award, and the Katha Award.

KULADHAR SAIKIA (1959), IPS and former DGP, Assam, is the current President of the prestigious Asom Sahitya Sabha, the premier literary body of Assam. A Fulbright scholar and Sahitya Akademi awardee, as well as the recipient of the President's police medals twice for his outstanding contribution to policing, he is also a Katha awardee for Creative Fiction. Among his short story collections is the well-known *Akaxor Sobi Aru Ananyo Golpo*. His writings are important for, among other things, their thoughtfulness and their deft combination of interiority and external reality.

RITA CHOWDHURY (1960), a Sahitya Akademi awardee, is one of the notable contemporary writers in Assamese. Among her other awards are the Asom Sahitya Sabha Award and Lekhika Xomaroh Sahitya Bota. She also has to her credit a number of research works, on subjects dealing with the Chinese diaspora, and communities in Assam such as the Tiwas. A fiery student activist during the days of the Assam Agitation, she was also sent to prison. Her fictional works often deal with historical events, through the lives and actions of beautifully conceived characters. An academic by profession, she was also the Director of the National Book Trust. Of her more than thirteen works of fiction, her best-known works are *Deo Langkhui* (The Divine Sword), *Mayabritta* (The Circle of Worldly Illusion), *Makam*, and also *Chinatown Days*.

MANOJ GOSWAMI (1962) is a print and electronic media journalist, a documentary filmmaker, and a recipient of the Katha Award for Creative Fiction, the Damodardev Award (2021), and the Sanskriti Award for Literature. He has several short story collections to his credit, among which are *Ishwarhinata*, *Swadhinata*, and *Samiron Barua Ahi Asey*. As a journalist, he has worked in and edited several well-known publications and newspapers of Assam. He is currently Editor-in-Chief of DY365, a popular television channel of Assam.

ANURADHA SARMA PUJARI (1964) is a journalist and is currently the editor of two well-known journals *Sadin* and *Satsori*, and is also a very popular writer of fiction. She is the recipient of the Kumar Kishore Memorial Literary Award conferred by the Asom Sahitya Sabha, among other awards. Her works reveal a keen sense of observation as well as of a sense of place, tight plotting, besides a conceptualization of apt and unique characters. Among her popular works are *Hridoy Ek Bigyapon*, *Mereng*, *Jalachabi*, and *Kanchan*. She has to her credit eleven novels, as well as four short story collections, and also autobiographical fiction, notable of which is *Kolikotar Sithi* (Letters from Kolkata).

IMRAN HUSSAIN (1966) is an academician, writer, and literary critic, a translator and lexicographer with four critically acclaimed works of fiction and short fiction. One of them, *Hudumdai Aru Ananyo Golpo* was published by Sahitya Akademi. Other collections include *Rupantoror Gadya* and *Asthir Pranto*. Some of these stories have been performed as plays, including the *The Water Spirit*. His works seamlessly blend folklore and myth with a deep compassion for the economically weaker sections of society, and rural citizens. His awards include the Katha Award for Creative Fiction and the Chandraprabha Memorial Award.

MONIKUNTALA BHATTACHARJYA (1966) is a prolific and popular award-winning writer, the recipient of the prestigious Munin Borkotoky Award as well as the Asom Sahitya Sabha Award for her novels. She has written nineteen novels, numerous short stories, poems, and essays: a total of thirty-nine books so far. She is also a regular columnist. Some of her best-known works are the novels *Arundhuti*, *Sandhya*, *Mukti*, among others, the short story collections *Borofor Beli* and *Kobigonga*. Her stories embody a variety of themes and locales, and are a realistic depiction of the various aspects of society.

MOUSHUMI KANDALI (1974) is a translator and writer who is regarded as one of the most innovative young short story writers writing in Assamese. She pushes the boundaries with her works. An art historian and art critic, she is an academic by profession. Among her short story collections are *Lambada Nasor Xexot*, *Tritiyottor Golpo*, and *Mockdrill*. She is the recipient of the Munin Borkotoky Award and the Bharatiya Bhasha Parishad Award for Young Authors.

NOTES ON THE TRANSLATORS

AMRITJYOTI MAHANTA is a writer in English and Assamese, and a translator between the two languages. He has thirteen published works to his credit, including translations, novels, and critical essays. He works in Doordarshan, New Delhi.

ARUNABHA BHUYAN is an Associate Professor (Retired) in the Department of English, Cotton University, Guwahati. She has been regularly translating Assamese short stories and poems into English for newspapers and journals. She has also been actively involved in providing the English subtitles for several National Award-winning Assamese films.

ATREYEE GOHAIN is an Assistant Professor of English at Bethune-Cookman University, Florida, where she teaches courses in academic writing, postcolonial literature, and diasporic American literature. She is also the Fiction Editor of *Jaggery*, an arts and literature journal with a focus on South Asia. Her translations have appeared in *Indian Literature* and *Muse India*, and in anthologies, namely, *Her Story* and *The Oxford Anthology of Writings from North-East India*.

GAYATRI BHATTACHARYYA worked in St. Edmund's College, Shillong, before joining Gauhati University. After retirement, she took up translation as a hobby, and has since translated many anthologies of short stories and novels written by eminent Assamese writers, into English, including works by Sarat Chandra Goswami, Bhabendra Nath Saikia, Mamoni Raisom Goswami, Anuradha Sarma Pujari, Dipak Barkakati, and Birinchi Kumar Barua. So far she has fifteen books to her credit, besides many short stories and articles published in anthologies and newspapers.

JIBAN GOSWAMI took up translation, both from Assamese to English and from English to Assamese, as a hobby, after his retirement as a bank executive. He has translated, among other works, John Steinbeck's *East of Eden* (which earned him the Amulya Kumar Chakrabarty Translation Award), Camus's *L'Etranger*, and Maugham's *Of Human Bondage*. He has translated the works of many Assamese authors into English, including stories of Saurav Kumar Chaliha.

MAITREYA PHUKAN is the pen name of Dhrubajyoti Borah who authored the story 'The Green Serpent'. He often translates his own works with proficiency and literary expertise.

MAITREYEE SIDDHANTA CHAKRAVARTY is a freelance translator, editor, and Assamese language consultant. Her translated novels include *On a Wing and a Prayer* (from Arun Sarma's *Aashirbador Rong*) and *The Hour before Dawn* (from Bhabendra Nath Saikia's *Ontoreep*), which was shortlisted for the Vodafone Crossword Book Award in 2009. She has dabbled in various professions ranging from marketing to teaching, but translation continues to be at the centre of her work, since she believes that it is the only way to bring good Assamese literature to people who do not read the language.

MEENAXI BARKOTOKI, a mathematician turned anthropologist by profession, has translated many articles, stories, and novels from Assamese to English over the last thirty years. Her translations have appeared in various newspapers, magazines, and periodicals as well as in many prestigious compilations, for example, *The Oxford Anthology of Writings from North-East India* and *Asomiya Handpicked Fictions*. She also writes articles of current interest, fiction as well as travel stories and is a founding member of the North East Writers' Forum.

MITALI GOSWAMI is a critic, translator, and educator. Her recent works include chapters in *How to Tell the Story of an Insurgency*, *Female Author-ity*, and the very well-received book titled *The Water Spirit and other Stories*.

MITRA PHUKAN is a writer, translator, and columnist. Her published works include four childrens' books, a biography, three works of fiction, namely, *The Collector's Wife*, *A Monsoon of Music*, and *A Full Night's Thievery*, several volumes of translations, and a collection of her newspaper columns. Her own works have been translated into several languages, and are taught in various colleges and universities. She writes extensively as a reviewer on music and theatre.

PARBINA RASHID is a senior journalist with *The Tribune*, Chandigarh. She has translated a number of books from Assamese to English, some of the noteworthy ones being *Painting of the Sky*, *Ballad of Kaziranga*, and

Echoes from the Valley. She has been associated with Sahitya Akademi in the capacity of a translator and a book editor.

PRADIPTA BORGOHAIN teaches English in Gauhati University. His notable works are *Scrolls of Strife: The Endless History of the Nagas*, co-authored with Homen Borgohain, and *Victorian Literature*. He also contributed to *Alice in a World of Wonderlands*. His work of translation titled *The Collected Works of Homen Borgohain* was longlisted for the Atta Galatta Prize. He also won the Katha Award for Best Translation in 1997.

PRAFULLA KOTOKY taught English in Gauhati University till his retirement. A well-known translator, scholar, and writer, and a Sahitya Akademi awardee, he was a renowned translator with major works in both Assamese and English. He was also a literary critic and commentator.

SURAJIT BOROOAH is a retired Professor of English. He is involved in various literary activities of the state and is a renowned translator of poetry. His works have been published in many well-known publications over the years. He has also translated several novels. He received the Muse India Award in 2017.

SUREKHA SACHDEVA is an editor of popular science books, with a deep interest in music. After a fifteen-year-long career in editing, the story which features in this collection is her first work of translation.

SYED NAZIM HUSSAIN is the eldest son-in-law of celebrated author Padmabhushan Syed Abdul Malik, and is engaged in translating his works. An orthopaedic surgeon based in Golaghat, Assam, he retired in 2016 as Joint Director of Health, Government of Assam. He has translated four novels of his father-in-law into English, namely, *Adharshila*, *Prachir Aru Prantor*, *Sumeru Kumeru Aru Eti Banhi*, and *Joya Monica Ityadi* and some short stories.